Where Dreams Meet

LYNDA M. NELSON

Other Books by Lynda M. Nelson

The Little Red Buckets
My Master's Touch

Where Dreams Meet

Published by Galleon Publishing

Cover & Interior Design by Charlotte Shirts

ISBN: 0-9645810-2-7

Library of Congress Card Number: 00-190362

9 8 7 6 5 4 3 2

A TALE OF LOVE...

A single entry in the journal of Carl Hennings Peterson intrigued me into finding out more about a woman named Selma, and her two daughters, Anna and Ruth. Their journal entries, like many bequeathed to us by our forefathers, provided only illusive clues to their lives and thoughts, challenges and successes. In the end, they left more questions than answers.

I have taken the opportunity to fill in the blanks as I wrote their love story - as it might have happened. In *Where Dreams Meet*, fact flows into fiction so fluidly that I will not endeavor to tell the reader where one ends and the other begins. I have changed their surnames because this is not a completely factual retelling of their story, but I have left their first names unaltered because it was their spirit and their love that brings this story to life.

For Ron & Betty

Journal Entry of
Carl Hennings Peterson
Superior, Wisconsin
1904

"It was Sunday afternoon. I was sitting in my room reading a book. I don't know if I was asleep or not, but it seemed to me that I was wide awake. A young woman and her two little daughters appeared to me in the room. I could see them just as plain as day. It startled me so, I gazed hard at them, but was unable to recognize them. I didn't know what it all meant. (Later)... Ruth, who was then five years old... asked, 'Is that man going to be my Father?'

"The realization of the vision or dream I had had in my room... came to a realization one night when Selma came through the kitchen door and I saw her for the first time... The minute I saw her come through the door, I knew beyond a shadow of a doubt she was the same woman with her two little daughters I had seen in my dream that Sunday afternoon."

CHAPTER ONE

The new Lord Wraxmore smothered a yawn as Lady Selma's husband was laid to rest on an overcast, drizzling English morning in the parish churchyard beside their illustrious ancestors. With this morbid addition, the family crypt was full, leaving Bruton Wraxmore, seventh Earl of Chycester, to build a new one. During the obsequies, the heir envisioned the future size and location of a marble edifice, ostentatious and befitting the entombment of his own remains one day. So engrossed was he in the finer architectural details that he felt mildly shocked when the service ended.

One fitful ray of sunshine broke through the clouds scudding overhead as the mourners filed past Selma. The new Lord Wraxmore had met the youthful widow only that morning for the first time and now he allowed his salacious imagination to roam at will as he admired her trim figure in the black crepe gown.

Lord Wraxmore was momentarily amused as, one by

one, the leaders of York society paused before the widow first, then came to him, expressing their sympathy in muted tones. But he was bored and yawning long before the first of his new tenants had a chance to tip their hats and welcome him to the district. As soon as the last of the local blue bloods climbed into their coach, Lord Wraxmore mounted his showy bay gelding and cantered through the gates of the cemetery, bound for the nearest pub.

Throughout the proceedings, a black gossamer veil hid Selma's face from prying eyes. The village tabbies were left to wonder later over tea and cucumber sandwiches whether the veil hid red, swollen eyes or a relieved smile at the passing of the Lord of the manor. It was noted and thoroughly discussed that the two little girls by the widow's side failed to show a proper grievance at the passing of their father.

"Well, Alice, it may be as you say, but I heard from my maid that the butler at the Manor told our John Coachman that milord never had a thing to do with the poor little tykes, because they were girls."

"I'm sure you're right, Cora. It's criminal, I say, how some men see value only in their sons." Alice swallowed a bit of tea, then set her Sevres cup on the dainty plate at her elbow." Pretty little waifs, they are, to be sure; the older one so dark like her father, the other fair like the mother." She touched a lace handkerchief to her shriveled lips, dabbing gently. "But how will her ladyship do, now that that young buck from London's come into the title? I heard the old Lord didn't leave her so much as a farthing, the greedy old boor."

"'Tis a crime, the way he willed the estate away from his own wife and daughters."

"It happens all too often, I say." Alice peered over the sweets plate and chose a plump tart. "And I, for one, can't see her taking up residence in the dower house. Wouldn't seem fitting, somehow, knowing the new Lord's reputation, what?"

"Happen the mother'll have something to say in young Mrs. Wraxmore's future."

"It's a shame," Cora shook her turbaned head back and forth, "how the mistress could be such a sweet, gentle creature with such a shrew for mother and beast for husband. Well, she deserves better and I'm not thinking she'll be getting it."

"I'm not disagreeing with you, my dear. I suppose there's nothing for her to do but find another husband." Alice extended a plate full of finger cakes to her friend, "Would you care for one of these, Cora? My new cook does so well with confections."

"Hmm. They look frightfully delicious. I envy you a French cook, Alice, truly I do."

"I must confess, though it breaks my heart to compliment the frogs higher in any endeavor than our beloved English," Alice paused to sip her tea, "but the French truly do know how to cook."

The young widow and her two daughters were forgotten in a lively discussion of the superior merits of French cooking as compared to solid British fare.

Selma's husband had been entombed less than a day when she unearthed her precious horde of pound notes and change. They had been saved at great pains through her married life for just such an opportunity. Selma had planned to run away almost from the day of her wedding. She tried once, but was hunted down and brought back, beaten and cowed, and was never again left unattended. Her entire savings equaled less than any of the hunters in the stable. Her late husband had been as clutchfisted as he was tyrannical. She wished it was more, but it would have to do.

Her bags, packed since the village minister had been called to pray over her husband for the last time, had already been spirited out of her room, down the servants' stairs, and hidden in the carriage barn.

She glanced once more around the room she had considered more a prison for the last seven years than a home and felt no regret about her decision. Without the smallest tinge of remorse, she left her grasping, selfish, overbearing mother asleep in the blue room at the end of the second floor hall and tiptoed down the broad, sweeping stairway. She carried Anna in her arms and held Ruth's small hand, keeping the silent child close to her side.

The breath caught in her throat as she and her daughters passed the library where the new Lord had already drunk himself into a stupor. One cautious glance revealed him slouched in a wing chair by the fire, shirt open at the neck, slack mouth hanging agape like a flycatcher. An empty decanter lay on its side on the floor at his feet.

Seth, her late husband's coachman, met her at the door. His gleaming coach stood hitched to a team of matched welsh ponies stamping impatiently in the starlit yard. She noticed the venerable driver had already strapped her single trunk and three small bags to the top of the coach. With a nod, Seth opened the door and lifted the little girls inside before turning to extend his hand to their mother. Her eyes flickered to his for a moment, gleaming sapphire in the coach torchlight as she nodded silent thanks for his help. Then she mounted into the plush equipage. Quietly, Seth folded up the steps and shut the door.

The horse's hooves clopped noisily on the cobbled driveway, setting Selma's nerves on end until they passed between the towering battlements surrounding the manor and reached the softer surface of the road.

A pale sun was rising behind a curtain of gray clouds when Seth finally pulled his tired horses to a halt. In the distance, a giant steamship towered above the wharf, its boarding planks overrun with excited travelers, uniformed sailors, and quayside workers ferrying last minute supplies aboard the ship. Selma descended from the coach, leaving her daughters in Seth's care while she stepped into the ticket office. With eager, trembling hands she bought the last three second-class tickets available on the first ship leaving England. The India Queen was scheduled to depart in forty-five minutes.

With the tickets safely stowed in her purse, Selma climbed once more into the carriage. Seth mounted to his seat and drove through the bustling crowds until he came to the berth of the India Queen. There he pulled his horses to a halt and opened the door for the last time for his mistress and her daughters. Selma nervously scanned the giant wharf, but recognized no one and breathed a sigh of relief. Quickly, she lifted Anna and Ruth down as Seth pulled the trunk and bags from the top of the carriage.

It was early yet, but the cold chill of morning had not deterred a huge throng of onlookers and well-wishers from crowding the splintered dock beside the ship. Seth hurriedly commandeered two sailors to carry his mistress' bags onto the India Queen and see them stowed in the cramped space they would call home for the next few weeks.

"I wish I were coming with you, milady." Seth stood before his mistress, turning his uniform cap around and around in his hand.

"Oh, Seth, I do too. But your life is here. You and Bertha have your home and friends..." Selma extended her gloved hand and Seth hesitantly took it between his own fingers. "Thank you...for everything, Seth. I could not have survived these past years without you... and your dear wife."

Seth blushed dark red in the golden morning light. "I only wish I could have done more." His harsh tones only served to emphasize his emotions. "There was many a time I wanted to..."

"Hush, my friend. He's gone now. No good can come of remembering dark days that are past."

Seth peered at Selma from beneath his bushy, silver eyebrows, recognizing the scars and fears, though she had buried them deep. "You're sure this is what you want to do, milady?

"Yes, Seth. I'm sure." Her voice was firm, her chin thrust out at a determined angle.

"Then here." He took a small box tied with string from an inner pocket of his uniform jacket and held it out in his gnarled hand. "This is from me and the missus."

Selma took the tiny box and felt a lump tighten her throat. She had to swallow several times before she could speak. "Thank you, Seth. For this, and for all you've done for me the last seven years."

"His grizzled brow furrowed in concern. "America is a wild, fierce country, littered with heathens and wild men. What will you do there? How will you live?"

A shrill whistle followed the clanging of a bell from the deck of the India Queen and a screeching bullhorn announced the raising of the gangplank. Anyone not already on board was warned to come now or be left behind.

"Even if I have to live with heathens and wild men, I'll have something I could never have if I remained here. I'll be free, Seth... free!" She flashed the old coachman a warm, bright smile that few people ever saw and lifted a fleeting kiss to that surprised gentleman's cheek. In a whisper, she confided, "Don't worry. I'm going to find my dream."

Bending, she scooped Anna into her right arm, quickly grasped Ruth's hand with her left, and started running for the ship. "Wish me luck, Seth. God bless you," echoed back along the dock. The skirt of her black dress flapped around her ankles as she dashed across the lowest gangplank and disappeared inside the ship. Seconds later, the sailors pulled the last walkways into the ship and clanged the doors shut.

"God bless you, milady," Seth whispered, one hand still raised in farewell.

The coachman searched the crowds of excited travelers lining the rails of the ship. At last, he was rewarded with a final sight of Selma, Anna, and Ruth, all waving excitedly from their perch in the bow of the giant black and white vessel. Selma waved ecstatically with one hand. Her other held firmly to Anna, who leaned against the highest rung of the ship's rail and waved enthusiastically with both hands. One bright, golden curl escaped the confines of her hat and hung almost to her waist, silhouetted against the deep burgundy of her velvet coat. In a rare moment of perspicacity, it occurred to Seth that Anna would grow up to look just like her mother.

He kept waving as his eyes moved to Ruth, the serious sister. Her mother's quiet shadow, Ruth looked more like her father, with her dark hair and eyes. But the delicacy of her features she owed to her mother and Seth knew she would grow into a beauty as well. As he watched, Ruth stepped up onto the rail beside Anna, their matching coats blending so that only their bright faces separated them into two children. Suddenly, Ruth's face split in a brilliant smile and her hand touched her lips, throwing an imaginary kiss down to where Seth waited on the wharf.

Two shrill blasts from the ship's whistle signaled the dockworkers to throw off the massive lines. They fell away as black smoke belched from the sleek, white boiler stacks. Miniature tugboats hooted their horns in response and slowly began to push against the black hull, straining to point the giant ship out to sea. Ponderously, the India Queen turned her bow away from the dock until Seth could no longer see his mistress and her children.

Still, he stood on the quay, watching until the entire length of the ship gradually disappeared, ghost-like, swallowed by the fog shrouding the bay. His shoulders drooped as he turned to mount the box on his carriage. When Seth turned the horses toward home, he was surprised to find warm tears trickling down the creases of his face. He lifted a mittened hand, brushed them away, and straightened his shoulders beneath the twin black capes of his driving uniform. The horses plodded along the near empty road and Seth squinted into the rising mist as his mind drifted back seven years to the first time he saw Selma Klintenberg.

The Wraxmore estate had been in an uproar for days. For the first time in almost twenty-five years, Lord Wraxmore was throwing a grand party. Bertha, who had been Lord

Wraxmore's housekeeper for most of those twenty-five years, received specific orders to have the maids dust and air out all thirty-two of the guestrooms in the sprawling mansion. The kitchen staff was ordered to lay in a daunting array of delicacies for the invited guests. When she ventured to ask how many would be coming, Lord Wraxmore informed Bertha that he was getting married and would be expecting fifty-two guests for five days. Still reeling from shock, Bertha immediately sent the cook's helper to York to hire extra girls to help with the cooking and serving.

Seth received specific orders as well. Every horse was to be washed and the stables cleaned. Every saddle, bridle, buggy, cart, and coach had to gleam from wheel to harness cope.

Two days before the guests were scheduled to arrive, a plain, black coach with no crest on the door, pulled into the cobbled yard. His lordship's very correct butler sailed out onto the porch to greet the arrivals, closely shadowed by the under-butler. Both were dressed severely in strict black, offset by stark white shirts and gloves. One stable boy ran to the horses' heads, another to stand at attention beside the door. Seth remained in the shadows of the barn door, silently watching.

A third stable boy, a red-headed lad of sixteen years, opened the coach door while the under-butler stepped forward to help two ladies descend from the carriage. The first woman made Seth's eyes start from their sockets. Tall, slender, regal, Mrs. Klintenberg alighted from the coach, not deigning to take note of the bowing servants around her and barely recognizing the butler of milord's establishment as she gracefully mounted the flight of steps. Seth had never seen a woman so beautiful; from her wide, luminous eyes, flawless skin, and high cheekbones to her delicately shod feet. If there was a flaw, it was in the narrow chin, too pointed for perfection, too high in the air for kindness.

Seth had served lords and ladies since the day he turned twelve and jumped up behind his first coach and hung on for dear life. He had seen women like this one before. Deeply in love with Bertha, his plump, humor-loving, down-to-earth wife, Seth wrote this woman down as cold, haughty, selfish, and more than a little grasping.

Then another woman stepped out of the carriage and Seth's brow crinkled in surprise. She was younger — more girl than woman — but they could have been stamped from the same press. Without doubt, he knew she must be the older woman's daughter. But the second her foot touched the cobblestones, Seth knew she was different. Her face was deathly pale and he recognized fear in the stiffness of her body as she moved. But she looked at each of those who offered her service and graced them with a gentle smile and a nod of thanks. Just before she mounted the steps behind her mother, she turned her head and, to his surprise and discomfort, discovered Seth in the shadow of the barn door. His breath caught in his throat at her tremulous smile. Then she was gone.

Getting ready for bed later that night, Bertha had told

Seth about the new arrivals: the widow, Mrs. Aurelia Klintenberg and her daughter, Selma. Seth assumed Lord Wraxmore would be marrying the widow, but his loquacious spouse soon set him to rights. She vowed it was a scandal, a disgrace, but the old lord was marrying the daughter, not the mother.

"You must be mistaken, m'love. She's young enough to be his granddaughter."

"And you think I don't know that, you old fool?"

"Well, does she want to marry him?"

"It's the mother's got the ordering of her life, I'm thinking. The poor little thing's got no say whatsoever — and scared out of her wits. It seems Miss Selma's been away at some private girl's school where her mother sent her when she was just little. She turned seventeen last May, graduated with honors, and the school sent her back to the mother."

"And just how do you know all this?" Seth lounged in his favorite chair, smoked his pipe, and watched Bertha let down her long hair. He still loved to watch her pull the brush through the silken, and now silvering, strands.

"From the mother's maid, of course; now don't interrupt. Ah, where was I?" The brush stopped in midair, then Bertha found her train of thought and continued.

"Seems the mother's fair jealous of the daughter and wanted to marry her off as soon as possible. No end of young beaus showed up in London wanting to court her, but... " she turned to stare straight at her spouse, "it seems Mrs.

Klintenberg's quite the gambler. Bets on the horses, cards, dice, and such." Her husband started to speak, but she waved him to silence. "Milord bought up all her IOU's and, can you believe it? Offered to trade them back if she would give him her daughter to wife. Seems he was quite taken with her at Lord Tinkerton's ball." Bertha's voice echoed her scorn.

"Why, that's barbaric! This sort of thing doesn't happen anymore! Mothers don't force their young daughters to marry miserable old goats."

"Just what I said myself. But the maid seems to think Mrs. Klintenberg is going do it anyway."

"Has the girl's father nothing to say in the matter?"

"Seems he's been dead since the girl was a babe. The husband's family disowned him when he married Mrs. Klintenberg."

"Has she no one else?"

"No, the poor, wee thing. She's all alone in the world — except for the mother."

"Some mother!"

The horses shied when a giant black dog suddenly erupted from a tall hedge beside the road. It chased merrily beside the horses, barking at their heels. Seth shouted at the hound until it bounded off, tongue lolling from the joy of the chase. Seth settled the horses down, then slowly drifted back to his reverie.

The noble guests had arrived, carriage after carriage, until the giant house overflowed with titled gents and their ladies. Seth didn't see Selma again until the day she stepped out of the house in her white wedding gown. He was driving the barouche and was required to maintain a posture of stiff attention at the reins. But when the door opened, he turned his eyes just enough to catch sight of the bride. Her terrified eyes were huge in a face as white as the dress she wore. Aurelia followed her daughter out on the porch and stopped her to pull the veil down over Selma's face. Then she took Selma by the arm and forced her into Seth's coach.

Seth felt tempted by a wild desire to gallop away from the ancient stone church, help the girl to escape. But it was only a fantasy and habit is a stern taskmaster. Within minutes, he pulled his shining team to a stop in front of the parsonage. An immaculate footman helped the bride-to-be to alight. Aurelia regally led the way into the church. Behind Selma, two young girls dressed in fluffy dresses of pale pink lifted the bride's train and held it aloft as they followed her slowly through the black oak doors into the shadowy chapel.

Seth watched Selma falter at the door, but her mother moved her inexorably inside. When she disappeared, Seth drove sadly forward to park his vehicle.

He watched the last guests hurrying into the church from his post in the shade of a grove of elm trees. It seemed only minutes later that one of the deacons rushed outside and gestured for Seth to bring his coach to the door. Through a flurry of cascading rice and laughing well-wishers, Lord Wraxmore practically carried his swooning bride down the shallow stone steps and lifted her into the carriage. Seth cringed at the lascivious fire burning in his master's cold voice when he ordered Seth to drive.

It was the first — but not the last time — that Seth thought about saving Selma from the life fate had dealt her. And sadly, it was the first, but not the last time he failed to do anything.

CHAPTER TWO

Selma stood at the bow of the enormous vessel and stared into the foggy expanse of the English Channel. Her arms were wrapped tightly around her only two treasures in the world, five-year old Ruth and four-year old Anna. A broad smile lit up her pale face as chill after chill rippled down her spine. She rubbed her arms where the skin raised like that of the chickens she had oftentimes helped the cook pluck and prepare for roasting in the ancient oven at Wraxmore Manor. Freedom, adventure — life — lay within her grasp. She hoped she was brave enough to embrace them all.

Wriggling loose from her embrace, Anna and Ruth eagerly began to explore the unfamiliar surroundings. Selma thought of the gift nestled in the pocket of her skirt and reached to take out the envelope and the tiny box. She turned them over and over in her hands, reveling in the final moment of mystery. At last, unable to wait longer, she carefully broke the seal on the single sheet and spread it open. The paper fluttered in her hands while she eagerly read the few words Bertha had written.

17 October 1904

Dearest Selma,

God bless you on your journey, my dear. We wish we could keep you near us. But we know it is best that you build your new life in a far land. God grant you health, peace, and prosperity. But most of all, we pray that you may find a place and time where your dreams of yesterday meet your dreams of tomorrow. We will miss you. Write as soon as you reach America for we will be waiting anxiously to hear how you fare. Give our love to Ruth and Anna. Kiss the little darlings for me. (Bertha wrote the last sentence sideways across the corner of the page.)

Respectfully and with all the love in our hearts, God bless you,

Bertha and Seth

P.S. As a small momento of our love, we had Scoresley fashion a special charm to mark the beginning of your new life. Add it to your bracelet. May it remind you that when the light at the end of your tunnel grows dim, your dream is not gone. All you need do is wipe away the soot of life for the light to glow as bright as ever it did before.

Selma's fingers trembled as she untied the string, then folded back the wrapping paper. Carefully, she lifted the lid from the tiny box. Hidden between folds of blood-red, satin fabric lay a golden charm. She gasped as it sparkled in a thin beam of light that finally lanced through the gray fog. Gingerly, she lifted it out, watching it twirl in the breeze blustering across the bow of the ship.

Precious gold had been molded into a tiny candle set in a plate-shaped holder, complete with a curled finger grip. A tiny, blood-red ruby, faceted in the shape of a heart, held the place of the flame resting upon the wick. Selma had never seen anything like it. Its intricate beauty took her breath away and she stood mesmerized, staring at it for a long time, thinking of the blessing Bertha was bestowing with this precious gift.

"Mother, Mother! Come quick. You must see what Anna and I have found." Ruth and Anna shattered her reverie with their excited babbling.

"I'll be right along," she called absently. Her head turned a tiny way toward the excited girls as she spoke, but her attention remained focused on the shimmering charm. Carefully, she removed her bracelet and securely attached the new talisman.

Anna and Ruth, shivering with impatience, finally began to tug at Selma's skirts. "Mother, come see, come see."

The girls pulled her toward two other girls who were playing with dolls on one of the deck chairs. As she listened with half of her mind to their excited chatter, Selma could almost feel the candle warm her wrist where it lay beneath the lace of her black glove.

Early the second morning aboard ship, a storm blew up. It ravaged ship and passengers relentlessly for days, tossing the India Queen violently through massive waves until she finally surged, tired and battered, into calmer seas. As though a gossamer curtain were raised, the cold fog of the British isles faded in the distance, replaced by the warmth and light of an autumn sun. From there the sailing was pleasant and rapid.

Slight skirmishes with seasickness for the girls soon gave way to racing up and down the steep stairways, from end to end of the wooden decks, and playing games with other children on board the ship. For Selma, the freedom of living without the brutality of her husband and the grasping, pinching ways of her mother opened new horizons promising a life full of wonderful possibilities. Gradually, she came to know many of her shipmates. Other mothers with children also had spouses. She soon found that difference served to set her apart from the women more nearly related to her own situation in life. But her youth and energy attracted several younger, single, women and happily, she found herself forming budding friendships.

Day after day, she walked the decks and stood tirelessly at the rail, watching dolphins play in the waves crashing outward from the ship's bow. In the solitude of her mind, she imagined herself as free as the sleek animals flying under and above the water. Turning around, her eyes studied the sweeping lines of the tall black and white stacks gushing inky smoke trails into the azure sky. Billowing white clouds floating high above the ship betokened her wings of freedom, signifying her flight from dark bondage into a life full of light, freedom, happiness.

For a few moments each day, she stood in the chilly sunshine and freshening breeze at the very bow of the ship and raised her arms out from her sides, as though she were a bird preparing for flight. With her head thrown back, she reveled in this novel sense of liberation. And for those moments, she didn't care if the India Queen never reached port.

Midway through the last week of the voyage, Selma left her daughters happily playing dolls with an older pair of sisters they had befriended while she strolled slowly along the now-familiar deck. She ignored the wooden guard rails and neatly packed lifeboats, invariably focusing her eyes on the far away clouds and that magical point where sky melds into ocean.

Captain Riley watched her progress along the deck. For the better part of his forty-two years, Captain Riley had been a seafaring man. A stern commander of men, he was more at home with his feet splayed wide apart to absorb the rocking of a ship than anywhere on land. He had always preferred the company of the officers on his bridge above even the richest of travelers mingling in the India Queen's cocktail lounge.

That changed the day he met Mrs. Wraxmore. His

straight shoulders automatically stiffened as she moved along the rail and stopped in the very same place at the bow of his ship where she had stood every day since the voyage began. One weathered hand unconsciously stroked his neatly shorn beard. Reaching a decision, he formally relegated command of the ship to his first officer, straightened the tunic of his uniform, and climbed down from his perch on the upper deck where passengers were not allowed. Nervously, he inhaled a deep breath of salty air then moved up beside the young woman and cleared his throat.

She turned her head and acknowledged the Captain's presence with a nod and a smile, but spoke no word. Inside, his composure crumpled, though outwardly he remained the same. When his eyes met the distant blue gaze of the beautiful widow, a betraying flush crept past the collar of his tunic, shading his face a ruddy color. She didn't appear to notice, but calmly returned her gaze to the sea. Silently, they stood side by side, staring out over the ocean until she moved away from the rail and began her return walk down the length of the ship.

Captain Riley had struggled to remain aloof since the first day Mrs. Wraxmore stepped aboard his ship and into his life with her deep, golden hair and sapphire eyes. He had met countless other women more beautiful than Mrs. Wraxmore. But none of those exquisite women, richly dressed and festooned with jewels, had made the slightest dent in his emotional armor. But something about the distant fear lurking behind her polite smile had touched an unsounded chord of chivalry buried deep in the Captain's seafaring heart. He glanced sideways at her profile and noted again the slight bump in her nose and wondered how it had been broken. His fingers burned to reach out and trace the pattern of a pale scar that extended in a thin, jagged line outward from her left eyebrow and down to her cheekbone. He didn't question why, he only knew that the imperfections in her face made her more attractive to him.

For twenty years, Captain Riley had enjoyed his self-imposed rule to never socialize with his passengers — even to the point of eating his meals in his own cabin rather than subject himself to idle chatter in the dining rooms. But day after day he had found himself struggling to ignore the fascination that kept him watching the young widow as she walked to the pointed bow of his ship and braced herself against the wind. Two days out of New York Harbor, he found he could no longer resist the urge to walk beside her, talk with her, look into her eyes. Now that he had succumbed to temptation, he felt like a gauche schoolboy, tongue-tied and insecure instead of the capable commander of a great steamship that he knew himself to be. Unaccustomed to engaging in simple small talk, he fell back on banal inanities and asked Mrs. Wraxmore how she was enjoying the voyage so far. Her answer was polite, but not expansive and he was left struggling for another topic of conversation.

For Selma's part, she was not seeking male companionship, nor was she ready for a man's company — any man. She did not wish to hurt the Captain's feelings, but she felt no desire to talk with him either. He was obviously a sincere, capable, hard-working individual, deserving of all common civility. But her heart and her body were raw from years of abuse. Despite knowing she was safe and this man meant her no harm, her skin still crawled from his nearness and she had to hold tight to every tether of self control to keep from cringing away from him. She answered his queries cautiously. And for half the length of the ship, she effectively concealed the nagging tension swelling in her stomach. But gradually, it mushroomed into a burning pain, firing a desperate compulsion to escape. Years of practice at hiding her feelings kept her countenance schooled to a neutral expression while she frantically inspected fellow travelers passing on the ship's deck, searching for a likely target where she could deliver her admirer.

At last! Miss Bordeston, that portly, energetic dame emigrating from Sussex, heaved herself up the final step and through the door leading from the lower passenger accommodations. Deftly, without the Captain ever sensing his imminent danger, Selma directed their steps toward the garrulous spinster. Not a single qualm disturbed Selma's conscience as she drew the older woman into conversation. Then she adroitly directed the topic of conversation until the Captain was inescapably entwined in Miss Bordeston's loquacious clutches. Giving no warning, Selma made her escape.

Smiling and waving, she excused herself on the pretext that she needed to check on her children.

Intense relief flooded through Selma and the pain in her stomach subsided as she rapidly threaded her way between other passengers, back along the deck to where Ruth and Anna still played contentedly. Safe again, she silently leaned her back against the ship's rail and listened to the stories woven by her daughters and their friends. Their fertile imaginations had transformed the ship into a romantic galleon overflowing with hordes of treasure, sailing in constant danger of attack by rogue pirates.

"Mother," Anna jumped to her feet and lifted her doll for Selma's inspection. "Samantha had a axadent. See her lace?"

"Oh, my. She surely did have an accident. It looks as though she trod on the lace while she was dancing?"

Anna beamed up into her mother's understanding eyes. "Yes, well, could you fix it for her, please?"

"Hmm, let me see what I can do." Selma sat on a deck chair and reached into her reticule for the simple repair kit she always kept with her.

Anna turned to her new friend and whispered behind one dimpled hand. "Georgette, my mother is the bestest sewer in the whole world. See my dress?"

Anna lifted a bit of the fine material in her fingers, emphasizing the hem of white lace. Her friend nodded.

"Samantha's dress is exactly the same as Anna's," Ruth

explained as Georgette looked from Anna's dress to the one Selma was starting to repair. "Mother made both of our dresses and the dolls' dresses to match."

Georgette's boundless imagination immediately took flight. "Maybe she could make us pirate clothes..."

Selma continued to set the tiny stitches until the lace was once again in place, then she handed the doll back to Anna. Their colorful fantasies brought a smile to her lips as she turned to face the lowering sun. Her mind flew away, soaring high above the waves, past miles of ocean to that great land of freedom — America. Unfettered, her own fantasies painted an idyllic picture of a tiny home surrounded by a white picket fence, where her daughters would play beneath green, spreading trees. Ruth and Anna would go to school, grow up, marry men they loved, and Selma would become a doting grandmother. In that pastoral scene in her dreams, she was her own mistress, growing older contentedly, year after year, never again living in fear of a man's footstep on the stairs, never feeling the cut of a lash, never having to endure...

Without warning, a dark cloud from the past overshadowed her bright vision of the future. Fiercely, Selma shook her head, forcing that black phantom back into the dungeon of her memory where she firmly locked the door against its escape. Her right hand stole to her left wrist where her fingertips caressed the charms on her bracelet, one by one. She knew it would take time, but Selma was determined to clear her mind of all such images. Every time they reappeared, she would force them away until one day they never came again. The man who had been the cause of those dreaded shadows was gone. Dead. She sucked in a deep breath and turned back to her daughters, the bright lights of her life; her sole reason for living. Silently, she vowed nothing and no one would harm her or her children ever again.

Ellis Island resembled a madhouse engorged with immigrants from many nations. Thronging crowds funneled together in a maelstrom of conflicting languages, smells, dress styles, and stations in life. Ruth and Anna clung determinedly to Selma's skirts so as not to become separated from their mother even as their wide eyes took in all of the strangeness of humanity shuffling beside them. Selma was not surprised to find that money and her title as "Lady Wraxmore" eased the way through the emigration sieve that left many poorer people standing in swollen lines and answering endless questions.

Finally ashore in her new country, Selma found the docks of America to be very much like the docks of England. Two enterprising young street urchins were soon carrying her trunk and leading the way between carts and carriages to the taxi of a street jarvey they swore was a 'right un'. That savvy gent peered at Selma through squinty eyes and listened to her request for a hotel. He looked from Selma to Anna and Ruth, then nodded wisely, saying he would recommend the Pantheon Arms. He vouched for it being a clean, quiet hostelry where he assured Selma that she and her daughters would be comfortable.

After he deposited her trunk in the quaint lobby of the small hotel, Selma made an appointment with the helpful driver for nine o'clock the following morning. He nodded, touched the brim of his hat with two fingers, and disappeared out the door.

A chill breeze whisked crackling leaves through the city streets the next morning when Selma directed the driver to the offices of Youngstrom & Youngstrom, a notable real estate firm recommended to her by her late husband's solicitor. As she stepped from the carriage, she asked the driver to wait for her.

The younger Mr. Youngstrom greeted her arrival with enthusiasm, eagerly asking how he might be of service. When she explained her desire to purchase a small piece of property somewhere out of the reach of big cities — a small house in a quiet town out west — his jaw dropped open in surprise. Selma watched him glance quickly up and down her body, assessing the stylish dress and hat she wore. She could almost hear his thoughts jostling around in his head. Why should a woman of obvious birth and station request a small house on the edge of the western frontier, far from more fashionable New York, Boston, or even Chicago?

She took a breath and carefully lengthened her countenance to tearful sadness. Keeping her eyes downcast, she confided that she was newly widowed and did not feel up to the excitements of a large metropolis. Perhaps later...

Suddenly, Mr. Youngstrom became all dutiful understanding. Of course, he said, he understood her desire to retire from the world during her period of mourning. Dollar signs practically leapt into his eyes as he assured her that he would find just the perfect situation for her. Then, when she was ready to again enter society, he hoped to have the pleasure of helping her find a more genteel location closer to the amenities of civilization.

She smiled at him, but was slightly disappointed, though not surprised, to see him melt. She had long ago grown accustomed to the effect a certain smile had on men — when she chose to use it. She had learned to use it as she would any tool at her disposal. But she could not respect a man who would look no deeper than the perfection of her skin or the brightness of her hair and eyes. It reminded her too closely of things she had watched her mother do and it repelled her as even the worst stench could not. For a short time, in the security of school, she had dreamt of a man who would love her for her heart and soul, not only her body. But that dream had died seven years ago. She shook away the chilling memories and centered her attention on the agent before her.

Mr. Youngstrom requested that she check back with him in two or three days. Or, if she would prefer, he could visit her at her lodgings to report his findings. Selma assured him that wouldn't be necessary, arranged to return in three days' time, and took her daughters away.

Three days later, the realtor was pleased to report he had found just such a situation as Selma had described in a lovely town called Missoula, in the western state of Montana. She studied the map on his wall and realized Missoula — Montana — was a bit farther west than she had envisioned. But when he described the home and the terms of sale, Selma knew she had to buy it and offered to pay cash right then.

Caught unprepared for such a quick sale, Mr. Youngstrom requested her to return in a week. By that time, he promised to have the paperwork prepared and they could complete the sale. The next day, Selma booked space for ten days hence on a train that would take the three of them to Missoula.

Winter in Montana, Selma learned, was often fierce. She evaluated their wardrobes and decided they would be well served with heavier coats, boots, gloves, and scarves. So it was that the day after the new American holiday, which had been dubbed Thanksgiving, Selma took the girls shopping.

The title transfer papers were ready when promised and Selma signed them, eagerly assuming ownership of a reputedly charming, two-bedroom home situated on three acres of land right outside the western city limits of Missoula. As they left the offices of Youngstrom & Youngstrom, Selma clutched the deed to her new home tightly in her fist and felt a thrill of solid accomplishment ripple up her spine.

The sign for a postal office caught Selma's attention from where it swung on the corner opposite the real estate office.

She stared at it a moment, then crossed the street. Sealing the deed in a large envelope, she addressed it to herself in care of General Delivery and posted it to Missoula, Montana. She was smiling when she stepped back into the street, one little girl holding to each of her hands. There was no turning back now.

CHAPTER THREE

Carl raced past the fishing vessels tethered safely behind the rocky headland that kept the stormy lake from bashing the wharves and moored boats to matchsticks. Merry Queen, the rescue vessel leaving the end of the pier, belched thick streams of black smoke into the dark, ominous sky as she eased away from her berth. Carl sprinted the last fifteen yards and launched himself off the end of the pier. His arms and legs flailed against the oncoming wind to keep his body upright until he smashed down onto the wooden deck and skidded toward the wheelhouse. A neat coil of heavy mooring line abruptly arrested his slide across the deck just as Henry Meisner stepped out of the wheelhouse. One side of his mouth twitched up and down while the weathered seaman stared down at Carl.

"Saw you tryin' to sprout wings." Henry stood short and powerful, legs spread wide from years of absorbing the waves of the sea, meaty fists firmly planted on narrow hips. The thick, rolled collar of his heavy knit sweater did nothing to disguise the breadth or power of his neck. "Didn't think you'd make it."

"I was wondering myself for a minute or two." Carl shifted around until the world was right side up again and gulped in a couple of deep breaths.

"Thought the boss told you to stay put." Henry pinched the butt of his cigar between the only two fingers left on his right hand and spat over the side of the boat.

"He did." Carl hauled himself to his feet and dusted imaginary dirt off his pant legs. The deck of the Merry Queen was spotless. When Carl finally straightened, he smiled sheepishly down into the older man's eyes and shrugged his shoulders.

Henry had to tilt his head back to meet Carl's gaze. "Hmm." The cigar clenched in his yellow teeth glowed red against the glowering black of the clouds beyond the top of the wheelhouse.

"Well, ya keepin' me, or throwing me back, ya old barnacle?" Carl smiled into Henry's stern eyes.

"Hmm."

Henry turned his head sideways, looking to see how much further the boat had to travel before it reached the lighthouse marking the end of the headland. His savvy eyes watched the massive breakers crashing over the rocky dike and rippling the bay waters.

"I reckon you'd drown if I threw ya off now," he growled.

"That's the spirit." Carl clapped Henry on the shoulder and stepped past him into the wheelhouse.

Muttering indeterminate ramblings, Henry shook his head and followed. Though only half Henry's width, when Carl moved toward the bridge door, Henry couldn't help but compare the younger man to some graceful alley cat on the prowl. His heart swelled with pride at the man the boy he'd known for so long had finally become.

"Hey, I thought management wasn't allowed on dangerous rescue missions." Max Vanderhoff laughed and shoved his giant hand out as Carl stepped inside.

"They're not!" Henry moved across the room and nudged Tristan aside then braced himself as he gripped the sleek, wooden helm. His two-fingered hand reached out and throttled more power to the engines.

Carl cocked an eyebrow at Henry as he shook Max's hand. "If you thought I was going to miss the maiden voyage of our newest and biggest rescue tug, you've been spending too much time with the mermaids."

"The old man'll have every one of our heads on the block if you get hurt, boy," Henry ground the words out around the fat, black cigar clamped between his teeth.

Carl glanced around at the grinning faces of the other six men in the cabin. "I'm two months shy of being thirty years old and I've been riding rescue ships since I was twelve — most of them with you, you old seahorse. So what's changed?"

"You weren't half owner of the biggest rescue and salvage

company in Twin Harbors." Fresh-faced, curly-haired Paul Higgins contributed from his corner near the heavy windows.

Suddenly, the bow rode high on a smashing breaker as the Merry Queen passed the Superior Entry Lighthouse and the protection of the breakwater barrier at Wisconsin Point. With no warning, she staggered back and pitched sideways. Seconds passed, then she righted herself and slowly battled her way into the open lake.

When the deck heaved, every man in the wheelhouse grabbed an overhead bar for support. Several of them flinched when green sheets of pounding water broke over the bow of the powerful vessel as it charged forward through the rising waves. Disrupted waves washed harmlessly down the sides of the sealed ship, foaming and racing away through the scuppers. Water sluiced in rivers down the giant glass windows, intermittently obscuring Henry's vision.

The tug battled the raging onslaught, headed east. Its powerful, 900 horsepower steam engines relentlessly drove the sixty foot vessel of steel and wood toward the Algonquin, a Great Lakes barge reported to be trying to make one last steel ore run before winter closed Lake Superior to barge traffic. The Algonquin was almost a day overdue in port.

The faces of the men in the tug's wheelhouse grew stern. Ninety-five years of hard-earned experience were shared by the men, most of those years earned by Henry, Max, and Carl. Every man wore heavy, waterproof boots, mackintosh coats over thick, wool sweaters, and canvas pants, wide-brimmed hats, and tightly woven woolen gloves.

Thirty minutes passed. Then an hour slid by while every eye peered through the stormy gloom, searching for some sign of the overdue ship.

"There she is," Paul suddenly shouted above the howling wind.

His eyes were keener than anyone else on board. Though not even sporting solid chin hair, all the older men had come to trust the boy's incredible eyesight.

"Two degrees to port, Henry! She's foundering in the waves. Her tender barge is already listing hard down to starboard." The boy rattled off the details through a dry, tense throat. "She's rolling," he yelled out, then the Merry Queen dropped into a gigantic trough and the Algonquin was lost to sight until the boiling water thrust the rescue ship high into the air again.

"No! She's righted herself again, but now the Algonquin is down hard to starboard as well." He squinted a moment longer through the lashing rain. "I don't see anyone aboard."

Henry canted the wheel two degrees to port and pushed the throttles full open. The Merry Queen surged forward under full steam, her pistons reverberating through the whole ship while the men struggled to stand against the heaving deck.

The Merry Queen was a hundred feet away from the Algonquin and the cargo tender coupled behind her when Henry shouted, "Time to get to work, m'lads." At his command, every man but Paul struggled out the door and into the storm.

Henry passed the foundering ship, then skillfully corkscrewed his vessel in a tight turn on the crest of a giant wave. Suddenly, the wind and waves were pushing him from behind instead of battering against him. He had only one chance and he drove his ship hard up beside the Algonquin as they rose and fell on the same wave, until their bows were almost touching. Three figures suddenly leaped through the watery gloom from the bow of his ship. Immediately, he throttled the tug ahead of the struggling barge.

Carl raced toward the stern of the Algonquin, his steps flung wide apart on the crazy deck. Even so, he stumbled and almost went down when the barge suddenly rose high on the sharp brow of a wave and staggered sideways down into the trough. He grabbed hard at an iron stanchion and held tight until the ship miraculously righted herself once again. He looked back, but the pounding rain almost obscured Tristan and Max at the bow of the ship where they were already reeling the heavy tow cable over the bow from the Merry Queen. In minutes they would have the Algonquin secured to the rescue tug where George and Paul stood ready at the winch, waiting to take out the slack.

Carl only had a few short minutes before Henry would be ready to take the Algonquin under tow. The trailing tender barge was twisting and rolling. Under the relentless heaving of her decks, the heavy load of iron ore had murderously shifted position and now pulled her toward the icy blackness at the bottom of the lake. The tender was the sacrifice Lake Superior demanded before she would relinquish her hold on the mother ship. If Carl didn't separate the two vessels, the Algonquin would follow her cargo tender over and down hundreds of feet. And once the Merry Queen was tethered to the Algonquin, the rescue tug ran the risk of suffering the same fate.

Carl was breathless, every muscle quivering from exertion when he finally reached the stern. Thunder crashed above him. White forks of lightning raced across the sky, flashing the lake's surface an eerie, silver green. Then it was dark again. Bracing his legs far apart against the roll and surge of the ship's canted deck, Carl pulled a blasting cap from the inside pocket of his coat. Quickly, carefully, he secured it into the coupling pin seats that secured the tender to the Algonquin. Eight seconds after he arrived, Carl raced for cover. He counted five and dove headlong down the slippery deck between two heavy stacks of cargo.

Thud! Carl barely heard the charge explode over the raging storm. He leapt up and ran toward the stern. In a series of violent shudders, the tender tore loose. Carl grabbed desperately for a rail as the Algonquin lurched sideways, reeling far over to the other side before finally righting herself again.

Prickles of hair rose on the back of Carl's neck. He turned at the feeling of warning and squinted sightlessly through the rain and darkness. Suddenly, a bolt of lightning flashed the scene into terrifying relief for a split second. The tender, free of her mother ship, had risen above the Algonquin and was charging forward on the crest of a gigantic wave. Carl staggered backward as the bow of the tender loomed fifteen feet above him in the air. In that instant, he knew he would die when it crashed down, splintering him and the Algonquin's stern deck together. Instinctively, futilely, Carl threw an arm up to shield his face.

A full second passed. Then another. Carl sensed more than felt the Algonquin surge forward. Then a second flash of lightning revealed the flat, steel bow of the tender launching higher and higher into the raging sky. Carl sent a final plea toward heaven to accept his soul. But even as he waited for the onslaught of cold steel to wipe out his existence, Carl was unable to drag his eyes from the spot where he'd last seen the dripping, black bow. He stared in terror through the rain-blackened sky, only to be blinded by bright spots flashing in front of his eyes, leftovers from the strobes of lightning.

Carl flinched. A terrifying rush of air slammed him hard as the tender finally collapsed downward. Just before he knew it would strike, Carl clenched his eyes shut and huddled into a ball. More terrifying seconds passed and Carl was still alive. Finally, unable to stand the agony any longer, Carl opened his eyes. Just then, another strobe of lightning highlighted the attacking tender where it had crashed into the sea, only inches behind the Alogonquin's stern plates. The Merry Queen, under Henry's desperate urging, had pulled the Algonquin out of harm's way just in time.

Carl shuddered with relief. For long moments, lightning played havoc in the heavens while Carl lay still, soaking up the falling rain and watching the barge tender retreat farther astern. Slowly, inexorably, she rolled over onto her topside, wallowing deeper and deeper in the rising waves. The Algonquin moved further and further away, obediently following the Merry Queen toward a safe harbor. Carl was mesmerized as he watched the tender founder farther and deeper. She was almost lost to sight when her bow end finally sank deep into the icy waters. Slowly, the stern tilted gracefully into the air, the relentless waves crashing white and attacking the hapless vessel from all sides. She offered no warning as she slipped suddenly, silently beneath the waves and was gone. One final blast of lightning and pounding thunder sent icy chills chasing each other down Carl's spine. The darkness returned and Carl jerked his eyes away from the watery grave and struggled to his feet. His legs felt like rubber as he staggered forward.

"No crew aboard!" Max yelled between cupped hands when Carl finally gained the pilot house.

Carl read Max's lips, but could barely hear him over the shrill howl of the wind and pounding rain.

"Abandoned ship?" Carl yelled back.

"Must have. Rescue boats are gone. Engines ain't workin' and she's taken a gutful of water."

"Think we can get her towed to Duluth?" The storm

threw the shouted words back into his face.

"It'll be chancy. If the wind stays at our back, we got a more than even chance. If the waves shift... " Max left the sentence unfinished.

Carl nodded. More than once, they'd been together on Lake Superior in the clutches of a raging storm and seen the waves suddenly shift directions, one minute pounding south, the next gigantic white horses crashing north.

Thunder boomed straight over their heads. A fiery stab of lightning strobed to the tallest mast of the barge. The strike hurled Carl and Max against a tarped bundle of wooden crates.

Tristan had been peering over the ship's edge to assess the strain on the massive cables when the lightning struck. Carl opened his eyes, frantically searching for the younger man. Between flashing, colored dots, he spotted Tristan precariously hanging from the side of the ship, struggling to hold onto a length of massive chain that served for a rail.

Carl leapt to his feet, but was immediately knocked over by a wall of water that rushed across the deck when a rogue wave rose over the Algonquin and crashed straight down. The ship staggered sideways. Frantically, Carl grappled for and caught hold on one of the tie-down ropes securing the cargo to the deck. His head ducked against the rushing water. When his eyes finally cleared again, he saw Tristan miraculously still holding on, but now with only one hand.

Carl lurched to his feet and staggered toward his shipmate, stumbling down onto his hands, then up again until he reached the side of the ship.

"Tristan!" The powerful wind whipped his voice into the storm. "Give me your left hand."

"I can't." Carl could barely hear the words. "It's broke."

More water sluiced over the two men and Carl lunged as Tristan lost his grip. Desperately, Carl grabbed for any hold he could catch. His fingers twisted into the collar of Tristan's coat and he felt a flash of victory. In the next instant, he was being ruthlessly pulled halfway over the side as the full weight of Tristan's body jerked him downward. Carl clung to his hold on Tristan and frantically wedged his right leg between the railing and the deck. His fingers were screaming in agony from the strain of holding the sodden weight of the injured man's body, when, without warning, the ship suddenly dropped a deep trough and a wall of icy water rushed up the side of the ship. Tristan's body shot up to come crashing over the rail and onto the deck.

Helplessly overbalanced, Carl felt himself rolling over and over in frothing water toward the wheelhouse. The ship dove forward again and Carl was flung helplessly back toward the edge with Tristan's hapless body madly tumbling with him across the deck. Carl thrust his legs wide, desperately trying to stop the roll while he grappled for another hold on Tristan.

Suddenly, Max was there, throwing his entire weight across Carl's body. One massive arm flung past Carl's shoulder to grab onto Tristan just as the two men slid to the edge and started overboard.

"Heave!"

At the command, Carl's arm instinctively tightened. One breathless moment passed before Tristan was safely back on their side of the rail. The three men lay in a soggy heap, gasping for breath.

Cold rain lashed sideways driven by the torrential wind, leaving them no time for rest. Carl and Max struggled to their feet. Together, they half dragged, half carried Tristan into the ship's wheelhouse and slammed the door on the storm outside. The three battered men flopped onto the floor, their lungs gasping hungrily for oxygen.

Tristan groaned and rolled slowly onto his side, hugging his broken arm to his chest. Suddenly, he gagged and retched, bringing up all of the water he had swallowed. His face glowed a pasty white against the dark wood of the deck as he slowly curled into a ball.

No one spoke. Their heavy breathing steamed the windows while each man considered the miracle that had kept them alive. Finally, Carl stood on shaky legs and swabbed a spot free of condensation. His eyes strained through the stormy darkness. During lightning flashes he could see Paul and George on the stern of the Merry Queen. They were holding tight to the wheelhouse stanchions, staring across the dark space between the ships.

Carl staggered to the door, forced it open against the ferocious wind, and stepped outside the wheelhouse long enough to signal that they were all right. He got a zealous signal in response from his worried shipmates then he let the wind blow him back inside.

Max was trying to get Tristan to uncoil from his huddled position on the floor. When he finally got Tristan's knees to lower, he feverishly worked to unbutton the waterlogged coat while the injured man trembled and clenched his jaws to keep his teeth from chattering.

Carl ravaged the cabin until he found a pry bar to use for a splint and a first aid kit containing bandages. He and Max carefully supported the broken bones as they stripped the coat and dripping sweater from Tristan's chest and arms. The boy could live through a broken arm, but shock from the cold and injury would kill him if they didn't get him warm.

Before they stripped off the rest of his wet clothes, Max wrapped himself around Tristan's torso and gripped tight to the upper part of his injured left arm. When Max was ready, Carl looked briefly into Tristan's eyes and got a nod. Grasping the young man's left hand and wrist between his own hands, Carl pulled straight out until the bone ends in the arm came into line. Tristan's piercing scream echoed above the sound of the storm and he fainted just as Carl felt the bone ends align and pop into place.

Carl released a bit of the pressure and the bones stayed put. Carefully, Max laid Tristan's inert body on the floor. While Carl held tension on the arm, he applied the splint and secured it in place with bandages.

Finally, they pulled the rest of the wet clothes from

Tristan's body and wrapped him in two wool blankets Max had confiscated from a footlocker. Protecting the unconscious man from rolling with the ship proved harder. They finally solved their problem by lashing Tristan's blanketed body to the supports between two locker doors.

"Glad he passed out." Max's harsh breathing punctuated each word.

"Yeah. Makes it a lot easier on him." Carl tied his last knot, then plopped down in a corner, bracing his feet against the pitch and roll of the deck.

"How long you figure 'til we reach port."

"Most of the night, slow as we're going."

"You think the crew got away safe?"

"I hope so."

"Pretty stupid to try to get a barge through this late in the year."

"Couldn't agree more." Carl brushed the wet hair up out of his eyes and turned his head toward Max. "But this is one of Beddlington's boats. And you know how he feels about his profits."

"Yeah. But losing this whole load and the barge along with it — can't be too profitable for the old man."

"He'll get Lloyd's to pay off on the insurance — probably even buy it back from us for the cost of salvage rights." Carl grimaced at Max through the darkness. "Don't worry about the old goat. He won't lose a dime."

CHAPTER FOUR

At three fourty-five on the afternoon of December 10, 1904, Selma and her daughters began what they thought was to be the last stage of their journey. Their favored hackney driver delivered them to the train station where Selma watched as her trunk was stowed in the baggage car. She pressed a handsome tip into the crusty old driver's palm and bid him farewell. Then she led Anna and Ruth forward and settled them in their seats. By the time the Great Northern train rattled out of town, heading north and west, Selma was tired and the girls exhausted from all the excitement. All three voted to inspect their sleeping berth. There they laid down for a nap and were asleep before the train passed the city limits.

Dark shadows crossed Selma's dreams and she tossed fitfully back and forth in the narrow bunk. She watched herself as though from a distance, begging something of a beautiful woman arrayed in an elegant green gown. The woman laughed and turned away, leaving Selma chained to a stone wall, naked and cold.

Selma forced herself to wake up, thrusting the familiar, frightening dream back into its dark box deep inside her mind. She hugged herself till the shaking stopped, then reached out to touch the tousled heads of her sleeping daughters; her touchstones to reality and strength.

For three days the train moved steadily westward, traveling just below the Great Lakes on its way toward North Dakota, Montana, Washington, and finally, the Pacific Ocean. The changing scenery fascinated Selma and she reveled in the majesty of her new country. The northern lands slept firm in the clutch of early winter. The rolling hills, low mountains, and trees were liberally covered with chilling, white crystals of untrammeled snow.

Passengers spoke of the Great Lakes just north of the rail line, bragging that they were the largest bodies of fresh water in the world. She heard of the massive barges that plied their trades in lumber, grain, coal, and iron ore from one end to the other. A young man, barely old enough to sport fuzz on his chin, introduced himself as Pratt Risely and quickly made friends with Anna and Ruth. Pratt had firmly attached himself to Selma's little family by the time they passed through the middle of Illinois. As the miles sped by, he regaled Selma and her daughters with descriptions of all the port cities on the Great Lakes. But he dwelt at length on the beauty and grace of Twin Harbors where the cities of Superior and Duluth shared a magnificent, natural harbor on the largest of the Great Lakes.

He spoke of the 158 ports from which cargo came and went, the shipyard where the world's largest grain elevators stood, and ore docks built sky high on pilings so that ships could dock right beneath them and the ore would pour into their holds from above. He bragged of a booming metropolis where more than 36,000 residents traveled streets paved with cedar blocks and sidewalks of wood planking.

He had worked for two years at the Daisy Mill before setting off to explore more of the world. But of all the cities he had seen in the six months since he left, according to Pratt Risely, no city outside of New York or Chicago could rival Superior, Wisconsin. He went on and on until Anna and Ruth felt life would not be complete if they did not see Lake Superior for themselves. Selma, fired with the same excitement, thought it could cause no harm to make a short detour to see one of the world's greatest natural wonders.

Accordingly, she stopped the grandfatherly conductor and asked about tickets and transfers for a loop to Superior. Nothing easier, was his reply. Change trains midway through Wisconsin, travel to Superior, stay for a few days and enjoy the sights. Then return to the main line where they could finish their journey to Montana.

When the train stopped that evening in Hutchison, Wisconsin, Selma and her daughters changed trains, adventurously bound for Superior. Few passengers boarded the single passenger car, leaving most of the seats around Selma empty. But just as the final boarding whistle screeched from the engine compartment, the door at the front of the car opened and two women stepped through. Selma glanced up and found her daughters staring at the new arrivals.

"Girls," Selma whispered, "don't stare. It's rude."

"We're not staring, Mother. We're just looking."

"Well, don't look, Ruth."

"But Mother..."

"We'll talk about it later, Anna. Now, keep your eyes to yourselves."

Selma glanced up as a short woman — not yet turned twenty and already thickening around the waist — led the way down the aisle. Her older companion held tight to her elbow with one hand while gripping a long, white cane in the other. The younger woman's face still held the first blush of youth, but the mousy hair pulled severely away from her face made her appear older.

In contrast, the older woman's face gracefully reflected her age in the fine lines radiating out from her eyes and mouth. Her soft skin was a creamy color and framed by neatly coifed salt and pepper hair confined in a soft bun at the back of her head. Bright, round hazel eyes stared blindly out at a world she could not see. But unlike the few other blind people Selma had seen in England, this woman's wide, unseeing eyes were wide and luminous.

Selma's gaze dropped to the long, bedraggled coat. The

frayed and worn garment was very long and stopped just short of the floor. It effectively hid the woman's dress, which Selma suspected was as disreputable as the outer garment.

As the strange pair passed, the younger woman stared in open admiration at the modish hat nestled on Selma's head. But when their eyes met, the younger woman blushed and forced her eyes forward. Then they were past.

Again, Selma urged her daughters to turn around in their seats and stop staring. But Anna and Ruth could not resist craning their necks to watch the two women get settled.

Then the door opened and a swarthy man in a conductor's uniform stepped into the car. The conductor on this train was a stern, sour-faced man who smelled of liquor and cigar smoke. When Selma extended their tickets for his inspection, he leered at her in a coarse, suggestive way that raised the hackles on her neck. He paused by her seat several times through the evening and always tried to strike up a conversation. When she did not respond, he whispered suggestive comments which she pretended not to hear nor understand. She fought down the icy terror his attentions evoked and consoled herself with the knowledge that twenty-four hours from now would see them in Superior, where they would spend a few days in a nice hotel endorsed by young Pratt Risely and explore the sights he had recommended. She could ignore the loathsome man that long. She was relieved when, after dinner, she finally escaped to her ancient berth, separated from the aisle only by draping, black curtains.

Selma hated the hours between darkness and dawn. Nightmares and dark memories that were easily controlled in the light of day took on monstrous proportions when darkness enveloped her world. She had hoped that in crossing the vast ocean they would be left behind. Not so. The end of each day came far too quickly, darkening the windows to a mirror surface that reflected her thoughts as they reflected her image back into the cubby hole, haunting Selma with ghosts from the past.

Finally, too tired to keep her eyes open, Selma nodded off to sleep. The girls sprawled between Selma and the window, contentedly dreaming to the clickety clack of the train rumbling across the metal rails. Selma tossed and turned for hours, fighting malevolent dreams that escaped to torment her rest. A slight bump in the night merely caused her to cry out in her sleep. Prisoner of a paralyzing nightmare, she mumbled incoherent words that no one heard.

Morning brought a blowing snowstorm. Swaying gently, the train cruised through the wall of white flakes, undeterred by their icy onslaught. Ruth and Anna were up and begging for breakfast when Selma discovered her purse was missing. She searched their berth over and over, growing more frantic with each turn of a pillow or blanket. Their sleeping cubicle was a small rectangle on the floor level with no place for a purse to slip away from sight. Their travel clothes were all accounted for. The bag in which she carried their night things was safe in the corner where she had left it. But the purse had disappeared.

Frenzied terror rapidly paralyzed Selma's body as the enormity of the theft bored its inexorable way into her mind. Finally, helpless, she huddled in the back corner of the berth, her eyes wide and staring. The bizarre look on their mother's face frightened Anna and Ruth. Hesitantly, they curled up beside her. Desperate for comfort and support, Selma opened her arms and pulled them close.

Selma was certain she had placed the purse beneath her pillow last night, as she did every night. But could she be mistaken? Was it possible she had left it somewhere else on the train — the dining car, perhaps? She determined to search every corner of the train, but she was loathe to ask the belligerent conductor if anyone had found a lost purse. She would face that last. Right now she had to feed Anna and Ruth. They had the whole day before they reached Superior and were safe in the train until then. Surely, she would find it. She had to find it! Her joints felt frozen and stiff when she finally forced herself to move.

Hour after despairing hour rushed by as quickly as the rails passing beneath the steel wheels. Selma searched methodically yet found nothing. She questioned the conductor and the servers in the dining car, but no purse had been found. The sky outside the windows grew dark again before the shrill whistle announced the train's arrival in Superior.

In quiet trepidation, Selma bolstered her courage and

sought out the conductor to ask for his help. Staring into his bleary eyes, she begged him to report her loss to the railroad officials and allow the three of them to stay on the train, return to the main line, then continue on to Montana.

His outraged response was to immediately order them off the train.

"But I told you! Someone stole my purse with all our money and our tickets," Selma cried in self-defense.

"Likely shtory," the conductor slurred his words as he pushed his unkempt face close to Selma. His insolent gaze moved slowly up and down her body and Selma shivered with disgust.

"I'm sure I could... ah... find another ticket... somewhere," he grinned suggestively at her, "fer a price." He whispered the last words and Selma gagged on the bile rising in her throat at the sight of his yellowed teeth and the smell of his foul breath.

"I told you. My money was stolen!" Selma tried to stay calm, keep her voice low and even, desperate to convince the foul man to attest to her loss to someone in authority.

"We had tickets — paid to return on this line, then all the way to Missoula. The other conductor sold them to me." Her voice quivered despite her tight control.

"Hmmph!" The train conductor kept pushing until he succeeded in herding them off the train. The scowl on his face spoke resplendent testimony to his lack of concern over the fate awaiting Selma and her daughters in a strange town in a new country on a freezing, cold night.

"Well, he's not here t' ask, now is 'e? 'Iss none of my business what you 'ad... 'rranged... with ol' Boris."

He leered suggestively at Selma until her hand itched to slap his face. "But you punched our ticket when we boarded the train." Selma felt close to panic. "Surely you remember!"

"I don' 'member nothin', lady. You don't got no ticket from S'perior to Missoula. You don' got the fare," he sneered as he looked down his crooked nose at Selma, "you don' got the ride. I'ss as simple as that."

"But we were robbed. The train company owes us..."

"The company don' owe you nothin'!"

He abandoned the three of them on the dark train platform, bereft and frightened. When he stepped up onto the lowest step of the passenger car, Selma rushed toward him. "But my trunk!" she begged.

"We have only the clothes we're wearing and our overnight bag. Nothing else! At least give us our trunk!" Selma's pleading voice shuddered. She felt burning tears clog her throat but she refused to cry.

"You ain' got no ticket that says you own no trunk on this train." Scorn laced his words. "You're the wors' kin' o' scammer, thinkin' the railroad's gotta s'pport you and yer brats — free food, free ride. Well, you ain' gettin' no free trunk!"

"But I... " Selma cringed at his harsh words.

"Lady, yer lucky I don' call the sher'ff and 'ave yeh lockt

up." He tromped up the remaining steps and slammed the car door behind him.

The faces of a few interested spectators who had just boarded the train peered through the glass windows, but no one made a move to help the mother and her two children. Without warning, the freezing wind suddenly whipped snow off the roof of the train station, pelting Selma and the girls with sharp, gritty flecks of ice. The rails clanged and the train began to move forward. Soon, a shrill whistle pierced the dark night. Its plaintive wail echoed back through the gathering storm, keening a poignant counterpoint to the fear in Selma's heart.

CHAPTER FIVE

thought I made it clear that you were no longer to participate in the actual rescue part of our operations!"

The old man glaring across the richly paneled room looked a decade younger than his sixty-two years, despite the wheelchair in which he sat and the rich burgundy quilt covering his shrunken legs.

"You made it clear, Uncle Thomas. But your phenomenal memory should also tell you that I never agreed to stay off the boats."

Carl looked resplendent in a black tuxedo as all six foot two of him lounged on a blue and rose sofa on the other side of the fireplace. The humor in his eyes glinted in the light from the fire as he watched the silver brows pucker above the old man's eyes.

"Then promise me now!"

"Your growls don't frighten me, Thomas. I was riding the

rescue boats long before you... took me into the family."

"And were barely making enough to live on, remember that!"

"But having a fine old time riding the high seas."

"You can't just go gallivanting off on some salvage operation for the sheer fun of it. Next time you might not be so lucky. Get washed overboard during one of the Lake's gigantic storms and there'd be no finding your body."

"You been talking to Max again?" Carl swung his long legs off the sofa and stood up.

"I talk to a great many people and they all tell me the same thing. If there's even the smallest hint of danger, you're right in the middle of it. If somebody gets in trouble, there you are, trying to save the fool."

The imperial old gentleman glared at Carl, expecting an argument but getting none.

"It's time you settled down, boy." He punctuated each sentence by slapping his right hand on the wheel of his chair. "Marry some girl from a good family. Start raising some children of your own."

"Uncle Thomas, how can you say that when you know I'm following in your footsteps?" Carl's silver-blue eyes crinkled with laughter while he tried to cajole the old man.

"What, by living alone all your life? Never having any children? Breaking your back so you have to spend the rest of your life in one of these da... dratted chairs?"

"Hasn't slowed you down any."

Thomas Mason brooded in silence long enough that Carl looked over to see if he had fallen asleep.

"You're the only son of my best friend." Thomas stared into the flames of the fire and his voice came as though from a great distance. "I have no children of my own, but I promised your father I'd take care of you like you were my own. Now you and Amanda are the only family I have left in the world."

His voice grew stronger and his eyes raised to deliver an icy blue message straight to Carl. "You're going to inherit everything I own when I die and I think that gives me the right..."

"No!" Carl interrupted. "Uncle Thomas. I love you... like a father. You've been good to Amanda and me the last twenty years. But if inheriting your money means you have to run my life, I can do without the money."

"And Amanda?" Thomas showed his trump card.

Carl hesitated, "I'll take care of Amanda."

"Not if you get yourself killed!"

A sudden knocking on the door interrupted them. The ornate, mahogany door opened and Thomas' butler entered.

"Mr. Carl, your coach is at the door. Miss Amanda will be waiting for you at the train station... " He left the thought dangling.

Carl took Thomas' right hand in his own and gazed down into wide blue eyes undimmed by age. "I'm good at designing boats. But if I don't go out on them — watch them in action, work with them with my own hands — how can I ever make the improvements that will keep our boats the best in the world?" A boyish grin split his face. "I'll try to be careful. That's all I can promise."

He let go of Thomas' hand and turned to go. "It was a great party, by the way. And now you'd better get out there before your guests think you've abandoned them."

Without another word, he swooped his hat and heavy dress coat out of the butler's hands and passed out of the room, leaving Thomas to grumble and mutter by himself.

"Would you like me to assist you to the drawing room, sir?" Dawson stood at aloof attention.

"No, drat you! I'm not helpless!" Thomas wheeled himself past the butler, not deigning to look up, so he missed the smile of understanding that momentarily split Dawson's face.

Shivering from cold and fright, Anna and Ruth huddled against their mother's legs. Selma leaned against the chill, clapboard wall of the station office so that she wouldn't collapse. Shock held every muscle in her body paralyzed. Her thoughts, frozen by the icy fingers of a fear more overwhelming than any she'd ever known, grappled uselessly against impending disaster. No matter how hard she tried, Selma could not focus on any solution, any course of action. Trembling with fear, she dropped to her knees and wrapped her arms around both girls. Desperately, her eyes coursed up and down the narrow platform.

"But what about our dreams, Mother? How will we ever get to Montana?" Ruth whimpered in fear while Anna clutched Selma's neck and began to cry.

"Hush, my darlings." Selma struggled to be brave and forced a cheerful tone into her words. "This doesn't change our dreams." She wiped the tears from Anna's cheeks and whispered in their ears. "Don't cry, my darlings. We'll work this out — somehow. I promise."

When the girls finally sniffled back their tears, Selma lifted her head and looked around. A wooden sign creaked in the wind above the dark, shuttered ticket office window. Even squinting, she could barely make out the printed words. But when she did, a dark depression enveloped her like icy water dropped from a bucket.

WELCOME TO SUPERIOR, WISCONSIN, read the sign, announcing the name of the city that had lured them from their safe path to Montana.

At last, she pushed herself slowly to her feet, still holding tight to Anna and Ruth. She tried to move, but her boots felt cemented to the wooden platform. Her mind raced futilely around in circles, like a rat in a maze with no doors. The train station, so busy only moments ago, was nearly deserted now. Only two other people remained on the platform.

The derelict blind woman who had shared their passenger car was sitting on the only bench outside the ticket office. Her companion waited beside her. Yellow light from a single gas lamp highlighted the older woman's vacant stare and long cane as she huddled against the cold inside her tattered coat and the swathing of scarves pulled up around her head and face. When Selma looked at her companion, the younger girl averted her eyes, seemingly embarrassed by Selma's predicament.

Selma's questing gaze touched the two women only fleetingly, then moved on. In the distance, perhaps three blocks away, she could see bright lanterns of a hotel where drifting snow flickered as it passed through the pool of light spilling out from the sheltered porch. Selma gulped a breath and told herself they must have shelter. Grasping her daughters firmly by the hand, she straightened her shoulders and lifted her chin. She took one big breath then commanded her feet to move toward the stairs leading down from the train platform to the street.

"What will you do?" The softly-voiced question surprised Selma into stopping.

"Excuse me?" Selma's voice carried the faintest trace of hauteur and disdain, shocked that the haggard woman had spoken to her.

"You have no money, no baggage, and I believe — are strangers in Superior?" As the blind woman spoke, her companion's eyes flickered to Selma, then away again.

"Yes. But don't worry. I'm sure we'll be fine." Selma was touched that the woman seemed to care, but could not face discussing her troubles with a complete stranger.

The blind eyes shifted in the direction of Selma's voice

and Selma experienced the oddest sensation that she was being appraised. She turned to go, but the woman caught her attention once more.

"I have a small home where you would be welcome to stay until you decide what you're going to do, if that would be of any help…"

"Th-thank you," Selma stuttered and a shiver ran up her spine when she imagined the type of home where this woman lived. She had passed many such destitute people living in their wretched little dwellings near the Wraxmore estate. She could not imagine herself or her daughters sinking to the level of sleeping even one night in such a hovel.

"I shall do well enough. You need not concern yourself with my affairs."

Selma cringed inside when she recognized the arrogant tones of her mother's voice issuing from her own mouth. Immediately, she regretted the words, but quailed at the thought of apologizing. She told herself that right now she had more important matters on her mind than the feelings of one ragged, old woman whom she would never see again.

The head wrapped in scarves nodded up and down in the shadowy darkness. When she spoke, her voice was so quiet that Selma barely heard the words. "If you would meet your dreams… you must live them each day along the way." Then louder, "I'm afraid you will find Superior is not a very… friendly… town. But good luck my dear."

Turning her head away, the strange woman resumed her

vacant contemplation of the snowy railroad tracks.

Selma stared at her a moment longer, slowly mulling over the bit of sage wisdom she'd let drop and instinctively applied it to herself. If I would meet my dreams. . .I must live them each day along the way. Something in the words touched a chord of understanding deep within Selma. She hesitated, but no reply seemed adequate to the moment. In silence, she led her daughters down the steps and into the street.

Suddenly, a tall man loomed out of the snowy night and almost ran into the little family. Selma flinched and staggered back in fear. Anna squealed.

"Excuse me, ma'am. Didn't mean to surprise you." Selma looked up and caught the briefest impression of sparkling, silver eyes set in a rugged face as the man touched the brim of his hat and nodded. Then he was past her, striding two at a time up the stairs of the railroad station platform.

Selma's frightened heart was still hammering against her ribs as she knelt in the snow to comfort the girls. Ruth recovered first and shouted above the wind, "Mother, why is that old woman just sitting there in the cold?"

"I don't know. She's probably waiting for someone — maybe another train. I'm more worried about us at the moment."

"Me too." The naked fear in Anna's voice carried clearly above the blowing snow. "That mean man on the train scared me!"

"He frightened me, too," Selma infused her voice with a cheerful tone, "but he's gone now and we're going to be fine. I promise." Selma kissed their soft, cold cheeks, then stood with their hands in hers. "Right now we need to get out of this storm."

Ducking their heads against the wind, they hurried toward the lights ahead. A set of cart tracks, rapidly filling with snow, led right to the door of the two-story hotel Selma had seen from the train station. She herded Anna and Ruth inside, then quickly stepped through and shut the door behind them. They shook off feathery clumps of snow and approached the youth behind the broad, polished wooden desk.

Howard, the pimple-faced night clerk, was engrossed in a book and did not look up until Selma cleared her throat. Startled, his eyes shot up from the page he was reading until he found himself staring into a pair of sapphire blue eyes ringed with dark lashes. His face shot red while he dropped his gaze and clamped his gaping mouth shut. His next glance took in her stylish dress of black, relieved only by the frothy white lace at her throat and partially hidden beneath a rich, claret colored coat. He stared briefly at the matching hat tied fashionably over her golden curls and his lips involuntarily formed a silent O. The woman before him represented a kind of wealth and style of which he'd only heard, but never seen. Her entrancing smile further weakened his concentration so that when she asked him in softly accented tones if he had a room for one night, he immediately fumbled the registration book around for her to sign and eagerly extended a key.

Howard did not start to breathe again until the hotel's newest guest turned toward the stairs. He was enthralled by the way she glided across the floor and gracefully mounted the carpeted steps. So spellbound was he that he barely noticed the tired little girls following in her wake. After she disappeared around the turn in the staircase, he shook his head, took a deep breath, then remembered he had not asked for payment in advance. His father would be furious. Howard knew he should follow the woman upstairs and ask for the money, but he just couldn't raise the courage to accost her. He worried for only a moment, then assuaged his conscience with the conviction that a woman 'like her' would surely be able to pay for a night in their hotel. Perhaps he would have the opportunity to collect payment tomorrow morning before his father realized his mistake. Entrusting tomorrow's problems to tomorrow, he picked up the book he had been reading and relegated the beautiful woman in room 203 to a distant corner of his mind.

"But mother," whispered Ruth as she peered out from under the covers, "how will we pay for the room?"

"I don't know, sweetheart, but I'll think of something." Selma spoke bravely as she tucked her daughters into bed and kissed them goodnight.

Like a caged animal, she paced the room for hours. Finally, she stopped before the mirror above the dresser and looked at herself in the lamplight. Her options were woefully thin. A diamond pin winked from the lace framing her chin. When she raised her hand to touch it, her eyes immediately focused on the charm bracelet daintily encircling her left wrist. Her right hand came up to touch each charm individually as she watched them glitter in the mirror. She held her breath for a long moment, then her lips clamped together in firm decision.

Her hand moved to the diamond pin. Drawing it out of the lace, she turned it from side to side, watching it sparkle in the dim lamplight. Carefully, she laid the pin on top of the dresser. Next, she emptied the pockets of her coat, but that produced only a few coins and a lace handkerchief. The diamond pin was her only asset; the coins would buy perhaps two meals. She must horde them carefully. Her tired mind could think of nothing more she could do tonight. Physically and emotionally exhausted, she finally readied herself for bed. As she crawled between the covers, a terrifying thought begged an answer. How soon would they sleep in a bed again?

"So, what did the doctors tell you?" Carl hung Amanda's coat and scarves in the closet by the door. He shook his head at the coat's disreputable appearance as an understanding smile curled one side of his mouth.

"They're just like a bunch of old men arguing about the weather!"

"Must have said something you didn't like?" He grinned

at his older sister while he crossed the room and dropped into his favorite, overstuffed chair by the fireplace. A pure white cat suddenly appeared at his feet and gracefully leaped up onto his lap.

"Now, they want to operate. All that fancy medicine I've been taking the last six months hasn't done a thing." Amanda felt in the basket beside her chair until she found her crochet needle, yarn, and the length of red and blue material she was weaving. She hooked a few stitches, then her hands dropped to lay idle in her lap.

"What kind of operation are they talking about?" The mischievous smile that seemed a permanent part of Carl's face disappeared as he stared across the short space at his sister.

"That bunch of old fools said I've got a tumor right at the back of my skull." She sighed and lifted her hand to massage the back of her head. "Dr. Frankenstein said it's putting pressure on some nerve and that's what's made my sight... what's made me blind."

"Dr. Funkelstine. Not Frankenstein." Carl looked down at the fur ball in his lap and allowed himself to be hypnotized for a moment by the opaline green eyes of the cat as she pummeled his leg with her dainty paws.

"Humph. He might as well be Frankenstein, the way he's wanting to cut holes in my head." Though she tried to hide it, Carl heard the tremor in her voice.

"What happens if they don't operate?"

"Well, I can't get any blinder can I?"

"No, but a tumor doesn't belong inside your head. I'm assuming if it's the cause of your blindness, it's not done making mischief." Carl struggled to keep his tone light, but his eyes bored blazing lines through the air to his sister.

"That seemed to concern them as well."

"I will never let you talk me out of going with you again!" The cat scurried for cover behind the curtains when Carl suddenly lunged to his feet and flung across the room. "Getting answers out of you is like pulling a dead barge against a forty knot wind in high seas!"

"Are you telling me my beam is as broad as a barge?" Amanda stifled the chuckle that rippled past her lips.

"You are so exasperating!"

"And you are overprotective." Amanda waited, but no response seemed to be forthcoming.

"Janet was a very fine companion on the trip. It did the poor girl good to get out of Superior and see a bit of the world. She was patient... attentive... never seemed bored to sit hour after hour in the doctor's waiting room..."

Carl shoved splayed fingers through his thick hair and heaved a deep breath. "Point taken."

Amanda smiled when she heard his soft chuckle, knowing his distaste for sitting still for any length of time. And she felt it when he grew serious again.

"So, are you going to tell me what the doctors said, or do I have to go ask them myself?"

"They gave me two years..."

Carl had started across the room toward his chair, but

stopped at her words and his face paled. "Two years? Two years for what?"

"Two years to live unless I let them remove the tumor." Silence followed her statement. Then she heard Carl's footsteps finish crossing the floor until she heard him slowly lower himself into his chair.

"Can they do it?" Carl tried to keep his voice steady against the icy chill that paralyzed his throat.

"They say they have a pretty good success rate; told me the Egyptians were performing the same surgery 2000 years ago."

"I'm supposed to find that comforting? Modern medical science hasn't improved on a surgical procedure in 2000 years?"

The fire crackled in the hearth while brother and sister listened to their own heartbeats and the whisper of blood in their veins. Carl stared into the rippling flames, choking on the tight fist of fear clenching his heart. Finally, when he could breathe again, he broke the silence.

"I take it you're going to have the surgery?"

"February 25, if Uncle Thomas will lend me the money." Still the yarn and needle lay still beneath her hands.

"Lend, nothing! He'll give you the money. I'll see to that myself." It was a promise Carl intended to fulfill tomorrow.

Suddenly, Amanda lifted one hand out toward her brother and he stepped across the intervening space to take it between both of his.

"If the operation works, Carl, I'll have my sight back."

Neither of them spoke of what would happen if the surgery failed.

CHAPTER SIX

Selma tossed and turned most of the night, worrying over her problem like a terrier digging at the hole of a rat. Early morning was shading from black to seal gray when she finally relaxed enough to doze off, only to have her dreams slashed with dark scenes rife with pain. Selma saw herself drowning in a black pool of freezing water while above her a beautiful face laughed. A hand with long fingers and bright red nails waved a cheery farewell, then left her trapped in the freezing darkness. Selma struggled against arms that held her beneath the water, desperately gasping for a breath of air. Her fists flailed and thrashed against the steel bands that held her frozen until a thundering noise echoed through her mind and she felt herself falling, falling, falling...

Suddenly, she jerked awake and bolted up in the bed. Ragged gasps echoed back from the flower-papered walls as she felt the sickening wave of terror slowly recede. She forced her eyes open and squinted at the early morning light filtering through flowered curtains. Heaving a relieved sigh, she wiped the beads of clammy perspiration from her forehead. Slowly, she closed her eyelids and lay back down.

The knocking came again, but in the waking world this time, growing louder with each impact. Selma forced herself upright again, struggling to come fully awake. Sluggishly, she pushed her arms through the sleeves of her robe, then padded barefoot to the door. Opening it a crack, she peered out.

"Excuse me, ma'am. Did I wake you?"

Mr. Stickle, the manager of the hotel, was getting to be an old hand at requesting payment from customers after his son forgot. One glimpse of the face beyond the crack in the door and he understood better why his son had forgotten. Well, he consoled himself, that's what happened when you hired your own child.

He apologized to 203 and presented a tray of rolls and hot chocolate, which he told Mrs. Wraxmore he had brought for their breakfast. Her radiant smile of gratitude almost caused him to forget his primary purpose in pounding on her door so early in the morning. However, after she had taken the tray into her room, thanked him again, and was preparing to shut the door, he interrupted the movement by apologizing for his son's oversight and requesting payment for the past night's lodging.

When her eyes slid sideways and her cheeks drained of color, he hoped it was just early and he had caught her unawares. But experience warned him there was a problem brewing in 203.

"Wait just a moment, please." The soft tones held him by the door as she disappeared for a moment. When she returned, her hand reached through the doorway and opened to reveal a diamond pin lying in her palm.

"Could you take this as payment?" Did he detect a hint of desperation in her voice?

He lifted the shining stiletto between his fingers and turned it back and forth, watching the lamplight sparkle in its facets.

"Well, I don't know, ma'am. A fancy bauble like this don't pay the bills or buy food for the table."

"I am aware of that," came the soft voice, "but it is all I have at the moment. We were... robbed... on the train. Our money was stolen. I... haven't had time... to... make other... arrangements."

Stickle transformed, chameleonlike, from obsequious landlord to haranguing judge. He wrapped his bony fist around the diamond pin and told her in no uncertain words that he would accept the pin as payment. But, unless she could produce cash to cover future expenditures — by eleven o'clock — she would have to gather her things and leave his hotel. He rounded out his tirade by announcing that his was not an establishment for vagrants nor a charity institution.

Selma desperately wanted to defend herself, protect her daughters, even beg for his mercy. But she was helpless before his outburst. Never before had she realized the difference money made in her life. She had been accustomed to budgeting and saving from what she considered a mere pittance. But never had she been totally bereft. Her social status alone had always guaranteed respectful treatment from persons of this landlord's station.

Instinctively, her breeding and training reasserted itself. Her chin raised on her pale, slender neck and she directed a bored gaze at the landlord, suddenly determined that he should not realize how desperate she felt inside. In frigid tones, she informed Mr. Stickle that she would quit his establishment as soon as she and her daughters were dressed. Then she closed the door in his face and leaned against it, trembling more and more until she could stand no longer. Slowly, she slid to the floor, one hand still twisted around the doorknob.

The trappings of British society were of no value here. She had never felt more helpless in her life. All of her goals, her plans, her dreams were under attack. She was scared. Terrified.

Looking across at her sleeping daughters, the hopelessness of her situation sank into her heart and mind like lead weights, ballast that held her spirit down, not allowing her mind to rise above the problems threatening to drown her. Her thoughts whirled around and around, gnawing uselessly at the same problem. Where would they live? What would they eat? Where would she get the money to transport her daughters and herself to the little home awaiting them? Montana might as well have been on the moon for all her little house could help her now. Oh, why oh why had she come to Superior?

Selma fought the morbid depression that began to spread its insidious tentacles through her mind, threatening to smother her in its foggy shroud. Even four years ago she would have dissolved in tears. But the fragile creature she once was no longer existed. With a will forged through years of practice, she called up the vision of her little house; the white picket fence, her daughters happily playing in their new home. She saw herself as a contented grandmother rocking her darling grandchildren. The vision deepened and she felt herself relax into her dream. Slowly, slowly, the steel grip on her lungs and heart loosened until she could breathe again. A clammy shiver raced over her skin and the moment passed. Then she gently tucked away her dream where she could touch it at need and turned her eyes and mind to focus on the real world outside the frosted windowpanes.

Selma's teeth were chattering. She realized she was cold and slowly crawled back beneath the covers of the bed. Lying on her side, she watched the growing light outside illuminate huge white flakes falling in heavy waves from the sky. The lacey wisps created an opaque curtain across the world beyond the little room. She had no idea how long she lay there, unable to return to sleep. Slowly, her body ceased shivering, though her mind continued to race.

At last, she pushed aside the blankets, walked over to the window, and looked down. A few people and several horse-drawn carts and wagons struggled through the snow on the street below. A yellow dog raced out of an alley between two buildings; just a momentary blur that disappeared behind the wall of white flakes.

Wrapping her arms around herself, she rocked back and forth, thinking, thinking. She must have money. But from where? Who? The only relation she had in the world was her mother. Abruptly, she straightened her shoulders, physically nauseated at the thought of begging her mother for money. She knew very well what that would cost. Never! She would work. Other people — most people — had a job of one sort or another. This was a large, booming city. Why couldn't she get a job? She would go from shop to shop until someone hired her. Surely working in a shop couldn't be that difficult. Yes. She could do this. A sudden spurt of new strength surged through her heart and mind.

A determined smile flickered for a moment at one corner of her mouth, then disappeared. The freezing cold in the world outside made it imperative that she get a job quickly; find a place to stay, a place to keep her daughters warm and safe. It wasn't much of a plan, but at least she could focus on a tangible goal.

"One step at a time," she breathed to herself. "Don't give up! Don't give in! We've made it this far. This won't stop us. We are free. We can do this! We will survive!"

Her fervent intensity waned. The more she thought about it, the more impossible this task seemed. She recognized the danger in following that path, so before her courage evaporated completely, Selma squared her shoulders and woke her daughters.

"Anna, Ruth, we have to talk," she pressed a kiss to each warm little cheek and forced herself to smile as their eyes slowly opened.

Anna yawned and stretched while Ruth smiled sleepily into Selma's eyes, "H'lo, mama."

Selma fed them rolls and the cooled chocolate while she explained their predicament as simply as she could. When she outlined her plan for their rescue, they were surprisingly enthusiastic about her plan to get a job. Their simple faith in her ability to solve all the problems the world could throw at them left Selma deeply humbled.

Thrusting aside the paralyzing fear of failure, she hurriedly helped the girls dress. When, just after eleven o'clock, the three of them descended the stairs, Mr. Stickle waited behind the desk. His face was a mask of disinterest, his eyes glittering like flint above arms that were folded across his dark vest. One glance at his immutable countenance and Selma turned for the door without looking back, a determined smile glued to her lips. No words passed between them, but the air was thick with disdain as Selma stepped out into the snow with Anna and Ruth trailing.

The door clicked quietly shut behind them.

"What's this I hear about you planning to go west?"

Thomas didn't even wait for Carl to get all the way into his office before launching his attack.

"I'd give a month's pay to know how you get your information." Carl laughed at Uncle Thomas' angry expression and tried to cajole him, "I've been meaning to tell you about it..."

"Well, you better get all that foolishness out of your head right now."

The old man's face suffused to an alarming shade of purple. A fist of iron clenched the center of his chest until Thomas felt the dreaded heaviness bearing down, forcing him to slump back in his wheelchair. Closing his eyes for a few minutes, he willed his heart to slow down.

The younger man stared at him in concern. "Calm down, Uncle Thomas, before you bust a gasket." Carl poured a glass of water from the pitcher on the corner of his uncle's desk and placed it in his hand. "Here. Drink this and take a few deep breaths. Then we'll talk about it."

Carl walked to the circular window behind Thomas' desk and stared out at the nearly deserted docks. Only a handful of workers could be seen in this area. Some were performing minor repairs to ships, some working near the storage bins and warehouses that lined the bay area.

"All right, Carl. Let's have it." Thomas' voice was more controlled now, quieter.

"The Columbia River Basin." Carl announced it as though he'd made a new discovery.

"What?" Thomas' fingers involuntarily clenched on the arms of his chair until he forced them to relax.

"It's the fastest route to ship goods into the inland regions of the northwestern states." Carl turned away from the window and returned to the chair in front of the massive desk. "The Columbia is a completely different river from the Mississippi. Needs different types of ships. I plan to explore the Columbia River and her tributaries with an eye to designing boats that can haul goods and people upriver. At least until the Rocky Mountains get in the way."

"What about the North American TransAtlantic Shipping contract?"

"I'm almost done with the designs for the new tug they want. I'll go to New York next week and discuss it with them. If they want us to proceed, I'll charge back here and get the prototype under construction."

His dreams were too big for the chair. Carl heaved himself to his feet again and started pacing the room. "It'll take six months to get the prototype built, and while..."

"It's your design. You need to be here, make sure it's built right."

"Steven can run the shop while I'm gone. He'd do that even if I stayed here, sitting in my office the whole time. You know there's no one better anywhere on the Lakes for building prototype ships."

Carl listened to Thomas grumble for a moment, then went on.

"By the time the prototype is ready to test, I'll be back — hopefully with ideas for new boats. Three years from now — two with a lot of luck — we could be the number one shipyard constructing boats specifically designed to navigate the rivers of the entire Columbia River Basin."

"You can't possibly expect to build boats here and ship them across the Rockies..."

"Nope. That's why we'll have to open a new shipyard on the West Coast. I was thinking Portland would make the best base of operations."

Thomas knew a sound business plan when he heard one. If anyone but Carl had proposed it... if he could only send another man to investigate. He fidgeted in his chair, silently cursing his useless legs and the broken back that bound him to his loathsome chair.

"Uncle Thomas. I know what you're thinking..."

"Well, you should. I've told you often enough," Thomas blustered. But for all his tirades, Thomas was a fair and honest man. Inside, he was intensely proud of Carl.

"It's a grand idea, son." Bitterness edged his next words. "If I weren't so old...and stuck in this dratted chair...I'd have thought of it first." A grudging smile lightened his stern countenance for a moment, then disappeared as he pounded one wheel of his chair. "But I need you here."

"No, you don't, Uncle Thomas. I'm just twiddling my fingers here. You handle everything — as you should. No one knows this business like you do." Carl was up and pacing, but stopped by the circular window to look out again. "And it's not like I'll be gone forever. Two weeks, three at the most, for the first trip. Then I'll be back. We can plan the West Coast operation after I make the initial survey..."

Thomas whirled his wheelchair until he was staring through the round window beside Carl. "Then you can run the West Coast operation while I stay here on the Lakes? That's what you're thinking, isn't it?"

"Well, you have to admit it's a good organizational strategy."

"I don't have to admit anything." The peevish tone in his voice did not escape Carl's notice.

Carl twitched the strained muscles in his tense shoulders and stirred the pot. "But you're right. I don't plan to run the West Coast operation. My ranch is still waiting for me in Montana. Once Amanda is well, that's where I'll be heading. I was thinking Finchley might be a good choice to run the Oregon operation once it proves out."

Carl watched Thomas carefully, relieved when the old man calmed down, and vaguely surprised that he avoided the subject of Montana altogether. That particular sore spot was usually good for a curse or two.

"When do you plan to leave?"

"Thought I'd make the initial trip week after next. Check on harbor space; get specifics on the rivers and towns; talk to freighters and shippers to get an idea of what's happening now. I need to get some idea how big an operation it could become. Figure it'll take a couple of weeks, then I'll be back in time for Amanda's surgery. I plan to go to Chicago with her. When she's well enough, I'll bring her back here. Then, later in the spring, I'll make a longer trip — when the rivers and roads are open so I can see them for myself."

And if she doesn't come back, you'll have somewhere to run to, something to keep your mind busy. Thomas kept the thought to himself.

Carl was surprised to see Thomas nod his head. Then the wheelchair turned to face him and the piercing, sapphire blue eyes bored straight into his.

"If you're going to go, you better get hustling on the Sea Tug design. You don't have much time left."

"Aye, aye, sir." Carl sketched a brief salute and sailed out the door.

hey're so pretty!" Anna unexpectedly buoyed Selma's spirits with her innocent delight in the graceful white flakes drifting out of a glowering sky. She held out her little mittened fingers and caught some of the flakes, then brought them close to her eyes to examine their perfect crystalline points.

"Oh, Mother," Ruth's surprised whisper brought Selma's head around with a jerk. "Look!"

Selma's eyes followed her slim finger. Shuffling along the shoveled sidewalk on the opposite side of the snow-covered street was the blind woman of last night, still shrouded in her tattered coat and plethora of scarves. If possible, her attire looked even more disreputable in the morning light.

The words spoken through the snowstorm on the dark train platform last night echoed through her mind as Selma watched the woman's halting progression down the board-walk. 'To meet your dreams... you must live them each day along the way.' She wondered what dreams the blind woman harbored in her soul and whether she had met them somewhere... along her way.

Unbidden, a flash of insight seared through Selma's introspective thoughts. Poor and ragged the older woman might be, but the fact that she was walking down the street today bore silent testimony that she did, indeed, have a home that had kept her warm and safe last night — and would again through the night to come. Meanwhile, Selma and her daughters, dressed in the finest clothes money could buy, had no place to call home, no corner of the world where they could escape from the cold, and barely enough money to purchase a few morsels of food.

Selma stifled a frantic desire to scream out her frustrations. Flitting through her mind came the urge to run across the street and beg for the woman's help. Simple pride held her back. She had depended solely on her own strength for so long that Selma found it impossible to ask for another's help. Instead, she straightened her shoulders, turned away from the blind woman, and began her search for a job.

Six shops had closed their doors to her by late that afternoon when the three of them — cold, tired, and hungry — stepped into a small, bustling, restaurant near the docks and approached a portly woman who looked to be the owner. As Selma explained her need for employment, she watched the same expression she had seen in each store today cross the woman's face. Her eyebrows rose in disbelief before her mouth turned down in disgust.

"Mighty fine togs for a woman needin' a job." Her aquiline nose pointed at Selma's hat and dress. "A woman like you wouldn't know how to wash dishes, let alone serve a plate o' stew to a customer. Nor clean up after he's gone." The woman sniffed and turned away.

"Madame, please! Judge me by what I do, not by what I wear." A pleading edge tainted her voice.

The woman paused and turned half way around.

Selma's brow furrowed as she plunged ahead. "I am penniless, no matter how much my clothes may say otherwise. And I have my two daughters to feed and care for." Her desperate eyes pleaded from the depths of her soul. "Please, I need to work... even for a few hours. Anything. Please?"

The stern woman's eyes moved past Selma. They came to rest on the pale faces of Anna and Ruth, quietly huddled close to their mother's skirts. Her face and her heart softened. Crossing her arms, the woman's shrewd eyes measured Selma from her toes to her hat while one stubby finger tapped her ruddy cheek.

"The dishwasher went home sick an hour ago. I could use some help in the kitchen, if you're willin'. But only for the rest of the day."

Relief washed through Selma, almost causing her knees to buckle. "Thank you," passed her lips in a tight whisper. "Thank you and God bless you."

Selma was stunned by an unfamiliar sense of humility

and gratitude that welled up in her heart until it almost choked her. She could barely force her stiff legs to hold her upright as she followed her new employer between crowded tables and through a swinging door into a hot, muggy kitchen.

Selma quickly settled her daughters in a corner where they would not get in the way. Pressing a kiss to each smooth forehead, she admonished them to be still as little mice. Their big eyes stared up at her and they nodded their understanding. The long hours of their first day of abject poverty had changed them. Their bellies were hungry, their bodies tired. And the growing understanding that there was no home to go to and no food to eat had thrust a cruel shaft of reality into their young lives. It held them silent and obedient as no other form of persuasion could.

Quickly, Selma stepped to the sink and rolled up her sleeves before plunging her hands in the deep, sudsy water. The girls snuggled close together on a wooden crate. Curious, they gazed at the charred cooking pots hanging from the center of the kitchen ceiling, and stack after stack of crockery lining cupboard shelves. Strings of onions, garlic, and dried peppers hung from the smoky rafters. Two slender Chinamen, dressed in black, loose-fitting pajama-like outfits, flitted between the giant cast iron stove and a massive, wooden, cutting block in the center of the room. They jabbered at each other incessantly in their high, birdlike language, but never spared a word or glance for the little girls or the new dishwasher.

Warmth emanating in waves from the big stove soon enticed Anna and Ruth to remove their coats. For the first time since leaving their bed that morning, the girls were warm right down to their toes.

Bang! The swinging door burst inward and Mrs. Guggenheim bustled through, carrying a tray overflowing with dirty dishes. She hauled them to where Selma scrubbed furiously, elbow-deep in warm, sudsy water, and stacked them on top of the mountain of dishes already waiting. She picked up several of the bowls Selma had already washed and rinsed. Her minute inspection earned Selma a grunt of approval.

A dark scowl drew the corners of the woman's mouth down when she glanced at the two girls sitting quietly in the corner. Lifting three newly-washed bowls from the counter, she turned to a giant pot on the black stove and ladled thick, steaming stew into each bowl. Two she carried to the girls. Thrusting the bowls at Anna and Ruth, she warned them not to spill any.

The third bowl she offered to Selma. "Here, girl. Dry your hands, sit down, and eat this. You're lookin' almighty pale and I don't want you faintin' on me."

Without another word, she turned and disappeared back through the doorway leading into the dining area. Selma squeezed beside Anna and Ruth and all three gobbled up the rich stew. One of the Chinamen walked over and shoved a small loaf of bread under Selma's nose and chattered words she could not understand. Selma looked into his face, but he kept his head bent as he waggled the bread at her again. She took the long, slender loaf from his hands and voiced her thanks. The little man merely turned and went back to work.

At closing time, Mrs. Guggenheim told Selma that she and her girls were welcome to sleep in the kitchen after she finished up with the dishes. She counted a few coins into Selma's outstretched palm and told her she could eat breakfast in the morning. By then the regular dishwasher should be back. She left the sentence hanging.

Selma met her eyes briefly, then looked down as she nodded her understanding. She was being dismissed. Then she raised her eyes again. Looking steadily at Mrs. Guggenheim, Selma thanked her sincerely for her kindness.

Mrs. Guggenheim suffered a momentary flash of guilt. However, she assuaged her conscience by counting the number of employees she was already supporting and knew that she could not feed every extra hungry mouth in Superior.

"Check back time to time. People come and go around here. If I have any openings, I'll be glad to talk with you. In the meantime, try Mr. Gibbons' hardware store over one street and down a block. He might have an opening."

It was the best she could do. In a moment, she had locked the doors and was gone.

Selma finished the dishes. Then she took a small handful of matches from the match holder by the stove and tucked them into one of the deep pockets of her skirt. She thought they might come in handy.

Through the long hours until dawn, the small family cuddled together on the narrow stack of wooden crates in the corner of the kitchen, warmed by the stove, their bellies full of food for one more day.

Early the next morning, breakfast eaten, the homeless trio continued their search. But Selma's step had a new spring in it. For the first time in her life, she had earned money through her own labor. It wasn't much, but she had proven to herself that she could do it. She was hopeful as she headed for the establishment of Mr. Gibbons. With a recommendation and a place to go, perhaps today she would get a real job; one that would last more than a single evening.

Snow did not fall through the day, but the freezing wind off Lake Superior howled down the streets. Mr. Gibbons was not hiring, but he referred her to Mr. Simpson. Selma maintained her composure and stepped out into the cold once more. Together, the trio trudged along the icy sidewalks for almost a mile. Halfway there, falling tears froze on Anna's cheeks as she held up her tiny hands and declared she could no longer feel her fingers. Selma picked up her youngest daughter and carried her, tucking her tiny hands between their bodies until Anna could feel her fingers again. Selma desperately wanted to run and had to force herself to walk slow enough for Ruth's tiny legs to keep up.

Mr. Simpson was not hiring, nor was Mr. Corey to whom he referred her. It was almost dark when Mr. Corey sent her to Mrs. Knightlington's Boarding House. The bustling woman had no job to offer and all of her rooms were full. Selma immediately recognized her aversion to the expensive clothes Selma wore, but her expression softened when she registered the cold and hunger in the eyes of the two little girls. She offered to feed the small family and told Selma they were welcome to sleep in her parlor; however, they would have to be gone before any of her boarders awoke in the morning. Selma swallowed her pride again and thanked the woman for her generosity.

The next night found Selma desperately clinging to the ragged shreds of her courage. Desperate thoughts fled to memories of England, her dead husband, their mansion home, her mother. And finally, her own bid for freedom. What had she said to her coachman? At least she would be free? How proud her words had been. How foolish? Tired shoulders slumped and her resolve began to evaporate in the freezing air.

Selma looked down at her daughters, shuffling stoically beside her, their faces pinched against the cold and hunger. Unexpectedly, her soul felt an influx of courage. Quitting was not an option. These two precious souls were depending on her. If she gave up, they would surely die.

She was free. And while she was free, she would never give up. Her chin lifted defiantly and she looked around for the first time in almost a mile of storefronts and modest homes.

They were trudging past a grocer's market and Selma

stopped to peer inside. Anna and Ruth listlessly plastered their cold faces against the windows, hungering for the bright things on the other side of the cold glass. Selma was suddenly overwhelmed with such an intense feeling of desperation that she imagined herself walking into the store and stealing food. She had taken two steps toward the door when she stopped herself. Fiercely, she thrust her hands deeper into her pockets and was surprised to feel the few coins she had been hoarding. Coming to a sudden decision, she opened the door and pulled the girls inside with her.

"Come on, girls. We're going to buy something to eat."

Anna and Ruth licked their lips while Selma spent a few of her precious coins on three seed cakes and a tin of canned milk. She asked the man to punch a hole in the tin, then led her girls back outside. Once around the corner, they huddled in the lee side of the building. Selma handed the milk to the girls and urged them to share the whole can. Then they ravenously devoured the seed cakes, their hunger making it impossible to eat slowly.

Repeated gusts of blowing snow sent the family in search of better protection from the wind. Selma urged the girls to follow as she led the way around the back corner of the store. They turned the corner and walked straight into a sheltered area enclosed on three sides and devoid of snow.

It was dark in the shed and Selma stumbled to a halt. As her eyes slowly grew accustomed to the gloom, she could just make out a tall wagon piled high with boxes and covered by a huge tarp. Eagerly, she led the girls around to the back of the wagon. Quickly, she untied the rope at the back of the wagon and peered beneath the covering. She could barely make out the vague shapes of boxes stacked around stuffed sacks. A narrow tunnel had been formed between the boxes on one side of the wagon bed and sacks stacked on the other.

"Girls, I think we've found a place to spend the night."

"Will it be warm?" Ruth, barely tall enough, peeked into the wagon bed.

Anna gripped the wagon bed with her mittened fingers and jumped up and down, trying to see. "Let me see. Let me see."

"Here... up you go, Anna." One at a time, Selma lifted her children into the wagon and urged them to crawl into the opening.

"We'll all snuggle real tightly together and make it all cozy and warm."

Selma followed them in and pulled the cover back into place. Inching along on her belly, she wedged herself snuggly between the crates on one side and Anna and Ruth on the other.

"Mama," Anna whimpered after they were all settled, "I'm still hungry."

"I am, too." Selma cuddled her girls close to share body warmth and security. "We all have to be strong until tomorrow," she whispered softly. "We'll find more to eat in the morning."

"It's okay," Ruth murmured through the darkness, "the milk and cakes tasted yummy."

Selma moved her hand until she touched Ruth's cheek. "You're being so brave. I'm terribly proud of you both. I want you to know how much I love you."

Alternately stroking one little head, then the other, she talked of their little house waiting in Montana, painting a vision of times ahead when their tummies would be full, when they would run and laugh under the trees around their house.

An hour later, the wind died away to a fitful breeze and the children finally drifted off to sleep. A lowering cover of dense clouds actually raised the temperature of the air a few degrees before midnight. But Selma worried for her children and spent the night constantly checking to make sure their skirts were pulled all the way over their feet to keep them as warm as possible. Gradually, she realized that their combined body heat had actually warmed up the tiny cocoon they shared. The temperature beneath the tarp had become almost comfortable. Selma fought her weariness, trying to keep herself awake by stroking first Anna's hair, then Ruth's, touching them alternately to continually reassure herself that they were all right.

She cocked her ears when she caught a familiar sound. Ruth was sucking her thumb. It was a habit she had discarded when she turned three, except in moments of severe stress. Selma's fingers moved to Ruth's tiny head where they twined around a soft ringlet. Gently, she rubbed the fine hair between her fingers. It stirred a memory of the day the doctor pronounced that her prolonged bout with the stomach flu was merely the first sign of pregnancy.

Selma had been stunned, appalled, disbelieving; then she wanted to kill herself. Oblivious to the horror his words had evoked, the doctor went to break the good news to her husband. Selma dressed slowly, slipped down the back stairway, and walked out the side door as though in a trance. Her feet led her blindly to the stable, her most favorite retreat on the whole estate.

When Seth saw her slip through the door, one glance at her face told him something was amiss. He shooed the young stable boy outside and stepped forward to attend Selma himself. Her voice was leaden when she requested that he saddle Sylvester. Her glassy eyes and pale face told Seth that something was far wrong. He ventured to ask if she was all right. He was rewarded with a smile, but one that only lifted her lips, never making it to her eyes. Nevertheless, Seth outwardly accepted her assurances that she was fine and merely needed to blow the cobwebs out of her mind. He offered to ride with her, but she firmly declined his company.

Once in the saddle, Selma did not wait for Seth to open the outer gates. When he released his hold on the reins, she set Sylvester at the side fence. The tall, chestnut hunter cleared the hurdle, taking it and the next one in his stride until the two were free and racing the wind across the south pasture.

Strangely, she didn't remember feeling the wind in her hair. Instead, the freedom in which she usually reveled while riding twisted into agony. Invisible chains wrapped around and around her chest, squeezing tighter and tighter until she could no longer breathe. Her mind felt trapped as her body and soul had been trapped. Riding instinctively, she held to the back of the horse as they sailed blindly over hedges and fences in a headlong rush to the sea.

Sylvester crested the grassy dunes and slid down the other side before Selma finally hauled back on the reins. The horse slowed to a halt, blowing hot air from flaring nostrils, white foam dripping from his lathered chest and flanks. For the first time in her life, Selma didn't consider the horse, but slid from his back and staggered into the surf, flinging herself through the foaming water until it reached her knees, her waist, her neck. Then she was swimming.

Without warning, a giant wave slammed over her head, forcing water into her open mouth. She felt herself sucked downward until her whole body pounded against the rocky bottom. Desperate and eagerly seeking oblivion, she relaxed and willed the waves to carry her body into the deep abyss.

Gradually, like a brightening light reaching deep into her mind, there grew a picture of a tiny girl with dark ringlets and brown eyes. Dressed in pink and white frills with a matching bow holding back her dusky hair, she was reaching snowy arms up toward Selma. With the vision came the dazzling revelation that Selma carried a new life in her womb; that from this day on, she need never again be alone.

Frantically, she began kicking and fighting against the whirling vortex until finally, her head breached the surface. Spluttering and gagging on the salty water, Selma came fully aware for the first time since receiving the doctor's news. She wanted to live. She struggled toward shore, but the heavy, waterlogged skirts entwined around her ankles and threatened to drag her under. Thrashing and kicking, Selma fought against the heavy burden, choking on more water, forcing her lips above the pounding surf. Just as her strength gave out, one foot touched the gravelly bottom.

More tired than she could ever remember being, Selma dragged herself out of the surf. Rising and falling and rising again, at last she flopped, exhausted, onto the rocky shore. Cold salt water gagged in her throat, retching out of her lungs and stomach. At last, she lay still, listening to the pound of the waves and the breath rushing in and out of her lungs.

When Sylvester began nuzzling her head and face, she heaved herself painfully to her feet. Grasping his bridle in her shivering hands, she leaned against his warm, musky neck and waited for strength to return to her shaking limbs. Then she started walking.

Her dreams for a future began that hour. Sodden and cold, deathly tired and vilely sick to her stomach, for the first time since leaving the seclusion and security of school, Selma viewed the dark tunnel of her future with a bright spot of light at the end. She formed no real intention of running away from her husband right then, but when she finally found a boulder big enough to help her get back into Sylvester's saddle, she turned the horse toward York. The Wraxmore Estate lay in the opposite direction.

She was ill prepared for flight, but once on the road, a hazy idea took shape in her mind. If only she could hide herself away, somewhere her husband could never find her, work at some menial task until she earned enough money for passage to — anywhere. She could sail away to — America!

It was the birth of a dream. America! The land of the free. Where men — and women — made their own destiny. Slowly, but with growing fervor, her heart flamed with a vision of freedom far from the loveless existence she now suffered, where she could bear the child growing in her womb and raise it in love and laughter. A burst of warmth surged through her heart and soul, warming her like a bright sun on a chill morning.

Amid a thunder of pounding hooves and crashes branches, six men on horseback, led by her husband, suddenly burst through the hedge behind and ahead of her. She was effectively surrounded. In one withering flash, the bright flicker of freedom died. She pulled Sylvester to a stop. The tired horse halted gladly, twitching his ears backward and forward.

Lord Wraxmore's minions kept their distance as he kicked his horse up beside Selma until he was almost face to face with his wife. The scowl on his dissolute face only emphasized the deep lines that creased his forehead and cheeks. Bleary, yellow-brown eyes glared through the fading light when she raised hers briefly to look at him. Immediately, she realized her error and dropped her gaze to stare at her hands where they held tight to the reins. For one mad moment she thought of kicking Sylvester and trying to out-run the men gathered around her.

No premonition forewarned her of the powerful back-handed blow that knocked her from the saddle. Grunting in pain, Selma landed heavily on her shoulder and crumpled into a heap. She lay in the dirt at Sylvester's feet, her ears ring-ing, her face numb from the blow. Tears started to her eyes, but she choked them back and sucked warm blood from a cut lip. Instinctively, she turned her mind inward, focusing on the light at the end of her tunnel, promising herself no more tears until she stepped into that light.

Wraxmore leaped from the saddle and strode around the startled horses until he stood towering over his wife's prone body. He drew back a foot to deliver a vicious kick, but was arrested by an anguished whisper from the man on the near-est horse.

"The baby, m'lord!"

The boot stopped just short of Selma's stomach. Cursing muttered oaths, Wraxmore whirled around and pulled him-self back into the saddle.

"You, Smith! Get her on her horse. Bring her back to the manor."

Without a backward glance he jerked his mount around and dug sharp spurs deep into the lathered and bloody flanks. The terrified horse leaped ahead and the men watched him gallop away.

Selma jolted herself out of the sleeping memory. She lay panting heavily, waiting for the dregs of horror to ease from her mind and body. It was a skill she had not yet perfected. But she was improving. The rest of the night, she lay awake, only nodding off in short spurts until the morning sun began to filter through the covering.

When at last they crawled out of their canvas cave, Selma tied the ropes back in place. Just as they rounded the corner at the front of the building, a man passed them, leading a team of horses straight toward the wagon. Selma's heart chilled when she realized how close they had come to being discovered.

CHAPTER EIGHT

he Truvier mansion had stood in the center of thirty acres of cleared lawn for almost 125 years. For
102 of those years, it had been a lively home overrun with the
numerous progeny of several generations of Truviers. But the
final heir lived his life alone and childless. In his early years he
had been an adventurous lad, always ready for a lark or spree.
Inheriting a sizeable fortune at an early age, he chose to seek
adventure in the far corners of the world. He traveled exten-
sively in the east, eventually spending long years in the orient.
In smoky opium dens, he developed a love for the fruit of the
poppy. Its beautiful flower disguised invidious talons of obses-
sion that first lured with feathery dreams of euphoria, then
tortured its devoted slaves until, at last, they died in the throes
of emotional misery, physical disease, and financial ruin.

Derek Truvier's once sizeable fortune was quickly
devoured by the rapacious drug parlors of China. When at
last he returned to Wisconsin, he was a mere shell of the man

who had recklessly sailed away, seeking adventure.

Upon the morbid demise of Derek Truvier, his nearest relative — far removed from the Truvier name — received notice from the Douglas County Tax Commission. He returned a boldly written letter directing the county to put the derelict house up for public auction. Any proceeds earned thereby were to be used to bury the man's paltry remains and pay off whatever debts the funds could cover.

A black-clad parson and two rough grave diggers, each paid for their services, were the only spectators as the simple wooden coffin was lowered into a muddy grave. Shovel after shovel full of cold, wet dirt crashed loudly down on top of Derek Truvier's final remains, hiding from sight and memory the last of what had once been a proud line of French immigrants.

In 1901, Thomas Mason purchased the Truvier mansion at auction and donated it to the county to be used as a shelter for homeless children. From the day of its inception, Mason took an active interest in the establishment. Requesting and receiving from the county commissioners an appointment to sit on the board of directors, he was assigned responsibility for fiscal maintenance of the home. In that capacity, Thomas Mason solicited contributions from business associates and wealthy friends. He also sponsored yearly fund raising campaigns aimed at supporting the orphanage. And from his own coffers, he made sizeable donations each year to its upkeep. Most people who knew Mason as a hard driving business man — as tough as the boats he produced to sail the Great Lakes — would have been shocked at his philanthropic commitment to the welfare of the twenty-seven children currently housed at the old Truvier estate.

Thomas Mason touched a napkin to his lips, then placed it on the table and leaned back in his wheelchair. He smiled at the woman seated across the table from him as he spoke. "I want to compliment you on the quality of the meals you serve, Mrs. Cutfield. You have justified every particle of faith I placed in your ability to run a first class institution."

The lady inclined her head and an answering smile creased her lips. "There is still much to do here, Mr. Mason. But coming from you, I take that as a prized compliment. Thank you."

She pushed herself back from the table and stood up. She stood just over five feet, two inches tall with a round figure that many men would turn to admire were she to pass them on the street. Her serious hazel eyes bespoke efficiency and dedication, but overlaying that was some indefinable expression that drew the children to her. That glow of sincere concern and interest sparkled behind round, wire-rimmed glasses. Tiny wisps of silver in the brown hair at her temples lent her an air of maturity belied by her unlined face.

"If you're ready now, let's remove to my office." She glanced down at the decorative watch face pinned to her bodice. "I think there is sufficient time to complete most of our business before you have to leave for the train."

Mason wheeled himself back from the table and turned the chair with a skill that betokened long incarceration in the vehicle. As he rolled quietly toward the door leading into the main hall, he noticed one small boy still seated at the center table. Mason stopped his wheelchair and peered at the little fellow from beneath silvering brows. Finally, he extended his right hand.

"I'm Thomas Mason. What's your name, son?"

"Drew Surrusco, sir," the boy answered, his eyes wide and nervous.

"And why aren't you out playing with the other children, Drew Surrusco?"

The pale face colored slightly, but before he could answer, a stocky man dressed in serviceable work clothes hurried through the door. When he saw Mr. Mason beside Drew, he stopped. His eyes moved from Mason to Mrs. Cutfield as he pulled the hat from his head and saluted with two fingers to his forehead.

"Excuse me, sir. Ma'am."

"Just a moment, Charlie." Mrs. Cutfield held up one hand, but addressed Mr. Mason. "Drew is like you, sir. He doesn't walk. Each day, Charlie carries Drew down from his room to eat with the other children for the noon meal. And now he will take Drew to the library for a while before carrying him back to his room."

Thomas Mason peered intently at Mrs. Cutfield while she spoke. Then he glanced briefly at Charlie. When his piercing eyes moved back to Drew, the boy's knuckles were white where his hands nervously gripped each other on top of the table.

"Rather inconvenient, I'd say." The deep voice reverberated from the walls, but in a warm, friendly tone. He paused, lost in deep thought for a moment, then lifted an eyebrow and addressed Drew.

"What you want is one of these, my boy." His right hand pounded firmly against the wheel. Drew's eyes flashed wide open as he looked from the chair to Mr. Mason.

"Yes, sir." He breathed the words reverently.

"Charlie," Mason looked up at the handyman and commanded, "bring Drew out into the great hall." He winked at the boy, then whirled his chair and rolled away.

Charlie looked for and received Mrs. Cutfield's approval, then nodded his head before scooping Drew into his arms and following Mr. Mason. When he reached the hall, the older man was waiting beside a solid wood deacon's bench to the left of the massive front door.

"Over here, Charlie. Put the boy—put Drew—right there and then help me."

"Sir?" Charlie stood rigid, confused by the commanding gentleman.

"Sit the boy right there," Mason pointed at the other end of the bench, "and help get me out of this da... dratted chair. I want Drew to take a ride in this buggy, but I have to get out of it first."

"Are you sure...?" Mrs. Cutfield started forward.

"Of course I am. I never do anything I'm not sure about, Mrs. Cutfield." He looked sharply up at her in surprise.

"What? You don't think I sleep in this contraption, do you?"

"Of course not. I just..."

"Well, stop your fretting. You sound like my butler." A chuckle removed any offense from his words.

Charlie settled Drew on the bench then moved back to Mason.

"You just do as I say..."

A moment later, Thomas was seated on the deacon's bench, directing Charlie to lift the boy into the wheelchair.

Drew's face exploded in smiles as he settled into the wheelchair. Though much too small for the adult chair, he gamely reached his hands out past the armrests and gripped the wheels right at the top of the circle. He pushed with all his might. But nothing happened, even though he strained so hard his face turned red.

"Can't do it like that, boy. Grip the wheels lower down on the front."

Drew moved his hands forward and pushed. Slowly, the chair moved ahead an inch, then another. His face lit up again and he pushed harder. Soon he was moving steadily down the long hallway with Charlie pacing a watchful step behind.

Mrs. Cutfield kept her eyes on Drew as she lowered herself to sit beside Mr. Mason. "Thank you, Thomas.

Sometimes you truly do surprise me."

"Surprise you? How?"

"Beneath that solid steel business exterior, there beats a heart of gold."

Mason started to bluster in disagreement, but she waved him to silence. "Don't worry. I won't let your secret out." She turned from watching Drew and stared into Thomas Mason's eyes.

"Actually, I had planned to speak with you about trying to find a used chair for Drew when we discussed new business this afternoon. He's a bright boy and he needs more freedom than just what Charlie can provide."

"You're right. But you don't need to find a chair. I know it's a bit too large for the boy, but I plan to give him the one he's riding in right now."

"Thomas, you can't do that!"

"Yes, woman, I can!"

His autocratic words took her aback for a moment. Her back stiffened and she stared at him, eyes wide and shocked.

"Excuse me?"

"Forgive me." His ruddy face turned a shade darker, but his eyes held hers steadily. "I just meant that I have another chair ordered for myself. That one may be too big for Drew, but it's a bit too small for me, so I've ordered a newer model. Should be delivered sometime next week. Soon as it arrives, I'll ship this chair out here for Drew. He'll grow into it, you'll see."

Mrs. Cutfield rewarded him with a blinding smile that made his face turn even redder. Then she leaned sideways and pressed a fleeting kiss to his cheek. "You're magnificent!"

Mason pretended nonchalance and rushed into speech to cover his discomfort. "Actually, he'll be doing me a favor. I hated to throw that chair away and didn't have any idea what to do with it once my new one comes."

The gruff tone of his voice didn't fool Mrs. Cutfield for a moment. He read as much in her eyes and turned away, trying to mold his face into a mask of businesslike attention as he called out to Drew, "If you want to turn around, pull one wheel while you push the other."

Mrs. Cutfield leaned back, smiling and shaking her head at the imperious man beside her. He cared so much for the orphans, yet wanted no one to know what a kind heart beat beneath his tough facade. She respected him all the more for his reticence.

Anna had given out hours ago. Selma carried her all the time now. She didn't know what hidden strength kept Ruth on her feet. She was so young and trying so hard to be brave. Selma felt an insane desire to scream her helpless anger and frustration at the world. Wasn't there someone in this cold, heartless town who would take them in? Help them? Save her children from starvation and freezing?

"Please, God," she prayed silently as she walked, "I need a job. I need a tiny corner out of the cold for my children. I'll work. I'll live in a stable. Anything. Anywhere. Please?"

In one glaring moment of clarity, she heard again the blind woman's offer and her own proud spurning of the very help for which she now begged.

"Oh, forgive me. I was so blind."

But now that Selma was willing to accept the proffered help, the blind woman was nowhere to be found. And no one else was offering.

Selma shuffled past door after door decorated with pine bows and wreaths of holly, each festooned with red berries and fluttering ribbons. Rows of candles stood in the windows of homes, ready to be lit when the sun went down. Every home and business outwardly displayed the owner's eager preparation to celebrate the birth of Christ. It made Selma wonder about that mystical spirit of love and giving that defined Christmas. Did it really exist? If so, where did it come from? Where had it gone?

Another store owner, this time a woman who advertised dresses and hats for sale, looked at Selma's attire and frowned over the rumpled condition of her bodice and the wet, muddy hem of her skirt. When Selma inquired about employment, the woman sternly showed her out the door — a red-painted door — gaily bedecked with Christmas decorations. When Selma stood once more on the snowy sidewalk outside Wanda's Chic Habberdashery and Dress Creations, she wondered what Christmas meant to Wanda.

Selma knelt down and pulled Ruth close. They cuddled

together as close as they could. Rocking her daughters, almost in a trance, Selma's memories suddenly laid open. She was momentarily transported back to a time when she walked on the brightly decorated streets of York, shopping with what she considered at that time to be a pittance, searching for Christmas gifts for Anna and Ruth.

A bedraggled street urchin, dirty of face and ragged of clothes, had piteously begged a copper from her as she stepped from a brightly-lit shop. She remembered staring at him and thinking he should take more pride in his appearance. She shuddered now, as she remembered how she had studiously ignored his desperate plea. Thinking him beneath her notice, that there were institutions to care for the poor, she justified her lack of charity with the knowledge that she barely had enough change in her purse to buy her own Christmas presents. A silent, agonized prayer formed in Selma's heart. In shame and humility, she begged for forgiveness.

A muscle cramped in her back. She gasped and forced her eyes open. She had to grip the wooden framing of the building to pull herself to her feet. Screwing her eyes shut in agony for long moments, she waited for the pulsing spasms to relent, willing her muscles to relax. Finally, the pain faded and her eyes slowly opened.

As though a sign suddenly lit up the sky, her eyes were drawn up to one tall, white, church spire where it rose above the surrounding shops and houses. The white beacon seemed even brighter against the backdrop of red brick buildings some distance behind it. Her eyes never wavered as she took the girls' hands and lifted them to their feet. As a family, they headed toward the spire.

Why hadn't she thought of a church sooner? Perhaps because she never went to church? But she had heard stories. Surely she would be able to find help in a sanctuary of God. A warm glow of anticipation filled her chest and the blossoming hope lightened her feet.

Ruth was energized by Selma's excitement. Anna tried to walk again, but could barely move one foot after the other. Selma and Ruth each held one of Anna's little hands as they climbed the tall set of wooden steps and hurried under a deep awning. Selma grabbed hold of the elaborate cast iron handle on the white wooden door and heaved. But it didn't budge. The door was firmly locked. All three of them knocked, their desperate pounding drumming for a full minute. When they stopped to listen, the echo of their pounding reverberated to silence beyond the door.

Selma's frantic eyes flew around the windy vestibule and were arrested by a fluttering piece of paper nailed to the post inside the entryway. She put her mittened hand up to hold the paper still against the tug of the cold breeze and read:

December 18, 1904

My Dear Parishioners:

I apologize for leaving with such little notice. My mother is very ill and I have gone to be with her. I hope to be back for the Christmas service, but if I am not, Father Lavigny will travel from his parish and lead a Christmas Eve celebration service. I am so sorry to leave you at this blessed time of year, but am sure you will understand and forgive me.

Your brother in Christ,
Father Bartholomew

Selma slumped against the doorway. Confused, Anna and Ruth snuggled beneath the skirt of her coat. She heard them whimpering as they tried to hide from the biting cold. Selma felt her strength evaporate and knew if she could not go on, her daughters would surely die.

"Oh, God. Why? What am I to do?"

She cried aloud as her eyes probed the silent, forbidding heavens. Snowflakes whirled into her open eyes until she finally dropped her head. As though through a haze, her eyes focused on a small food store across the street, one she had not even noticed in her determination to get to the church. Haggard courage inspired her, giving her strength to rise again. Lifting Anna into her arms, she headed down the steps with Ruth trailing behind.

The pungent aroma of spices, bread, dried meats, and fruit struck like a physical blow to Selma's starving belly. The same shadow of desperation twisted Ruth's tiny face. Selma felt her heart tearing to shreds when the proprietor accosted them with a surly frown from behind a counter overflowing with foodstuffs. Bolstering her courage one last time, Selma begged for a job, laid her soul bare, and pleaded for work so that she could feed her children.

His lips twisted downward, but a softer gleam crept into his eyes when Selma expected anger. Silently, he considered the two little girls, one holding desperately to Selma's coat, the other clasped tightly in her arms. He stared for a bit, then turned to a wooden box and pulled out a loaf of bread. He wrapped it in brown paper and offered it across the counter to Selma. Though he inclined his head, he spoke no words.

Selma understood and could barely swallow the lump threatening to choke her. How badly she wanted to refuse his charity. She wanted a job, not a handout! But she could ill afford false pride. She had to think and act for the two precious little girls depending on her for their very lives.

Tears welled up in her eyes until the shopkeeper swam out of focus. She nodded her thanks while her lips twisted into a travesty of a smile. Her chin began to tremble as the corners of her mouth dragged her lips downward. She stuffed the loaf of bread into her coat pocket, then returned to the cold, blowing wind and frozen world outside the warm store. Selma resolutely swallowed salty tears and forced her eyes dry by sheer will power. Solemnly, she turned and watched the cold winter sun reflect off the glass separating her tiny family from the bright room full of food and warmth, then turned away and shuffled down the boardwalk.

Her resolve only lasted a few minutes. Deathly tired and

soul sick, Selma collapsed in the protected corner of an ornate bank building. She pulled Ruth in close and tried to wrap both girls inside her coat. Anna made no sound, but Ruth cried very quietly. Selma rocked her daughters and murmured words of love over them while her haggard eyes moved from one doorway to the next.

Holly wreaths. Candles. Tinkling bells. A separate part of Selma's mind considered the Christmas decorations. For the third time in as many days, she felt bewildered that Christmas could be nearing in the rest of the world while she and her children were dying for lack of shelter and food.

Ironically, the only Bible story she'd ever heard — read to her by a childhood friend late one night by the light of a single candle — now blossomed in her memory. Selma closed her eyes and tried to fit together the vague tidbits of the story she remembered. Hadn't there been an expectant mother? Her husband had walked the streets of a strange town, desperately seeking a place of rest for the woman to bear her first child. Yes. That was it. She remembered how he had knocked on door after door after door. But all of the inns in the little town turned them away.

The cold numbed her mind but she didn't care anymore. Suddenly, it seemed inordinately important that she remember the rest of the story shared in the forbidden attic room at Miss Shiboleth's Boarding School for Young Women.

The baby had been born in a stable. A son—the Christ child. Somewhere, the father had found a stable and taken his wife there. Oh — she licked her frozen lips at the thought — how good a stable sounded right now. Warm, fragrant straw. Warm animal bodies to heat it. Selma's lips curved in a smile at the thought and she relaxed as though she really were in a warm, cozy barn.

Suddenly, a whirling breeze sifted freezing snow into her face and her eyes struggled to open. A frantic voice in Selma's mind clanged a warning that the three of them would freeze to death if they didn't keep moving. Deathly tired, Selma gathered her last shreds of resolve and struggled to get up. She was so weak and Anna so heavy that she almost failed to rise. She urged Ruth to get up, but the poor little girl had finally reached the end of her endurance. Huddling miserably at Selma's feet, she refused to stand again.

Selma bent down. Drawing strength from a source only mothers possess, she lifted the shivering five-year old into her arms and straightened again, holding both girls to her breast.

Numbly, she stumbled down from the wooden sidewalk. At the next corner, she turned up Harbor Street, almost resigned to the feeling that she was looking for a good place to die. This section of town ended at the frozen shore of Lake Superior. She was almost to the docks. From where she stood, Selma could see that the enormous shipping and storage buildings up and down the street were almost completely devoid of activity.

For no reason other than one direction is as good as another when one is looking for a place to lay down and die,

Selma shuffled down the street toward the great lake she had come here to see. Vaguely, she noticed that the gigantic buildings completely blocked the wind from reaching the street where she now walked. Confused, Selma stopped, swaying drunkenly on her feet as she gazed around. Something had caught her eye, but she didn't know what it was. Her head swiveled slowly back and forth. The mouth of an alley drew her attention and she turned into it.

Beyond the brick walls of a boat repair shop, she shuffled through virgin snow for another fifty feet down the dead-end lane. Her arms ached painfully from carrying Ruth and Anna. Slowly, her eyes lifted, searching for a soft spot to lay down. Snow-covered mounds were everywhere.

Then something out of the ordinary caught her attention. She looked closer and saw what appeared to be a rough shack sloppily stuck on the outside corner of a brick warehouse, like a wart on a toe. Its roof started high and sloped away from the larger building. No holes showed in the sturdy walls. A single pane of glass was still intact and the door appeared tightly shut. It looked completely derelict, unwanted, surrounded by piles of refuse, as though it hadn't been used in eons.

A pitiful surge of adrenaline sent Selma struggling forward until a thigh-high pile of snow-covered debris barred her way. She stopped and lowered the children to the ground.

Frantically, Ruth cried out. "Where are you going?" Anna only slumped in a heap in the snow, neither speaking nor moving.

"Wait here, Ruth. Hug Anna tight to you. Try to keep each other warm. I'm going to look at something and I'll be right back." Her frozen lips could barely form the words and they came out in a drunken mumble.

The sound of Ruth's feeble sobs wrenched at Selma's heart as she stumbled away. Even unhampered by the children, Selma still struggled to climb over the barrier. On the other side, she stumbled toward the little shed. Her feet plowed a narrow path through the heavy snow, past more stacks of old wooden crates, and around rusted barrels and snow-covered mounds of debris that nearly hid the small structure from sight. She noted the lack of human attention to this portion of the alley and a dim sense of hope flickered in her heart, pounding it against her ribs until she could barely breathe.

She reached the wall of the shed and hurriedly dusted away the snow from the window so she could peer through. Nothing. The interior was dark. She tried the door. Surprisingly, the latch lifted easily. Ancient leather hinges swung outward silently, holding the door on a tilt as it brushed snow away from the entrance.

"Mama…" Anna wailed piteously, shivering and cold, held tight in Ruth's arms.

"Wait, sweetheart. I'll be right there." The vibrant enthusiasm in Selma's voice jerked Ruth's head up from where it had been resting on Anna's blue knit cap. She blinked through her tears and the falling snow. Her eyes were dull from cold and hunger, but her arms tightened around her little sister in hopeful anticipation.

Selma stepped carefully through the doorway and found herself standing on a dry, hard-packed, dirt floor. Out of the freezing wind, the air was noticeably warmer. Wild with excitement, she searched for signs of recent use. There were none, but right now she would have fought a bear for the privilege to bring her daughters into this little shelter. She whirled around and raced back to the girls.

"Anna! Ruth! We've found a home… " Selma breathed the words quietly, almost afraid this glorious ray of hope would vanish if she spoke the wish too loudly. Selma lifted them both over the barrier, then scooped Anna into her arms and led Ruth the last few yards to the shed and through the doorway.

CHAPTER NINE

Invitations to a party thrown by Thomas Mason were highly coveted by every woman who prided herself a member of high society in Superior. In their turn, the men considered such parties a rich venue for furthering their business interests and were equally eager to attend. With only a few exceptions, this guest list had been carefully selected by Thomas Mason with an eye to established, influential families that all met one specific requirement: they had at least one daughter of marriageable age.

Thomas greeted each of his guests as old friends. Then he introduced them to Amanda where she stood next to his wheelchair, acting as hostess for his party. Though many of the invited guests had heard of Amanda and her recent loss of sight, most had never met her. However, they were all familiar with her dashing brother, Carl. Their prospective inheritance of Thomas Mason's fortune would have made the brother and sister acceptable to all of Superior society, even if they had not been endowed with good looks and charming manners. Each lady and her spouse greeted Amanda with honor and respect, then proudly introduced their offspring.

Through with introductions, the guests moved on into the giant ballroom where huge tables offered dish after dish of culinary delights. Uniformed waiters glided silently between the guests, offering an assorted array of drinks in crystal glasses on silver trays. Chatting in small groups around the vast room, many of the ladies agreed that the eminently desirable Carl Stanton could have been Amanda's son.

"It seems odd that she is so much older than Carl," Mrs. Willis whispered to her friend and confidante.

"I believe she's more than twenty years Carl's senior. In fact, I understand she raised him after their parents died," Katherine Dempsey nodded wisely.

"Died?"

"Oh, my yes, haven't you heard? It was terribly sad. The influenza epidemic of 1876, you know." Teresa Willis spoke as though she had been right there the whole time. She nipped a fresh drink from the tray of a passing waiter and sipped it before continuing. "Then Amanda's husband died a year later, poor thing."

"What a tragedy." Mrs. Dempsey was sincerely sympathetic. "Any children?"

"No, more's the shame. Now it's just the two of them."

She drew her friend to a striped love seat and invited Mrs. Dempsey to sit beside her where the two ladies could eagerly peruse and discuss the growing crowd of shipping magnates and their wives and daughters.

Suddenly, Mrs. Brackenstock, a fellow mother sans child, sailed up, resplendent in a gown of black silk glittering with threads of gold interwoven in the material. Gold beads were handsewn on the bodice that covered her enormous bosom.

"Well, if you ask me, it looks very much like the king giving a ball so the prince can choose a bride."

Teresa Willis and Katherine Dempsey both smiled at the woman's outrageous comment and declared she must be mistaken. But, however much they dissembled, all three women knew it to be very nearly the truth.

"Where is Carl?" Thomas Mason growled aside to Amanda when none of his guests were within hearing range.

"I don't know, Uncle Thomas. I thought..."

But what she thought remained unspoken for at that moment Carl's name was announced by the butler. Amanda's brother sailed through the drawing room door, looking dashing in a black tuxedo and flashing the two greeters a roguish smile.

"Where have you been?" Thomas did not wait for Carl to respond. "I said the party started at eight o'clock and everyone has been asking where you are for the last hour!" He made no effort to keep his gravely voice quiet, and several heads turned to see what had upset him so much.

"Carl, is it you?" Amanda interjected, holding out both hands.

"Yes, it is your truant brother," Carl took her hands in his and pulled her into a quick embrace. Then he released Amanda and held her at arms' length while he looked her over. "That is a beautiful dress. You've been shopping."

"You like it?"

"I love it."

Thomas almost exploded. "Drat you two! Have you no respect for my wishes, boy?"

"Immense respect, Uncle Thomas," then he bent over and whispered conspiratorially in the old man's ear, "except when you try to sell me off to the highest bidder. I told you I'm not interested in getting married — and especially to any of these blue bloods."

When he stood, his charming smile was firmly fixed to his mouth, but his eyes flashed like inflexible steel into Thomas' smoldering blue gaze. Immediately, he was sorry for his defiance as a choleric hue purpled Thomas' face.

"Calm down, Uncle. I'm not saying I'll never get married, just that I'm not ready right now." Carl's apology fell on deaf ears.

Amanda sensed the strain between the two men and reached out to Thomas. Almost immediately, her soothing touch on Thomas' shoulder and whispered words in his ear seemed to soothe his frustrated soul. The deep color ebbed slowly.

Thomas was habitually incensed when his will was crossed. But he had more at stake tonight than just his authority and he knew he had to play his cards right. He truly had conspired to provide Carl with sufficient opportunity to find a suitable wife. A girl who would be able to curb his wanderlust, convince him to settle down right here in Superior. Someone who could help Thomas keep Carl close to him. The adoptive uncle acknowledged that he was acting for his own selfish interests, but there wasn't much left in the world that Thomas Mason wanted and didn't already have. Twenty years of being a millionaire had taught him that the most important things in life can not be purchased. Amanda and Carl were his family and he wanted them close. Amanda, at fifty, had no children and likely would never have any; so his burgeoning dreams of grandchildren were centered solely in Carl.

Blithely unconcerned with Thomas' paternal expectations, Carl excused himself and moved away with Amanda, adroitly mingling with the crowds. Without appearing obvious, he singled out his favorite people at the party and furthered their acquaintance with his sister.

Meanwhile, Thomas brooded from his favorite spot beside the fireplace. He alternately fumed at, then admired Carl's easy camaraderie as he moved from group to group. Until his attention was claimed by his old friend, Bradley Burdock. When Thomas again searched the room for sight of Carl, he failed to find him. He wheeled his chair to where Amanda sat beside the grand piano, chatting cozily with a pretty young lady, and immediately demanded to know where

Carl had disappeared to.

"I think he's gone back to his office, Uncle Thomas. He mentioned something about having to finish the plans for his sea tug..." She stopped when she heard Thomas' chair whirl around and glide away.

"Why is he so angry?" the young debutante asked in a bewildered tone.

"I couldn't say, Prescilla. I really couldn't say."

Anna and Ruth stared around the room, at the stack of baled straw in one corner, and old, canvas feed sacks haphazardly thrown in another. Curry combs, hoof picks, and a curved hand-scythe hung from nails driven into the shed walls beside a rusted saw. An ax with a broken handle and two dented feed buckets lay scattered about the floor. Two rusty lanterns hung from hooks in the ceiling rafters between three dilapidated, dust-covered saddle blankets that were thrown over the wooden ceiling beams.

As soon as she shut the door, Selma stood on her tiptoes and stretched high, but she couldn't reach either lantern. Quickly, she inspected the meager collection of tools and chose the ax. Holding the metal head, she extended the broken haft above her head. The extra two feet were enough to reach the handle of the nearest lantern and lift it away from the nail where it hung. She lowered it carefully, then shook the lantern and grinned at her daughters' upraised faces.

"It has oil in it. That means we'll be able to have a bit of light when it gets dark."

The girls huddled together, watching with wide, expectant eyes as Selma worked in a fervor of excitement to drag bales of straw from the stack and push them into a rough rectangle against the back wall. She used the scythe to hack apart the twine on one bale. Feverishly, she stuffed loose straw into a dozen feed sacks and laid them in a criss-cross pattern across the top of the bales. The feed sacks were longer than Ruth, so Selma had each of the girls step into one, then she pulled it up around them before lifting first Anna, then Ruth, up onto the soft, cushiony bed she had made. Selma talked excitedly with her girls while she covered them with more sacks filled with straw.

"Mama, can we eat the bread?" Ruth's huge, round eyes glittered at Selma through the shadowy light.

"The bread!" Selma shoved her hand into the deep pocket of her coat and pulled out the loaf. She tore apart the brown wrapping paper, broke half of the loaf into pieces, and handed one to each of the girls.

The window provided a tiny bit of light. But while Selma worked, the dwindling day had given way to increasing darkness until they could barely see each other. Before it was too dark to see, Selma pulled one of the matches from her pocket and struck it on the side of the lantern. Its bright flicker cheered Selma's soul. The growing flame mesmerized her. She stared at it as though at a fantastic magic trick until the flame burned lower on the match and threatened to burn her fingers. Selma shook herself awake and quickly thrust the flame to the wick of the lantern. Hungrily, the wick caught fire and the lantern glowed to life.

Selma turned to the girls, thrilled to show them the light. Ruth's bread was already gone but Anna held hers listlessly in her mittened hand. Only a tiny bit of it showed chew marks.

Selma hung the lantern from a nail on the center post, then hurried over to the girls.

"Anna, darling, please eat the bread."

"Too tired," came the feeble reply.

"Please, my love, you need to eat a few more bites." Selma pinched off a small piece and touched it to Anna's pale lips. "The bread will make you warm and strong, sweetheart." She lay down and cuddled close to both girls. "Then you can go to sleep."

Slowly, Anna nibbled at the tiny pieces Selma fed her until most of it was gone. Then Anna turned on her side and fell immediately to sleep. Ruth's eyelids nodded heavily over her eyes. She murmured sleepily, "I'm getting warmer."

Selma watched her daughters and listened to their gentle, even breathing. What began as a flicker soon expanded into a tingling, upwelling feeling of gratitude that surged through her entire body. Humbly, gratefully, she turned her eyes toward the ceiling. Her eyes did not focus on the rough wooden timbers of the roof. They saw beyond to the bright windows of heaven where someone had heard her prayer.

When she was sure both girls were asleep, Selma carefully wiggled off of the straw bed, pushed herself to her feet, and headed for the door.

Instantly, Ruth bolted upright, all sleep gone from her eyes. "Mother! Where are you going?"

Selma rushed back to her daughter's side. "Outside for firewood, Ruth. I think I can build a small fire in the corner right over there and it will warm us up." She smiled soothingly into the dark, frantic eyes. "Don't worry, sweetheart; I'm not going far and I'll be right back."

Ruthlessly, she banged the snow from a wooden crate pulled from the huge stack outside the door, then wrestled it into the shed and proceeded to hack it to pieces with the ax. Selma could never remember being fired with so much intense energy. She couldn't work fast enough and an idiotic smile felt permanently plastered to her lips.

Using the paper from the loaf of bread, it was only minutes before Selma had a small fire lit. She kindled it in the corner where the two brick walls met, at a safe distance from the straw bed and wooden walls. In seconds, a curling tendril of smoke rose to the ceiling. Selma watched it creep along until it found one of several holes in the roof slats where it filtered outside. An hour later, the air inside the shed was still clear, but considerably warmer. Selma felt she had achieved a miracle. The golden light of the fire was bright and welcome. Its flickering waves transformed the cold, dark shadows of the room into a warm, inviting, almost magical atmosphere.

Sometime later, Anna woke up, crying out for water.

Selma had discovered an empty tin can in the corner beneath the feed bags. While the children slept, she had melted snow in the buckets over the fire, then cleaned both the buckets and the little can. When Anna awoke, Selma was proudly able to offer her a drink. Ruth awoke and both girls guzzled the water eagerly, their bodies needing liquid even more than food.

Tummies full, thirst quenched, Anna and Ruth quickly fell back to sleep. At last, Selma lay down beside them and stared at the fire. The warming air in the shed charmed her with feelings of security. The dancing flames entranced her mind, relieving it of care for a few moments. Then she broke the spell and gazed around at the shadowed walls of the abandoned shack as though at the walls of a palace. She marveled at how little she really needed to be happy. A little water. A portion of food. The merest shelter and a tiny bit of warmth. Humbly, she bowed her head and voiced another silent prayer of gratitude towards Heaven. Finally, completely exhausted, she too slipped through the veil of dreamland and slept.

CHAPTER TEN

A morsel of food, a drink of water, and one night of warm sleep worked miracles on Anna and Ruth. They woke up bright eyed and elated by their new home. Selma warned the girls to make very little noise. She went on to explain that they must cover the window at night to hide the light of their fire, lest they be discovered and thrown out. And never... never, she emphasized, were they to get the straw too close to the fire.

The girls nodded enthusiastic understanding and agreement. While Selma emphasized the danger of fire, her own worst fear was that someone would find them and evict them from their simple home.

Throughout the day, they nibbled on the second half of the loaf of bread and remained snuggled together, thankful to be warm and secure. Selma only left the little shack to bring in more crates for the fire.

Having obtained shelter, food now became Selma's chief

concern. She wracked her brain for hours trying to think of how to feed the three of them. For several introspective moments, she seriously considered robbery. In the end, she was forced to accept the simple fact that she was incurably honest. Besides which, she had no idea how to successfully — and she would have to be successful — steal food.

Just as she was dropping off to sleep that night, her mind opened on a vision of the resplendent tables she had set in her husband's home. Course followed course, fish and fowl, vegetables and desserts, sweetmeats and candies. Her stomach growled when she recalled the food their servants had thrown away from every plate at that ornate table after the guests were done, and how little concern she had felt in its disposal.

Suddenly, she came awake, excited and breathless, wondering if people in this American town might not be discarding scraps that would be palatable, even life saving to her little family. Excitedly, she woke Ruth and explained her idea. It took a long time to reassure the little girl that she and Anna would only be alone for a short time.

"You're hungry. I'm hungry. Ruth, darling, I have to go. But I'll be back soon. I promise." Selma kissed both of Ruth's soft cheeks, then tore herself away and slipped out the door, heading for the back of Mrs. Guggenheim's restaurant.

Ruth lay fidgeting nervously in the dark until she could stand to be alone no longer. She woke Anna and together they waited expectantly, their eyes moving from the door to the flickering fire and back again. It seemed an eternity and the fire was dying down before they heard footsteps crunching in the snow outside. Huddling beneath the straw-filled sacks, they waited, expectant yet fearful.

With a whoosh of cold air, the door opened and Selma hurried inside. A small bundle wrapped in her handkerchief was clutched to her bosom. Pushing and shoving in their excitement, the girls scurried out of the straw to see what treasure their mother had brought.

Selma unwrapped the lace handkerchief to reveal crusts of bread, pieces of potato, and a single, large chunk of frozen meatloaf. Not even for a moment did Selma feel repulsed. Instead, she voiced a prayer of thanksgiving, then placed the food in one of their buckets and warmed it over the fire. They were all drooling and eagerly licking their lips by the time the food was warm. Laughing and joyous, Selma shared with her daughters and thought nothing in the world had ever tasted so good.

Carl stood before the broad window, gazing out at the silent ships bound immovable in the ice. Far beyond the sea-wall barrier, white caps showed where the wind kept the last bits of water from freezing. Carl moved his gaze slowly along the entire waterfront. Few people were out in the winter cold. The bustling activity along the shores of Lake Superior quickly subsided to become almost nonexistent during the cold winter months when the giant barges were frozen in their docking berths.

A flutter of movement caught his attention and he swiveled his head to see what it was. For a bare second, he caught sight of a woman before she disappeared behind the machine shop just east of the main office. He looked back in the direction from which she had come and was surprised to see a slender spiral of smoke issuing from a hole in the roof of the sturdy old shack once used to store grain for the horses before steam power made them obsolete.

Vagrants. A frown creased his forehead. Too many homeless people had been lured to Superior in hopes of finding jobs in the mines, logging, or shipping industries. But this time of year, even fully employed men were often out of work for months at a time. It was not unusual, even in these frozen, northern latitudes, to find vagabonds camped out in any likely spot that would afford shelter from the wind and cold. But vagrant women were fairly rare. In an offhand way, he wondered what her story was. She was probably following her husband from job to job. But Carl had problems more pressing than a pair of vagrants camped out on the fringes of his shipyards. At the same time, he decided not to inform the security chief of her existence. In his mind it was no crime to be poor. If they caused no damage to any of the properties, they were welcome to what shelter they could find. He knew they would probably move on when the weather warmed.

Easily putting the strange woman out of his mind, his thoughts returned to contemplation of the schematic drawings spread across his desk. His innovative designs for Great

Lakes rescue tugs had caught the attention of the Great Northern TransAtlantic Shipping Company. To his surprise and delight, they had contracted with him to design a vessel tough enough to take on rescue operations for ocean-going vessels in the midst of violent storms. Vessels rugged enough to win the battle against wind and waves. He settled behind his desk, picked up a pencil, and starting making notations on the engine design.

Thomas Mason wheeled through Carl's office door at half past five. "Time to call it a day, young man."

Carl looked up, startled at Thomas' arrival. Slowly, he stood and stretched both arms high and backwards as he watched the man in the wheelchair maneuver up beside his desk.

"Hello, Uncle Thomas. I hadn't realized it was so late."

"Been working hard, I see." Thomas pulled a magnifying glass from his pocket and peered through it at the penciled markings and notations on the schematic.

"Looks like a different chair, Uncle. Something new?"

Thomas peered at him over the top of his reading glasses. "That other one was too small. Didn't fit. Inferior product. Schuster advertised this one and I thought I'd give it a try." Thomas turned his eyes back to the plans spread across Carl's desk.

"Hmm." As Carl walked over to the windows that ringed the north wall of his office, he continued to work his stiff muscles until they loosened. He listened half-heartedly to

Thomas' mutterings for a moment, then something moved outside the window and immediately all his attention was focused in the alley below.

The woman he had seen earlier in the day was returning to the little shack. As he watched her trudge through the snow, it occurred to him that she was quite young. For no particular reason, he found himself squinting through the failing light, trying to determine her hair color beneath the stylish hat she wore. He was disappointed when she opened the door of the shack and disappeared inside. It was then he realized her clothes, as well as the hat, did not fit those of an ordinary vagabond.

Carl shook the mystery aside. The woman's plight was no business of his. Pushing the question to the far recesses of his mind, he turned back to Uncle Thomas, the drawings, and the important puzzles he still had to solve.

Just after midnight three days later, Selma crept through endless dark alleys heading for the restaurant again. She shook her head and grinned beneath the scarf pulled tightly across her face, fantasizing about what the fashionable women in London's drawing rooms would say were she to walk in, looking and smelling as she did right now. She imagined herself greeting them as old friends. Mrs. Kiddle would faint — she always fainted. Lady Hester would look down her nose, raise her chin, and turn away. Actually, she would never get as far as a drawing room because the footmen would have thrown her out long before any of the society dames could even catch a glimpse — or a whiff — of her ragged attire.

A cat screeched in the night, immediately focusing Selma's attention on where she was right now. The night was calm and icy beneath sparkling stars. Her breath froze and almost crackled the instant it left her mouth. Steathily, she entered the alley behind the restaurant and realized that what would have been unthinkable only a week ago, now made her mouth water in anticipation. Forcing her thoughts away from how low she had sunk, Selma concentrated on the need to feed herself and her children. They had shelter. And they had a source of food. Beyond that — well, she would continue searching for a job until she found one. Until then, she was grateful to have a means to provide for her children.

Selma jumped when another cat screeched at her then raced away, its inky black shadow disappearing through a hole in the wooden fence. Her heart pounded so loud she was sure others could hear it. Pausing in a shadowed doorway, she listened to sounds in the night, always fearful a light would suddenly blossom in some nearby window. She dreaded getting caught.

Nothing. She waited a moment more. Still nothing. Her heart slowed and she breathed a sigh of relief, then continued on, her boots making a squeaky, crunching sound on the frozen snow. Twenty more feet. Now just fifteen. There, she saw the back of the restaurant. Then she was at the back door and began searching in the darkness.

But there were no buckets tonight. With a sinking heart, she realized the day just past had been Sunday. The restaurant had been closed. Her heart shriveled, she felt her soul shrink inside her body. The tense excitement she had felt since leaving the little shed flittered away, leaving her cold and depressed. Selma turned to retrace her steps back to the little shack, trying to comfort herself with the thought of tomorrow — a new day full of new opportunities.

Suddenly, a shadow moved in the darkness ahead. Her heart hammered painfully against her ribs and she didn't know whether to go forward or retreat. But her daughters were ahead of her, so she had no choice. She inched a step forward, holding her breath as she placed her right foot silently onto the snow. Nothing. Another step. Pausing, she held her breath and listened. She whirled at a sound from behind. Silently, a giant shadow melded from the darkness into the frosty moonlight. Fear stabbed through her when a hulking man in ragged clothes took another step toward her.

Instantly, she whirled around and fled down the alley, running for her life. She heard the scraping of ice and snow as he came pounding after her. His breath beat a harsh rhythm bare inches behind her ear. Her shoulders recoiled away from the hand she felt reaching out to grab her.

Crashing sounds suddenly reverberated from the brick alley walls, immediately followed by the sound of a falling body. One massive hand wrapped around her ankle, tripped her, and she fell. She kicked backward with all her strength and felt her feet thud against flesh. Then she was up and running again. Grunts and heavy groans faded to silence as she rounded the corner and fled down the open street.

Fear leant wings to her feet and she fairly flew around the next corner. Her feet pounded quiet whispers through the snow until she had covered almost three blocks. Her lungs cried desperately for rest as the icy air froze the delicate tissue of her throat. She jerked her scarf up to cover her mouth and warm the air she breathed. Finally, she slowed and craned her head to look back. A giant sigh of relief exploded from her mouth when she saw that the street behind her was empty. Silently, she crept back into the shadows and cautiously made her way home.

CHAPTER ELEVEN

idnight was twenty minutes away and Carl was supposed to take the nine o'clock train to New York in the morning to deliver his plans to Great Northern. But he still wasn't happy with several details on the port engine diagram for the sea tug. He had been working nonstop for twenty hours and the figures and lines were starting to blur. A huge yawn twisted his face as he stretched his arms high into the air and groaned. Time to call it quits.

He flicked off the desk light and walked to the window. Clear indigo skies stretching across the lake were speckled with myriad shiny points of light. No moon dimmed their brilliance and he gazed at them in awe for long moments. Suddenly, a light on the ground snapped his eyes downward. Startled, he saw a shadow slip through a faint sliver of light then all was dark again. He strained his eyes, but could see nothing else on the ground. It was the young woman. He was sure of that. But what was she doing going out in the middle of a freezing, winter night?

Carl had seen the strange woman almost every day for a week now, but only for mere seconds at a time as she crossed the narrow space between his building and the little shack. He had begun to look forward to seeing her, much as he would a wild animal that frequented the same watering hole or salt lick.

Unexpectedly, he felt his sense of adventure piqued and he struggled against an overwhelming desire to follow her, find out where she was going, what she was doing. In the next moment, he was berating himself for a fool and forced his attention away from the window. He pulled on his coat and black cowboy hat, then wrapped a woven scarf around his neck. Just before locking the heavy office door behind him, Carl glanced back out the window and noticed the moon peek above the eastern headland. He knew it would be a blistering cold night out and shivered in anticipation.

Quickly, he descended two flights of stairs, passed through the front door of the building, and turned east onto Harbor Road. He shivered for real in the sub-freezing night air, tucked his chin deeper into the scarf, and hurried toward home.

He'd gone only a few yards when he was startled by a figure that stepped silently out of the alley ahead of him and turned east as well. He was intrigued and excited when he recognized his fellow traveler to be the woman he'd been watching from his window. She moved rapidly toward some unknown destination and when she turned off of Harbor Street, he didn't think — he just followed.

In the starlight, she seemed to flow along the ground, the hem of her long skirt just skimming across the packed snow in her wake. She moved like a ghost, a tantalizing wraith that beckoned him toward the unknown. She never looked back and Carl found himself relaxing, unafraid that she would discover him following her. He had trailed her through block after block of winding streets when he glanced up to see the tip of a bright moon peek into the street below. When next his gaze returned to street level, she had disappeared.

Quickly glancing left and right, Carl cautiously crept forward and stopped to peer around the corner into the next alley. All was in shadow, but faintly he heard her footsteps ahead. Silently, he stepped into the alley and flattened himself against the side of the building, waiting for his eyes to become accustomed to the deep, black shadows.

Tentatively, he started forward. Suddenly, he heard footsteps approaching and froze, feeling naked and exposed, even in the darkness. The footsteps grew nearer just as the moon, drifting further through its arc in the sky, sent a thin shaft of silver light creeping past the edge of the building. In an instant, the far side of the alley was bathed in its cold light. Carl flattened himself in the inky shadow against the wall, held his breath, and watched the mysterious woman glide toward him. For one instant, he stared at her classic profile, stark white on one side, inky black on the other.

Suddenly, a huge shape loomed out of the shadows behind her. The woman heard him and whirled around, a frightened cry escaping her lips. The man lunged forward. She screamed and stumbled backward, then whipped around and started running.

Carl's heart was pounding when the woman dashed past him, her derelict assailant thundering two steps behind. No time to think. Carl gauged his distance and leaped at the same instant the man launched himself forward to tackle the fleeing woman. Carl's surprise attack catapulted both men into a stack of barrels. At the same instant, he saw the woman fall. In a flash, Carl saw her feet smash backward into her assailant's face. Then the two men tumbled painfully across the frozen ground, rolling together through the snow, punching and kicking. Carl swung again, but hit only empty air as the foul-smelling tramp suddenly jerked free, scurried sideways, then lunged to his feet and sprinted painfully around the corner of the building. His flight led in the opposite direction from where Carl and the woman had come.

Carl lay on the ground, panting billowing clouds of steam until the cold of the snow penetrated his back and legs. Finally, he pushed himself to his feet, dusted off the snow that clung to his pants and arms, then headed back toward his office. He was sure the woman would return to the shack in the alley.

Carl had followed her on a long, circuitous pathway to this alley, but now he raced back along a shorter route. His curiosity had been fully piqued and he wanted at least one answer before he went home to sleep—had she made it back to her haven safely?

He arrived first, but was forced to wait for so long that his feet were almost frozen by the time she finally rounded the corner into the alley where he was hiding, silently squatting behind a tangled stack of snow-covered debris.

She didn't make a sound and he almost got caught blowing warm air into his freezing hands. But a flash in the moonlight alerted him and Carl froze, watching intently as she glided down the alley and up to the shed doorway. She lifted the latch and the door swung outward. He wasn't surprised by the gentle glow inside the shed, but he was stunned when he glimpsed two tiny girls and heard their excited little voices call "Mama!" before the door shut.

The terror Selma escaped in the moonlight outside of Mrs. Guggenheim's restaurant left her trembling for hours after she snuggled into bed with Ruth and Anna. By the time morning light crept around the edges of her makeshift curtain, she had decided that night time forays in search of food were far too dangerous. She determined it was time to once again search for a job.

"Please don't leave us alone, Mother." Anna's wrenching cry almost shredded Selma's resolve to leave them in the shed while she ventured out in search of a job.

"It's terribly cold outside. You'll be together and much

more comfortable here, Anna." Selma included Ruth in her glance as well. "Here you'll be warm and safe. And I'll come back to you as soon as I can."

"But what if you don't come back?" Ruth's lower lip trembled and she bit it to keep from crying.

Selma pulled them close in her arms, squeezing them tight to her chest, as though all her love could burn from her heart into theirs. "I'll always come back, my darlings. You are the world to me. I could not live without you."

Selma felt her own eyes fill with tears and she swallowed them with a forced smile as she settled the girls back into their nest of straw.

"I'm frightened, too. So you must be extra brave to help me. Hold each other tight while I'm gone and I promise I'll be back before you know it."

Selma pulled herself away. As she crossed the room and opened the door, her courage almost failed her. She stared back at their wide, terrified eyes and felt something shrivel inside her chest. Quickly, she blew them a kiss and shut the door.

Selma's fine, stylish clothes were filthy and bedraggled now; her ragged and dirty hair looked unkempt even though she had combed it and shoved it up under her sagging hat. She realized, after the owner of a harness shop sniffed and covered his nose with his handkerchief, that her chances of obtaining a job now were probably even more impossible than before.

A kind woman in a candle shop apologized for not being able to hire Selma, but wished her a Merry Christmas and pressed three candles into Selma's hands along with a dozen cookies wrapped in brown paper. Selma impulsively hugged the plump little woman and wished her a Merry Christmas as well.

She was very tired and cold, carrying her little bundle of gifts, when she heard a group of children singing in the distance. Selma recognized the song and began to hum along with them.

"God rest ye merry gentlemen, let nothing you dismay..."

Tiredly, she trudged along the last row of houses before the street that led to her alley, humming until she could no longer hear the children's voices. The deepening snow tugged at her feet until she was almost too weary to go on. But more singing in the distance lifted her soul and she paused to hear the end of the new song. Suddenly, a door to her left burst open and a woman ran out of her house and down the steps where she stopped in front of Selma. She said nothing, but smiled crookedly at Selma and handed her a bundle wrapped up in a dish towel.

Hesitantly, Selma reached out for the gift and thanked the woman. Then she watched her disappear back within her comfortable little home; a house like the one waiting for Selma and her daughters in Missoula. With a lighter heart, Selma tramped the last yards to the corner of the bank building, then turned into the alley, dreaming of the home still waiting for them five days' train ride to the west. Her dream shone like a bright beacon on a dark night. They would get there. Somehow, someday, they would get there.

Ruth and Anna's frantic greeting woke Selma from her reverie as she slipped through the door with the bundles of food. Their tears turned to joy as they eagerly explored her treasures. In moments, they settled down to ravenously devour a crisp meat pie and sugar cookies while Selma explained about the kind-hearted women who had fed them tonight. Then she selected one of the candles and held it to a corner of the fire until it took the flame. Selma set it on a wooden ledge where they all watched its tiny flicker of light brighten the dark corner. Selma stared at it, thinking it was much like the glow from her dream, throwing light into the gloomy corners of her mind.

Later, Selma snuggled next to her daughters, holding them close to her heart. Silently, she sent another prayer of gratitude winging to heaven, a new practice that was quickly becoming a habit. Just before she dropped off to sleep, she decided to visit Mrs. Guggenheim's restaurant again—but this time she would do it during the day.

Mrs. Guggenheim was aghast at the change in Selma since the day she'd first met her. She held the door open and stared at Selma for a long time. The last of Selma's pride was stripped from her when Mrs. Guggenheim told her she was too filthy to wash dishes in her restaurant. But the formidable woman told Selma to wait. Then she shut the door.

When she returned, Mrs. Guggenheim carried a battered metal wash tub in which she had placed a bar of soap, three towels, a loaf of bread, and a crock full of stew. She thrust the tub at Selma and told her to come back when she was clean, promising to hire Selma to wash dishes again, but bluntly guaranteeing only three days of employment.

Anna and Ruth cried and hugged her desperately when she returned. The strain of their daily existence was starting to take its toll. Selma hugged them to her breast and rocked them until they calmed down. When she finally lifted the lid on the crock full of stew, a delicious aroma wafted through the air. One whiff and their frantic tears turned to gasps of drooling anticipation.

After their tummies were full, Ruth inspected the tub and picked up the bar of soap as though it were a treasure of some sort.

"Is this soap?" she breathed the question.

"Yes." Selma set a bucket full of snow on bricks around the fire. "We're all going to take a bath tonight."

"A bath?" Ruth opened her eyes wide at Anna, then looked into her mother's eyes.

"You remember what a bath is, don't you?"

"Of course I do. But how?"

"In our new bathtub." Selma indicated the tub Mrs. Guggenheim had sent.

She looked skeptical and shook her head back and forth.

"It's not very big."

"It'll work. You'll see." For two hours, Selma melted water over the fire in the two buckets and a battered pot she had scrounged from a junk pile on one of her midnight forage runs. The girls took turns in the tub while Selma scrubbed the dirt of the past two weeks from their bodies and hair. They huddled around the fire, wrapped in the towels Mrs. Guggenheim had sent while their mother washed their dresses and laid them across the slats of a wooden crate outside to freeze.

"Why are you freezing our dresses, Mama?" Anna wrinkled her little nose.

"Because I saw a woman do it in town a few days ago. After the water freezes, you beat the dresses with a stick and the frozen water cracks and falls off."

"Will the clothes be dry then?" Ruth was having a hard time envisioning wet clothes freezing dry.

"I think so. In any case, I think it's worth a try."

Two hours later, Selma beat the ice out of the two little dresses and brought them back into the shed. Anna was already asleep, but Selma and Ruth were very impressed with the results. Selma waved the dresses over the fire for a few minutes to warm them up and found that they truly were dry. After she helped Ruth dress, Selma woke Anna enough to slip the dress back onto the tired girl.

At last, when her daughters were asleep, Selma worked on cleaning herself. It wasn't an exotic bath in a porcelain tub, but no Roman bath full of honey and milk could possibly have felt better than the one Selma took that night. She found that washing the filth from her skin and hair brightened her whole outlook on life. Last of all, she washed her own dress. Wearing her coat over the towel, she tiptoed out the door and threw the dripping garment across the crate then rushed back inside. The warmth inside the shed was a relief after the freezing temperature outside, but she had to practically stand in the fire to warm up again. When she finally put her washed, frozen, beaten, and dried dress back on, Selma felt like a woman reborn.

Mrs. Guggenheim met Selma at the back door of the restaurant the next day and nodded her approval. As promised, she hired Selma to wash dishes for the next three days. But each passing hour compounded the torture Selma suffered. Soul-wracking guilt and worry over leaving Anna and Ruth alone seemed to constrict the heart in her chest, making it beat abnormally. Nor could she get an entire breath into her lungs from the time she left them in the morning until she raced home after the lunch hour rush to check on them. Then the whole cycle began all over again when she returned to the restaurant in the afternoon. The only peace Selma knew was when once again she held her little girls in her arms.

At the end of those first three days, Mrs. Guggenheim hired Selma steady. For three days a week she would scrub floors, clear tables, wipe chairs, and help in the kitchen wherever she was needed. And each night when Selma made her way back to the little shack, she carried a basket full of food from the restaurant. Slowly, time and practice worked to ease the pain of separation for Selma and for the girls until it had become their way of life.

CHAPTER TWELVE

rs. Guggenheim slammed through the door into the kitchen, muttering dark curses beneath her breath. Shock whirled Selma away from her dirty pots and pans to see what had caused such an emotional outburst. Her employer carried what looked like a set of the dining room's blue and pink striped curtains balled up in her hands.

"What..." Selma began, but Mrs. Guggenheim cut her off.

"That no good Hank Chichester came in here drunk — again! He no more than got through the door before he started falling all over himself — again! And what does he do? He grabs my beautiful curtains to save his sorry... a... self from falling and rips them right off the rod. Look at this!"

Selma was surprised to see the forceful woman almost moved to tears as she held up the ripped and frayed material.

"Oh, no," Selma soothed, "it's all right." Drying her hands, she hurried across the room, "I can fix those for you if you want me to." Gingerly, she took the material from Mrs. Guggenheim's grasp and inspected the damage. "I can sew these so you'll hardly know Mr., um, Mr. Whatshisname ever got his hands on them."

"You can do that? Really?" Mrs. Guggenheim's eyes widened with surprise.

"I have hidden talents," Selma's eyes sparkled at the startled lady. "But I'll need some thread and a needle?"

The startled restraunteur did not reply. Instead, she bolted back through the door to reappear in less than five minutes with needle and thread. She hovered over Selma until, laughing, she told her employer to tend to her customers while she worked on the curtains. Selma was glad to have her hands out of the dishwater and thoroughly enjoyed carefully setting each tiny stitch so that they were almost invisible.

"I never knew anyone to sew such fine stitches." Mrs. Guggenheim fingered the mended spot. "This is beautiful. I can hardly tell where the material was torn." The delighted woman raved on for several minutes, then took the curtain back through the door to hang it up. Selma returned to the stack of dishes.

Mrs. Guggenheim paid Selma the coins she had earned that day, then impulsively pressed another one into Selma's hand and wished her a gruff 'Merry Christmas'. Selma hugged the woman and wished her a Merry Christmas in return, then she stepped through the door and started on her way home.

She had almost reached the street that led to her alley,

when, across the road, Selma was startled to see again the woman whose offer of help she had snubbed at the train station her first night in Superior. She hesitated a second, then deliberately stepped off the sidewalk and crossed the street, heading for the blind woman dressed in her ragged, old coat and using her cane to feel her way along. When she caught up, Selma put her hand on the woman's shoulder.

"Excuse me."

The older woman turned and stared blindly at Selma through greenish hazel eyes. "Yes?"

"I don't know if... I mean... I'm sure you don't remember me, but... " Selma was surprised to discover the woman was not nearly as old as she had assumed that night at the train station.

"Of course I remember you," the rag woman interrupted, "you are the mother of the two little girls... you were evicted from the train a few weeks ago on a very cold, very snowy night."

"Why, yes." Selma was amazed. "How did you know?"

"I never forget a voice... and you have such a lovely voice, it would be hard to forget."

"Oh, well, thank you." Selma cleared her throat and started again. "What I wanted to say was... well... thank you... for offering to help." She lifted one gloved hand from where it held lightly to the long cane and pressed into its palm the extra coin Mrs. Guggenheim had given to her.

"I just wanted to wish you a Merry Christmas and tell

you how sorry I am for having been so rude."

"You weren't rude, my dear. You were frightened." Amanda smiled and nodded as her fingers read the coin. "Merry Christmas to you and to your daughters."

"Thank you." Impulsively, Selma leaned forward and pressed a kiss to the soft cheek, then turned for home. She had reached the other side of the street when she turned to look back one last time. Just then, a tall, well-dressed man wearing a black cowboy hat stepped out of a doorway and stopped beside the blind woman. Selma stared until, without warning, he looked her way. His gaze crossed the distance, holding Selma captive with his eyes until she felt the breath catch in her throat.

Quickly, she whirled away, intensely embarrassed by her worn clothes, ragged hat, and the tattered scarves wrapped around her neck. Hurrying, she stepped around the corner of the bank and disappeared.

"Do you know that young woman, Amanda?" Carl spoke to his sister, but his eyes remained fixed on the point where the mysterious woman had disappeared.

"Remember the young mother and her two daughters who got evicted from the train the night you picked me up at the station two weeks ago?"

"That was the same woman?" He pulled his eyes around to stare at his sister.

"Yup." Her tone was thoughtful and Carl continued to stare at her.

"She certainly didn't look very proud just then. In fact, I would have thought her..." Carl's voice paused while his stunned thoughts turned in circles. He had recognized his 'tenant' by the clothes she wore. But the minute she turned around and her eyes met his, he felt his whole world tilt off balance. His sister was still speaking, so he struggled to pay attention.

"Poor?"

"What?"

"You thought her poor?"

"Um. Yes, I suppose I did."

"Life has not been kind to her. But she's surviving."

"How could you tell?"

"Oh, Carl. You obviously looked at her clothes, not her heart." She smiled and moved her hand over from where it held to his elbow and tapped him in the center of his chest. "This is where you must look to see who a person truly is."

"You know, sometimes I think the world would be better off if we were all a little blinder," Carl smiled though she couldn't see his face.

"She gave me this." She held out her hand and the coin glittered in her open palm.

"She gave you this? She doesn't..." Again he stopped his tongue from uttering words he thought it best not to say.

"She doesn't what?" Amanda cocked her head sideways at the strange tone in her brother's voice.

Carl cleared his throat. "She doesn't look..." He paused,

trying to imagine the kind of woman who could barely eke out an existence in the shed in his alley, but whose heart was big enough that she would give away so large a part of what had to be a mere pittance to a blind stranger on the street.

Amanda finished the sentence for him. "As if she had enough change to spare?"

Carl was silent so long, Amanda thought he was not going to answer. Then he covered her hand with his own and turned to lead her home. "Something like that," his voice was low when he finally spoke.

"That makes her gift all the more precious, wouldn't you agree?"

"Um hmm."

"Carl! What are you thinking? Your body is here. I can feel it walking beside me. But your mind, dear boy... your mind is a million miles away."

"No, it's not that far. Just a few short blocks."

Two days later, Mrs. Guggenheim bustled through the kitchen door with a lady who was as small as Selma's employer was large. Mrs. Guggenheim introduced her friend as Mrs. Staples, then shocked Selma by explaining that the dear woman had a daughter getting married in two days. She went on to explain how the fancy wedding dress they had ordered from the fashionable New York catalogue did not fit the bride to be. Mrs. Staples sniffed audibly until Selma was afraid the little woman was going to cry.

"I'm so sorry." Selma didn't know what else to say.

Mrs. Guggenheim charged ahead. "I told Cora here about what you did with the blinds out front, and..." She stopped, suddenly unsure of what to say next.

"And you'd like to know if I can fix the dress; make it fit?" Selma's eyes began to sparkle.

"Yup, that's about the size of it." Mrs. Guggenheim stared right at Selma and Mrs. Staples' eyes burned with a hopeful light as well.

"I can't promise until I see the dress, but I should think I could..."

"There, see Cora? I told you not to worry." Then she turned to Selma. "Dry your hands, girl. There's no time to waste. You just go along with Cora here and I'll worry about the dishes."

Fitting, tucking, and sewing took Selma the better part of the two hectic days remaining before the wedding. But the bride walked down the aisle on time and in a dress that fit perfectly. The bride's grateful mother sat in the front row of the church and cried tears of joy.

Selma did not attend the wedding. She saw the bride dressed, then quietly slipped away and walked home. As she followed the well-worn path that now wove between the piles of snow-covered debris, her mind dreamily focused on their little dream house in Missoula. In a can on a shelf in the little shed she had stashed almost enough money to buy one train ticket to Missoula. She would keep working and saving, and one day soon…

Then she rounded the dwindling pile of snow-covered wooden crates and her startled eyes fell on a small, wooden crate sitting in the snow by the door. It was overflowing with food. Her eyes shot wide open and she whirled to look up and down the alley. No one. Rushing to the door, she yanked it open.

In the center of the straw bed, Anna and Ruth were chattering and playing with the dolls Selma had fashioned from straw and bits of material. Immediately, they jumped up to greet their mother, their excited voices welcoming her home. Thankfully, she swept them into her arms and kissed them both till they begged to be put down. Then Selma turned back to the door. Once more, she looked around the alley. Seeing no one, she finally picked up the crate, took it inside, and shut the door.

Carl stood in his darkened office, peering down from the window that overlooked the alley. When the two little girls rushed out to hug their mother, Carl realized it was the first time he had really seen the children. From his lofty view, they looked like mere babes. He smiled when his tenant whirled around, looking for who had left the crate of food. He'd never played the role of guardian angel before, but he found it to his liking.

CHAPTER THIRTEEN

"Tomorrow is Christmas," Selma's cheery voice caught the girls' attention, "and I think we should have a tree."

Ruth and Anna stared at their mother. Then their widening eyes swiveled around to look at each other.

"Christmas?" Anna squealed.

"A tree?" Ruth crowed.

Excitement flitted across the eager little faces, staring out at her from the new blanket bought with the money Mrs. Staples paid Selma for altering her daughter's wedding dress.

"Yes, a tree." Selma shared their joy and grew more excited just watching them. "Part of the forest comes right up to the end of Juniper Street. It's just a short walk, and not too far to drag a tree."

"Will there be presents under the tree?"

"I don't know for sure," Selma bent down to kiss Anna's creamy cheek, "but if there is no tree, there can't be presents

— right?"

"Yup." Ruth erupted from the bed. Anna trailed right behind her.

"What are we going to decorate it with?" Ruth's cherubic face radiated enthusiasm as she brushed bits of straw from her hair and straightened her crumpled dress.

"Whatever we can find in the forest." Selma shared out some of their food, but the girls were so excited, they hardly took time to chew.

"There are berries still hanging from some of the bushes, and we'll just have to see what else we can find. This year, we'll decorate au natural."

"Huh?" Anna and Ruth traded confused looks.

"Nature will provide us with the decorations. We just have to use our imagination."

Anna nodded faithfully, but Ruth still looked perplexed.

"We'll make our tree beautiful. Just wait and see."

Selma carried the old ax and Ruth and Anna each carried a metal bucket. They had hardly started when they reached the end of Juniper Street where the forest began. Bright sunshine warmed the frigid air. Sparkling, feathery, frost crystals glittered as they fell between the trees to join the snowy floor. The gleaming, cerulean sky seemed so unreal that it looked as though a mad painter had mixed cobalt and turquoise together. Adding a drop of magic, he then splashed it on the canvas, creating an azure mixture never before seen.

Young trees ringed a small clearing where their boughs

struggled to rise above the deep snow piled at the feet of towering conifers. Regal and forbidding, the old giants of the forest formed an impenetrable curtain that shadowed the deeper forest. Sculptured drifts of snow soon inspired a mythical, magical kingdom inhabited by gallant knights invented by Ruth and Anna to save them from fire-breathing dragons.

However, before the snow became too deep to trudge through very far, Selma selected a young tree and declared it to be perfect. The girls helped her clear snow away from the tree trunk and Selma swung the ax.

"Mother. You're a very good tree cutter-downer," encouraged Anna.

"I think chopping up those crates for firewood," Selma breathed heavily as she swung the ax, "has definitely helped me acquire a new skill."

With enthusiastic help from her daughters, Selma dragged the tree home along with the buckets carrying their meager collection of wrinkled berries and a few colorful, dried leaves. By far their most valued prizes were the four bird nests they found still clinging to the branches of low bushes.

Alternately laughing and arguing, they worked tirelessly to set up the tree and decorate it. At last, they all lay back on their straw bed and admired their handiwork. The tree was barely three feet high. Narrow, but fully limbed, it fit perfectly into the corner beside the door. They all agreed that the shriveled, red berries and tightly woven bird nests added just the right festive touch. The girls were delighted with Selma's last-minute addition of bows tied from long wisps of straw and balanced carefully to fill up all the barren spots.

Tired, but contented, the girls snuggled into their mother's lap. Selma wrapped her arms around them both and kissed their tiny ears. The firelight crackled gently from the corner and she began to hum as her eyes moved slowly around the walls of their home, at their meager possessions, the bright fire, the magical little Christmas tree. Gradually, she realized that she felt calmer, more at peace at that moment than any time she could ever remember.

Softly at first, she began to sing. "Silent Night... Holy Night... all is calm, all is bright... " Ruth joined her, humming when she forgot the words. Anna smiled contently and just watched and listened until she fell asleep.

Later, when both girls were snuggled in their blanket, Selma rose and slipped out through the door. Walking slowly, she gazed up at the narrow ribbon of stars glittering beyond the tall buildings. She stared at the frozen points of light sparkling in the velvety sky until the cold air raised chills on the flesh of her arms. Just as she turned to go back, the round face of a full moon peeked into her part of the world. Rooted to the ground, she watched it move inch by inch across her small slice of sky until the entire circle, glowing white, floated free between the dark, silent, towering buildings.

A vision opened in her mind of another night, long ago, when a young mother-to-be searched for a place of sanctuary where she could have her baby. That woman was turned from door after door until her husband at last found respite in a stable.

The irony of her own situation galled bitterly on her soul when she realized how little that story had meant to her before now. Her soul cringed to a depth of loneliness she'd never thought possible as she recalled many times in her life when she had turned away those in need of the simplest help. Then, one by one, she relived each time she had been turned from similar doorsteps during the past weeks. How desperate she had grown. How precious a bit of human kindness had become.

Her eyes turned heavenward and she sent a prayer winging upward, pouring out her gratitude for the small stable where she and her children had found sanctuary; gratitude for the tidbits of human kindness that had blessed their lives and for their mysterious benefactor who had left the crate of food.

Shivering till her teeth chattered, she finally turned and retraced her steps back to the little shed. She put more lumber on the fire, carefully banking it for the night. When she looked at the bed, Anna and Ruth were peacefully snuggled together, warm and safe. Feeling like a child herself, Selma smiled as she tiptoed to where she had hidden six round, precious oranges. With great care, she arranged them on a fragrant evergreen bough laid beneath the tree. The rich scent of orange intermingling with fresh pine tantalized her nostrils. A wave of nostalgia swept through her heart as she stepped back and looked at the nest of oranges.

With a stab of irony, she realized that she felt more joy at this moment than on any other Christmas in her memory. She asked herself why that could be when she compared this meager celebration to the ornate ones of the past; and knew it was because she had come to appreciate each little thing. She no longer took life and its myriad blessings for granted.

A chilling sense of insight washed across her soul. Clearly, with a kind of twisted appreciation, she realized that before the thief had stolen her money on the train she would never have known such hardship and misery; nor would she have known of or trusted the strength of her own determination. Unthinking, she fondled the bracelet on her wrist, her fingers moving from one charm to the next until they paused on the ruby candle. She could feel the dream that had carried her so far was expanding into something richer than she had ever imagined. Now she saw not only a little house full of love that would protect those within its walls, but she envisioned a home and a life that would radiate love beyond its own walls.

She thought of Bertha and Seth. From the place where she kept it tucked safely away, Selma pulled out the last letter from her friends in England. One sentence seemed to jump off the well-worn page as she reread the words.

... But most of all, we pray that you may find a place and time where your dreams of yesterday meet your dreams of tomorrow...

Quivering chills raised gooseflesh on her arms as, ringing

through her memory, she heard again the words spoken by a blind woman on a cold train platform almost three weeks ago: "To meet our dreams... we must live them each day along the way."

CHAPTER FOURTEEN

arl cut short his second trip to New York. He remained in the noisy, bustling city just long enough to present his plans to the North American TransAtlantic Shipping Company and receive their enthusiastic response. The chief engineers were very complimentary and assured him they would go over his plans and cable their final comments after the first of the year. Then Carl went shopping.

When he caught the Red Eye heading west, Carl told himself he wanted to get back in time for Christmas with Amanda. Less than two months were left before her surgery and he was deeply concerned. However, as the darkened sleeping car rattled through Michigan, he admitted to himself that he was also anxious for someone else's Christmas. The brightly wrapped boxes beside him had a date with a certain shack in an alley by the bay.

Christmas morning arrived quietly. Selma woke early and added more broken lumber to the smoldering coals of the fire, patiently coaxing forth a bright flame before warming some water to wash her face.

She flinched when her serenity was shattered by the crunch of footsteps on the snow outside. She froze. Her ears strained until her head hurt while her eyes darted to the children, praying they would not make any noise. They slept soundly, leaving Selma to face her fear alone as the footsteps crunched closer. And closer.

Suddenly, they stopped. Selma could not breathe while she listened for a knock at the door, petrified with fear that her family would be forced back out into the cold.

She held her breath until her lungs burned with fire, but still no fist sounded on the door. Then, just as unexpectedly as they had come, the footsteps retreated. Hurriedly, she raced to the window and inched the drape aside to peer out with one eye. The still morning air was so thick with a dense, white fog that Selma could barely make out the side of the building. Barely discernible, the ghostly form of a tall man wearing a thick coat and black cowboy hat glided across the snow until he disappeared into a wall of mist that closed about him.

Selma stared into the landlocked cloud until her eyes burned and she had to close them; but he never returned. Curiously, she tiptoed to the door and inched it open until she could peer outside. Shock held her frozen. Her eyes widened in amazement. Right before her door, entwined by the drifting fog, sat two gigantic baskets. The first held a tumble of boxes wrapped in bright paper and tied up with bows. Two beautifully dressed dolls were snuggled daintilly between the presents as though they had brought them personally for Selma's family. The second basket fairly prickled with loaves of bread, tubes of salami, rounds of cheese, apples, oranges, and chocolate bars.

Selma's head swam. She felt faint and gripped the door tightly to keep from falling. A silly grin split her face from ear to ear, but she was helpless to stop it. Excited and feeling more like a child than any time in her entire life, she rushed out the door and into an enchanted wonderland. She dropped to her knees in the snow and looked raptly at the packages, fearful that she was dreaming and would wake to find them gone. One doll had long golden curls, the other had long, dark tresses. Both dresses, the first forest green, the second cranberry red, were made of velvet with hats to match and rich petticoats of white lace. Shiny black shoes adorned their tiny feet. Selma tilted her head sideways and read the direction on a paper tag tied to one ribbon.

'Goldilocks,' the jaunty printing read. Selma felt her heart flip over when she read the tag on another package. 'Rapunzel.'

Quickly, she looked around again, as though someone might be watching her. Thick fog had isolated her small world until Selma felt there were no other people, no world beyond this magical bubble surrounding her.

She turned the card on another gift so that she could read it and her hand began to tremble. 'Cinderella,' was printed in strong, black characters. Other gifts in red and green, blue and silver all had tags with the names printed on them.

She remained kneeling in the snow, spellbound, feeling that she was living in a dream world and not sure she wanted to wake up. But soon, the cold air penetrated her clothes, the snow chilled her legs, and she started to shiver. The young mother shook her head and struggled to climb back to her feet.

It took two trips to carry the baskets into the shed. When at last they were bunched up around the tiny Christmas tree, Selma hugged herself, then flung her arms wide. She danced and twirled around the dirt floor like a fairy with no cares in the world. Whirling to the window, she pulled aside the makeshift curtain and let in the muted light of day. She did not see gray light from a hazy dawn because enchantment sparkled in the air. In one euphoric moment, the little shed had been transformed into a palace of radiant magic.

"We wish you a merry Christmas," burst out of her mouth, loud and ecstatic, matching the smile exploding all over her face. Two small bodies began to stir and Selma sang it again, laughing at the same time.

"We wish you a merry Christmas." Both girls sat up at the same time. "We wish you a merry Christmas, and a happy New Year."

Four sleepy eyelids flew open wide, followed by squeals

of delight that reverberated from the rickety walls when Anna and Ruth's astonished eyes focused on the Christmas that had come while they were sleeping. They jostled against each other in their efforts to reach the basket full of presents. Selma's eyes filled with tears as she watched them cooing in delight over the elegant dolls. Their tiny fingers gingerly explored the soft material, the bright feathers in the hats, the tiny shoes — as though they were almost afraid to touch. But they kept the dolls close and giggled in ecstasy as they turned their attention to the wrapped presents.

Selma joined them as they took turns caressing the paper and shaking the boxes. Whatever was in the packages would be appreciated, but much of the magic lay in the wrappings themselves, the mystery of an unopened present, the knowledge that Christmas had come from... somewhere. Anna and Ruth turned imploring eyes to her and asked permission to open the presents.

Ruth's dark hair made her 'Rapunzel'. Anna, they all agreed, was 'Goldilocks'. And the girls thought it great fun that the very largest package was addressed to 'Cinderella'. Selma watched them carefully remove the first ribbons and paper and could almost imagine they were in their little home in Montana.

Anna got the wrapping paper off of a box first and pulled out a pair of thick, blue, woolen stockings followed by a pair of matching gloves. "Ooh. They're so soft." She held them out for Selma to inspect.

Ruth opened an identical box and lifted out her own pair of dark green stockings and matching gloves. "They're so pretty. They'll keep my feet and hands nice and warm." Her little fingers brushed up and down the soft material. "Your turn. Open a present, Mother."

The bow fell away, then the wrapping paper. She lifted the lid and parted the soft paper inside to reveal a thick, luxurious scarf woven from the softest yarn Selma had ever held between her fingers. Its rich, cranberry color matched the color of her own coat while a black stripe ran down both edges and ended in black fringe on each end of the scarf. A matching pair of gloves lay snuggled in the folds of the scarf. It was the most beautiful ensemble Selma had ever owned. But more importantly, it was a gift chosen with a great deal of thought and care. They would protect her face, neck, and hands and keep her warm on cold, blustery days.

Selma peeled an orange and shared out the wedges. Then the girls opened a chocolate bar and broke it into little pieces. Each tiny morsel brought oohs and ahs. Then sticky and happy fingers flew to the ribbons on more packages.

Ruth and Anna both received a new dress, a new pair of boots, and a downy pillow. Selma watched them in awe. She almost forgot to open any of the packages addressed to Cinderella until Ruth and Anna insisted. Her fingers moved slower and slower as one by one, she untied colorful bows and folded back the rich paper to reveal a round mirror with a long handle, a tortoiseshell comb and brush set, and a luxuriously soft, thick blanket.

Ruth and Anna chattered incessantly until the floor was covered with bright piles of colored paper and ribbons. Uncovered now, Selma lifted out the final present. The girls watched excitedly as she peered closely at the tag. "This one is addressed to all of us."

Moments later, the wrapping paper added to the mayhem and Anna, Ruth, and Selma sat gazing at the wonder before them. Cautiously, Selma picked it up and turned it over very gently. A metal key in the base turned easily at the pressure from her fingers.

Carefully, she set it back down and pulled out the tiny brass ring. Instantly, beautiful, haunting music filled the room while four intricately carved and brightly painted carousel horses rose and fell in their journey around the twirling platform of the music box.

Anna reached out to touch the horses. But Ruth grabbed her fingers and held them tight in her own. "No, Anna," she breathed. "We have to be very, very, very careful." Her brown eyes lifted to Selma in question. "Don't we, Mother?"

"You're so wise, Ruth," Selma said as she pushed in the brass ring, "but it is Christmas and I think we should touch it — very carefully."

Little fingers gently caressed each mane and tail. Then they traced the bridles and saddles on each miniature horse. Selma watched and wondered at the identity of someone kind enough to bestow such bounteous gifts, to give things they needed, yet thoughtful enough to envision a gift that would bring hours, even years of beauty and delight to their eyes and music and comfort to their souls.

Chills sizzled up her spine as she realized that, in some mysterious way, the wise men had again traveled from afar, bringing gifts to the Christ child — in the form of her tiny family. Though not of gold or frankincense or myrrh, these gifts were just as valuable and every bit as deeply appreciated. Surprised, Selma reached up to touch a flood of warm tears coursing down her cheeks. She struggled to breathe and felt her heart tighten in her chest. Someone in heaven and someone on earth cared what happened to her family.

Carl accompanied his sister to church on Christmas morning. The pastor's eloquent, hour-long sermon encouraged his parishioners to open their hearts to their neighbors in Christian charity; to remember the poor at this blessed Christmas season. Following the service, Amanda chatted with a few friends on the front porch. Carl waited. When at last his sister was ready to leave, Carl escorted her to Christmas dinner at Uncle Thomas' mansion.

The butler, properly attired in severe black and starched white shirt, opened the door and welcomed them in deferential tones. First, he removed Amanda's coat from her shoulders without even blinking at the unusual garment. Then he took the coat and scarf Carl held out to him.

"I can't even begin to imagine what the servants say about you." Carl's whisper carried the smile from his face to

Amanda's ears.

"Because of my coat?" Her tone betrayed a hint of worry. "I suppose I should wear the new coat you gave me last year…"

Carl chuckled and patted the fingers that held lightly to his arm. "That old coat is your signature, Amanda. Anyone who knows you, knows the coat. And no one would recognize you if you wore anything else."

"I can't tell if you mean what you say or if you're just patronizing me."

Carl had no chance to answer as they entered Uncle Thomas' immense drawing room where the guests were already being seated at the vast dining table. Thomas had been keeping watch and imperiously waved them forward. The lavish table was heavily laden with china and crystal. The sparkling silver reflected the glow of ornate candles elegantly adorning the center of the table. Carl relaxed in a plush chair and listened to the enthusiastic chatter of happy people. Tinkling of crystal glasses clinking one against another highlighted the cheerful atmosphere.

Carl watched platter after platter of rich, succulent, food being placed on the table. He compared this fabulous repast and opulent surroundings to the humble alley shed where he had delivered his simple Christmas gifts to 'Cinderella' and her daughters. He was surrounded by friends and acquaintances, family and business associates, relaxing in the most luxuriant surroundings Superior society could offer. Yet his thoughts and desires were miles away. He did not hear his Uncle addressing him while he found himself wishing he could have watched the little girls and their mother open their presents.

CHAPTER FIFTEEN

The day after Christmas, Selma described the man who had left the gifts by her door and asked Mrs. Guggenheim if she knew who he might be.

"Sounds like young Carl Stanton. He's the only one I know wears a hat like that. He spent some time out west after his father died. I heard he went cowboy, working on one of them horse and cattle ranches in Montana for a couple of years. Then one day he showed up back here to take care of his sister."

"His sister?"

"Mm hmm." Mrs. Guggenheim scooped chili into heavy crockery bowls and placed them on a tray. "She's probably twenty years older'n him — raised him after the parents died in the influenza epidemic when he was just a boy. Been slowly going blind the last five years. Wears a tattered old coat around town. Looks hard up, but she's got a real nice house over on Grover Street. The brother came back about the time her sight give out completely."

Stunned, Selma paused as she hung her coat on the hook by the door and lifted an apron over her head. Her mind whirled at the information and she was astounded by her misjudgment of the blind woman's situation.

"Oh, I almost forgot to tell you," Mrs. Guggenheim lifted the heavy tray to her shoulder and headed for the dining room, but paused with the door halfway open. "Mrs. Gordon came by this morning. Wants to know if you'd sew a couple of new dresses for her daughters. Her address is on that piece of paper tacked to the board by my lists." She winked at Selma, "I told her I'd send you over to her place first thing this morning, so shuck that apron and get going." She chuckled good-naturedly. "You're gettin' such a fine reputation so's pretty soon you won't be wantin' to wash my dishes no more." So said, the door swung shut behind her.

Selma found the paper with Mrs. Gordon's address and was removing her apron when the door flew open again. Mrs. Guggenheim stuck her head through and hissed, "That young Carl Stanton's out here right now if you want to see if it's him." Then she was gone again.

Selma stood undecided for several moments until Mrs. Guggenheim burst through the door carrying another tray loaded with dirty dishes. "If you want to see him, you'd better hurry. He's about to leave."

"Selma hung the apron on a peg and hurried to the door. Swinging it open just a few inches, she cautiously peered through the opening. No one in her view resembled the man she'd seen. Bravely, she pushed the door open a bit further. Her eyes examined each gentleman in the room, but she recognized no one. She was about to ask Mrs. Guggenheim to point out Mr. Stanton when a rugged man, almost as tall as the door, with broad shoulders and wavy black hair stepped into the restaurant. Her eyes followed him as he walked across the room to retrieve the black cowboy hat still hanging on the back of a chair.

Selma clamped her lips tight and started to move backwards into the kitchen. Just then, the man turned his head and their eyes met. Electricity fairly crackled across the room. Selma didn't know how long she stood staring before the door swung shut and she was secluded in the kitchen again, trying to breathe. Call it female intuition. Call it fear. But some sense warned Selma of his approach. Quickly, she scurried into the supply closet and lifted one finger to her lips as Mrs. Guggenheim stared after her in surprise.

Suddenly, the door to the dining room swung open again and Mrs. Guggenheim's eyes shifted from the partially closed closet door to the young man framed hesitantly in the entry. His questing eyes rapidly searched every nook of the kitchen.

"Can I help you?" Selma was impressed at the normal tone of Mrs. Guggenheim's question.

"I thought I saw... " He stopped and started again. "Is there a young woman working back here?"

"Well, I don't consider myself young anymore, but I

work back here." Selma stifled a chuckle at the coy expression that softened Mrs. Guggenheim's formidable countenance.

A deep, rich chuckle followed her joke. Selma clamped both hands over her mouth to stifle an answering laugh. She held her breath and didn't move or make a sound. Another man's voice echoed from beyond the door, "Carl. Come on, let's go."

"Um, well, thank you anyway." Carl nodded at Mrs. Guggenheim and allowed the door to swing shut behind him.

Mrs. Guggenheim's eyes shifted to where Selma sagged inside the doorway of the closet. "And what was that all about, may I ask?"

"I just... I didn't... I wanted... " Selma paused, unable to formulate her thoughts.

"Oh, I see. It's all very clear now." Mrs. Guggenheim raised her eyebrows while a knowing smile flitted across her face. "Truly, I believe I do understand. But if a young gentleman like that one was ahuntin' me, I wouldn't go hidin' in no closets."

"You don't understand."

"I understand enough. And I'll tell you this, young lady. If that young gent wants to find you, I think he's the kind who'll get the thing done." Grinning, she picked up the tray loaded with fresh food, but stopped before going through the door. "Mark my words if he don't." Then she sailed into the dining room.

Selma slipped out of hiding, threw on her coat, and

dashed out the back door. She half expected Mr. Stanton to come back through the other door any minute. Her face flushed anew. The tall, handsome stranger didn't have to find her in Mrs. Guggenheim's kitchen. He knew where she lived. For a moment, her old sense of false pride flared up, stinging her with acute embarrassment that he would associate her with such humble surroundings. She'd been too embarrassed to meet him, or say 'thank you' for the generous Christmas presents — while her hands were buried in soapy dishwater.

She hadn't walked a block before she was heartily ashamed of herself for feeling embarrassed that he knew she lived in the little shanty. Next, she harangued herself for being afraid to get caught washing dishes. She was performing an honest labor for an honest wage. It might not be easy, but she determined that if she ever met Mr. Carl Stanton again, she would hold her head high and express her thanks.

As it turned out, that opportunity presented itself much sooner than she expected. Almost a week later, on a blustery, snowy afternoon, Selma went shopping at the Crusted Hen Drygoods Store with the money she had earned sewing for Mrs. Gordon. She purchased tinned milk and dried beef, salt, potatoes, one small bag of flour, and another of sugar. She was reveling in the joy of being able to buy food when she stepped back into the howling wind and blowing snow. She ducked her head against the icy flurries and started across the street.

Without warning, she smashed right into a man as he unexpectedly stepped around the corner, directly into her path. One of the bags dropped from her hands, splattering flour and sugar all over the icy street. For a moment, her full concentration was centered on the loss of the precious food. All the color drained from her face so that when she looked up to apologize, her eyes were huge in her ashen face. When she recognized the man she had run into, she felt like shrivling into her boots. Her eyes dropped immediately, but lit upon the splattered flour and sugar again. Selma could have screamed in her frustration, embarrassment, misery!

"Excuse me. I didn't mean to run into you..." His voice reverberated through her soul and he stood so close that she could smell the clean scent of his soap. Suddenly, she couldn't breathe and she didn't know why. She only knew that she lacked the self-confidence to face him in her ragged clothes, and she couldn't face standing there, trading polite apologies. Desperate to escape, she gripped the other sack tight, turned, and ran.

"Missoula, Missoula, Missoula," she whispered the name again and again to the beat of her feet pounding over the snowy ground. "I'll go to Missoula in the spring. I'll live in my little house. I'll work. I'll watch where I'm going. I'll never run into a handsome stranger again as long as I live!"

The humor of the situation finally occurred to her, but not before she had raced around the last corner and turned into the alley that led to her little shack. She had run almost a mile without stopping and her gasping breaths were freezing her lungs. Slowing to a walk, she pulled her beautiful new scarf up to cover her mouth and warm her face. A fresh flood of embarrassment colored her cheeks when she realized where the scarf had come from.

Then she determined to stay away from the Crusted Hen Drygoods Store — forever!

"Well, young man, what have you got to say for yourself?" Thomas Mason wheeled himself into Carl's office.

"Good evening, Uncle Thomas." Carl leaned back in the leather chair and stretched his arms over his head, twisting his hands out and back toward the giant map of the Great Lakes that covered the wall behind his desk. "Arrgh," he growled, "that felt good." He pushed the chair back and stood up. "I've been sitting in this chair way too long."

"That's not what I asked."

"I apologize. What did you ask?" Carl turned his innocent gaze on the smoldering old man.

"I thought we agreed that Reeves would go west to survey the Columbia River Basin. Now I hear from that incompetent nincompoop that you are leaving first of next week. And without so much as a 'by your leave' to me."

Carl noted the all-too-familiar color changes in Thomas' face and wondered again how long his heart could stand the stress.

"We didn't agree on Reeves, Uncle Thomas. You told me you would rather he went, but I never agreed. I told you way before Christmas that I intended to go."

"I thought you were waiting until after Amanda's surgery."

Carl pushed long fingers through his thick hair as he turned to look out the window into the dark of early evening, instinctively searching for a sign of light in the alley below.

"I decided to go now. I'll only be gone two weeks this trip. That way I'll be back in time for Amanda's surgery. I figure I can plan for our new venture out west while she recuperates."

A small shaft of light glowed in the alley for a moment then disappeared and all was dark again. A mischievous smile had lifted the corners of Carl's mouth when he turned back to face Thomas.

"I can't stay and talk, Uncle Thomas. I have an apology to make." He strode across the room, pushing his hands into the arms of his coat as he spoke. Then he picked up a package from the credenza by the door, waved a cheery farewell at his confused, spluttering partner and sailed down the stairs two at a time until he reached the main floor.

Thomas watched him go, then wheeled across the room until he was right next to the window. He peered into the alley below where his adopted nephew spent so much time staring, wondering what the attraction was.

The sun had long ago settled beyond the towering buildings when Selma snuggled into the bed with her two wiggling, giggling bundles of energy and tried to tell them a bedtime story. But she had been gone most of the day again and they missed her; and she them. Giggles and laughter accompanied massive bouts of tickling and wrestling until the covers were all messed up and bits of hay were sticking out in all three heads of hair.

"Now, I'm going to have to remake the bed, you little raggamuffins!" Selma laughed as she escaped their clutches and stood, hands on hips, looking at the messy bed.

"It's all right. We'll help." Ruth started to hop off the bed when Anna tackled her. Selma hesitated a moment, but couldn't resist jumping into the fray.

Suddenly, the door rattled under a knocking fist, shocking them to silence. Two pairs of wide eyes stared at her and Selma's face washed as pale as theirs. Together, they waited silently, hoping against hope that whoever was out there would go away.

Knock, knock, knock.

Trembling, Selma untangled herself from the arms that had quickly wrapped around her. She stood on shaking legs and straightened her clothes. Gathering all of her courage, she forced her feet to walk to the door. Once, she glanced over her shoulder at the terrified children and tried to flash them a reassuring smile. It failed miserably. So she stiffened her back, grasped the latch, took a deep breath, and flung open the door.

She had no idea who would be on the other side. But the man standing there was the last one she expected to see. Selma gasped as her face flushed dark red, then paled to the color of untrammeled snow.

"Hello again." His face and voice were so familiar, Selma would have recognized him even without the black hat gripped in one strong hand.

Selma stood rooted to the ground, her tongue so thick in her throat that she couldn't have spoken to save her life.

"May I come in?" The deep tones made the request seem natural and normal. It helped Selma come back on balance.

"Yes," her voice croaked through her dry throat. "Please, come in."

Selma moved aside and the tall stranger ducked to step through the door. As he entered, the little shed seemed to shrink. She shut the door carefully behind him, all the while desperately wishing she could sprout wings and fly away.

"My name is Carl Stanton." He lifted his hand into the space between them. Selma stared at it for agonizing seconds, working up enough courage to put her own hand in his.

When she tentatively touched his fingers, a tingle of electricity raced up her arm, making her voice squeak, "I'm Selma Wrax... Wraxmore."

"Pleased to meet you." The words were perfunctory, but the warm hand that closed over her own was anything but detached. She could feel the blood pulsing in his palm and her betraying heart tried to match its beat.

Selma started to pull her hand back, but Carl held firmly to her fingers. She could feel his eyes looking down at the top of her head, waiting for her to look up. She dared not raise her eyes above the top button of his shirt. Instead, she studied the strong line of his neck and the dark shadow on his chin. Insanely, her hand itched to reach up and touch the pulse she could see pounding in his throat. Instead, she swallowed hard and dropped her eyes to her feet. But there were his feet, shod in leather boots, much larger than her own.

She felt trapped in the small room and could feel him staring at her as though the children didn't even exist. The children! How could she forget them! Her hand jerked free of his disturbing grasp as she turned toward the other end of the room.

"Girls, I want you to meet... Mr. Stanton. I think," finally, she flickered a glance up at his face, "that he is the man who brought our wonderful Christmas presents."

Carl felt strangely embarrassed that she would know the gifts were from him, then forgot everything as a chill of de ja vu passed through his soul when he focused on the two small girls curled up on a straw bed in the corner.

"I thought Santa Claus brought the presents." Anna's confusion was mirrored on Ruth's face.

Selma didn't know what to say, but Carl stepped right into the breech.

"He did, but I surprised him up in my office. And when he told me he had been having trouble finding you, I told him I knew right where you were."

"You talked to him?" Four little eyes were riveted to

Carl's face.

"I sure did. And when he told me how busy he was, I volunteered to deliver your presents for him."

"Wow!" Ruth was obviously impressed with Carl's credentials.

"I love my doll. And my stockings," Anna pulled up the hem of her dress to show him the stockings that adorned her tiny legs. "See? Aren't they pretty?"

"They certainly are." Carl moved across the small room and squatted down in front of the golden-haired child and looked into her blue eyes. "Do they fit all right?"

"Oh, yes. They're just perfect. 'cept I have to roll them down a bit above my knees." Anna looked over at Ruth, "But Ruth doesn't have to roll hers down. Her legs are longer than mine."

"Where's your office?" Carl turned his head at Ruth's question and met two deep, brown eyes beneath dusky curls held back with a frayed, pink ribbon.

"Two stories up in that building right there." Carl pointed one finger toward the ceiling above the doorway.

"Wow!" Ruth and Anna mouthed together.

Carl found himself enthralled with the two little girls, but almost afraid to turn and face their mother.

Finally, he stood and turned slowly around. His glance moved along the walls, noting the bits of rickety, makeshift furniture neatly placed around the walls, boxes, tins, a metal tub, and a tiny horde of food in a wooden crate near the fire.

The woman standing beside the fire and staring into the flames looked far too young to be the mother of the two children behind him and he could only guess at what circumstances had left her alone. Perhaps she still had a husband, waiting for her somewhere, coming back to her someday. He wondered what insanity had brought him here. Slowly, hesitantly, Selma turned toward him and her eyes lifted to meet his, solid and strong. Then he knew why he had come.

For the third time in his life, Carl felt an electric jolt that had nothing to do with Mr. Edison's new light bulb or the electricity he used to power it. He had felt this sensation the first time across a snowy street before Christmas when his eyes first met hers. Later, he convinced himself he had imagined the feeling. But then he'd seen her from across a crowded room, standing in the doorway of Mrs. Guggenheim's restaurant kitchen and the same thing happened. It was the exhilarated sensation for which he had yearned earlier in the day when the flour and sugar suddenly spilled around his feet and he realized whom he had run into. He had waited in vain for her to look up outside the drygoods store. Instead, she turned and ran away, leaving him standing alone, feeling hollow inside.

Now she stood before him in the dim light of a small fire with part of her face in shadow. No street lay between them, not even the length of a room; but coursing between them he felt that same unmistakable power, but from only inches away.

His voice came out husky, the words inane, mundane. "I brought these."

He held out the parcel he had been carrying. When at last her eyes moved from his face to his hands, he started to breathe again. "It's flour. And sugar. You dropped yours earlier today... when I ran into you. I... wanted to apologize and to... replace them."

Selma couldn't get her heart to stop racing or her breathing to even out. She reached for the package. Their fingers touched for the breath of an instant.

"Thank you." It was a whisper.

"My name is Carl Stanton."

"Yes, you already said that."

Carl took a breath and turned his eyes to the children. He forced his shoulders to relax and his lips to smile. "I thought if I started the introductions, I might get you to properly introduce me to these two beautiful young ladies."

Ruth and Anna giggled, then hopped off the bed and stood waiting for their mother to introduce them. They smiled while they formally shook his hand, then quickly jumped back under the covers on the stack of hay bales. Carl could see their mother in their features and clamped his teeth shut against the questions he desperately wanted to ask. Why were they here in this tiny shed, fighting every day against starvation? Where was the father of these tiny girls? Would she marry him? Was he crazy?

CHAPTER SIXTEEN

n the alley?"

"Don't repeat everything I say or I'll think you a fool!" Thomas thundered at the slight, bespectacled gentleman sitting before his desk.

Gunther Strauss didn't flinch, only because he had worked off and on for Thomas Mason anytime the past fifteen years and was no longer shocked by his outbursts. Instead, he concentrated on the notes he had jotted in the small notebook in his hand.

"Just find out and get back to me as soon as you can."

"Doesn't sound too complicated. I should be able to get some information fairly quickly." He stopped at the door, placed his hat carefully on his head, lifted a hand in farewell, then disappeared through the doorway without making a sound.

Selma bid goodbye to her latest sewing patron. She carried two candles and a dozen cookies which Mrs. Hoffman included with her payment — an extra bonus, she explained. Selma looked back when she reached the street and smiled at the new curtains hanging in Mrs. Hoffman's bay window. They looked lovely and brought a thrill of pride to Selma's soul. This was the third sewing job she'd completed and she was as happy as the woman smiling and waving from the window.

The aroma of fresh baked bread and sweet cakes tantalized her nose as she passed a corner bakery and her face beamed with a vivacious smile. The sun shined brighter and a new bounce lightened her steps. All because Mr. Stanton had knocked on the door of their 'house' again last night and surprised them with a basket overflowing with oranges, licorice, and peppermint sticks for the girls. She could remember no more than ten words they had exchanged with each other, but just having him near and watching the magic he worked with her children warmed Selma's soul deeper than the huge stove in Mrs. Guggenheim's kitchen warmed her body.

When at last he stood to go, he took her hand in his own and turned her wrist, gently drawing her nearer until her arm was intertwined with his, the back of her hand pressed against his chest. Suddenly she was trapped and felt a familiar, desperate urge to flee. But he held her tight, gently forcing her to look up into his eyes. For a moment, the fear melted away and she felt the magnetism of his gaze drawing her toward him. Warmth flooded her body and she felt herself swaying. Then she remembered another man's smiles turning to brutality, his cultured voice to profane words.

Carl felt the shudder run through her slim frame and saw her eyes narrow in fear. He searched her eyes for a moment longer, then released her hand, nodded in farewell, and stepped through the door. When he was gone, the gentleness of his touch and the understanding light in his gaze stabbed at her heart with poignant intensity. Later, as she lay awake watching the flames lick at the wood of the fire, the warmth of that moment returned to torture her mind and leave her with a dreadful longing she was helpless to define.

Selma shook off the memories and concentrated on finding 441 7th Street. Today she was answering a newspaper advertisement whose solicitor, a Mr. Henson, was seeking a seamstress to sew outfits for children living in the county orphanage. For the first time, Selma felt a sense of gratitude that her husband had set more store by the saddles and bridles worn by his stable of hunters than the clothes adorning his wife and daughters. Because of his antipathy, Selma had cultivated her ability to sew and turned it to good use for herself and her children. She quickly became a notable seamstress, thus laboriously acquiring a salable skill that she now hoped to turn into a career.

Seventh Street. A carriage waited outside number 441, but the driver pretended not to notice her as she stepped past and knocked on the ornate door. A stout woman in severe black and wearing wire rimmed glasses below a tight beehive hairdo, admitted her to the offices of Henson, Warder, and Jorgensen, attorneys at law. The woman asked Selma to take a seat beside three other women waiting in the room. Then she disappeared through an inner doorway.

Selma stared nervously around the rich, wooden paneling of the walls and framed pictures of old men in long, white beards. She waited for so long that she started in surprise when a door opened and the woman came out. She was followed by a venerable gentleman with a mane of silver hair and bushy eyebrows shading a pair of piercing blue eyes. He moved through the door in a wheelchair and she wondered if he was Henson, Warder, or Jorgensen. His head was turned to the side as he spoke to a man walking behind him; a very rotund gentleman in a tight, striped waistcoat, whose reddish hair was parted in the middle and slicked down the sides of his head.

The men bid each other farewell, then the corpulent gentleman in the striped waistcoat retreated back into the office. A powerful man in a severe black suit moved from where he had been silently standing in a corner. Grasping the handles of the wheelchair, he pushed the silver-haired gentleman toward the outer door.

"Sally McBride?" One of the waiting women stood and the secretary led her through the door. The burly man helped the gentleman in the wheelchair don a heavy winter coat, then he turned the chair backward in preparation for descending the stairs outside. Just as he opened the outer door, the secretary stepped back into the outer office and called Selma's name.

"Mrs. Selma Wraxmore?"

"Yes. That's me." Selma turned toward the secretary, but not before she saw the old gentleman jerk his head toward her and lock his piercing eyes on her face.

"I need to have you answer a few questions. If you would just step over by my desk for a moment, we can take care of the formalities." As she moved briskly to sit behind her desk, Selma turned to see that the man in the wheelchair was still staring at her. Then his servant wheeled him backward through the doorway and out of sight.

An hour and a half later, Selma listened hopefully to Mr. Henson, the man in the striped waistcoat. A partner in the law firm, he also acted as Chairman of the Board for the Douglas County Orphanage. He rushed through the information that several wealthy families had donated bolts of material for use in the orphanage. The Board of Directors had determined to use that material in the manufacture of as many children's outfits as could be squeezed out of each inch of material. When asked, Selma assured the warden that she was indeed capable of undertaking such a task. To prove her point, she lifted from her handbag a dress she had made for Anna, working all day yesterday and late into the night, using material Mrs. Guggenheim had been storing 'since before time,' as she put it.

Mr. Henson fingered the garment, inspecting the seams

and hems, then handed the dress back to Selma, informing her that she was hereby awarded the job at the wage of $11.00 per week, plus room and board.

Selma's face flushed with happiness until Mr. Henson explained that the orphanage lay forty-two miles south of Superior near the small town of Douglas. She sat stunned while he explained that Selma would be expected to reside at the orphanage, where a set of rooms would be prepared for her own use until the project was completed. Selma swallowed her fears and asked if it would be possible for her to share the rooms with her two daughters.

She was taken aback when Mr. Henson's corpulent face flamed red and puffed up. His eyes threatened to bulge out of his fleshy forehead. He launched into a sudden tirade, accusing her of hiding the fact that she was married, with children.

Stunned, but holding tight to her self-control, Selma defended herself calmly, informing him that, though she did not see that it was in any way his concern, her husband was deceased. And the fact that she had two daughters would not affect her work. Her hard-won self-confidence kept Selma's chin level and shoulders straight while her cool blue eyes met Mr. Henson's disgruntled gaze.

Unexpectedly, the lawyer deflated like a balloon losing air. His anger ebbed and his expression turned apologetic. "I'm sorry, but that would not be possible. You'll have to find other accommodations for your children while you are working at the orphanage. You can visit them on weekends, of course."

"But Mr. Henson, I can't leave them alone. Please, I promise they won't be a problem; they could stay with me in my room..."

"I apologize, but we simply cannot allow you to take your children to the orphanage. It would be very... disheartening... to the children who live at the orphanage. I'm sure you understand."

Selma silently sought for a solution to her problem. She needed this job badly. The pay she would earn would be enough to buy the final train tickets to Missoula. She had learned first hand how difficult it was to find a job. And the little house beckoned.

"May I have a few days to make arrangements for my girls?"

Mr. Henson looked at the young woman across his desk and enjoyed the feeling of power his position granted him. He had interviewed several other ladies, all older matrons who had long ago lost their first blush of youth. Now, across from him sat a beautiful young woman who could clearly use a benefactor in her life, someone to help ease her burdens. He resisted the urge to smile.

"I have business in Duluth that will keep me occupied until the first of next week. I'll expect your answer when I return. Does that give you enough time?"

"Yes. Thank you."

Selma walked out of the oak and marble offices into a

bright winter morning. As she tip-toed cautiously across frozen puddles and between horse-drawn buggies, a pair of fine lines creased her smooth brow. Part of her mind guided her footsteps unerringly back toward the alley she called home, but a deeper part wrestled with the logistics of fulfilling this badly needed job.

With the money she was earning at the restaurant, she could now afford to feed her family. Her sewing provided extra that Selma was saving toward train fare. Stashed in a tin box in the little shack she now had enough money for two tickets. The money she had received today would go in there as well. But Selma calculated that if she could just find a way to make the job at the orphanage work out, by the end of February she would have more than enough money to pay their way to Montana with a tiny bit extra to help them get settled in Missoula. True to Bertha's advice, Selma had been wiping away the soot that covered her dream. Her reservoir of inner strength grew each time the light at the end of her tunnel grew brighter. Four short weeks was all she needed — and a miracle.

A chill raised the hair at the back of her neck and Selma unaccountably felt a desperate need to hold her children. Her speed increased. She hurried around the corner into her alley and squinted ahead through the shadows.

A flickering movement caught her attention. Her eyes flew wide as a tendril of flame flickered through a hole in the shed wall, then another. Screaming, she dropped her bundle, picked up her snowy skirts, and ran. Her feet felt like lead, her strides slow and painful as she watched red flames lick higher on the dried wood and the reflections of fire dancing eerily on the single window pane.

She tripped over something and fell hard in the snow, cutting herself on a chunk of ice when she tried to catch herself. She didn't feel the blood dripping down her arm as she scrambled up and ran on. She wrenched the door open. Immediately her arm flew up against the flames bursting in her face. The interior was completely engulfed in fire. Straw-filled sacks in the corner writhed in one massive inferno, like something ferociously alive. The wooden walls rippled with dancing flames. Blistering heat drove her back, cringing from the burning blast. A child's screams reverberated through the air and she charged forward again. Suddenly, the entire shed exploded in one gigantic fireball. Selma was catapulted backward into a tangled pile of debris. Her head collided with something hard and she crumpled into a heap as blackness deeper than night dropped its curtain over her mind.

Carl's ears were still ringing from the familiar tirade Uncle Thomas had unleashed as soon as he came into the office. Today, it took every ounce of self-control Carl possessed to keep from flinging his share of the partnership in Thomas' face and leaving the company for good. When his anger seethed white hot and he was ready to burn every bridge between himself and the ancient plutocrat, the thought of his sister's upcoming operation and her need for continuing medical care kept his tongue between his teeth until he felt his blood boil.

However, no matter how much Thomas ranted, Carl would not succumb to the older man's efforts to dictate his actions. Even before Thomas finally reached the end of his blustering tirade, Carl walked stiffly to the door and calmly interrupted to announce his determination to be on the train in two days' time. Then he stepped through the door and quietly shut it in his seething partner's face.

Back in his own office, Carl paced up and down in front of his windows like a ferocious, caged animal. Longingly, he stared across the bay at the frozen lake, wishing the waters were free and the wind blowing up a storm so that he could charge into the foaming breakers in one of the rescue boats. He longed to pit his strength against the elements. Instead, he flipped open his briefcase and threw in tablets, rulers, and pencils, then slammed the lid down, locking the catch before picking it up and striding to the door. Out of habit, his eyes dropped to the alley below. Instantly, his eyes flew open and his racing heart froze.

Throwing down the briefcase, Carl tore out of his office like a madman. He raced past his secretary's desk, sending papers flying in his wake. Down the wooden stairs he bounded, two and four at a time, barely holding the ornate rail in his breakneck flight to the ground floor. He crashed through the back door and burst into the alley, his legs pounding at a sprinter's pace.

Flames were creeping up the western wall of the shed when he threw the door open and heard Ruth and Anna whimpering in terror from the corner against the far wall. Unheeding of the heat and fire, Carl charged through the flames licking at the door and threw a blanket over the girls before he gathered them into his arms. Turning, he saw the flames had reached across the doorway and were starting to devour the southern wall. The intensity of the heat burned his eyes and seared his throat. The little girls clung to his neck through the protective blanket so tight he could barely breathe. With one hand, he grabbed up an old feed bag and wrapped it around his head and face. In the same instant, he charged through the flames where he thought the opening should be.

CHAPTER SEVENTEEN

Selma awoke slowly, as though she was struggling up a steep incline and the rocks and brush kept ripping away in her hands, making her fall backwards time and time again. A terrifying memory lurked at the edge of her consciousness and each time she neared the precipice, she lost her grip and slid back down into the dark, tangled depths of forgetfulness.

When she finally forced her eyes open, Selma found herself staring out an unfamiliar window at a dark sky that held no stars, no moon, no light of any sort. The pain in her chest spiraled downward into her stomach, cramping her insides until she pulled her knees up in a ball, hugging herself. Her eyes were wide and staring. Long moments passed before she considered the question of where she was. She turned her head, then shuddered at the pain lancing through her skull. When she dared open her eyes again, she noticed a single candle burning in its holder, reflected in the mirror on top of an ornate, wooden bureau. The tiny flame hypnotized her, drawing her eyes to focus on its finger-sized teardrop of light.

A wretched sob broke from her chest and she turned away from the flame. Its flickering light, held captive to the candle, brought back a raw memory of other flames; flames that had taken from her all that she held dear. She rolled away from the flame. A clean fragrance exuded from her hair when she turned. She lifted a hand to find that it had been washed. Was she dreaming? Could it all be a terrible nightmare? She touched her chest and found a soft, silky nightgown in place of the newly-altered dress she had been wearing when...

Her soul cried out in agony and she thrust the memory away. This had to be a dream. Desperately, she pressed her thumb and finger together, pinching the soft flesh of her arm. The sharp pain was real. This was no dream. Futilely, she fought against the tears that filled her eyes and wet her cheeks. She was clean. Lying in clean clothes. In a clean bed. But she would have gladly taken back her ragged and stained dress, have traded anything in the world for the lives of her children.

Immersed in her own misery, Selma did not hear the door open. A woman stood in the doorway and listened to the ragged sobs coming from the figure huddled in a heap beneath the blankets on the bed. She took two steps nearer.

"Don't worry so, my dear. They're safe. They're here."

The words repeated several times before the soft voice penetrated Selma's grief. She gulped and held her breath for a long moment.

"Here?" Selma envisioned two little bodies lying cold, in wooden caskets, and her heart felt as though it was being squeezed between a giant vise. The dreadful pain behind her eyes filled her entire skull, threatening to rip her head apart.

"Yes, they're asleep in another room."

"Asleep?" The pain in her head was so intense that Selma could barely focus on the words. She repeated it again. "Asleep?" Her stunned mind tried desperately to understand what the soft voice was telling her.

"I promise." The voice was soothing and gentle, "Would you like to see them? I think you would feel better... ?"

Fragile hope surged through Selma's chest, encircled by a tight fear that she might now be dreaming. She pinched herself again and found it hurt as it had before. She prayed that her children were indeed asleep in another room as the voice promised. Struggling against the blinding pain in her head, Selma turned over and sat up, swaying back and forth as she faced the owner of the voice.

Selma squinted at the woman and her head threatened to explode, forcing her to lay back down. More than ever she felt she was dreaming. She stared at the woman, trying to formulate a question, but her mind didn't want to work and she was left speechless, numb.

"Yes, it's me — the woman from the train depot." She held out her hand, searching through the darkness with her blind eyes in Selma's direction. "Come now and see the children. We can talk later."

The blinding headache blurred Selma's vision. But, at last, she managed to follow the woman down the hallway and into a bedroom on the other side of a broad stairway. She passed through the door and waited for her eyes to adjust to the darkness. There were two beds in the room, but both little heads stuck out of one set of covers. A cry escaped her lips as Selma fell to her knees beside Ruth and Anna.

Gently, hesitantly she reached out to touch the curls on their heads. Then she held her breath and listened. Their peaceful breathing was the sweetest sound she'd ever heard. She pressed gentle, tear-filled kisses onto their smooth, clean cheeks, desperately wanting to wake them and hold them in her arms, but knowing she should let them sleep.

Her head felt like a thousand miners were wielding pick axes to chisel away at the inside of her skull. The pain nearly blinded her as she tried to rise. Stars burst before Selma's eyes as she staggered to her feet and wove her way toward the door. Grasping her head in her hands, she tried to hold the sides together against the pain that threatened to tear it apart. She struggled to force her feet to carry her through the doorway before the scream building in her throat escaped.

The woman was speaking, but Selma couldn't decipher her words against the background of agony in her ears. Just before all the lights flashed out, she opened her eyes and saw Carl in his distinctive hat standing at the top of the stairs. She reached a hand toward him as though he could save her, then the world turned dark and Selma felt herself falling.

Carl leapt forward and caught her as she toppled. He lifted her in his arms, holding her limp body tight to his chest, and carried her back to her room.

"Amanda," he spoke over his shoulder, "she fainted. I'm taking her back to her bed." He heard his sister walking behind him down the hall and spoke without turning his head again. "What were you thinking, letting her out of bed? She's practically split her skull open and you're giving her the guided tour?"

"I know she shouldn't be up and walking, but she woke up and was in so much misery, thinking her little ones were burned alive. I just had to tell her," Amanda explained. "Then she needed to see for herself."

"Well, of all the stupid, foolish excuses for..." he broke off the unjustified tirade and Amanda smiled to herself and forgave her brother for his anger. She thought she understood the reason for it.

Gently, Carl laid Selma on the bed and drew the covers up to her chin. He couldn't resist touching the soft skin of her face, something he'd wanted to do for a long time now. Then he stroked the silky hair where it lay on the pillow while his sister stopped in the doorway and listened to his movements.

"Is she pretty, Carl? She sounds pretty."

"No, she's not pretty," his throat constricted on the next words, "she's beautiful." He cleared his throat and kept talking, "But she's very, very thin, because she works too hard and probably doesn't have enough to eat." Bitterness edged his words as he sat beside the unconscious girl and saw for the first time the telltale scars that marred the perfection of her face.

He spoke as though he'd forgotten his sister was still there. "Her eyelashes have been singed and a little bit of the hair around her face looks like it has melted. The skin of her face looks like she has a bad sunburn. But I don't believe it's too serious."

Amanda counted her steps to the rocking chair in the corner and sat down, listening, waiting for Carl to say more.

Carl stared down at Selma. When he spoke, his voice sounded far away. "Did I ever tell you about a dream I had about six months ago?"

Amanda cast back in her mind for the memory, but found none. "No, I don't think so..."

"It was a Sunday afternoon. I was sitting in my room reading a book. I don't know if I was asleep or not, but it seemed to me that I was wide awake. A young woman and her two little daughters appeared to me in the room. I could see them just as plain as day. It startled me, so I gazed hard at them, but was unable to recognize them. I didn't know what it all meant — then."

"But you do now?"

"That woman was Selma. I thought I recognized her from across the street the day she put that coin in your hand. But I told myself my imagination was running wild. Then a few days later, I was at Mrs. Guggenheim's restaurant. The door to the kitchen opened and I saw her standing there. It was Selma — I had no doubt that she was the same woman I saw in my dream. Then I found the little... house... where they're living and met her daughters. As soon as I saw them, I knew Ruth and Anna were the same little girls that I saw in my dream."

Amanda felt a chill sizzle up her spine and tingle across her scalp. "What does it all mean?"

"It means this is the woman I'm going to marry," was on the tip of Carl's tongue, but he couldn't force the words out, as though saying them would jinx the wish. "I don't know." The words sounded lame, even to Carl's ears.

"Have you gotten to know her at all?" It seemed like a logical question to Amanda, considering the circumstances.

"I've tried, but I think she's afraid of me."

"Afraid of you? What have you done?"

"Not me! I would never harm a hair of her head," Carl couldn't resist touching her hair again. "But something else, someone else... " he couldn't finish the sentence and they sat in silence for several moments, each alone with their thoughts.

"I wish I knew where she came from. How she managed to be all alone."

Carl longed for Selma to open her eyes and look at him. Her face was lovely, but her soul held the beauty that attracted Carl and he wanted to lose himself in it again. Then his sister's words jerked him back to the present.

"I probably scared her the night she was thrown off the train. If I had known how badly things were going to turn out for her, I would have tried harder to bring her home with me. Then, the day before Christmas when she stopped me on the street and pressed that coin into my hand... wished me a Merry Christmas... Well, I could have cried, I was that touched."

"It's that ragged, old coat you wear. Makes people think you're a beggar." Carl spoke lightly, only part of his mind on the words.

"In my eyes that coat is still as beautiful as the day Joseph gave it to me."

"I know, but... " Carl started to argue, but his heart wasn't in it.

"You're probably right. He's been dead a long time and it's a foolish thing to hold onto. But I still love him and wearing that coat makes me feel as though he's nearer."

"You loved him a lot. I don't think I ever realized what that meant..."

... before now? Amanda silently finished his sentence to herself.

Selma stirred and moaned. Her hands escaped from the blankets and grappled above her in the air for something only she could see. Carl caught both hands in his own and held them tight to his chest, caressing them gently with his fingertips while he cooed soothing words. Finally, she relaxed and quieted.

He held her hands a long while before tucking them back beneath the covers. At last he stood. He gazed down at her for another moment, then reached for one of his sister's hands and pulled Amanda to her feet.

"Let's go downstairs and I'll make you some of my world famous hot chocolate. Then you can go to bed. I'll keep an eye on our fair maiden and you can spell me in the morning."

"You've got yourself a deal. Who knows? Maybe she's Sleeping Beauty and you'll fall in love. You'll wake her with a kiss, get married, and live happily ever after." Amanda teased as she placed her hand in the crook of his elbow.

"A-man-da!"

"Ooo! I know I've touched a nerve when you call me 'A-man-da' like that," she chuckled a rich, deep laugh. "Can't blame a sister for trying."

Arm in arm, they descended the stairs and drank hot chocolate while Selma and her children slept soundly between warm, clean sheets on comfortable beds in the rooms upstairs.

CHAPTER EIGHTEEN

I t burned to the ground. I haven't found a soul who knew anyone was living there."

"But you're sure someone was?" Thomas peered sharply over his shoulder at Gunther Strauss.

"Without a doubt. I sifted through the ashes after the place burnt down. Found a few things — a charred doll, couple of pots, stuff like that. Tin can full of what looks like burnt money. Figure it was a family of vagrants waiting out the winter."

"Any sign of... ?"

"Nope. No bodies. Whoever lived there got out in time. Some blood in the snow outside. Somebody got hurt, but that's it. Want me to keep looking?"

"Yeah. Spend another day snooping around; see what you turn up." Thomas tore his eyes from the blackened scar in the alley below and wheeled away from the window of Carl's office. "Got something else I want you to do for me."

Gunther turned to a new page in his notebook. "Go."

"Woman named Selma Wraxmore. Lady Selma Wraxmore, unless I'm mistaken. Living here in Superior somewhere, now. But when I saw her picture in the paper seven years ago, she had just gotten married to an English peer name of John Christopher Wraxmore. Had holdings in York, if I remember correctly." Thomas leaned back and stared at the ceiling. As he thought back over the years, his voice turned brittle. "Beautiful young thing — married off to an old goat."

"What's your interest in the lady, sir, if I may ask?" Gunther peered myopically through his thick glasses at the shipping magnate.

"Not what you're thinking, I'll guarantee you that!" Thomas thumped his balled fist on Carl's desk and glared at the little man. "I saw her in the offices of Henson, Warder, and Jorgensen two days ago, looking for a job."

Gunther looked into Mason's eyes but realized his employer was miles away. "I'm just wondering why the beautiful, young wife of an English peer is dressed in hand-me-downs and looking for a job in Superior, Wisconsin. Call it curiosity."

"You're paying the bills, Mr. Mason." Gunther stood and moved to the door. "I'll get back to you in a couple of days." Then he was gone.

Thomas Mason slumped down in his ornate wheelchair. A brown stupor whisked his mind back twenty-five years into the past. Twenty-five years ago to the first time he met Aurelia Klintenberg — Selma Wraxmore's mother. He had been young and ambitious; a cocky, outspoken fire-eater, determined to carve his own niche in the burgeoning world of Great Lakes shipping. He gambled his scant life savings on a fancy suit and a ticket to the British Isles in search of investment capital. Luck smiled on him midway through the voyage across the Atlantic when he walked away from a smoky card table in the ship's lounge with substantial IOUs signed by Lords Crippenden and Marsh.

Unknown to Thomas, the two impoverished noblemen had played far beyond their means. When Thomas presented himself at their respective establishments in London for payment of the debts they had incurred, he walked away from one with cash, but something far more valuable from the other — letters of introduction to three of the most powerful shipping men in England. Within two weeks and by sheer force of personality, Thomas Mason had convinced two of those men to back his daring Great Lakes enterprise. He never looked back.

The only scar he bore from his time abroad was carved on his soul by a green-eyed seductress named Aurelia Klintenberg. Thomas was bowled over the first time he watched her glide into Lord Crippenden's ballroom. His host informed him that she was newly widowed, but that didn't stop Thomas. He went after Aurelia with the same aggressive tactics he used in business. And, for a short time, she seemed to welcome his advances. But Thomas made one fatal error in his calculations. He thought her cold, glittering emerald eyes masked a warm heart. After two weeks of mad, passionate, lovemaking, he discovered how wrong he had been. By the time Aurelia convinced him that she truly had been toying with his affections and cared no more for him than her butler's cocker spaniel, Thomas went away a scarred and bitter man.

Through twenty-five years, not another woman had ever tempted him from his celibate state. He harbored no love for Aurelia and the cold bitterness had certainly served him well in business. But it had also left him unfulfilled. Only recently had he faced his mortality and felt the loss of a wife and the family he might have had. If only...

He jerked out of his trance. His broad shoulders straightened and he pushed a heavy hand through his mane of silver hair while his questing eyes stared out past the lighthouse into the gray, frozen bay. That day in Henson's office. He thought he was dreaming when he saw her. But only for a second did he imagine he beheld Aurelia. It wasn't her youth that told him he was mistaken; but the look in her eyes, the gentle molding of her features. Even when he imagined himself in love with Aurelia, he was not blinded to the calculating glint in her eyes, nor the hard set to her features. He had only fooled himself into thinking he could change them. And the girl's eyes had been sapphire blue while Aurelia's were cat-eye green.

Selma held one hand of each little girl and gazed ahead at bookshelves lining the walls, at cluttered stacks of memorabilia that filled every corner of the room. Quilts, crocheted in bright hues, were draped over chairs and every seating space in the room. A kaleidoscope of colors intermingled before her eyes, different shades and textures blending and merging from floor to ceiling. She closed her eyes against a dizzy feeling, then opened them again while commanding the room to hold still. It didn't work and she was forced to close her eyes again.

One hand lifted to massage the ache stubbornly plaguing the back of her head. Gently, she rubbed a lump the size of a very large egg beneath her thick hair. Gradually, she lowered herself into a large, overstuffed chair while Anna and Ruth helped settle her in by stuffing cushions behind her back until she protested she was comfortable. Then they spread a rose and green colored afghan across her legs and Selma, eyes closed, explored it's silken texture with her fingertips.

When her head finally stopped spinning, she ventured to open her eyes again and watched the room slowly settle into focus. Her girls were chattering away, obviously having the time of their lives. They hadn't quit smiling since she woke up three days after the fire. Ruth wasted no time confiding that every day they awoke in Amanda's house felt like Christmas.

"Look, Mother," Ruth held up a brass statue of an elephant.

"See this Mommy?" Anna extended her hands, wrapped around a carved crocodile.

"And this... and this... and this... " The list went on and on as the girls lifted one treasure after the other for her to see. Ruth held up crystal balls with cityscapes and forest scenes tranquilly sprawled beneath feathery showers of snow. Anna proudly displayed a long cane with a sparkling crystal on the end. They all watched the prism colors dance on the walls and ceiling when Anna passed her treasure through a beam of sunlight. Selma felt her head start to pound in rhythm with the beats of her heart just as Amanda came into the room and told the girls to quiet their voices because of their mother's headache.

Ruth and Anna were immediately contrite and lowered their voices to whispers. Beckoning with one hand, Amanda invited them to follow her to the kitchen. Selma smiled at the enthusiasm her daughters showed toward their hostess. She had warmed to Amanda immediately too, finding in the older woman a maternal instinct and genuine concern that had been pointedly lacking in her own mother.

Mrs. Guggenheim came to visit on Selma's fourth day in Amanda's home. She had received a message from Amanda explaining about the fire, Selma's injuries, and telling her that Selma was now living at her home in Grover Street. Mrs. Guggenheim was sincerely happy to see Selma in a comfortable home and added her urging to Amanda's that she stay with the blind woman until she was ready to travel west. Tired and soul-weary, it didn't take long before Selma was convinced that Amanda was more than happy to have the young mother and her daughters stay for as long as they wanted.

"I have an ulterior motive, my dear. I like the sound of the children and I love the company. They give me a reason to get up in the morning."

Six days after the fire, when the girls were asleep upstairs and the two women were sitting in quiet companionship, Selma finally asked about the fire that destroyed her tiny home. Amanda's sightless eyes seemed to stare into the distance as she related the story she had pieced together from Carl and the girls.

Ruth had been trying to build the fire up so that Selma wouldn't have to when she got home from work. She piled on a few sticks, but they seemed to smother the fire. Afraid she had put the fire out, Ruth threw on more sticks. Suddenly, the whole stack caught fire and the blaze grew until flying cinders chased the children back. Suddenly faced with a towering wall of fire, Anna and Ruth had no idea what to do. Terrified, they cowered in the farthest corner by the wall. Then an exploding spark ignited a mound of straw and before they knew what had happened, the walls were on fire and the shack was filling up with smoke.

Selma's heart raced with renewed fear as Amanda calmly told how Carl had looked from his office window and seen smoke rolling out between the top of the door and the frame. She described his race down the stairs and outside to the shed where he charged through the burning door and whisked Anna and Ruth to safety. He had just carried the girls through the back door of his building when Anna and Ruth — both looking back over his shoulder — saw Selma race up to the flaming shed and throw open the door. They both screamed and Carl whirled around just in time to see the explosion that hurled Selma back and knocked her unconscious. He left the girls and bolted back to lift Selma and carry her to safety as well.

"We were very relieved when the doctor told us you just had a concussion. He cleaned the gash in your arm, wrapped it up, and told us you'd be good as new in a week." Amanda left out the part about how Carl sat faithfully at Selma's bedside through the first trying nights, comforting the delirious mother as she thrashed in pain and relived the nightmare of the fire.

"Four days after the fire, I finally convinced Carl to get on with his trip to Oregon. He's working on a new project to open up a big shipyard in Portland. He's been planning this trip for some time, but he didn't want to leave until he knew you were all right. If all goes as planned, he should be back by the end of next week."

Selma was relieved to hear that Carl was away and felt comfortable asking a question. "Does Carl live here with you?"

"For now. He bought a cattle ranch in Montana when he turned twenty-one. He went out there on a hunting trip with our father when he was only ten and came back all fired up about the lofty mountains and clear rivers and a sky he said went on forever." She smiled happily at the memory of a beloved brother's enthusiasm. "Said he'd go back there to live one day.

"Then our folks died and he came to live with Joseph and me. He inherited our father's share of the shipping business with Uncle Thomas, but he was too young to run his own affairs. Though he started going out in the boats when he was just a small boy, he never loved it like our pa. But after our parents died, Carl went berserk for the danger, always riding the rescue boats out into the wildest storms, even though it infuriated Uncle Thomas. Carl had been very close to our father, almost inseparable. I often wondered if he wanted the Lake to take him, close out the pain." She sighed at the memory. "Instead, he earned the respect of even the most hardened boatmen and developed a reputation for never losing a ship he set out to save.

"Uncle Thomas thought he'd forgotten about the wide skies and tall mountains of Montana. But when Carl came into his inheritance, he bought that ranch, packed his bags, and moved out west." She turned her face toward Selma as though she were watching her reaction. "I suppose you noticed the cowboy hat?"

"Couldn't miss it. But what brought him back?"

"Me, I'm sorry to say. My eyes started going bad five years ago. I didn't tell him. Didn't want him to worry. But dear Uncle Thomas wrote him, even though I told him not to. And Carl came right on back to be with me. Thomas has always wanted Carl back here, close to him. Thomas is a good man, but a hardheaded businessman who's used to getting his own way. He's come to think of Carl as the son he never had. Carl loves and respects him, but goes his own road anyhow." She chuckled, "Oh, my goodness, the arguments those two men have had. But mostly it's Uncle Thomas haranguing and Carl quietly going on about his business. I think the fact that Carl won't argue with him infuriates Uncle Thomas almost as much as the fact that he won't knuckle under to his dictatorship."

Selma found herself warming to Amanda's brother. She knew what it meant to have a dream and she understood his desire to follow it to the very end.

"He went to college in engineering and since he's been back in Superior, he's been designing ships for Uncle Thomas again. That's his side of the business. The 'thinking up new ideas and designing' part. He's always got to be doing something; can't hardly hold still for two minutes. Carl went back to Montana in September and October to check on his ranch, help with the roundup and branding the calves. He's got a good foreman running the place for him while he's gone, so he doesn't really need to worry.

"When he first came back, he said he planned to return to Montana as soon as my eyes were better." Amanda's voice took on a dreamlike quality, as though she was thinking aloud and had forgotten Selma was even in the room. "But now, when he talks about the boats and the Lake — and even Uncle Thomas — I get the feeling he's glad to be back. Truly glad. Perhaps he left the pain out there in those wild mountains."

Amanda sighed and was still for a moment before she went on. "I truly want the best for Carl. I want him happy, and if Montana is where his happiness lies, well, then Montana it'll have to be. But I get the feeling he's... happy... to be home. I guess it's that simple. A few comments he's let drop from time to time make me think he's seriously considering staying here." She chuckled and shook her head, "But he's not going to tell Uncle Thomas that; not till the last minute. He's a naughty boy, and I think he gets a kick out of riling Uncle Thomas."

Selma felt completely relaxed and was thoroughly enjoying listening to Amanda's story and did not want her to stop. "If he goes back to Montana, will you go with him?"

"He asked me to once... " She paused in thoughtful contemplation. "But my friends are here. My life is here. And I'm too old to go adventuring in a strange land." She sighed and a sense of sadness seemed to settle over her. Then she smiled and shook off the reminiscences as she stood up. "Well, my dear, it's time we were getting you back to bed."

CHAPTER NINETEEN

wo more days passed before Selma's headaches subsided enough that she could spend any amount of time away from the darkness of her room. After that, she healed rapidly. Each day saw her increasingly eager to find a way to repay Amanda for saving her life and the lives of her children. Each morning that she awoke to see the beautiful, flower-paper covered walls of her room, Selma felt she was waking in a dream world. In one terrifying moment, she had gone from living like a starving gutter rat to being a pampered guest in a beautiful home. In a strange way, the past months seemed merely a dreadful nightmare. Then, in the middle of the night, she would jerk herself out of horrible nightmares where she saw her children dying of starvation; screaming in flames; freezing from the cold.

But dream or reality, the experiences through which she had lived had left their indelible mark imprinted on her soul. No longer the same woman who set sail for a new life in a new world, she was forever different; braver, wiser, more self assured, stronger. In quiet moments, Selma analyzed the changes and found them of value. Even the brutal nightmares that had ceaselessly haunted her night hours for so many years had become mere ghosts, flitting silently at the edge of her sleep.

After the children fell asleep, the women spent the evenings together, gradually getting to know one another. At first, Amanda would sit quietly in Selma's room, telling her about the day just past and relating tidbits about Anna and Ruth. By the third evening, Selma hobbled carefully from her bed to sit for an hour in Amanda's cozy parlor where the cushions were fat and soft, the fire warm and enticing. Snuggled in front of a cozy fire, Selma at last tried to express her gratitude to Amanda while berating herself for refusing Amanda's help that first night at the train station.

Amanda smiled and kept crocheting. "It is a sad fact that often we learn life's most important lessons by walking the most tangled path. When we start down that road, we take a terrible chance that we may fail. But if we succeed, no one can take away from us the lessons we learn or the strengths we gain." Her hands stilled and lay silent in her lap as she leaned her head against the high back of her chair. "If we're poured from the right metal, the hardships of life act like a blacksmith's hammer and pound out our impurities — while shaping us into stronger people."

She turned her blind eyes toward Selma as though she

could see the younger woman. "And from what I've seen, I think you're made from some pretty strong stuff."

Amanda's eyes turned back toward the fire, leaving Selma to consider the impurities in her soul that might have been pounded out. A thoughtful sigh escaped her lips. "I can assure you that I never want to go through anything like it again. But when I consider the good with the bad, I realize I have learned invaluable lessons I might never have learned any other way."

Her mind revolved around the great and small changes she felt in herself and Amanda could hear the smile in her voice. "By far the most valuable, I hope I never forget to be grateful for even the smallest of life's blessings."

"They are often easily overlooked. But without them life would quickly come unraveled." Amanda lifted the yarn and needle and started hooking stitches again.

Selma paused, unable or unwilling to discuss the deeper lessons she had learned. The women sat in companionable silence for some time. The white cat appeared from behind the curtains and jumped into Selma's lap. She petted the plump, purring animal for some time, then tentatively unlocked her heart a tiny bit more.

"On the train platform that night... I felt my dreams wither and die in the cold and snow. At that moment, losing our money, our tickets, our possessions, meant losing any hope of our future or happiness. I can't begin to describe the dark horror that... that paralyzed my mind." She stopped and only the crackle of the fire echoed in the room.

"Despite that, when you offered me refuge, I was... too proud... to take it." Selma reached across the short distance to lay her fingers on Amanda's arm. "As I was leaving, you said something that pierced that terrible fear for just a moment. Do you remember what you said?"

"My mind isn't what it used to be," Amanda chuckled. "You'll have to remind me."

"You said 'To meet our dreams... we must live them each day along the way.' Your words burned into my mind and I never forgot them. But I was too distraught to consider their meaning until days later. But after we found the little shed—and finally had a tiny corner we could call our own—your words came back to haunt me."

Amanda could hear Selma relax into her memories and waited expectantly. "The girls were asleep. We were warm and relatively well fed. I lay snuggled up to Ruth and Anna, looking around at the humble walls, the stack and sacks of straw, and feeling the blessed warmth of the fire. Suddenly, I realized that destitute as we were, I knew a peace and contentment I had never experienced."

Selma stared into the blazing heart of the fire in the stone hearth as she traveled back in her mind to that night. "The thought of our little house was even brighter in my dreams than it had been in England. But I suddenly realized that if I lived my whole life waiting for that one dream to come true before allowing myself to be truly happy, to fully live each day... I never would be happy."

She squeezed Amanda's arm and the older woman laid her own hand over Selma's fingers. "I saw how I had kept my happiness on hold, waiting for that future day when the safe, controllable dream I had created would come true — as though on that day I would suddenly be happy, contented, fulfilled."

Selma stood up to pace slowly around the room. Held securely in her arms, the white cat purred as Selma scratched behind her ears. When she spoke again, it was almost to herself.

"Out of self defense, I had learned to depend only on myself. But one can learn that lesson too well. One shove by a mean-hearted train conductor forced me to realize how easily my dream could be shattered and lost."

She laughed mirthlessly, "Granted, it's hard to find joy when you're freezing and starving to death. But if I could not find some joy in each day along the way — no matter where all my struggles took me, no matter if I was rich or poor, I would never be happy or content."

Selma shook her head and sighed in frustration. Carefully, she lowered herself back into the chair, the cat still held in her arms.

"I know I'm probably not making a whole lot of sense..."

"You're making perfect sense, my dear. Great philosophers have struggled for centuries, searching for the perfect way to say just those same things. In many different ways they have each tried to explain that the joy of life is truly in the journey, not in reaching the destination. If we rush over the simple steps in our headlong race to get to the finish line, we will reach the end and realize that we've rushed over life itself. The prize will be empty."

Selma shivered as a chill ran down her spine. "As strange as this may sound, I've had moments where I felt... almost a fear... that if we hadn't been kicked off the train... I may never have learned the most important lessons of my life."

Amanda nodded as though in perfect understanding, a tragic smile tilting her lips at her own unspoken memories.

Selma shook away the premonition. "But I can assure you — the next time I'm in trouble and someone offers me a lifeline, I won't be too proud to grasp it with both hands."

"What are your plans now, Selma?" Amanda hooked a few more loops, but her heart wasn't in the afghan and she stopped to listen with her whole mind.

"I must earn enough money for train fare to Montana. Then, once we get to Missoula, the deed to our little house will still be waiting in the post office. That dream hasn't disappeared; it's just grown up a bit. I'm thankful every single day that I decided to mail the deed on ahead, or it would have been stolen along with everything else. When we get there, we'll have a home and we'll have each other."

"Do you ever think of romance, Selma? You're young, vibrant, just starting out in life. Surely you hope to find a man to share your joys and hardships?"

Selma didn't answer and the long silence made Amanda wonder if Selma could possibly be mourning her lost husband. "I'm sorry. Perhaps I shouldn't have spoken of... another man. I know you lost your husband not too long ago. But you'll get over that in time and I'd like to think of you remarrying some day — find a man for you, a father for your children."

Amanda feared more than before that she'd hit a nerve when Selma still did not respond. She waited, trying with all of her senses to detect what emotion Selma was feeling, but could tell nothing. She had to wait for the younger woman to confide in her.

A jolt of cold dread had made Selma realize all of the pain was not gone. All of the impurities had not yet been beaten from her metal, for a twisted bitterness galled her throat when she thought of her dead husband.

"A father for my children?" Her voice sounded hollow. "A man for me?" The white cat leaped to the floor as Selma pushed herself to her feet and began to wander around the room again. She picked up an object, inspected it, replaced it, then moved on to another. "My children had a father. I had a...man." The depth of loathing in Selma's voice shocked Amanda. "I think one is enough in any woman's life."

Amanda started to speak, but Selma changed the subject and kept going. "I'm so inconsiderate, Amanda. All we've done is talk about my problems. But I want to know about you. Would you mind if I asked how long you've been blind?"

Amanda felt the fences go up around the subject of men and took her cue from Selma. "Not at all. In fact, I wish more people had the courage to talk about it. Seems to scare folks, like it's a taboo subject. But my blindness is part of my life and I can't ignore it. I don't know why others should."

The crochet needle paused a moment, then started moving again as Amanda spoke. "I started losing my sight almost five years ago. But I quit seeing much of anything at all just about six months ago."

"Six months? You get around as though you'd been blind all your life." Selma was shocked and stared in awe at the woman beside her.

"I determined not to give up on life any sooner than I must. I got a cane and started paying attention to where things were set long before my eyes were gone completely. It's been a... challenge. But I've learned a few valuable lessons myself through it all."

"You say 'challenge', but it's more than that. It must be terrifying to face such a life-altering change. Most people faced with such a disaster would become bitter and withdrawn. But you're just the opposite."

Amanda just smiled mysteriously.

Selma stared at her, truly in awe of the older woman's undaunted spirit. Then she shook her head to clear her muddled thoughts. "What did the doctors tell you?"

"In the beginning, it started with headaches and occasional blurred vision. Our old family quack gave me some medicine and said it was normal for my age. But the medicine didn't help any. My sight grew worse and so did the headaches. I have to admit I hid it from Carl the few times he came back to visit. But when Uncle Thomas finally wrote him, Carl rushed back from Montana. By the time he got here, he was absolutely furious. He cussed me for a fool five ways from Sunday." She chuckled at the memory. "He loves me, you see. Even before he got here, he'd burnt up the telegram wires sending inquiries around the country, searching out the best eye doctors. Turned out, they're in Chicago. So, he packed me up and sent me to Dr. Funkelstein right after Thanksgiving."

"What did Dr. Funkel…what did the doctor say?" Selma leaned forward in her chair, hanging on each word.

"Said I've got a brain tumor."

Selma's face drained of all color and she felt her throat tighten. "What does that mean, Amanda?"

"It means that in about six weeks the doctors are going to operate on my head and take the dratted thing out."

"But isn't that dangerous?"

"Well… my options are fairly limited. They tell me I'll die in two years, maybe less, if I don't have the surgery. The pain will get worse until it drives me insane long before I die." Amanda spoke in a matter of fact voice, as though discussing the price of bread instead of her future.

"If it works, I'll live and have an even chance of getting my sight back." A humorless chuckle escaped her lips. "Some choice, don't you think?"

Selma suddenly considered her own troubles insignificant in comparison.

The cheery tone surfaced once more in Amanda's voice. "But I don't like to dwell on it. Makes me worry. Now it's your turn to tell me something, Selma?"

"I will if I can." Selma was still reeling from Amanda's revelations and it was a moment before she could focus on her question.

"While you were delirious, Carl said you kept talking about an orphanage."

"Carl... said that?"

Amanda heard Selma's voice warm at her brother's name and she silently cursed her blindness. She wanted so badly to see into Selma's eyes.

"You were too much for me to handle when you were delirious, so I had Carl help me in your... wilder moments."

"I see. Well, just before the... the fire... , Mrs. Guggenheim showed me a notice in the newspaper where the Douglas County Orphanage was advertising for a seamstress. I applied. Mr. Henson, the man who hires staff for the orphanage, told me I could have the job. The money he offered to pay me would be enough to buy train tickets to get the three of us to Montana. I thought I'd finally solved our problems. I was thrilled.

"But then he stipulated that I couldn't keep Ruth and Anna with me at the orphanage. He gave me until," she mentally counted the days, "tomorrow, actually, to find someone to care for Anna and Ruth during the weeks while I would be away."

Selma leaned back and rested her head on the high cushion of the chair. "He said it would be okay with him if I visited them on the weekends, as if that would solve my problem. But I can't possibly leave them... so I'll just have to find something else."

Suddenly, Amanda was fired with a burst of energy, but she considered her words carefully before she spoke. Her first thought had been to offer Selma the money outright for the tickets. But something — a premonition, maybe — made her withhold the offer. She didn't take time to analyze her motives right then. Instead, she offered a different solution.

"Selma, you are welcome to live here with me. I would love to have you and your girls in my home—you bring life back to this lonely old house." She felt Selma stir and rushed ahead. "If you want to work, I could watch the children while you go to the orphanage. They wouldn't be alone; you wouldn't be alone. You'll be back to visit them on weekends..."

Selma almost opened her mouth to decline Amanda's offer. Then she remembered a cold, terrifying night at the train depot when this kind woman had offered her shelter. How differently the past weeks would have been for Anna, Ruth, and herself had she swallowed her pride and accepted Amanda's help when it was first offered.

Amanda's quiet, contemplative words broke into Selma's

reverie. "Joseph — my husband — and I wanted children. Desperately. We had been married thirteen years when my parents died and we took Carl to raise. Our parents had only Carl and me, born twenty-two years apart. I think Carl was a surprise." She grinned and kept talking. "My Joseph loved Carl, took him into our home, loved him, treated him like his own till the cancer took him. Fourteen years of marriage and we never had any children of our own. We never stopped trying, right to the end. If I'd only known... I would have talked Joseph into adopting. But, like most young couples, we thought we had the world and our whole lives in front of us. Then he was gone and it was too late. But I've never stopped wishing for children... all these years... even knowing I could never have any.

"Now, here you are, an answer to prayer." Her blind eyes glistened with unshed tears and her voice pleaded. "I would love to play grandmother to Anna and Ruth. So please don't say 'no' until you've thought it over."

Selma's mind whirled through the possibilities placed so invitingly before her. A home with this warm, caring woman—a friend, a grandmother to her children, someone else to help, someone on whom she might rely. Then, unbidden, her mind conjured the picture of Amanda's handsome brother and the powerful magnetic force she felt when she gazed into his eyes. She shook the image from her mind, frozen by a desperate fear that wove icy tentacles through her heart. She feared losing her independence; that all the strength she had gained would be lost; feared the blossoming, radiant feeling she felt in his presence might be fleeting, might turn to the cold brutality she had escaped when the coffin lid closed upon her grim past. Worse than living without that feeling would be having it turn cold, bitter, ugly. Did she have the courage to find out, to give it a chance? She had no answer.

Amanda interrupted Selma's fevered introspection. "At least let me care for Anna and Ruth while you work at the orphanage. The timing would be about right. If you are still determined to go, you would have the money for your tickets to Montana by the time Carl takes me to Chicago. You wouldn't be alone. And I would love the company. You'd be doing me a huge favor. Caring for the girls will help keep my mind off my surgery. There's time enough to face our futures after that."

"Thank you, Amanda. You'll never know how much this means to me." Selma's voice faltered and she swallowed hard before continuing. "But I can't let you think I plan to stay here. I've had my heart set on this dream for so long that... " She paused, uncertain now where the end of her dream actually lay. "Through all of the hardest... darkest... moments in my life, this dream has been like a shining beacon glowing through the dark, giving me the courage to go on. To give it up... ?"

"Not give it up. But perhaps to change it. Maybe even make it better." Amanda was surprised at how important

Selma's decision had become to her. She spoke the simple truth when she talked of the joy Selma and her children had brought back to her house. The mere sound of children laughing, arguing, running through the halls and up and down the stairway—ah, she thought, that was life at its best.

"You would be blessing my life, Selma. Please believe me. Leave the girls with me, work at the orphanage. That's all I ask for now. Then, when it's time for you to go, we'll talk again. And I hope you'll decide to stay."

Selma moved to kneel beside Amanda's chair and wrapped her arms around her motherly friend, hugging her in a tight embrace. "Thank you, Amanda. You'll never know what a blessing you are in my life. I'll take the job. And I promise to think very hard about the future."

Amanda returned the embrace and smiled over Selma's head, as though she was looking into the future and liked what she saw. "Thank you, my dear. And don't you worry too much about the future. Take it one step at a time. It'll all work out for the best. I promise."

CHAPTER TWENTY

arl stretched his stiff muscles and stared at the surrounding hills and mountains. Missoula lay nestled between rolling grasslands to the east and steeply rising hills that rapidly cascaded into forested mountains to the west. It was a young city, still booming from the mining rush, complete with rough edges and poor manners. It took him the rest of the day to find out where Selma's house was located, so he decided to wait until morning to ride out there.

Right after breakfast, he borrowed an old plug from the hotel owner and rode out of town — at a leisurely walk. A trot or gallop seemed beyond the old nag and Carl quickly found that if he didn't constantly urge the horse to move, it would stop and dig through the snow to find last summer's grasses. He was thoroughly disgusted with the animal by the time they reached their destination. He stayed in the saddle, fearful the horse would turn and race for home if given even the slightest opportunity. But the nag seemed content to paw for grass while Carl stared at the small house.

It looked to be in good repair. A pole fence encircled the front yard, but the gate hung crazily from only a single hinge. The roof was straight and solid, the walls white clapboard and painted probably the summer before. Giant trees rose behind the house and would provide shade during the hot afternoon hours of summer. He urged his sluggish mount around to the back of the house and found it to be much the same as the front. Selma had made a good purchase. He looked longingly at the tall mountains rising in a scenic backdrop, then turned the horse toward town. He had judged the animal correctly. One nudge with Carl's heels sent the horse charging full speed toward his barn and bin of oats.

Later that night, Carl boarded the train for the last half of his trip to Portland. As he stared out at the quickly darkening landscape, he was unsure whether he was happy or sad that he had detoured to see Selma's house.

Selma visited Mr. Henson's offices just before noon. He seemed pleased to see her and almost excited when she formally accepted the position. But she was stunned when he instructed her to be ready to depart in two days' time. The monthly supply wagon was leaving at eight o'clock Saturday morning and he expected her to be on it. Straightening her shoulders, she promised to be ready.

Without really intending to, she took a detour on her way back to Amanda's house. She relaxed in the afternoon sun and her feet unerringly followed the familiar path back to the alley. Worries kept her mind focused elsewhere until she felt vaguely surprised to find herself staring at the charred remains of the little shack that had been their home. Gazing sadly around, she realized that nothing was left but the memories.

A familiar shape caught her attention and she knelt and brushed fresh snow away to reveal the charred remains of the music carousel. A rush of poignant emotions left her reeling from twinges of happy, sad, bitter, and sweet pains. A quiet, melancholy reverence seemed to fill the alley until Selma could almost imagine she was attending a friend's funeral. Finally, the penetrating cold reminded her she had a warm home and people who loved her. And they were waiting for her return. She stood up, feeling stiff and cold, and turned to leave. She would mail her letter to Bertha and Seth. Then she would go home to Amanda's house.

"The weeks will pass quickly. You'll see."

The way Amanda said the words somehow made it easier for Selma to believe. She was standing on a chair and reaching into a high cupboard for the suitcase Amanda insisted she borrow for her trip to the orphanage.

"I've never been away from Ruth and Anna overnight. Tell me again that you're sure they'll be all right with me gone five days at a time?" Selma's voice betrayed her intense agitation as she stepped carefully down off the chair and shut the cupboard door.

"You're a good mother and they know you love them. They've been through a lot for such little girls and they've come through it all just fine." Amanda squeezed Selma's arm reassuringly. "They'll understand and I'll love them all I can while you're gone. I promise."

Amanda tried to turn the young mother's thoughts in another direction. "I have a surprise for you."

"A surprise? Ooh, I can hardly wait! What is it?"

Amanda rummaged in a low cupboard for several moments. Finally, her searching fingers found a box and lifted it off the shelf. She pushed the cupboard door shut, then held the box for Selma to take. Amanda held her breath in anticipation as she heard Selma open the lid and lift back the tissue paper. Her face split in a wide grin at Selma's surprised exclamation.

"Oh, Amanda! It's beautiful. How in the world did you manage to find such a perfect dress — the size, the color... ?"

"I didn't. Carl picked it out."

"Carl?" Selma choked on the name, then went silent.

"He went shopping just before he left for Oregon." Amanda explained as she led the way to Selma's bedroom. "I sent him to the woman who helps me with my dresses. I realized it was taking a chance, but he volunteered to do it. Mirabelle is very dependable and I had faith that she'd give him good advice. He picked it out, but it needed to be altered or I'd have given it to you a few days ago. Go ahead. Try it on. See how it fits."

The younger woman followed her down the hall to her bedroom in silence. She carefully laid the dress out on her bed and worked to unbutton the dress she was wearing. Amanda sensed Selma's discomfort. As she moved to the chair in the corner, she desperately sought for the right words to ease Selma's distress.

"Please understand that you and your girls seem almost like family to us. I can't explain why that is, but having you and Ruth and Anna here makes this house a home again. Carl wants you to be comfortable here as much as I do. And you must admit, you do need a new dress."

"You're right." Selma tried to forget Carl and spoke in a lighter tone. "And I am grateful." She exchanged the dress of Amanda's that she was wearing to the new rose and cream creation she'd just unwrapped. As she twirled in front of the long, ornate mirror, a wave of unfamiliar emotions surged through her body.

"The dress is perfect, Amanda. I wish you could see it." She stopped twirling, knelt before her benefactress, and took the wrinkled hands in her own. "I've just never had anyone care so much, or thought it could be so difficult to have someone give me... so much. It makes me uncomfortable in ways I can't even begin to explain."

"If it makes you feel any better, Carl was a bit uncomfortable picking out a woman's dress." She chuckled and returned the pressure of Selma's hands. "But he was better for it, and you will be too."

She knew her next suggestion was going to be hard for Selma, so she plowed right ahead. "In fact, I thought perhaps we'd go shopping tomorrow since you're leaving the next day. You'll need some clothes for your new job." She left the invitation hanging.

"I couldn't... " Selma tried to object.

"Yes, you can. And don't you go getting all uppity on me." Amanda infused her voice with all the love and understanding in her heart.

"I'm not... I don't... I can't..."

"Not another word. You just look at it as making an old woman happy and allow me to have my fun."

Selma stared at the blind woman's eager face, but unbidden came the memory of a different invitation to go shopping, on a long ago day in another country.

"No, please. I'd rather have the blue dress. This one makes me feel almost naked."

"Don't be missish!" Aurelia Klintenberg chided, her eyes sparkling in a disturbing way. "That blue dress will never attract any attention. You look positively dowdy with the neckline almost up to your chin and those ruffled sleeves." A theatrical shiver accompanied her dark frown.

Selma had been seventeen, fresh from school, and accustomed to wearing a very modest uniform. Her mother, all too eager to marry her off quickly, immediately took Selma shopping for a gown to wear at the season's first society ball.

"But I feel so... indecent... in this, Mother. Mrs. Coriandor would consider this dress... vulgar." Selma blushed and dropped her eyes; afraid she had been too forward in expressing her opinion.

"Tut tut, child. Mrs. Coriandor is a fine teacher, but her world is limited to books and the acquaintance of other equally boring educators. Allow me to be a better judge of fashion. Now, stop fidgeting, girl, and hold your head up. No man likes a wilted flower. And shyness does not become you."

One long finger lifted Selma's chin and another straightened her slumping shoulders. Then Aurelia walked slowly around Selma, looking critically at the creamy skin rising above the dipping neckline. Just the right amount of décolletage emphasized her budding charms and elegant neck. The only covering on Selma's arms were the long white gloves that stopped just above her elbow. The tight waist and draping skirt of filmy material left just enough to a man's imagination to incite intense interest. Aurelia nodded her head in approval and turned to the matron of the shop.

"We'll take this one. Please deliver it to 23 Curzon Street."

"Yes, Madame."

Lords and ladies gossiped in small salons, danced in the ballroom, and played cards in small anterooms from ten o'clock until the wee hours of the morning. Selma thought it a hideous party. She felt like a horse at auction as her mother introduced her to every eligible bachelor of her acquaintance, none of them under forty years of age. She almost expected to be asked to show her teeth to prove she was in good health. Of the young men who solicited her hand to dance, her mother allowed only one to escort her onto the floor. Selma later found he was the eldest son of the Duke of Eddington and likely to come into the title soon because of his father's declining health.

By the third such ball, Aurelia Klintenberg had narrowed the prospective field to three gentlemen, chief of whom was Lord Wraxmore. Selma did not care for any of the men of her mother's choosing, and naively thought she would have some say in the matter of her husband. Not so. The first week in October, Lord Sefton threw a weekend hunting party at his lodge and invited Mrs. Klintenberg and her beautiful daughter. Over the poker table at three o'clock in the morning, Aurelia found she had gambled herself past the brink of financial ruin. Lord Wraxmore, also a guest and winning player at the table, suggested they take a stroll in the garden to discuss repayment of her debt. In the rose arbor, he suggested trading Aurelia's IOUs for Selma's hand in marriage. Aurelia readily accepted.

Her mother broke the news to Selma when she came to her room at noon in response to a summons delivered by Aurelia's maid.

"Mother, don't do this! Lord Wraxmore terrifies me." Selma was horrified at the announcement of her betrothal.

"Look at me, Selma." Aurelia had been peering at herself

in an ornate hand mirror, poking disgustedly at her puffy eyes. She threw the mirror down on the bed and faced her daughter. "I'm 38 years old, in the prime of my life! I'm too young to have a daughter trailing after me for who knows how many years. It's high time you were married. I've merely found you a suitable husband who can take care of you in style."

"But he's so old." Selma's voice echoed the horror she felt. "And he's cruel to his horses."

"Lord Wraxmore is old enough to not chase around after other women; old enough to appreciate a beautiful young wife; old enough to have sufficient money to keep you in elegance and style. And what he does with his horses is his own affair."

"But I don't care about money," Selma pleaded as welling tears trickled down her pale cheeks.

"You will. Take my word for that. Life without money, my foolish daughter, is no life at all. You'll learn wisdom as you grow older."

Aurelia threw back the covers and swung her long, shapely legs out of bed. "Now, go get dressed. We must go shopping for your bride clothes. We have much to accomplish in the next two weeks."

"Two weeks!" The room reeled around Selma and she clutched a chair to keep from falling. "Don't do this to me, I beg of you!"

But no amount of begging, pleading, or crying moved

Aurelia from her determination.

Selma shook off the horrible memories and concentrated on the present. "I can't tell you how grateful I am, Amanda — for everything. I'll pay you back somehow, someday."

"Don't worry about me. I told you I'd love taking care of your children. I love taking care of you." Her voice took on a dreamy quality and her blind eyes stared at the wall as though she was reviewing her own private vision of the past.

"Joseph would have loved your girls. We used to talk about the children we would have. We even came up with names for them."

Selma watched the tears gather in Amanda's eyes and wondered about a love that remained undimmed after so many years of separation. Then, as quickly as it came, the moment of reverie passed.

"Just see that you do a good job for those little homeless waifs at the orphanage and that'll be payment enough for me, my dear."

"I better go check on the girls... and show them my new dress." Selma stood to leave, but Amanda called her back just as she reached the door.

"Oh, I almost forgot to tell you. I received a wire from Carl this morning."

Selma felt her face flush and was grateful that Amanda could not see the betraying color. "What did he say?

"The snow is deep, the rivers landlocked with ice, and

he's probably going to be gone a week longer than he origi-
nally planned."

Selma breathed easier, even though she felt an unac-
countable loss at the news.

"But he emphasized that he still plans to be home in time
to take me to Chicago."

"I'm glad he's doing well." Selma didn't know what else
to say, so she moved toward the door. Amanda's next words
made her stop and turn back again.

"He said to tell you he stopped off at your house in
Missoula."

Selma's eyes widened and her heart beat faster at that
news.

"He said it is a lovely house, in good repair, and that
there are tall, beautiful trees all around it."

"Thank you, Amanda. That was very kind of him."
Amanda waited for Selma to say more, but she heard only soft
footsteps pass out the door and echo along the hallway.

Anna and Ruth were just waking up from a nap when
Selma walked into their bedroom. She watched them wiggle
and stretch, then slowly open their eyes. She sat on the bed
and cuddled them close while she told them about her job.
Cheerfully, she emphasized how much fun they would have
staying with Amanda.

They received her news unhappily, protesting they did
not want her to be so far away from them. It was some time
before she could impress upon them the importance of her

taking this job. She finally had to resort to reminding them of the days she had tramped around Superior, desperately seeking employment, and their starving condition when she could not find a job. Immediately, she regretted her words as they wrapped their arms around her, shivering and tearful. The old fear revisited their innocent minds more forcefully than Selma had intended.

"No, no, no. Don't worry. I'm sorry, my darlings. I didn't mean to frighten you. But just think," she held them at arm's length and smiled from one pair of eyes to the other, "you'll get to stay here with Amanda, live in her beautiful house, and play with the white cat's new little kittens. Amanda says she's going to have them any day now. And I'll be back before you even know I've gone."

Ruth looked at Anna. Anna stared back at her sister. Solemnly, they turned their eyes to Selma and nodded in unison. "Okay. All right."

"Thank you." Selma lifted her hands to one cheek on each little girl. "Now, I want you to promise me that you'll help Amanda and be little angels all the time I'm gone."

"We will." Anna sniffed.

"Promise." Ruth crossed her heart, but her lips quivered as she brushed sparkling teardrops from the corners of her eyes.

"Mommy, when will Carl come back?" Anna asked.

Selma was surprised by the question. "He sent a cable saying he would be gone longer than he thought, so I'm not sure when he'll come back." She paused, then had to ask. "Why, my darling? Do you miss him so much?"

"Oh! Yes!" The vehement response from both girls took Selma by surprise. But she positively reeled at the next question.

"Is Carl going to be our daddy?" Ruth asked while Anna nodded enthusiastic encouragement.

The frilly canopy over the bed seemed to whirl around Selma, reminding her of the first day she opened her eyes after the fire. She clamped her eyes shut for a moment and her fingers gripped the bedspread to hold herself steady. After several ragged breaths, she braved opening her eyes again.

"Why do you ask that, Ruth?

"Because," she cupped her hands around her mouth and whispered in Selma's ear, "I had a dream that he brought me a beautiful, shiny black pony for my birthday. It had a bright, red bow tied around its neck. He led it around and around while I rode on its back. Then he took Anna for a ride, too, and then our little brother." Her eyes fairly glowed in her eager little face. "And you were there and we were all a family."

Selma looked into Ruth's glowing brown eyes and every inch of her skin prickled with gooseflesh. Anna clasped Selma's right hand in both of hers and leaned against her arm as she looked into her mother's eyes. "I think he'd make a really good daddy. Don't you?"

Selma could not answer.

CHAPTER TWENTY-ONE

he orphanage loomed into sight through a curtain of heavily falling snow. The driver pulled up where ancient lanterns hung from graceful pillars, shedding warm light in front of the old mansion. He climbed down, cold and stiff, then helped Selma to alight. Her frozen feet threatened to crack and fall off as she hobbled up the steps and across the porch to the massive wooden door. Leaving her alone, the driver climbed back into the wagon and drove around to the delivery entrance.

Selma looked upward at the half-moon window glowing above the entryway, took a deep breath, and lifted the heavy brass knocker. The door swung inward almost immediately and she was met by a small boy of some five years. Eagerly, he lifted his huge brown eyes to Selma's face, shocked her with a wide, toothy smile, and asked in an excited tone if she was going to be his new mommy.

Selma shook her head silently from side to side as she

stepped through the doorway. The light in his eyes dimmed, but he rallied quickly, flashed her another brilliant smile, and held tightly to her hand while promising to show her all around the orphanage.

Mrs. Cutfield, treading lightly down the long hallway, quickly shooed the little fellow away, then asked in what way she could be of service. Selma introduced herself and the gracious woman immediately overwhelmed her with gratitude for accepting the position and cheerfully welcomed Selma to the Douglas County Orphanage.

Introductions out of the way, Mrs. Cutfield led Selma on a brief tour of the facilities. It wasn't long before Selma felt completely bewildered by the intertwining maze of halls, rooms, and passageways. Finally, she was led up a narrow flight of shadowy stairs and along a cramped corridor on the second floor of the antiquated mansion.

"Before I show you to your rooms, I want you to meet a very special inmate here at Douglas." Mrs. Cutfield rattled a quick tattoo on the door at the end of the hall. "I know I shouldn't have favorites, but sometimes I make an exception. Drew is one of those." She heard a soft voice bid them enter and opened the door, allowing Selma to pass through first.

"Good evening, Drew."

"Oh, is that you, Mrs. Cutfield? I'm so glad to see you."

Mrs. Cutfield closed the door in her brisk way, then led Selma across the room.

"Drew, I would like you to meet the newest member of

our staff." Mrs. Cutfield smiled at Drew, then nodded toward Selma. "This is Mrs. Wraxmore. She has come to sew clothes for the children here at the home."

Selma stopped beside the bed and looked down at a bright-eyed young boy of some ten years, propped up among innumerable pillows. His bed was higher than normal and positioned where he could easily look outside. The broad windowsill was stacked with a plethora of young boy treasures: partially carved blocks of whittling wood and an old knife; bottles bristling with sticks and dried grasses; marbles, string, and a myriad other things all tumbled together. A premonition took her eyes to the thin legs beneath the covers of the bed. Her flickering glance told her this little boy would never walk. Selma met his eager young gaze and was immediately enchanted by the rich highlights in his brown eyes.

"How do you do?" His high, enthusiastic voice charmed Selma with disarming candor. "Ooh, I love the color of your eyes. Hmm. They remind me of someone else... " In a flash, his soft cheeks blushed a rosy color for fear he'd said the wrong thing.

Mrs. Cutfield chuckled and Selma's face lit up with a rare smile that few people ever saw. "Why, thank you. You're a most observant young man. My eyes remind you of someone else? Who would that be?"

Selma smiled disarmingly and Drew relaxed again. But his brow wrinkled in thought as he tried to recall the memory.

"I dunno. I can't remember right now. But I'll think of who it is and tell you later. Okay?

"I look forward to it."

Drew dazzled her with a blinding grin of his own. In that one twinkling of a second, an indefinable connection was formed between the boy with the twisted legs and the woman with the crippled heart. Their fingers touched to shake hands and the bond was cemented as though they shared thoughts when no words had been spoken.

Carefully watching Selma from the corner of her eye, Mrs. Cutfield was pleased with what she saw. She allowed them to talk for a moment, then took Selma's arm and led her to the door while telling Drew she would check in with him again later. Selma glanced back, caught his eye, and winked before the door shut.

Mrs. Cutfield then led Selma to the other end of the hall to a set of small rooms. Each wall was covered in faded wallpaper featuring winged fairies cavorting amidst droopy flowers in a riotous garden. A single dormer window overlooked the front of the property. During the daytime it would allow light into the humble room. But at the moment, a chilling breeze was its sole contribution. Selma ignored the cold draft and expressed her delight at the quaint charm of the dropped ceiling and ancient four poster bed.

Mrs. Cutfield's lips crimped in a wry smile, then she started to chuckle. "The whole house is quaint. It's positively overloaded with grace and charm. But experience has taught me that newspaper stuffed in the cracks around the windows helps with some of that." She raised one eyebrow as her eyes met Selma's. "Too much charm, as anyone can tell you, can produce detrimental effects... over an extended period of time."

Both women laughed and a friendship was begun.

The wagon driver had carried the bolts of cloth to what would become Selma's sewing room, adjacent to her bedroom. When they entered the tiny room, Mrs. Cutfield frowned at the unsightly stack of donated material.

"Don't touch any of that tonight, my dear. Ugh!" Her nose crinkled at the pungent, moldy aroma exuding from the stacks. "We'll attack it together tomorrow. Messy chores are always more pleasant when shared. Don't you agree?"

"Yes, ma'am." Selma could barely repress a chuckle at the disgusted expression on the matron's face.

"I look forward... to seeing if there's really anything of value here." Mrs. Cutfield rolled her eyes at Selma as she closed the door on the sewing room.

"Well, my dear. Get settled. I'll bring you up a bedtime snack before I turn in. And I promise," she tilted her head forward and smiled at Selma over the top of her tiny glasses, "it'll all look better in the morning."

Unpacking her few belongings took only moments. A tight fist slowly clenched Selma's heart in its ruthless vice as she ceremoniously set the small pictures, drawn of themselves by Anna and Ruth, on top of the chest of drawers in her room. Gently, she pressed the tip of her index finger to her lips, then touched a kiss to each picture. "Patience, my darlings," she whispered silently into the empty room.

The first five days at the orphanage were very difficult for Selma. She spent nearly every waking moment wondering how her children fared, praying she'd made the right decision. But she soon found that spending time in Drew's company assuaged part of the pain she felt in being away from Anna and Ruth.

By bits and pieces, his life story unfolded; a childhood spent in orphanages, none of them happy experiences until he was sent to be with Mrs. Cutfield. He'd never known his parents nor any life outside of an orphanage. But his single wish, as with all orphaned children, was to have a home and family to call his own.

Under his gentle inquisition, Selma found herself sharing tidbits of her own life in England and every detail about her daughters. Sharing the dream of her little house in Missoula seemed a cruel thing to do, so Selma kept that part of her heart closed to him. His intelligent eyes told her he knew she was hiding something, but was willing to wait until she was ready to share it.

She was in his room, hemming a little skirt and watching him carve a piece of wood into something resembling a dog when Mrs. Cutfield came personally to tell him his wheelchair had arrived. He exclaimed with delight and begged to see it. Together, Selma and Mrs. Cutfield carried the excited boy downstairs and placed him in the still cold chair. The other children from the orphanage lined the walls of the vast hall and watched him wheel back and forth. Soon they were all begging to take turns riding with him and pushing the chair.

Late Wednesday afternoon, Selma was exploring the dark, musty attic with two little girls, 'oohing' and 'aahing' at the ancient furniture, stacks of moth eaten pillows, and battered furniture when she discovered a treasure. It was an old, over-stuffed chair that looked disreputable but turned out to be very comfortable.

"This would be perfect in my sewing room." Selma stood with her hands on her hips, surveying the battered relic through dusty beams of light.

"Why would you want that old chair in your room, Mrs. Wraxmore?" The little girls wrinkled their noses in disgust. "It's ugly."

"It's not that ugly, Mary." Selma countered.

"Not if you close your eyes." Mary laughed and Josie giggled behind her little hands.

"If I throw a blanket over the top, it will serve nicely... for visitors." The little girls giggled even more.

But Selma was not to be deterred. She went in search of Charlie, the handyman, as soon as she had descended the narrow flight of stairs and shaken the dust from the skirt of her dress. She found that gruffly friendly gentleman in the kitchen, attaching the blade of an ancient shovel to a new handle he'd carved. When she told him about the chair, he gave her a penetrating stare, then nodded and agreed to drag the old relic out of the attic and down to her room.

Selma was hemming another skirt the next evening when Mrs. Cutfield sent her a message. Mr. Henson had arrived on a surprise inspection and would honor them by dining at the orphanage with several members of the staff. Selma was invited to join them in the formal dining room within the half hour.

Her mouth immediately went dry and her stomach clenched in a knot. She supposed that Mr. Henson had timed his visit to see what progress she had accomplished in her first week. She nervously checked her hair in the cracked mirror above her bureau. Several wayward wisps refused to tuck into place and she felt like screaming. At last, she forced herself to take a calming breath and straighten her shoulders before stepping into the hall. Beneath her calm exterior, her heart refused to stop hammering against her ribcage and she could barely breathe as she made her way to the dining room at the back of the house.

Mrs. Cutfield and Mr. Henson were speaking together when she entered the long, elegant room. Her heart pounded faster when she saw that no one else had arrived. Suddenly, she feared that her precious job might be in danger. Gathering her tattered courage, she gulped in a deep breath and schooled her face to an expression of polite greeting. Then she stepped forward and shook Mr. Henson's hand.

He smiled and appeared pleased to see her. Selma breathed again and relaxed a bit. However, when she tried to release his hand, Mr. Henson held onto hers a moment longer, adding an extra bit of pressure at the end, much as an old acquaintance might do. Selma was stunned. Mr. Henson was not an old acquaintance and such an intimate handshake went well beyond the polite bounds acceptable between employer and employee. Blushing, she turned to greet Mrs. Cutfield and surprised a look of concern on her face.

"Thank you for coming, Selma. I'm pleased you could join us," Mrs. Cutfield said.

Just then, the cook announced that dinner was ready. Mr. Henson immediately took hold of Selma's elbow and guided her to the table where he held her chair as she sat down. Mrs. Cutfield was left to seat herself.

Selma raised surprised eyes to those of her friend as she said, "Is everyone else late, or am I just early?"

Mrs. Cutfield began to speak, but Mr. Henson interrupted. "I thought it would be a good idea for Mrs. Cutfield and myself to take some time to get better acquainted with our newest employee."

Selma turned to face Mr. Henson and was about to ask why Miss Higley had not been invited, since she had started work only two days ago in the nursery. But Mrs. Cutfield's quick sideways glance made her pause. She coughed instead, covering her mouth with her napkin. Mr. Henson looked at her in concern and started to rise from his seat.

"Excuse me, I, er, I swallowed something wrong." Selma cleared her throat again and took an audible breath, half-afraid from the concerned expression on Mr. Henson's face that he would jump out of his seat to rush around the table and pound on her back.

Dinner was a most unusual affair. Mr. Henson asked only in a perfunctory manner about her job, then dismissed the subject in favor of regaling her with tidbits of political and social gossip. He showed her a marked degree of attention that bordered on rude, to the point of almost completely ignoring Mrs. Cutfield. If Selma hadn't continually included the older woman in the conversation, the headmistress of the orphanage would have sat silent through the entire meal.

Mr. Henson grew very gregarious over dessert and positively flirtatious after his third glass of wine. Disconcerted, Selma found herself torn between the desire to laugh at the oddity of Mr. Henson's brazen efforts to impress her and an overwhelming urge to slap his rubicund face; the whole time endeavoring not to offend her employer.

When at last they rose from the table, Selma tried to excuse herself. But Mr. Henson insisted that both women accompany him to the music room where they were subjected to an impromptu piano concert, featuring Mr. Henson and his personal interpretation of several Bach cantatas.

Selma was just thinking how much Mr. Henson reminded her of 'Humpty Dumpty Who Sat on a Wall' when Mrs.

Cutfield took the opportunity, during a particularly obstinate phrase in Mr. Henson's recital, to reach across and squeeze Selma's hand. Surprised, Selma turned her head to look at Mrs. Cutfield and immediately choked down a laugh at the humorous expression lurking in those hazel eyes.

Later, after profuse compliments and many thanks for an enjoyable evening, the ladies finally escorted Mr. Henson to the carriage that would convey him to a small hostelry not far distant from the orphanage. When that equipage rounded the corner in the road and disappeared into the cold night, Mrs. Cutfield invited Selma into her office. There, she lowered herself into her high-backed chair with a tired sigh.

"Selma, my dear, I hope I am not speaking out of turn..." Mrs. Cutfield hesitated as she met Selma's pensive gaze.

"Do not guard your thoughts; I think I know what you're going to say."

"Yes. Well, you're not a green girl fresh out of school, thank goodness. And I probably don't have to warn you to be on your guard with our... kind... Mr. Henson..."

"No, you don't have to warn me. And I want — most sincerely — to thank you for not allowing him to have that private moment he tried so hard to insist upon."

"Alas," sighed Mrs. Cutfield, "the children are not the only ones I feel obliged to protect in this establishment." Her expresive eyes mirrored her concern. "But I'm afraid this will not be the last time we see the... um... amorous side of Mr. Henson."

She paused, considering her next words. "Though I've heard... stories... , smitten suitor is a role I have never actually seen him play before."

"Oh, I hope it's not that serious. I was sure he was merely setting up a mild flirtation to pass the evening. I've known many men to do that when they are bored."

Mrs. Cutfield paused, a thoughtful light shining in her eyes. "Perhaps we should hide the port next time he comes to visit?" But she shook her head as Selma laughed. "He looked anything but bored, my dear. I think you rate yourself too lightly. A beautiful young woman such as yourself is likely to attract quite a bit of attention." Mrs. Cutfield made the observation without any hint of derision. "But I wouldn't feel I had done my duty if I didn't warn you that our dear Mr. Henson is a bit of a lady's man, if you know what I mean." Her brow wrinkled. "If you give him any hint that..."

"No!" The word exploded from her lips. Selma hadn't meant to speak so emphatically and apologized. "Please don't worry, Mrs. Cutfield. "I'm a mother... with two daughters to care for. My only purpose here is the job for which I was hired. I'm not looking for any kind of relationship... with a man. I just want to work and support my children and myself without worrying about..."

She paused, a troubled frown creasing her brow. "I need this job... and..."

"Don't worry, my dear. I understand... probably better than you think. We'll just have to keep Mr. Henson at more than arm's length when he comes to visit. Or better yet," she sat back and took a deep breath, her eyes twinkling, "surround him with children all the time he spends here."

Selma laughed with her. But Mrs. Cutfield had not missed the change in Selma's expression when she spoke of men, nor did she think Mr. Henson was the man to change Selma's opinion on 'relationships' with men. She didn't know Selma well enough to pry into her history, but she felt a strong kinship to the younger woman and was more than willing to protect her from the unwelcome advances of ardent suitors, be they never so much her employer.

CHAPTER TWENTY-TWO

"MOTHER!" Anna and Ruth launched themselves at Selma as soon as she stepped down onto the railroad platform late Friday night.

Selma hugged her precious daughters and smothered their soft hair with kisses. Some strange premonition made her look quickly over her shoulder and she surprised a small, bespectacled man watching her as he stepped down from the train. His gaze moved on past her almost immediately, but she had the feeling he was still watching. She kept her eyes on him until he passed out of sight along the other side of the building. Then she shook off the feeling and turned her attention back to the girls.

Looking over their heads, she saw Amanda sitting in the same place, on the same bench where she'd been that first night they arrived in Superior. A wave of déjà vu swept over Selma, prickling shivers that ran down her spine. The feeling passed, but only slowly. Then Ruth wriggled free and took possession of her single suitcase. Anna held tight to her right hand and together they crossed the platform to Amanda.

Selma reached down and lifted one of the blind woman's hands in her own. "Amanda, it's Selma."

"Yes, I thought it must be you from the way the girls were going on." Amanda smiled and pushed herself to her feet. "Welcome home, my dear."

"Thank you," Selma wrapped her arms around the blind woman and received a warm embrace in return. "Thank you... more than I can say."

Amanda patted Selma on the back, then took her elbow with one hand while she used her cane with the other. "Shall we go home? We've got a nice meat pie in the oven — the girls even helped me make it."

"Oh! Cooks are we, now?" Selma laughed in sheer delight to be back with Anna and Ruth — and Amanda. Talking over one another, her daughters started regaling Selma with newsworthy events of the week they had been apart.

On Monday, Mrs. Jones' cow got loose and ravaged Amanda's frozen raspberry patch behind her house, leaving a very smelly calling card right on the back porch steps.

"Mrs. Jones?"

Tuesday, Mr. Clifford got drunk and dropped his drawers right in front of the dry goods store to answer nature's call. It was the talk of the neighborhood because his wife had come out of the store just as he was getting started. She screamed loud enough to wake the dead, then grabbed her inebriated spouse by his protuberant ear and dragged him, bellowing, down the alley and out of sight, with his pants snaking around his ankles through the snow.

"Mr. Clifford?" Her children were obviously getting to know the neighbors.

Selma was afraid to hear what happened on Wednesday, but the girls were on a roll and thoroughly enjoyed her shocked reactions. On Wednesday, Ruth's doll — one illustrious Josephina, adopted from Amanda's sizeable collection — was lost until Anna noticed the two boys next door preparing for a hanging — using Josephina. There had been quite a tussle. Anna and Ruth insisted they had been winning until Amanda came out with her rolling pin and threatened to wallop the whole bunch of them if they didn't quit.

Ruth and Anna giggled continuously as they related each event to their mother and Selma couldn't help but contrast this week in her daughters' lives to the ones just before the fire.

Thursday was noteworthy because Mrs. Guggenheim had come to visit and enlivened their afternoon with her animated version of the fight her Chinese cooks had with the temperamental Irish dishwasher she had hired to replace Selma.

"Mrs. Guggenheim asked me to give you her best wishes on your new job. She said she misses you very much, but she's happy for you as well." Amanda counted the steps up to

the broad porch in front of her home. "I told her we would
try to come by the restaurant sometime during the weekend
so you could say hello."

"I would love that. Thank you, Amanda."

Selma opened the front door and the older woman
stepped through, followed by the girls.

"And Carl sent us a wire," Anna chimed happily.

"I plumb forgot to tell your mother. If my head wasn't
attached... " Amanda clicked her tongue. "He said he'd done
about all he could right now and couldn't see much sense staying longer."

"Did he say when he would get back?" Selma was
shocked at her heart's reaction to the sound of his name.
Suddenly, that faithful organ was performing flipflops in her
chest.

"No, just that he's on his way." Amanda stood her cane
in the corner, turned to hang up her coat, and almost tripped
over a doll laying on the floor.

"Anna, Ruth, you can't leave things laying around on the
floor." Selma felt mortified. "Amanda can't see them. She'll
fall and hurt herself."

Anna scooped up the doll while Ruth apologized, and
both girls fervently promised never to leave anything on the
floor again.

"Ah, don't fret, my dear. The girls are like a fountain of
youth making me a younger woman. They force me to pay
attention to life again. I like it. I haven't had this much

excitement since Carl was a little tot." Amanda hung her scarves over another peg by the door.

Selma clasped her hand and squeezed tight.

"You're an angel, Amanda."

"Not an angel, just a want-to-be-grandmother."

"Mother! Amanda said we may call her 'Grandma'. Is that all right with you?"

An unexpected lance of pain stabbed through her heart, and it was a moment before Selma could trust her voice.

Amanda misunderstood her silence and spoke, "If you're uncomfortable with that... .?"

"No. No, I... it's just that it surprised me and... I love it, Amanda. Thank you." Selma's voice broke and she stopped. How could she tell Amanda how badly she had wished for a loving grandmother for her daughters?

Satisfied, Amanda patted her arm, then let go and headed for the kitchen.

Knock. Knock. Knock.

Selma jumped. Amanda stopped and turned her head in the direction of the sound while Ruth raced Anna to the door. Squabbling, they struggled to open it. Finally, Selma had to separate the girls from the doorknob before she could open the door. When she recognized the visitor, she started back in surprise.

"Good evening, Mrs. Wraxmore."

"Mr. Henson." Selma had to force her jaw shut to keep it from dropping open. "What a surprise." She stood rooted to the same spot for so long that Mr. Henson finally cleared his throat.

"Oh, excuse me. Won't you please come in?" Selma stepped to one side to allow the portly gentleman to enter. Anna and Ruth immediately hid behind her skirt, barely peeking out to see who the visitor was.

"I enjoyed our little chat at dinner—that night at the orphanage—so much that I thought I would be so forward as to come calling and inquire about your return trip to Superior." Mr. Henson passed into the house, then turned and extended his hand for Selma to shake.

Remembering the last time she shook hands with Mr. Henson, Selma was hesitant to put her hand in his. But good manners required her to respond to his civil greeting, so she allowed him only the tips of three fingers to shake, then quickly pulled her hand back. Apparently unruffled, Mr. Henson removed his coat as though he belonged there. He laid it and his hat on the deacon's bench by the door, straightened his collar and tie, then pulled down on the lapels of his buff colored jacket. Apparently satisfied, he moved further into the room while Selma fought down a wave of irritation at his assumed familiarity.

"The train ride was very pleasant, compared to my first trip to the orphanage on the wagon," Selma spoke evenly while only good breeding and the knowledge that she owed her job to this man kept her from asking him to leave.

"And are these your daughters?" Mr. Henson spotted the

two little faces peeking from behind Selma's skirts.

"Girls, come out and meet Mr. Henson, my employer." She emphasized the last word for his benefit. "This is Ruth. And this is Anna."

"How do you do?" Ruth shyly stepped out beside her mother and extended one little hand. And though Anna came out of hiding, she flatly refused to shake the pudgy fingers extended toward her.

Mr. Henson bent a disapproving stare upon the little girl, but quickly wiped the expression from his face when Selma turned to introduce him to Amanda.

"Mr. Henson, may I introduce you to Mrs. Reeves, my kind benefactress."

"She's our Grandma!" Anna announced vehemently.

Mr. Henson's narrow brows rose as he stepped forward and took Amanda's hand in his own. Selma breathed a sigh of relief when Amanda asked Mr. Henson to sit and indicated the solitary chair directly across from her. Good manners required that Mr. Henson sit where she invited and he did so, leaving Selma to occupy the sofa with her daughters, forming a cozy little semicircle.

Amanda took control of the conversation so adroitly that Mr. Henson had no recourse but to converse with her, thus leaving Selma able to sit back and relax, even to find humor in the man's discomfiture.

When their visitor had been there for half an hour, Amanda rose and thanked him for visiting. He stood with her, but his eyes darted to Selma. It was plain to see that he wanted time alone with Selma. But when Amanda extended her hand, he took it perfunctorily. To his surprise she held tight to his fingers. And so skillfully that he did not know how he was thus maneuvered, she turned Mr. Henson until she could hold his arm. Then the blind woman irresistibly guided him to the door, leaving him unable to do more than murmur his farewell to Selma and her daughters over Amanda's silver head.

CHAPTER TWENTY-THREE

manda leaned one ear against the closed door and waited until she heard Mr. Henson reach the bottom step of the porch outside before turning around.

"Well, that won't do!"

"Whatever do you mean?" Selma tried to keep the laughter from her voice.

"That is not the man for you, Selma! I don't care how badly you want him. I simply won't have it!" The adamant lady kept a straight face until Selma feared that she was serious.

"Oh, Amanda. No! I wouldn't..."

Unexpectedly, Amanda relented and started laughing. "I know dear. I know you wouldn't. How could you? What a pompous fool. Estimable, I'm sure. But still, he's not the man for you."

"I don't like him either, Mama," Anna tugged at Selma's skirt. "He's fat!"

"And he has little, mean, pig eyes." Ruth, normally so soft-spoken, shocked her mother.

"My darlings," Selma reassured them, "Mr. Henson is just my employer. I'm not going to marry him."

"Well that's good 'cause I like Carl better."

"Carl?" Selma stiffened and tried not to meet Amanda's eyes, then realized how silly that was when Amanda could not see the color of her face or the discomfort in her expression.

"Yes, mama. I think you should marry Carl. He's nice to us. And he's funny."

"And he likes us, Mama." Ruth's expression took on an almost pleading demeanor.

"My darlings." Selma knelt and pulled both little girls into her arms, looking from one set of blue eyes to the other of brown. "I'm not going to marry anyone. So, don't you worry. All right?"

Ruth traced one of Selma's eyebrows with her little finger as she hesitated before agreeing, "All right." But Selma did not miss the tone of disappointment in her voice.

"I still think you should marry Carl," Anna announced with finality. "You'd be the Mommy, Carl could be the Daddy, and Amanda would be our Grandma. Then we'd all be a real family."

"Dinner, girls, " interrupted Amanda, "I think it's time we fed this hungry mother of yours." Selma sighed with relief, grateful for the interruption.

Meat pie and fresh bread filled up Anna and Ruth's tummies. They grew sleepy and not much later, were ready for bed. Selma kissed their soft, warm cheeks and tucked them under their covers after listening to their prayers. She had missed them so much that she stayed in their room until long after they fell asleep, simply listening to the sound of their gentle breathing and watching the way their lashes lay against their soft cheeks.

Amanda was sitting quietly in the living room when Selma finally descended the stairs. Her hands were folded in her lap, her sightless eyes staring toward the heat from the fire. When she heard Selma approach, she turned her face and smiled. "Are they asleep?"

"Yes. But I've missed them so much that I could hardly leave them, even after they were asleep. Oh, Amanda... how can I ever thank you enough for keeping them safe for me?" She warmed her hands at the fire as she spoke. "The children at the orphanage... so many of them remind me of Anna and Ruth. It makes me so grateful that my daughters have you to care for them while I'm away."

She moved over to sit down next to Amanda on the curved sofa. "There is nothing quite as wonderful as belonging to a good family." She squeezed Amanda's hand for a moment. "And I'm thankful every day that you included us in yours."

Amanda laid her other hand over Selma's and felt again the bracelet that Selma wore.

"Where did you get this bracelet that you wear? Carl told

me about it and made me wish I could see it."

"My bracelet?" Selma raised her brows in surprise as she looked at the unusual piece of jewelry. A gentle smile lit up her face. "Hmm. How do I describe it? It's a charm bracelet — sort of a personal record in a way."

"Really? Do you mind telling me about it?"

Selma unclasped it and stared at each piece as it lay in her hand. "It marks all the brightest moments in my life... and to me, it's priceless."

Amanda sensed that Selma was opening a very private door and held her breath lest any noise cause her to shut it again. Carefully, Selma placed the first charm between Amanda's fingers and began to speak.

"The bracelet itself is formed of tiny silver links. Only it never tarnishes, so I don't know what it's really made of. Meredith, my very best friend at school, gave it to me the last day we were together."

Amanda listened hard to Selma's quiet voice and realized Selma's mind was as far away as her voice sounded.

"The first charm is made with a button from the uniform blouse I wore at Miss Shiboleth's Boarding School for Young Women. Those years at her school make up my earliest memories. When I graduated and had to leave, it felt like I was leaving my family... instead of returning to it."

A thin slice of bitterness edged her voice. Then Selma moved Amanda's fingers to the second link. "This is the key that locked my diary where I wrote all my thoughts and dreams while I was growing up."

"Do you still have the diary?"

Selma paused so long, Amanda cursed herself for interrupting the reverie with the wrong question. When Selma finally answered, her voice sounded lifeless, wooden.

"My mother threw it in the fire the day I unpacked in her house. She told me it was time to put aside childish things." Amanda's heart cringed at the brutality of the blankly uttered words. "But I had already put the key on the bracelet. She never knew."

The young mother's tones emanated quiet joy at her next words. "The third charm is Ruth's baby ring — it's made of gold. All the servants in my husband's household pooled their money to buy it when she was born. It was an unforgettable day. When John found that I had born him a daughter," her voice turned dead, merely words stating facts as they happened, "he walked to the head of the bed and cursed me in foul, disgusting language. That still didn't seem to... to soothe... his disappointment. With no warning, he lashed out with his fist and struck me over and over in the face."

Amanda recoiled from shock, then bit down on her lip to silence her horror as the litany continued.

"It broke my nose and knocked me out." She lifted one hand to touch the tiny bump in the middle of her nose. "They told me later John slammed out of the house and galloped away on one of his horses. The horse died two days after he brought it back. The stable boys said he ran it to death. I was only grateful that he hadn't hurt Ruth. Later that day, the servants came to see the baby, one at a time, and to wish us both well. Bertha — she was John's housekeeper and my best friend, my midwife, my... solace — took Ruth into the other room so that the servants could not see my face. When she brought Ruth back to me, a tiny gold ring was on the first finger of her right hand. Bertha told me it was a gift from all of the estate employees."

"They must have loved you very much, Selma."

"They treated me well. I could have been happy there, except for..."

"All men are not like him, Selma."

"No, I suppose not." Selma paused. "Seth... Bertha's husband... was never like John. Could never be like John. He was kind and thoughtful, and I loved him like a father."

Amanda took a breath and her heart started to beat again. "And the next charm?"

"The fourth one is a real, store-bought charm that Seth and Bertha gave to me. John had been drinking very heavily for several months. I think he lost a lot of money on several horse races, but I only suspected that because I overheard snippets of conversations he had with his friends. He never talked to me about... he never talked to me at all. November had been a particularly... difficult... month. I found myself spending more and more time in Bertha's little home behind the mansion. One day she asked me the oddest question." Selma paused again, her mind drifting backward in time.

"What was it?" Amanda prompted.

"She asked what my dreams were; how I wanted my life to be in the future. I thought it an odd question, but very perceptive — because I did have dreams that went far beyond my marriage; hope for a home much different from the mansion where I lived. Before I knew it, I found myself telling her about my dream of escaping to America and living with Ruth in a little house far away from Wraxmore Manor."

Selma shook off the abstraction as she guided the charm between Amanda's fingers. "Bertha and Seth gave this to me the third Christmas after I was married. It is a miniature house fashioned in pewter. When they first gave it to me, it had tiny, white paste jewels in each of the windows — like diamonds. But over the years, all of them have been lost except one."

Amanda's sensitive fingers traced the box form of the tiny house until she could see it clearly in her mind's eye.

"Bertha told me to never lose sight of my dreams. She is a lovely woman and it was incredibly difficult to leave her. But when Lord Wraxmore died, she encouraged me to go, told me I would never find happiness if I stayed."

"Have you written to her yet?"

"Twice. When we first arrived in New York and just before I went to the orphanage. But I need to write again. She'll be worrying."

Amanda moved her fingers to the next charm. "And this one? It feels like another ring?"

"Yes. Anna's baby ring. Made from silver instead of gold. Looking at it now, it's hard to believe her fingers were ever so small."

"They grow up too quickly." Amanda was afraid to ask the father's reaction to a second daughter, and hurriedly moved her fingers to the last charm. "And what is this one?"

Selma took a breath and shivered. "This is the last gift that Seth and Bertha gave to me. Seth handed me a little box just before I went on board the ship heading for America. The note Bertha wrote said they had it made especially for me by a jeweler in York. I know it cost them far more than they could afford."

Amanda could feel the love Selma cherished for the couple she had left behind in England.

Selma lifted the bracelet from Amanda's hands and held the last charm up to the light and stared at it as though for the first time. When she spoke, her words came slowly, almost reverently.

"It's a candle with a flame. Only the flame is a ruby in the shape of a heart."

Amanda caught her breath. "Why that symbol?"

"Bertha's note said it was to remind me of the light at the end of the tunnel. She said no matter how dark the tunnel of life might sometimes appear, if I would just wipe away the soot, the light would still be there."

"And the heart-shape of the flame?"

"After Lord Wraxmore died, Bertha told me I had more

than just a chance to start over; I had a chance to build a new life full of light and love. But, she told me that my light could never shine its brightest until..."

"Until what?" Amanda urged.

"I know this sounds fanciful, but... until I find another soul whose dreams meet mine. Someone to love. Someone I could share my life with."

"That doesn't sound fanciful to me at all. There's nothing quite as glorious in life as finding someone you can love with all your heart, body, and soul."

Selma placed the charm bracelet in Amanda's hand and guided her fingers to the candle charm. "I used to believe that..."

"But not anymore?"

"No, not anymore." Selma spoke softly, slowly — almost convincingly.

Amanda changed the subject. "Tell me about Seth and Bertha? They sound like wonderful people. I wish I could meet them."

"Seth was Lord Wraxmore's coachman. He is a kind and thoughtful man, married to jolly, round, little Bertha. They sort of... adopted me... looked after me when I came to live at the Wraxmore Estate."

Amanda detected that familiar strain return to Selma's voice. "Until I met you — and Carl — I thought they were the only ones like that in the world."

"Like what?"

"Understanding. Willing to give to someone in need. Loving, caring people."

"There are a lot of folks just like that. Actually, I think most folks want to help. Biggest problem is they just don't know how to go about it — don't know how to offer."

Amanda traced the outline of the candle, wishing she could see it. "Then lots of times, people have to be ready themselves to take the help when it's offered."

Selma thought back to that fateful night on the train station platform when Amanda had offered Selma the hospitality of her home. Clearly, she saw her pride for what it was. It pained her to admit to herself that she had felt herself above Amanda and was unable — unwilling — to accept help from someone so far beneath her social station. As humble as Selma had felt herself to be, despite the problems and abuses of her marriage, the dysfunctional relationship between herself and her mother, Selma had still been too prideful to accept the simple help offered by a woman in a ragged, old coat.

She spoke as though Amanda had heard all her thoughts. "I was thoroughly at fault, Amanda. I know that now."

"Not at fault, Selma." Amanda's voice carried love and understanding. "You had been depending on yourself for so long that you didn't understand the kind of help you needed."

"I think I was too proud... " It was painful, but Selma felt she had to say what was in her heart, "... to take help from a woman in a ragged coat. I'm so sorry! I can never express how badly I feel for so misjudging you — for judging you at all."

"Yes, that old coat has led many a stranger to think me different than I am." Amanda's eyes closed and she leaned her head back on the chair, thoughtfully fingering one charm at a time.

"Do you mind... if I ask... ?" Selma paused, unsure if she should ask the question in her mind.

"Why I wear such a ragged old coat when I could have a newer, finer one?"

"Yes."

"Joseph gave that coat to me the third winter after we were married. He saved all year to buy it for me and it was a beautiful garment when I unwrapped it. We didn't have much money. He was going to medical school and we were as poor as church mice. But he saw me mooning over that coat in the window of a store in Chicago and decided I had to have it. He worked extra jobs through that entire year, saving every spare dime, even though his pants were threadbare and he needed new shoes. When December came, he placed a beautifully wrapped box under our pitiful little tree. I still remember how excited he was... like a child that could hardly wait until Christmas morning."

Amanda hesitated for a moment and a nostalgic smile creased her face. Selma watched the wrinkled hands lovingly caress the white material on her lap, and wondered if Amanda was imagining the new coat under her fingers again.

"I was shocked when I unwrapped the coat — it was so beautiful back then, all soft and luxuriant, rich, velvety, midnight blue, with black fur trimming around the hood and cuffs and down the front. Big silver buttons." She shook her head back and forth while a lopsided smile tilted her lips. "I remember I scolded him for the extravagance. I had only bought him a small trinket of some sort. I don't even remember what it was now. All I remember was the coat." A soft sigh punctuated her thoughts. "But that's as it should be, I suppose."

Amanda paused and Selma watched the firelight flicker on her face, breathlessly waiting for the older woman to continue.

"I hardly wore the coat at all. I felt too extravagant, didn't want to hurt it. Joseph told me I was foolish. The next summer he started to feel ill. Sore throat, aches, pains. A cough that wouldn't go away. Finally we went to a doctor. Then lots of other doctors; until we'd seen every cancer specialist in the country. I turned 34 that year. My parents died and Carl moved in. Carl and I were mourning the death of our parents and Joseph was wasting away, a bit more every day."

The pregnant, white cat jumped up into Amanda's lap, startling the woman for a moment. Then she relaxed and began to stroke the animal's silky fur. "Then I received the inheritance my parents had left for me. At first I believed it was God's way of making up for taking my parents. He'd sent the money to save Joseph. Like a miracle, only backwards."

Amanda stopped talking. Her head shook slowly back

and forth. Her shoulders began to heave silently up and down. Still Selma waited. Painful moments passed, but Amanda fought her memories in silence. Finally, Selma reached out and grasped one hand with both of hers and squeezed tight. Another moment of silent bonding passed, then Amanda went on.

"We spent every cent of the inheritance on doctors and their fancy medicines." Her voice trembled with remembered impotence. "But nothing helped. He gave up the struggle just as the crocus buds were opening in the snow. April 6. The sun was going down." Tears coursed down Amanda's face, but she didn't lift a finger to wipe them away. "The last thing he said... " she choked on a breath, "... his last words were... 'I'll be... waiting... for you.'"

A wretched smile trembled on her quivering lips and Selma's heart twisted at the last words of comfort from a beloved husband to his grieving wife.

Selma watched through her own veil of grief as Amanda delicately wiped her eyes with a lace handkerchief and swallowed several times. Her swollen eyes were red and her cheeks still damp and glistening from the trail of her tears when a radiant smile lit up her face and brightened the entire room. She took a ragged breath.

"I started wearing the coat and have never stopped. Every time I pull it on, I feel as though Joseph is near me again. I feel his arms around me and imagine the first time he lifted it onto my shoulders." She drifted away in thought for a moment before she spoke again. "I could wear a newer, fancier coat, but it wouldn't carry Joseph's love."

She turned her head and stared blindly straight at Selma. "My eyes don't see the coat as it looks now. I see it — and always shall — as it looked the day he gave it to me, rich with all the love of our life together, all the sacrifice he dedicated in getting it for me."

The two women shared the silence, listening to the fire crackling in the hearth. No more words were said, but Selma wondered if ever in her life she could love as Amanda had loved. Would she find a man who would love her as Joseph had loved Amanda? Carl's face flashed into her mind. Or had she already? The thought created a piercing ache deep in the dark, empty, well of Selma's heart.

CHAPTER TWENTY-FOUR

ngine 29 screeched to a grinding stop and Carl bounded off the train into a brilliant, sunny, winter day and shivered in the cold chill of the wind blowing across Lake Superior. He threw his bag over his shoulder as he stepped off the platform and headed for Amanda's house. He ignored the line of waiting hackney carriages and stretched his legs into a long stride, relieved to exercise his stiff muscles after the interminable train ride.

He had returned a week early, unable to stay away one day longer. Every waking moment he spent thinking not of his Columbia River Project, but about a beautiful, young, blue-eyed mother and her two daughters. He found the intricate details of ship design and water drainage tables increasingly trivial when all he could think about was: What was she doing? What was she thinking? How did she spend her time every day?

Finally, afraid she would slip away where he might never

find her again, Carl could stand it no longer and hopped on a train headed back to Wisconsin.

Long strides carried him around the last corner onto Grover Street where his eyes immediately sought out Amanda's house. Surprise stopped him dead in his tracks. Four houses away, Selma was just stepping out onto the porch, followed closely by a man Carl did not recognize. He fought the jealousy that reared its ugly head until the blood began pounding in his ears and he felt his face grow hot. He started walking again and did not take his fierce gaze from the two people on the porch. As he drew rapidly nearer, he saw the portly gentleman reach out and grab Selma's hands with his own. A thrill raced through Carl's heart when Selma drew back, gently at first, then tugging harder, obviously struggling to free her hands from the man's grasp. Carl's speed increased.

Selma moved backwards and the stranger followed until she had retreated as far as she could go. Carl was two steps from the gate when she was effectively cornered and the man followed up his advantage by trying to take her in his arms and kiss her. Carl's temper flared to boiling point when he heard Selma cry out in distress. He dropped his bag, vaulted the fence, and hit the ground running.

Selma pushed futilely against the man's chest. Then Carl was charging up the steps three at a time, a loud, grating roar announcing his arrival and the fist that closed on the stranger's shoulder jerked him around. The shorter man, realizing his danger, loosed Selma and whirled right into Carl's fist as it smashed into his bulbous nose and knocked him flat on his back.

Terrified, Mr. Henson scuttled backwards until he reached the stairs. Then he bumped and bounced ignominiously down the steps before he realized the tall, threatening man standing on the porch above him was not following.

Henson looked up into the cold, dangerous eyes beneath the black cowboy hat and his face paled at what he saw. He missed the relief that flooded Selma's face because his eyes were glued on his antagonist. When Carl took one step down from the porch, Henson frantically heaved himself to his feet and scurried through the slushy snow until he reached the street. It was then he noticed the blood gushing from his battered nose and quailed in distress. Pulling a large handkerchief from his pocket, he held it over his nose. Hurriedly, he scrambled into his buggy and frantically hollered to the horse to "git up."

Carl's anger was still red hot when he turned to face Selma, but she found the blazing passion almost soothing after Mr. Henson's unwelcome advances. She murmured her thanks and thrilled to the transformation she saw take place. One moment he was the noble rescuer, furious conqueror; but when he turned to her, the wild man tamed and he transformed into her kind benefactor, gently asking if she was all right.

He was so near, so alive. So protective. A primal, instinctive force lifted her right hand to lay against his chest where his coat parted and fell to the side. She felt his heart racing and heard his breath coming in ragged gasps. His hands came up to gently grasp her shoulders as she lifted her eyes to the dark stubble outlining his chin. She held her breath and raised her eyes up to his. An alien sensation stirred in her heart at the banked fire in his eyes and she felt herself invisibly drawn to him.

Out of nowhere, Anna and Ruth came charging up the steps, clamoring for Selma's attention. They'd been watching the whole episode from behind a friend's tree, two houses away. When they burst on the scene, Selma's hand fell and she dropped to her knees to embrace both little girls. Then, Ruth and Anna turned to enthusiastically welcome Carl home and proclaim him a hero.

"You sure gave that old wind bag the 'get go'," Selma was shocked to hear such a phrase from her tiny Anna.

Ruth raced to the door, grinning, "I gotta tell Amanda about Carl socking Mr. Henson."

"No, I get to tell her," Anna was right on her heals.

The door banged shut, leaving Carl alone again with Selma. But the heat of the moment had passed. "Thank you, Mr. Stanton. I don't know how... I...I was...he…"

"Call me Carl." His voice came out deep, raspy. "You don't have to try to explain. I could see he was getting pretty carried away." Carl didn't explain that it would be easy to get carried away in the presence of a woman as beautiful as the one blushing before him now. A vision flashed through his mind, not for the first time, of how it would feel to kiss Selma and he fought the urge to take her in his arms.

"What was that old windbag doing here, anyway?"

Selma dropped her eyes to the dimple in his chin, then smiled crookedly. "Mr. Henson is my... employer. He hired me to make clothes for the children of the Douglas County Orphanage. He mistakenly... I... didn't..."

Selma sought desperately for the words to tell Carl that Mr. Henson meant nothing to her, but ended lamely "... I don't know what to say, except — thank you." She tried to shift the subject. "You seem to have an amazing habit of arriving just in the nick of time." She drew a deep breath and smiled at him, a smile that covered her entire face, sparkled from her eyes, and curled his toes.

"If your boss is going to treat you like that, my advice is to get another job." Carl tried to keep his voice neutral, but a possessive tone flavored his words.

"He only hired me; I don't work near him. His office is here and I work at the orphanage for a wonderful woman named Mrs. Cutfield. I rarely see Mr. Henson." She felt she was almost pleading for his understanding. "And I need the job badly." Selma braced herself and looked up into his eyes. "When I finish the contract I've made to sew the clothes for the children, I will have enough money to purchase train fare for Anna, Ruth, and myself to go on to Montana."

The magnetic light that glowed from his eyes tied her stomach in knots until she had to drop her gaze. "Then we won't be a burden on your sister any longer."

"You're no burden. I'm sure Amanda has told you no different." Carl surprised himself at the harsh edge on his words. He had no right to tell Selma what to do and he chafed against the urge to beg her to quit, to stay here, let him take care of her.

"We'd best get inside and save Amanda from the girls." She turned toward the front door, hugging her arms tight against the cold. Carl fought an overwhelming urge to pull her against his chest, protect her from the cold, share his own body heat. Instead, he opened the door for her to pass inside.

Selma looked toward the street as she started through the door, but stopped. Carl whirled to see what had caused Selma's face to pale. His eyes searched up and down the street, but found nothing. When he looked at her face again, Selma's brows were pulled tight across her eyes and her lips tensed.

"What is it?" Carl looked at the street again.

"A man. I've seen him three times now."

"Where?" Carl turned all the way around and searched the street again.

"He was there, peeking out from behind that huge tree across the street. But I..."

Carl started toward the steps, but Selma caught his arm and stopped him. "No, don't go. I'm sure it's nothing. Let's go inside."

Carl stared across the street for several minutes, but still saw nothing. Selma tugged at his arm again and he finally followed her into the house.

"Where else have you seen him? Do you know who he is? What does he look like?"

Selma couldn't help but smile at his protective attitude. "He rode the same train when I went to the orphanage and was on it again when I came back from the orphanage. He's fairly short, well dressed, wears glasses, and a bowler hat."

Carl chuckled as he hung his coat in the closet and turned to look into her curious eyes. "Sounds relatively harmless. But tell me if you see him anywhere else, all right?"

"Okay." Selma turned away, but his words charmed her heart with waves of unaccustomed warmth and security.

They found Amanda in the kitchen, directing Anna and Ruth in setting the table.

"Hello, Amanda." His deep voice reverberated from the flower-papered walls.

Amanda whirled around at the sound of her brother's voice. "Carl! You're home." Her face exploded in smiles as she held her arms out for his embrace. "The girls told me you were out on the porch…with Mr. Henson…but I didn't know if…" She paused a second and tilted her head sideways before continuing. "I didn't know you were going to get here today." His tall shoulder muffled her voice. "Did I?"

"Sorry. I didn't take the time to cable you. I got lonesome and just felt like getting back here a little early. So I hopped the first train out of Portland and pulled in just a few minutes ago."

"Does Selma know you're here?"

"I'm right here, Amanda." Selma spoke from the doorway.

"I found her out on the porch flirting with some man named Henson."

"Mother!" Anna and Ruth both looked accusingly at Selma.

"I was not... " Selma started to defend herself.

"Selma! I told you not to flirt with that man." Amanda's mock-serious tone took Selma by surprise.

"I wasn't! I promise!" Selma's face turned scarlet when Carl turned his questioning eyes on her.

Amanda spoke as though to a recalcitrant child, "I knew I shouldn't let the two of you out of my sight."

"Amanda! How could you?" Selma spluttered in her own defense.

"I'm just funnin' with you, dear." Her mischievous smile brightened the whole room.

"The girls told me a story about fisticuffs on my front patio. Now, Carl…" she began to shake her finger at him, but Carl interrupted.

"Speaking of 'sight', sister of mine, how are you feeling? Heard anything from the doctors?"

"My headaches have been getting a bit worse, but they still come and go."

While Amanda shared her news with Carl, Selma placed a hot pad in the center of the table. When she moved to lift the heavy pot of stew from the stove, Carl was suddenly beside her. Gently taking the hot pads from her hands, he nudged her aside as he lifted the pot and carried it across the room.

Amanda spoke in a light tone. "I received a letter from Dr. Frankenstein on Tuesday. He told me to check into the hospital on February twenty-first. He wants to run a few more tests before they actually do the surgery."

Amanda felt Ruth beside her. Gently pulling the little girl onto her lap, she wrapped Ruth in a warm embrace.

"The twenty-first? That's only a week away!" Carl stared hard at his sister.

"I know. But let's not discuss that right now. Instead, tell me about your trip."

Carl suddenly caught the concerned expression in Ruth's eyes as they moved from Amanda's face back to his. Again, he marveled at how Amanda perceived the world around her much clearer without her eyesight than he often saw with his perfect vision.

Dinner was a lively affair. Anna and Ruth listened with wide eyes while Carl and Amanda discussed preparations for Amanda's upcoming surgery. Then Carl regaled everyone with an animated account of his journey.

"I didn't even begin to travel the entire distance a ship could sail. In that part of the country the roads simply close down in the winter. Once the snow gets two feet deep, people just stay put in their homes until spring comes."

"Doesn't that make your shipping idea even more attractive?" Amanda queried.

"You're not only beautiful, but you're smart."

Selma relaxed in her chair and, for the first time, realized how very comfortable she felt around these two people; how much they made her feel at home, secure, welcome. A warm, passionate feeling enveloped her whole body, complete with chills and a shiver. This was the way families were supposed to be. Work hard. Come together at the end of the day to share trials and triumphs, laughter and love. The feeling came very close to what she saw in her vision of the light at the end of her tunnel. She felt an intense sadness, indefinable and untouchable, and didn't know why.

It was almost dark outside when Selma hugged and kissed Anna and Ruth, promising to return in five days — the last week she would ever be gone from them. Carl was waiting for her after she bid farewell to Amanda, his coat on, hat in hand, ready to walk her to the train station. She looked up at him in surprise, but he merely lifted her bag and opened the door. Her shoulder brushed against him as she passed through the opening, making her heart skip a beat.

They walked the first block in silence while Selma tried to calm her breathing. Then Carl asked her about the woman she had mentioned from the orphanage. Hesitant at first, Selma soon lost her reserve in sharing warm memories of Mrs. Cutfield. Then, laughingly, she tried to portray the crabby Mrs. Poulson. She was just describing her newest friend, Miss

Calver — the plump, talkative, lovable, young woman who had newly come to teach the youngest children — when they arrived at the train station.

Selma flinched when his hand protectively gripped her elbow to support her up the icy steps. She didn't start breathing again until he released her when they reached the platform.

A stiffening breeze whistled out of the north, flinging bits of snow through the darkness. Selma raised her eyes to the sign that read Superior, Wisconsin. The weathered sign creaked back and forth in the wind. A sudden flashback sent a chill trickling down her back and she shivered.

"Is something wrong?" Carl's deep voice warmed Selma through the cold darkness.

"This night feels very much like our first night in Superior... " she left the sentence hanging.

"I wish... " Carl started to speak, then paused at the enormity of all he wished.

"So do I... in a way." Selma felt a kinship to his thoughts. Somehow it was easier to talk with him in the darkness. Slowly, a tiny corner of her soul opened toward Carl.

"Yet, through... " Selma spoke slowly, "... maybe because of... everything that's happened…I've grown. I'm better for it. Does that make sense?"

"No! I don't understand that!" Carl's blunt tone said, more than words, that he could not find it in his heart to think any hardship for Selma to have value.

"But one day, when you've come to trust me, I hope you'll share your thoughts with me."

"Trust you?" Selma repeated.

Two magic words, spoken through the darkness, awoke a sleeping chord in Selma's fragile soul.

The gusting wind dusted more ice flakes from the roof and Carl moved closer to shield Selma from their frosty touch. She shivered as she gazed up into the dark pools where his eyes were hidden, astonished at how powerfully his request had touched her heart.

Without warning, she was in his arms, pressed against his powerful body, hungering for the fiery kisses he poured over her face and lips. The cold of the night was forgotten. All that had gone before did not exist; just now, here, this moment. Selma melted in the heat of his embrace, giving herself fully to his questing lips, finding blissful sanctuary in the muscular arms crushing her to him.

Gradually, the puffing, clanking train rattled into the station and screeched to a halt. Still she clung to him, lost in the passion that warmed her body, her heart, her soul.

The conductor's voice shrilled across the platform, "All aboard."

Immediately, Selma awoke to her surroundings. Her arms loosened where they were clasped around Carl's neck and she struggled to pull away.

"No. Stay here." Carl's voice was husky, deep, vibrant. "Don't go."

"I have to," she whispered against his lips.

"No, you don't. Stay, please," he was almost begging. "You don't have to work. I..."

"Last call! All aboard... " The conductor droned for the last time.

Suddenly, the weight of her world came crashing down. "I can't!" Selma wrenched herself from Carl's embrace and turned away.

Scooping up her bag, she raced toward the slowly moving train. In a flash of skirts, she disappeared through a door and was gone.

Alone on the platform, Carl watched the train chug noisily into the night. Its lonesome whistle shrilled back through the cold, black night, echoing in the hollow space of his heart.

CHAPTER TWENTY-FIVE

Selma finished fitting the dress onto her little model. "Perfect, Margaret. You look like a princess," she smiled at the child.

The six-year old's broad, toothless smile proclaimed her joy and pride in the new dress. She flung ecstatic arms around Selma's legs in a great big hug, then let go to twirl about the room. Selma laughed, held out her hands, and soon they were dancing a jig together.

The sudden opening of the door brought them up short and they stood together, gasping for air. Miss Poulson stood at rigid attention and stared in obvious displeasure from the doorway.

"Mrs. Wraxmore," began Miss Poulson, in a voice of icy censure, "Mrs. Cutfield requests that you visit her—at your convenience." With a swish and twirl of her severe black skirts, Miss Poulson shut the door and was gone.

Margaret looked fearfully up at Selma only to find mischievous blue lights dancing in her eyes.

"Miss Poulson reminds me of one of those old crows that squawk so loudly in the cherry trees out behind the rectory," Selma whispered loudly, her head bent down so Margaret could hear. "Don't you agree?"

Margaret's lips formed a silent "O" in shock. Quickly, she clapped her hands over her mouth to stifle an explosion of giggles. Her head of dusky curls bobbed up and down in agreement, her eyes sparkling with delight.

"Now, you better run along, Margaret, and I had best go see what Mrs. Cutfield wants."

Margaret skipped happily out the door, intent on telling her best friend Cally about her astonishing afternoon with Mrs. Wraxmore.

Selma found the garrulous Miss Calver just reaching the top step of the stairway. She smiled at the woman, "How are you?"

Selma didn't have to say another word. Miss Calver's good will bubbled over like an ever-flowing, effervescent pool. Selma heard about the cook's accident in the kitchen, the new batch of kittens born in the barn, the dairyman's niece running off with the new postal employee, and the fact that Mr. Henson was supposed to visit sometime this week.

A tremor of fear raced up Selma's back at the mention of Mr. Henson. Then a daring idea burst in her brain, like a bright light on a dark night. Ruthlessly, she interrupted Miss Calver's discourse.

"If Mr. Henson stays to dinner, as he most always does when he visits the orphanage, would you be willing to join us? You know, help even out the numbers? Perhaps tell Mr. Henson about your students and those new reading programs you've established?"

"Would I? Oh, Mrs. Wraxmore! That would be simply divine!"

"I can't promise, of course, so don't say anything until I make sure it's all right with Mrs. Cutfield," she smiled at her loquacious friend. "But I think you would be a delightful addition to such dull evenings."

They parted and Selma tripped down the stairs to Mrs. Cutfield's office. She knocked on the office door then entered to find the woman seated in front of the tall windows at the end of the room. She seemed to be studying a sheaf of papers that lay spread across her desk.

During the month she had been working here, Selma had come to deeply admire Mrs. Cutfield for dedicating her life to helping the children without families who found their way to this house. Many were sent here because their parents died. Some were found abandoned on doorsteps. Many were left right at the orphanage itself. Mrs. Cutfield took each one in and tried to provide them all with love and security while she searched for families to adopt them.

Glancing up, Mrs. Cutfield recognized her visitor and motioned Selma forward with a wave of her hand and a smile. "Come in and take a chair, Selma. I've been wanting to talk with you... to thank you, especially, for the wonderful outfits you've been creating with all that old, rubbishy material..."

Selma chuckled as she thought back to the half-moldy, mismatched bolts of unwanted — donated — cloth she unwrapped the day after she arrived at the orphanage.

Mrs. Cutfield sighed as she took off her glasses and polished the lenses. "Forgive me. I realize I shouldn't be ungrateful, but... well, I know you understand." A smile flashed across her normally serious countenance. "When I saw what Mr. Henson deemed a 'blessed contribution to our dear little orphans', I was quite sick with worry. For you know, my dear, that children don't like to look like hags any more than anyone else. And, if I hadn't seen it with my own eyes, I would never have believed that pile of rubbish could ever be transformed into the beautiful pinafores and dresses I've seen on the girls and the shirts and pants you've made for our boys."

"Thank you, Mrs. Cutfield. I'm so glad they meet with your approval. But really, the material wasn't nearly as bad once I had washed the mold out of it and cut around the worst spots." Her fine, bright eyes sparkled with humor.

"However, I must admit to a moment of near-panic after I unwrapped those first bolts."

"You're a miracle worker, that's what you are, Selma, and I bless the day Mr. Henson hired you." Mrs. Cutfield dropped her eyes while she made a pretense of straightening the papers on her desk.

"Selma..."

Selma waited curiously, patiently, wondering what would cause such intensity.

"... very few people are made to work in a place like this." Mrs. Cutfield waved her hand broadly in a sweeping gesture at the surrounding walls. "But you seem instinctively to understand what the children need. I would like you to stay here, work with us, with the children." Now her serious eyes studied Selma for her answer.

"I'm flattered, Mrs. Cutfield." Selma's brain whirled through a kaleidoscope of new possibilities. Could she sell her home in Missoula and purchase another here? It wasn't what Selma had planned. But then hadn't her plans been reshaping themselves since a thief made off with all of her money? Would a little house right here be as good as a little house further west?

"I want you to know how deeply honored I am with your confidence. I...I can't answer you right now, but let me think about it."

"There's no hurry. I normally don't offer a position like this to young, unmarried women, because I assume they will get married sometime soon and I will just have to start again. But in your case..."

"You're right, Mrs. Cutfield," Selma cut her off, "I have no intention of marrying again."

"That's not what I meant, Selma. What I was going to say is that I would be willing to have you for as long as I could because of the kind of person you are. Of course I expect you to meet some young man and marry him. I'll miss you when you do go, but I'll wish you the utmost happiness."

Selma did not try to discuss that subject any further, but addressed the job offer instead. "I need time to consider your offer, but I'll let you know soon."

Mrs. Cutfield studied the top of her desk silently for a moment, weighing her words. Then she decided to just say what was on her mind.

"Selma, from what little you've shared with me about your life before you came to America, I know your marriage was not a happy one. But I want you to know that not all marriages are like yours. Many are truly happy, with both husband and wife working together, sharing and loving throughout their lives."

"I know, Mrs. Cutfield." Selma's thoughts were all jumbled and she found it painful to discuss this subject. "But unless... until…I find a man with whom I can share that kind of marriage, I would much rather depend only on myself."

"Well," Mrs. Cutfield placed both hands flat on the desk and looked straight at Selma, "we would be glad to have you stay here with us... where you have friends and support."

"If I decide to stay in Wisconsin, I would love to work here." Selma paused and her brows drew together, forming a small furrow of wrinkles between her nose. "But there is one real, major... sticky... problem that I don't know how to handle." Selma wasn't sure how to phrase her concern, but Mrs. Cutfield took the words right out of her mouth.

"Mr. Henson?"

"Yes." Selma sighed with relief at her quick understanding.

"Hmm. His... um, attentions... do present a ticklish problem. Has he visited you at Mrs. Reeves' home again?"

Selma laughed mirthlessly. "Yes! Every time I go home to see my daughters, he's there on the slenderest of excuses. He's practically laid siege to Grover Street! If it weren't for Amanda, I don't know what I would do." She paused, not sure whether to tell Mrs. Cutfield about the latest episode, then decided she had better know it all.

"Mr. Henson was getting rather too... forward... in his attentions last Sunday... " Selma shook her head in memory. "He asked me to step out on the porch, because — he said — he had to tell me something about my job that he particularly did not want anyone else to hear."

"Oh, no. And did you go with him?"

"How could I say no? He puts me in the most outrageous situations." Selma flushed at the memory.

"Did he try to kiss you?" Mrs. Cutfield was appalled.

"Y...yes, and I admit I was... having trouble... controlling his... ardor..."

"Why, that vulgar man!" Mrs. Cutfield positively fumed with anger.

"I was rescued," Selma chuckled, "just in the nick of time. By Amanda's brother, Carl Stanton." She started to laugh, then forced herself to stop, yet couldn't repress the silly grin that lifted her lips.

"What did he do?" Mrs. Cutfield leaned eagerly forward across her desk, agog with curiosity.

"He bashed Mr. Henson right in the nose!" Selma doubled up her fist and demonstrated. "Blood all over everything. Knocked him down. Kersplatt! He practically rolled down the steps. Then he got up and tottered off to his buggy." Selma laughed at the stunned expression on Mrs. Cutfield's face.

"If I thought his intentions were honorable," Mrs. Cutfield fumed, "I could almost — almost — forgive him. But I've known Mr. Henson for ten years and he consistently shows a weakness for beautiful women, though he usually chooses ladies who are largely blessed with wealth."

"I suppose I should be flattered?" Selma grimaced at the unspoken compliment.

"Perhaps." Mrs. Cutfield tried to keep a straight face, "But I would still advise you to be on your guard to give him no encouragement for his fantasies." She raised her eyebrows in question, "Unless, of course, you have developed a tendre for him?"

"No!" The word burst from Selma's lips, then she shook her head, smiled sheepishly, and spoke with more control, emphasizing each of her words. "I certainly esteem all the virtues possessed by Mr. Henson... " Selma hesitated and Mrs. Cutfield finished the thought.

"But he's a pompous boar, with barnyard manners, and it's all you can do to treat him civilly. Do I have that right?"

Selma burst into laughter again and Mrs. Cutfield joined in, laughing until tears squeezed from their eyes. "Thank you, yes. If he weren't so particular in his attentions..."

"But he is and that's a problem." Mrs. Cutfield spoke with severity and the laughter calmed.

"Yes."

"Well, we'll just have to devise some strategy to frustrate his schemes. I certainly don't want him driving off my best employee."

"Oh. Speaking of schemes, I meant to ask you… Would it be all right if we included Miss Calver at dinner next time Mr. Henson makes an appearance?" Selma looked innocently at Mrs. Cutfield.

"Why you devil, Selma. That would be perfect. I only wish I'd thought of it myself."

"And how about featuring him in a concert for the whole orphanage, children and staff alike?"

"I look forward to it." Mrs. Cutfield's eyes twinkled her appreciation.

Selma rose and took her leave, a huge smile lightening her face and her heart, while Mrs. Cutfield returned to her paperwork. But when Selma reached the door, she turned back and cleared her throat gently.

"Yes, my dear — was there something else?" Mrs. Cutfield peered over the top of her narrow reading glasses.

"Um, yes, actually, but it's a serious topic. After I hem Claudia's dress, I will be finished with all but one of the outfits. I wanted to ask if you thought it would be all right if, after Prissy's dress is made, I make an outfit for Drew. Of all the children here, his clothes are the most threadbare... and I just... he deserves... he needs..."

"I think that would be wonderful, Selma." Mrs. Cutfield sat back in her chair and clasped her hands on top of the heavy wooden desk. "As you know, I do not approve of Mr. Henson's attitude on that subject and I'm sorry I couldn't intervene on Drew's behalf earlier. But he's not here now and you have accomplished so much in such a short amount of time that I feel justified in making that... executive decision."

"Mr. Henson never sees Drew anyway, so he'll never know," Selma's eyes narrowed with determination.

"Bless you, Selma. I wish more people understood the needs of these children as you do."

unther eased through the door and crossed the room while Thomas surreptitiously watched from the corner of his eye. It never ceased to amaze him that the man could move so silently that not a breath of sound announced his approach.

Gunther sat down in his usual chair, facing Thomas Mason, and waited.

"Well?" Thomas growled.

"Turns out Mrs. Selma Wraxmore is the dowager Lady Selma Wraxmore."

"What? You mean widowed?" Thomas bellowed and his eyes popped wide open.

"Yup. I sent a cable to an associate of mine in London. He confirms that Lord John Christopher Wraxmore, sixth Earl of Chychester, died October 25 and the widow disappeared the very next day. According to her mother," Gunther's notepad was open, but he looked straight at Thomas, "one

Aurelia Klintenberg — to whom I also sent a wire — Lady Wraxmore was spirited away by one of the household servants and hasn't been heard from since."

"You contacted Aurelia?" The harsh pitch of Thomas's voice alerted Gunther's curiosity. His sharp eyes narrowed, but he kept his thoughts to himself.

"There's more. There were two daughters, Ruth, five, and Anna, four. The servants at Lord Wraxmore's estate are as tight lipped as a pack of oysters. I'd say they were very attached to Lady Wraxmore. If they knew where she was going, they're not saying a thing."

He spoke almost as though to himself. "Most unusual to find a whole house full of servants that can't be bribed in one way or another. Speaks highly of the woman, I'd say."

"I agree." Thomas almost whispered. His eyes were pointed toward the ceiling, but looked far beyond the walls of the room. "What's she doing in Superior?"

"That's the interesting part. Unless I'm mistaken... and I don't believe I am... Lady Wraxmore was the tenant in your alley until the fire forced her out."

"What?" Thomas' eyes shot back to Gunther's face.

"Yup. Had a real interesting conversation with a little girl by the name of Anna Wraxmore." Gunther couldn't stop a smile from creeping onto his face. "Cutest little girl you've ever seen."

"By all that's mighty..."

"Yes, sir. The way she tells the story, they have a little

house in 'Tana'... Montana... as close as I can make out, and were traveling there by train. Seems all of their dreams are tied up in that little house, according to the girl. Then a 'bad man' — I'm quoting here — 'stole all their money one night on the train' — and they were kicked off right here in Superior."

"You don't say..."

"Lived on the streets for a few days. Just about starved to death if you believe Anna, and I do. Then they found the shack in your alley and made a home... 'til it burned down."

"Where are they living now?"

A broad smile covered Gunther's entire face and he paused theatrically before delivering his piece de resistance.

"Well, man, out with it! Do you know where they're living or not?"

"At 279 Grover Street."

"Grover Street?" Gunther savored an intense sense of enjoyment at the stricken look slowly chilling Thomas Mason's face. "279 Grover Street?"

"That's the place."

"But that's..."

"Yes, sir. It is."

"Amanda?"

"Yup."

"How'd they get there?"

"Give you two guesses." Gunther hadn't enjoyed himself so much in years.

"Carl!" The name exploded from Thomas. "That's

why..."

"I believe so, sir."

"Well, I'll be..."

"Yes, sir!"

Selma closed the door gently and stepped back into the shadowed hallway of the great, rambling house. A determined smile touched the corners of her mouth as she mounted the narrow steps to the second level and hurried along the creaking corridor to the last door on the right. She knocked gently before she opened the door and heard a faint voice bid her enter.

Drew, propped up on his tall bed, was gazing through the window at the children playing outside. He turned his head and smiled when he saw who had entered his room.

"Mrs. Wraxmore, I'm so very glad to see you." The chipper little voice carried a peculiar lilt that Selma found irresistible.

"And I'm glad to see you too, Drew." She pulled a heavy wooden chair up beside the boy's bed and sat down. "And how are you today, young man?

"Much better! My butterflies are starting to hatch. Five of them already today — two large yellow and black ones," he extended his fingers to show their size, "a tiny blue fluttery one, and two dark orange and black butterflies." He fluttered his little hands, mimicking butterflies in flight as he pointed toward the row of bottles standing on the table beside his bed.

Selma enthusiastically peered into the bottles and exclaimed at the newly hatched butterflies gently waving their wings back and forth.

"They're beautiful, Drew. I don't know how you got so many of them to actually hatch."

"All the kids brought me bunches of different caterpillars in the fall. It wasn't hard after that. I think they were all ready to make their cocoons for the winter anyway and now they're finally hatching."

"What are these big yellow and black ones called?"

"I don't know."

"How about the blue ones?"

"I don't know any of their names. I've been wishing I had a book to tell me what kind of butterflies they are. Wouldn't that be grand?"

"Tell me, Drew," Selma's eyebrows raised in awe, "did you wish on any of the stars last night? Or rub an old lamp like Aladdin's?"

Drew chuckled and two dimples peeped out of his pale cheeks. "I did wish on the very brightest star when the clouds cleared off last night, but I don't have an Aladdin's lamp — you know that."

"Hmm, I'm not sure just wishing on stars is enough magic to make a wish come true."

"I said my prayers too, Mrs. Wraxmore. That counts, doesn't it?" He turned his earnest gaze from the bottles toward Selma. "I particularly asked for a butterfly book so I could name all of these as they hatch out."

"Well, I don't know if it was the wishing or the praying, but I have a surprise for you, so close your eyes."

Selma was rewarded with a blinding smile below tightly closed eyelids. She reached into the pocket of her pinafore where she retrieved a burnished orange book, then placed it gently into the eagerly outstretched hands.

Drew's eyes shot open. They grew even bigger and rounder as he recognized the flying insects that graced the cover of the book. Above the drawing were nine large letters in black ink that spelled out 'B-U-T-T-E-R-F-L-Y'. Selma watched with simple pride and thankfulness that one of the two books she had bought at the second hand store over the weekend just happened to be on Drew's favorite subject. Luckily, she had noticed the bottles last week and thought he might be interested in the book.

All of a sudden, two skinny arms stretched out wide and he leaned as far forward as he could, every inch of him begging for a hug. Selma grasped the frail little body to her breast and hugged him back. His strong, young arms squeezed her tight and she felt his lips press a fervent kiss on the side of her cheek. Then he let go and settled back onto the bed, holding the book tightly clasped in his slender hands.

"Mrs. Wraxmore, this is the most... bestest... present I've ever had. I love it. Thank you, thank you, thank you!

"Well, I don't know if you'll thank me after you see all the gigantic words that book uses to describe simple butterflies. I looked through it on the train ride and decided my poor brain needs simpler reading."

Drew thought she was funny and laughed. Then he chattered enthusiastically about the book and butterflies while Selma listened and fought back pangs of love and sorrow. Despite, and perhaps because of his twisted legs, Selma loved this little boy more than all the others. From the day she had met Drew, virtually locked away in his tiny room, staring down at the other children playing in the yard below his window, she had felt a strange affinity for him.

Often, she carried him to her own room so that he could talk with her while he watched her sew. He exhibited neither jealousy nor signs of envy that the other children received their clothes first. She had saved back some of the best bits of cloth for the outfit she planned to make for Drew; but knew she must bide her time. Mr. Henson had made it clear to Selma that she was not to make clothes for "that crippled boy" unless there was extra material left over after everyone else had a new outfit, because...

No! She refused to allow herself to remember the degrading words of that pompous bigot. Selma gave herself a mental shake and turned her attention outward again to see that Drew was leaning heavily on the edge of the table, examining individual butterfly bottles. Before him lay the new book and he eagerly turned page after page in search of an identifying picture that would tell him the name of his fluttering friends.

"Look, Mrs. Wraxmore, that orange one with the black

stripes... it's a Mon... Mon... Monarch?"

"Monarch, Drew... the ch sounds like a 'k'."

"Then why didn't they just spell it with a 'k' instead of a 'ch'?"

"I don't know, Drew. That's one of the great mysteries of life. Everyone who can read wonders the same thing."

"Well, when I grow up, I'm going to invent an alphabet and make words so that everything sounds just like it looks, or looks just like it sounds. You understand, don't you Mrs. Wraxmore?" Drew spoke to her without turning, his eyes still searching for butterflies inside the bottles and between the covers of the book.

"I surely do understand, Drew. And I have another surprise for you."

At her words, Drew pulled himself back from his study of the bottles and turned expectant eyes on Selma.

"I'm sure you won't think it's quite as grand as the butterfly book, but this afternoon I'm going to start making you an outfit."

"You mean like the ones you made for the other kids? I get a new outfit just like everyone else?"

Drew's excitement made Selma glad, for the hundredth time, that she had saved the best bits of cloth for this sweet boy. He hadn't expected an outfit and didn't begrudge the other children theirs, just like he didn't begrudge them the ability to walk and run and play. For that very reason, Selma had wanted his outfit to be the finest.

One day, when he was older, Selma feared that he would understand more fully and come to hate his infirmities; afraid also that he would be shunned by adults for being different. She had trod this mental pathway before and it led nowhere but depression. She was determined not to succumb to that temptation again. Instead she smiled and asked if he wanted to come to her room.

"Oh, yes. More than anything. Thank you."

Drew wrapped one arm around Selma's neck as she bent and lifted him into her arms. He clutched the butterfly book tightly in his other hand while gripping three bottles precariously to his chest with his forearm.

Selma's room was on the same floor, which made it easy to carry Drew back and forth. She passed five doors, then turned left into her sewing room and lowered Drew to the battered sofa chair Charlie had wrestled out of the attic for her. It had turned out to be the perfect size for Drew.

Selma had just seated herself at her sewing table when a knock sounded on her door. "Come in." She and Drew both looked at the door.

The door opened and Mrs. Poulson stepped into the room. She started to speak, then stopped when she noticed Drew curled up in the old sofa chair, looking at her with his liquid brown eyes. Selma felt her temperature surge as Mrs. Poulson raised one eyebrow and frowned, first at Drew, then at Selma.

"What is he doing in here, Mrs. Wraxmore?" Her frigid

tone matched the icy daggers in her eyes.

"Watching me sew, Mrs. Poulson, and discussing an interesting division of the common Rhopalocera as compared to the order of Lepidoptera." Selma stared innocently at Mrs. Poulson while a vapid smile covered her face. "It has really been a very lively discussion."

Mrs. Poulson looked thunderstruck, then angry, her caterpillar brows pulling together to form a bridge across her nose. Her loose mouth flapped opened, then smacked shut again, reminding Selma of a landed fish.

In a slightly bored voice, Selma continued. "Perhaps you could enlighten us as to their proper categorization; you see, we can't seem to agree." Selma's limpid blue eyes gazed innocently at her steaming visitor. "Do you think the common Lepidoptera are of the genus arthropod or genus anthropomorphic?"

Mrs. Poulson's ears turned the color of beets and her eyes narrowed to mere slits in her face. "I'm sure I couldn't say." She cast a withering glare at Drew, then turned her eyes back to Selma. "I came here to inform you that three members of the Board of Directors have arrived. Mrs. Cutfield asked that I inform you that they expect you to dine with them at six o'clock this evening." So said, she huffed back through the door and slammed it behind her.

"Thank you, Mrs. Poulson," Selma raised her voice so as to be heard through the closed door.

"Stiff necked, pompous old crow... " Selma muttered

softly, laughing to herself. A fiery flush highlighted her cheeks as she turned her eyes to meet Drew's. "I apologize. I should not have said that."

"I never heard you say a thing," Drew tried to smile, but it came out crooked. He tried to hide the hurt, but the lancing pain ran too deep and his shell was not yet hard enough to deflect barbs like those thrown by the Mrs. Poulsons of the world.

Selma crossed the room to sit beside her friend. She folded the boy into her arms, wishing she knew what to say to take away the hurt.

"Does she think I made my legs this way on purpose? To irritate her? To make more work for everyone else? Does she think I enjoy living like... this? Does she really think I wouldn't rather get up and walk and run and play like the other kids?" His voice caught. Tears flowed over his eyelids and followed each other down his smooth cheeks. "Why do people like her look at me as though I'm an inferior human being?"

"It's not you, Drew." Selma held him tight, trying with all her heart to shut out the cruel world. "It's them, Drew, them! Not you. Their souls have shriveled into tiny little wads inside their hearts, so small they have no room for love or empathy. There's only enough room left for a sort of self-righteous judgment that they pass out on the world around them. It's as if they need to pull others down so that they can feel higher. It's almost a sickness; one they use to infect the world around them until it weakens and destroys it. And all the while, they're pretending to try to make it better."

They held each other for a long while, then Drew let out a watery chuckle. "Common Lepidoptera — a genus arthropod or a genus anthropomorphic? The first is an insect, the other is a man or ape."

"Really?" Selma lifted innocent eyebrows above twinkling eyes.

"Do you even know what you were talking about, Mrs. Wraxmore?" Drew pulled back to look up into Selma's eyes.

"About half the time, Drew." She smiled and Drew's world was back on course. "I'm no genius like you, young man, but sometimes I really do know what I'm talking about."

"Well, you were great! Thanks."

"Anytime, my friend. Anytime."

CHAPTER TWENTY-SEVEN

"Ruth!" hissed Anna. "Carl is coming down the street." Anna turned from where her nose had been plastered to the window. "Let's go and see him."

Ruth's serious face brightened noticeably. She was two steps behind Anna when they burst through the door into the second floor hallway and smashed right into Amanda.

"Anna! Ruth!" Amanda's strident voice stopped both girls in their tracks. "Is something wrong?"

"No, why?"

"Well, I heard all sorts of noise from your room. Then you come pelting out and run over me..."

"We didn't run over you, Amanda. We ran into you."

"Um hmm. So what's the hurry?"

"Carl is coming. We have to talk to him before Mother comes home tomorrow." Anna blasted Amanda with a devastating smile calculated to make her forget any wrongdoing, then remembered Amanda could not see her face.

"From the sounds I heard, I believe you two need to pick up a few things in your room. Your mother will not want to find that her two beautiful, young daughters have been transformed into little piglets when she comes home again."

Anna laughed at being called a piglet and Ruth turned to go back into the room, tugging on her sister's sleeve as she went. No frown on Amanda's face could extinguish the twinkle lurking in her wide, staring eyes, but both girls knew she meant business. They marched back into their room and Amanda shuffled on down the hallway.

Bouncing down the stairs at last, they found Carl standing in the hall, glancing at a newspaper story concerning a brewing dispute between the Lake ship owners and dock workers in Twin Harbors.

Carl's serious expression lightened and his silver-blue eyes crinkled as the girls flew down the last steps. "And how are my two loves this fine evening?"

Carl laid down the paper and turned his full attention on the girls. With grace and gallantry, he first held Anna's, then Ruth's petite fingers and raised them in a courtly manner while he bent to drop a light kiss on each little hand. Both girls colored right up to the roots of their hair. Anna giggled delightedly. It was always easy to make Anna laugh. But Carl felt inordinate pride when he saw Ruth's lips break into a smile and her serious eyes light with gentle laughter.

"We don't want to be your loves, Carl," began Ruth, a twinkle still lurking in her eyes.

"Now, how am I to take that, Ruth, my darling. Have you found a suitor you like better than I?"

"No, Carl! I don't have any suitors." Ruth's clear gaze met Carl's laughing eyes. "You know that! But Anna and I had an idea. A very important idea! And we want to tell you about it."

Anna's bright curls bobbed up and down again, framing her cherubic smile. "Yes, we want to talk to you about..."

Suddenly, Ruth clamped her hand over her sister's mouth and hissed, "Shhh! Anna! Wait until he sits down and gets comfortable. Then she leaned her head back to look up at Carl, "Would you sit in the parlor with us, Carl?"

"I'd be honored, Ruth, but you better let go of that little piece of dynamite before she blows."

Ruth released her sister, who glared at her then raced for the parlor.

When Carl was finally settled in a comfortable chair, Anna climbed right up and snuggled into his lap. The white cat leaped onto the lap of Anna's lavender dress and the little girl began to pet the proud mother of four white kittens. Ruth stood resolutely before Carl for a moment, analyzing again his dark, curly hair, hypnotic blue eyes, and strong, but gentle hands. Yes, she thought, they had made a good choice.

"Okay, Ruth. I'm ready. You've certainly got my curiosity aroused. What's this all about?" The understanding light that first drew her to him flashed in his eyes.

Ruth opened her mouth to speak, but before she could

utter a word, Anna grabbed Carl's chin determinedly between her own small hands and pulled his face down so that she was looking right into his eyes. Nose to nose, in a tone most serious, she whispered, "We want you to fall in love with our mommy, marry her, and be our daddy." Her head nodded vigorously to punctuate her words.

Carl was stunned to the soles of his feet. He hadn't known what to expect, but this shocked him more than he thought possible. It took a moment for him to recover. Then his mouth started to twitch. It was a great tribute to his self-control that he maintained a serious expression, but he couldn't stop his eyes from dancing with shocked humor.

"Anna! You shouldn't ought to blast him with it like that!" Ruth moved a step closer while glaring daggers at her sister.

"Please, Ruth, don't be angry with Anna." Carl attempted to maintain the peace. "I've told you before, I like the word with the bark still on it. You don't have to make any fancy speeches for me."

Ruth scowled at her sister for another moment, then gasped in shock as Anna turned her cherubic face toward her, flashed her a blinding smile, then stuck out her tongue.

"Now, don't you two get into it... " Carl stiff-armed Ruth and held the angry little girl a safe distance from her unrepentant sibling.

"Ruth, why don't you just ignore Anna here and tell me if what she said is true. Do you really want me to marry your mother?"

Ruth backed up; primly tilting her delicate chin into higher air, she turned, and settled her pink skirts gracefully onto the chair next to Carl's.

"Actually, Carl," Ruth assumed a much older voice and her eyes took on an expression which spoke more than mere words, "what I really wanted to say was... we would like you to court our mother," Ruth's eyes were serious and businesslike while Anna's opened wide in eager anticipation, "just to see if she likes you enough to fall in love with you."

Ruth hurried ahead to avoid any confusion on Carl's part. "She works really hard and she loves us a lot. But we think she needs someone to love her and take care of her like she takes care of us. And we like you. And we think you would do that really good." She paused as her little nose wrinkled in thought. "But she might not fall in love with you. Then we would be in a fix if you had already agreed to marry her... mightn't we?"

Carl gaped from blue eyes to brown, completely speechless.

Selma paused on the threshold of the dining room Thursday evening and her heart cringed. Mr. Henson, resplendent in a pale yellow waistcoat and striped pants stretched past breaking point over his vast stomach, stood near the blazing fire, his head thrown back in laughter, conversing with two gentlemen she had never met.

She held her breath, but no one in the room looked her way. Silently, she slipped backwards out of sight, then tiptoed to the kitchen. She found Charlie there sipping a cup of coffee at the battered wooden table while his wife stumped around the room, muttering dark curses on inconsiderate men who just 'showed up', without so much as a by-your-leave, and expected an honest woman to be ready to cook a big, fancy, dinner for them.

Selma listened in amiable agreement for a break in the tirade. Finally, the cook took a breath, and Selma quickly addressed Charlie, outlining the task she had in mind. When she finished, a slow smile spread across his face and he touched his brow in a brief salute. "Yes, ma'am, it'll be a pleasure."

Next, Selma climbed the back stairs and knocked on Miss Calver's door, praying her garrulous friend would be in her room. She breathed a sigh of relief when she heard heavy footsteps and the door opened.

Twenty minutes later, Selma trod down the stairs once more, but this time Miss Calver walked by her side. The two women entered the dining room and Mr. Henson, already chafing at Selma's failure to appear, turned expectantly. His smile of pleasure at seeing Selma quickly evaporated when he recognized Miss Calver. His thin brows snapped together over a bulbous nose and his lips froze in a rigid line as the two women advanced into the room, heading straight for him.

"Mr. Henson, how are you this evening?" Selma inno-

cently greeted the stunned gentleman before turning to introduce her companion. "I'm sure you remember Miss Calver. I
took the liberty of inviting her on your behalf. I was sure you
would enjoy hearing of her progress with the primer classes."

Selma kept her mouth schooled in a polite smile. But she
was helpless to stop the laughter that sparkled in her eyes at
the stunned expression on Mr. Henson's face when the ebul-
lient Miss Calver gushed her appreciation over being invited
to dinner. When that redoubtable dame took Mr. Henson's
hand in her enthusiastic grip, she thoroughly rattled his teeth
before letting it go.

Mrs. Cutfield, trying valiantly to hide her appreciation
of Mr. Henson's discomfiture, soon interrupted to introduce
a gentleman wearing a religious collar. Father Bartholomew's
name shocked Selma and brought a flood of memories
avalanching through her mind; frigid visions of a desperate
night when she walked up the steps to a locked church and
found no sanctuary in its hallowed halls. She shivered and
shook off the picture. She greeted the reverend gentleman
briefly, then turned when Mrs. Cutfield introduced Mr.
Southby, a noted banker who also lived in Superior.

"Mr. Mason sends his apologies. He couldn't be here
with us tonight, but we bear his deepest regards and hopes
that you'll excuse him." Mr. Southby intoned in a dry voice.

Miss Calver, thrilled to be included in such select company and enjoying a captive audience, was all that Selma had
hoped she would be. With the best of good will and enthusi-

asm, she forcefully monopolized the conversation, periodically including each of the gentlemen in her discourse. Selma and Mrs. Cutfield were left to watch in humorous satisfaction.

"Oh, Selma. Thank you," Mrs. Cutfield whispered. "Once they arrived, I couldn't escape long enough to warn you."

"Well, as you know, I was brought up to maintain equal numbers of ladies to gentlemen at the table," Selma lifted her eyebrows and pretended innocence.

"Mr. Henson will be furious," the older woman hissed, trying not to laugh.

"What can he do? Fire me? I'll finish the last suit of clothes tomorrow morning, then... " she left the sentence hanging but her eyes sparkled.

Mrs. Cutfield saw the cook signal from the doorway and called everyone to the table. She took the Reverend's arm as Mr. Henson stepped quickly to Selma's side, leaving Mr. Southby to squire Miss Calver to the dinner table.

Selma expected Mr. Henson to remonstrate with her for including Miss Claver in the company. But she was not prepared for the heartfelt apology he expressed for his 'deplorable behavior' at Mrs. Reeves' home, Sunday last.

Selma was left speechless. She did not want to accept what she felt was a false apology and asked, instead, what role Mr. Southby, the Reverend Bartholomew, and the absent Thomas Mason played in the Douglas County Orphanage.

"First and foremost, Southby, Bartholomew, and myself have been lifelong friends. I was best man at Southby's wedding and instrumental in getting Bartholomew appointed as head rector of the First Lutheran Church in Superior."

Puffing up with self-importance, he looked sideways at her demure countenance. Observing her calm demeanor, Henson convinced himself that his behavior had not been as deplorable or unwelcome as he had feared. His self-disdain quickly faded away. In an arrogant voice, he went on to explain that Father Bartholomew and Mr. Southby were fellow members of the Board of Directors and were visiting the orphanage on their bi-annual inspection of the facility.

"Thomas Mason also sits on the board. Though he is a cripple and confined to a wheelchair," Henson spoke with deprecation, "his membership on the board is welcome because his contributions are largely the reason we are able to maintain such a fine facility when other orphanages are barely able to feed their inmates."

Father Bartholomew had been listening and now nodded his approbation toward Selma as she took her seat at the table. "And of course, we were most anxious to meet the young woman who is sewing so many clothes for the children here."

Over chicken and creamed potatoes, Mr. Southby regaled Selma with an account of his seven children and pregnant spouse. Selma maintained an interested smile as Southby warmed to his theme, mistakenly assuming the sparkle in Selma's eyes came from her interest in his third child's bout with croup.

Barely listening to the man, Selma could not help but be entertained in observing the hard-pressed Mr. Henson who was unenthusiastically receiving the brunt of Miss Calver's eager discourse and hearty appetite.

When Mr. Southby stopped talking to fork a piece of chicken into his mouth, Selma took pity on Mr. Henson and asked Miss Calver how her reading class was progressing since receiving their new primer books. It was all that enthusiastic dame needed to switch conversation partners. Mr. Henson mopped his brow in relief while Selma listened appreciatively, sincerely enjoying the woman's love of her work and enthusiasm for the welfare of the children she taught.

Almost lost in the clink of silverware and prattle of conversation, Selma noticed her name being mentioned and was shocked to overhear Father Bartholomew whisper aside to Mr. Henson, "She's all you said she was. A fine choice. She'll make the perfect wife for you, my friend."

Mr. Henson nodded proudly as his eyes flicked possessively across the table at Selma.

Flaming indignation rose in Selma's spirit and her eyes flashed daggers, causing Miss Calver to pause in her dissertation. Then it was gone and Miss Calver thought she had imagined the fire in her friend's eyes. For the rest of the meal, it took every ounce of Selma's self control to maintain her composure and focus her attention on Miss Calver's flushed countenance.

Dinner ended with a chocolate cake for dessert. Then Father Bartholomew and Mr. Southby stood and thanked Mrs. Cutfield for their enjoyable stay. They were profuse in their compliments of her continued smooth running of the orphanage, then they departed to catch the 8:30 train and return to their respective homes. Mr. Henson waved to them from the porch as their carriage wheeled down the snowy drive, then he turned to Mrs. Cutfield and steadfastly announced his intention to spend the night at the orphanage.

"Would you not be more comfortable at the Comstock Inn, away from all the children and fuss of the home?" Mrs. Cutfield was caught unawares by his request and left disconcerted.

"There are one or two more things I would like to... do... before I leave." Mr. Henson ended the debate. "I can sleep in the spare gardener's room down the hall from the kitchen."

Following Mr. Henson back through the mansion door, Selma shared a speaking glance with Mrs. Cutfield. In response, she found that dame's eyes fuming with frustration and overlaid with wry humor. Her comical expression caught Selma unaware and suddenly she was choking on her laughter and trying to turn it into a coughing fit. Conscious of Mr. Henson's concerned stare, she kept her gaze lowered until she could dash the tears away from her eyes.

"If I may, Miss Wraxmore, I would like a moment of your time... " Mr. Henson walked toward the door to the library and held it open. However, Mrs. Cutfield's next words caught him off guard.

"Dear Mr. Henson, we would so love to hear you play the piano for us again. That is, if you're feeling in the mood?" Suddenly tense, Selma relaxed again and turned wide eyes on the unsuspecting gentleman, watching him puff up with pride.

Miss Calver immediately expressed her delight with the scheme. Mr. Henson bridled for a moment, then said he would be glad to play a number or two for the ladies' entertainment. Though his eyes bored straight at Selma when he spoke, Mrs. Cutfield moved forward and claimed Mr. Henson's escort. Selma took Miss Calver's arm and the four of them slowly made their way to the music room.

Charlie passed the group in the hallway and tipped his hat in Selma's direction, the lurking smile in his eyes immediately mirrored in her own. Indeed, she was not surprised when Mr. Henson threw open the door to the music room and found every chair filled with the children of the orphanage interspersed with the adults who supervised them. The entire group erupted in applause at Mr. Henson's entry.

That dumbfounded gentleman paused upon seeing such a large crowd and grew alarmingly rigid. Miss Calver tittered delightedly that it was to be a real concert and sailed into the room to be greeted enthusiastically by all of her pupils.

Mrs. Cutfield gently urged Mr. Henson toward the piano, while all the time showering flowery compliments on him. Before he could protest, she had left him standing before the instrument and turned to address the audience.

"Quiet everyone. Quiet." She waved the room to silence, then announced: "Thank you all for coming. We have a special treat tonight. But I must tell you, this is a surprise for our dear Mr. Henson. I'm sure you're all familiar with our kind and generous administrator here at the Douglas County Orphanage." She paused until a smattering of polite applause quieted, then went on.

"Often, after a hard day of helping us here at the home, Mr. Henson regales just a few of us with his wonderful musical talent. But tonight I thought it would be a delightful surprise for all of you—and for Mr. Henson—if we were to ask him to perform a small concert for everyone's benefit."

Enthusiastic cheering erupted from students and faculty alike.

Mrs. Cutfield turned to Mr. Henson and found him struggling against conflicting emotions. His eyes passed across the excited crowd and for a moment she feared he might storm out of the room. She, more than anyone else in the entire county, knew the depth of his antipathy towards all children. When his seething gaze finally stopped on her face and bored straight into her wide, innocent eyes, she wondered, in a purely detached way, if he might not explode.

Then Selma moved up to sit in the front row, right beside Drew in his wheelchair. Mr. Henson's eyes swiveled to watch the younger woman and Mrs. Cutfield suddenly saw his expression change. She knew the exact moment he decided it would further his suit more to stay and play than to storm angrily from the room.

When she sat down beside Selma, Mrs. Cutfield was fully prepared to enjoy herself. During the opening bars of a Mozart prelude, her hand moved over Selma's and squeezed her fingers firmly, sharing the victory of their campaign, before returning to her own lap. In her turn, Selma held Drew's fingers in her other hand and shared a smile with him from time to time.

Mr. Henson, finding himself trapped, and with no gracious way to escape, had indeed decided to use this opportunity to impress the woman of his choice. Cudgeling his memory, he resurrected and played every piece he could perform with any virtuosity.

At the end of the concert, Miss Calver, flanked by most of the teachers and a group of noisy children, moved forward to surround and congratulate Mr. Henson. Enthusiastically, they complimented him on his skill and thanked him for his kindness in providing an evening of such elevated entertainment.

Selma watched for a moment from the doorway at the back of the room. Drew observed Mr. Henson for a moment, then grinned up at Selma from his wheelchair. She shared a mischievous smile with the boy, then they made their escape.

CHAPTER TWENTY-EIGHT

You don't have any more time. Four days from now, we leave for Chicago. Selma and the girls will be off to Montana before we get back. If you're going to do something, it better be quick."

"She's still scared of me, Amanda. I see it in her eyes... I don't know how to fight that." The cat watched from a safe spot beneath the round table by the window as Carl paced back and forth in front of Amanda. The rhythmic twitch of her tail matched the tension in his strides. A kitten mewed from the box beside the fireplace and she raced over to see what the problem was.

"You can't fight it, Carl. You just keep on loving her until she can work all the way through the pain from her past. If you don't love her enough to wait until that day, well..."

"So what are you saying?"

"I'm saying tell her. At least don't let her leave here without knowing how you feel. She's not the same girl who stepped off that train before Christmas. She's come a long way and she's possesses an incredibly strong spirit. She'll come back all the way…under the right influence. And I know you've got what it takes. She needs you as much as you need her. Believe in that!"

Carl paced back and forth in front of Amanda's chair. From the dark shadows above, Ruth and Anna silently watched and listened through the rails of the upstairs landing. Anna turned her wide, apprehensive eyes to stare at her sister. Ruth held one small finger to her lips, urging Anna to keep quiet. The blonde ringlets nodded fervently and Anna held up both hands, showing all of her little fingers crossed over one another.

Gunther pulled the lapel of his jacket aside and extracted a folded sheet of paper. Almost ceremonially, he pressed open the creases in the document and silently passed it across the desk to Thomas Mason.

"Look at the third name on the registry." Gunther's left eye twitched spasmodically, the only sign of his excitement and agitation.

"By all that's holy!" Thomas' face paled but his eyes remained glued to the printed page held in his shaky fist.

"I thought you would want to know."

"You were right." He dropped the paper on the table as though it burned his hand. Nervously, he began drumming the fingers of his left hand on the cherrywood desktop. "I'm too old to believe in coincidences, Gunther."

"Yes, sir." Gunther reached up and held his left eye closed with two fingers while Thomas continued drumming on the table and staring at the ceiling. Long moments passed while neither man spoke. Suddenly, the silence was broken by the bong, bong, bong of the grandfather clock against the far wall. The deep tones seemed to awaken Thomas from his hypnotic state.

"I could be wrong, but I don't believe in taking chances." His fingers stopped their agitated dance.

"No, sir."

Thomas slapped both hands flat on the table, leaned forward, and glared straight into Gunther's eyes. "Have you a good man you can trust?"

"Yes, sir."

"You're a prize, Gunther. Now, here's how I think it'll play out..." Neither man knew they were already one step behind.

Selma was up early Friday morning, finishing the outfit she had made for Drew. By noon she was packing her bags for her final trip back to Superior. Finished, she glanced around the empty room for the last time, then stared out through the window, willing the bright winter sun to warm the cold knot in her stomach. Selma set the bags just outside her door then turned toward Drew's room for the last time. Her feet dragged as she walked down the hallway to the door of the last room.

She stood with her hand on his doorknob for long minutes, struggling to find the courage to turn it. During the last month, the boy on the other side of this door had become almost as dear to her as one of her own daughters. Having to say goodbye was like a knife hacking and slicing away at the ragged edges of her heart, creating an unrelenting pain that was almost more than she could bear.

She had lain awake night after night trying to plan a way, devise some scheme whereby she could adopt her little friend. In the end, she had to admit defeat. If love was all that he needed, she would whisk him away today. But taking on the care of a child like Drew became out of the question. He needed more than just her love. He needed a stable, secure home and adequate medical attention. Right now, Selma wasn't certain how she was going to support just herself and her own children. Her heart had enough room to include Drew, more than enough. But her purse was woefully slim. She knew it would be wrong to give the little boy false hope for the future.

She felt rootless herself, desperately trying to decide what to do now, where to go from here? At last, she had enough money tucked away to purchase three train fares to Missoula. But could she leave Amanda, not knowing if her eyesight had been restored, or...

She leaned her head against the door of Drew's room and tried to concentrate on her dream. But each day it became harder and harder to focus on the single bright ray of hope that had sustained her through years of hardship and despair. The tunnel that for so long had seemed eternally dark, with only a point of light at the end, had expanded in the past few weeks to where it was now wide and brightly lit; until she had difficulty focusing on just one bright pinpoint of light at the end.

Her little house. She willed her mind into the cherished dream of herself and her children living in their dream house in Missoula. But strangely, instead of feeling like a sanctuary, the little house now felt lonely. Leaving Amanda, Mrs. Cutfield, Drew, and all of the other people whom she had come to love — she dared not dwell on Carl — made her dream home suddenly appear cold and lonely.

Should she follow through with her plan? Take her children west? Find a job in Missoula? Start their lives all over again? Or should she sell the house and stay with Amanda for a time, find a home near the orphanage and keep working for Mrs. Cutfield? She could repay some of Amanda's generosity by helping after her surgery. Warmth flooded her soul at the thought of staying in Amanda's home. She lapsed again into the slippery spiral of unending possibilities. Finally, she allowed open the one door in her mind that was growing harder and harder to keep locked.

Carl. Where did he fit into her life? Did he fit anywhere at all? More and more her mind and heart tangled itself around memories and feelings, new and old mashed together. She could no longer force thoughts of him out of her mind, was not even sure she wanted to. Selma allowed herself a tiny glimpse of the times she had looked into his hypnotic eyes; the simple acts of kindness he had shown her; his caring voice, gentle touch, the way he treated Anna and Ruth — his kisses. She felt her knees weaken. She couldn't force the door in her mind to close, so she turned the knob and stepped into Drew's room.

He sat in his accustomed place beside the window, watching the children building snow forts and throwing snowballs outside. He turned when the door opened and his face lit up with the pure joy he felt whenever Selma came to see him. She crossed the room, holding her hands behind her back.

"Pick a hand," she said.

"Your right one." Drew's eyes sparkled with anticipation.

Out came the pants.

"Oh, Mrs. Wraxmore," he whispered in awe, "they're beautiful."

"Pick another hand," she said again.

Drew slowly pointed to her left hand and she brought out the matching shirt. The look of wonder and appreciation that lit his face brought a poignant smile to Selma's lips. But her joy was only momentary, for she had come to tell her friend she was leaving.

The visit with Drew was painful and left her drained. They both struggled to be brave in their farewells, but it didn't work and soon Drew was in tears, his arms wrapped around Selma's neck as she held him close. Selma whispered promises to write and to visit; Drew hiccuped promises to write back and to be there when she returned.

Selma was almost relieved when the sour-faced Mrs. Poulson barged into the room and informed her that Mrs. Cutfield wished to see her in the library. Selma kissed Drew on the forehead and hugged him tight one last time. When she stood up to leave, her aching heart felt as though it would break.

Just as she opened the door of Drew's room, two little girls raced past her to jump up onto Drew's bed. They were chattering excitedly, some oddment held in their hands which they had come to share. Drew was immediately all smiles and joined enthusiastically into their chatter.

Selma stood in the doorway and watched for a moment, a tortured smile tilting the corners of her mouth. Gradually, a peaceful feeling warmed her soul and she knew Drew would be all right. He had friends at the orphanage, and as long as Mrs. Cutfield loved him he would never be alone. Selma knew she could not offer him as much. But the crooked smile remained on her lips as she walked slowly down the stairs.

Passing the main dining room, she listened to the happy chatter of children eating at the long tables. Selma had heard stories of other orphanages where love and happiness were not considered essential to the growth of the children. Mrs. Cutfield was ahead of her time. She believed, heart and soul, that children needed to feel love and security in order to grow into responsible adults. She ran her orphanage with that goal in mind.

Selma chuckled to herself at the thought of Mrs. Poulson, the only adult who did not seem to fit Mrs. Cutfield's requirements for staff members. Perhaps, she mused, Mrs. Cutfield was trying to help Mrs. Poulson.

Selma set her suitcase by the front door, took a deep breath as she squared her shoulders, then turned aside to the library to bid farewell to another dear friend. Everyone else was in the lunchroom and the hallway was empty. A lonely feeling, almost of impending doom, swept over Selma. She shook it off and pushed open the heavy oak door.

The room was dim. The shutters had not yet been opened. Perhaps Mrs. Cutfield had a headache and needed to shield her eyes from the bright sunshine outside. Selma did not see her right away, so she closed the door and advanced further, calling her name.

Slowly, a man — hidden by the high back of the chair in which he sat — rose and turned to face Selma. His eyes glinted in the shadowed room as they looked up and down Selma's stiff body.

Selma forced her taught muscles to relax, but her temper soared. She struggled to control her smoldering anger at the childish subterfuge Mr. Henson had used to get her alone.

"Mrs. Wraxmore — Selma," he breathed her name, throaty and low, while his eyes glittered. He'd always loved the thrill of the hunt and his prey was neatly trapped.

"Mr. Henson," Selma's voice was stone cold and unyielding as she interrupted, "excuse me, but Mrs. Cutfield requested me to meet with her and I understood she was in this room." Cooly, Selma stepped back towards the door. "I did not mean to disturb you. I'll just go see if she's in her office."

She turned and grasped the doorknob with her hand. Suddenly, he was beside her. Without warning, he slammed the door shut with one meaty fist and grabbed for her with the other.

Frantically, she skittered out of his grasp, flying around a rectangular book table and trying to keep its broad surface between herself and her amorous employer.

Mr. Henson charged after her, the buttons of his figured waistcoat straining against the force of his protuberant belly. Again and again she avoided his grasping hands, but he just kept coming. By now, Selma was really and truly frightened.

"I am a wealthy man." He paused and faced her across the table, his voice low and ominous. Slowly, he began inching around the end of the table, slowly, cautiously, waiting for her to bolt. "I have power, prestige in my community..."

Selma shuddered at his words while she cast her eyes around, desperately seeking another avenue of escape. She found none.

"I could make you a very wealthy woman... " He jerked forward, surprisingly quick and agile for a man so large. She leaped away from him, but too late. He caught his prey and pulled her back and around until he could wrap both arms around her struggling form. Selma thrashed in his arms, but he only grew more excited as she pushed, twisted, and pulled her head back and forth to avoid his seeking lips.

"I want you!" his voice was a growl. One hand grabbed the back of her head and his fingers twisted in her thick, golden hair, forcing her head still. Ruthlessly, his lips smashed against her own.

Revulsion shuddered through Selma and she felt vilely sick. Her strength was no match for his and her struggles merely seemed to inflame his excitement. Horrible memories flooded her mind until she was frozen with terror, her body trapped, her mind desperately seeking a way to escape.

Thud. Thud. Thud!

Relief flooded through Selma when her assailant partially released her and whirled around, a savage snarl escaping his throat. Without warning, the door flew back on its hinges and slammed against the wall. Selma struggled to escape, but Mr. Henson's fist held her tight while his face suffused with angry color.

Panting and disheveled, Selma looked past him. She saw who stood in the opening and without warning, her knees buckled completely as she felt the blood drain from her face. Mr. Henson only gripped her tighter, pulling her firmly against his fleshy chest until his arm around her waist was the only thing keeping Selma from slipping to the ground.

"May I help you?" Mr. Henson's enraged voice transposed from angry to ingratiatory in just those four, short words.

The cause was easy to ascertain. Before him stood a tall, striking woman, dressed in the height of French fashion, her face rouged and powdered in the latest continental style. Entirely overwhelmed by the extraordinary vision before him, Mr. Henson stood gawking like a schoolboy enthralled by the strange sights of a traveling circus.

Strength flowed back into Selma's legs just as Mr. Henson's grip completely loosened about her waist. Her knees were shaking but she grabbed for a chair back to support herself while she commanded the room to stop reeling around her. She sucked in a deep breath. A second only, then her mind came back into focus. Her legs strengthened, her spine grew rigid, and her chin lifted higher in the air.

The strange woman glided through the door and looked Mr. Henson up and down with a disdainful stare, then her eyes traveled beyond him to where Selma stood straight and proud, like a statue carved from fine marble.

"Hello, my dear."

The woman's tones were deep and sultry, and Selma watched Mr. Henson's face flush and his eyes bulge even further. She was not surprised. This was not the first time she had seen Aurelia Klintenberg have this affect on a man.

"Did I interrupt... something?" Her voice purred, conjuring in Selma's mind the familiar picture of a cat happily playing with a particularly fat mouse.

CHAPTER TWENTY-NINE

ello, Mother." Selma was not too disheartened to appreciate the appalled expression rapidly overtaking Mr. Henson's flacid features.

"Mrs. Wraxmore?" Shock depleted the ruddy color from Mr. Henson's face, leaving it an ashen gray.

"My name is Aurelia Klintenberg." Selma's mother surveyed the awe-struck man before her, assessing his expensive clothes and possible value before extending one neatly gloved hand. "Wraxmore is my daughter's married name."

Gingerly, Mr. Henson took her long, slender hand in his own, staring with undisguised awe at the vision before him, "Oh, my g... goodness, I m..mean…excuse me."

He cleared his voice and remembered his manners. "What a pleasure to meet you." He turned a small, perfunctory bow into a grander gesture, then lifted her hand to his lips.

Aurelia raised her eyebrows and stared disdainfully at

him a moment, then freed her hand and glided past. His eyes followed slavishly as she moved further into the room and paused beside Selma.

Mrs. Klintenberg lifted one graceful finger and gently flicked Selma's cheek. Slowly, her eyes traveled up from the scuffed boots on Selma's feet, taking in every detail of her simple, blue, second-hand dress to her slightly ruffled hair.

"You're looking positively... domestic." The word issued like a curse as she walked slowly around her daughter, her eyes moving up and down Selma's slim figure. "Simple cotton, my dear. How could you?" A theatrical shudder emphasized her contempt.

Selma remained silent under the blistering scrutiny. Failing to elicit any response, Aurelia's eyes returned to Mr. Henson. She allowed a haughty smile to crease her perfect mouth, though it never quite reached her eyes.

"I am so sorry." Her finely arched brows rose slightly as she looked from one to the other. "How thoughtless of me. I do believe I've interrupted a love tryst." Selma's face flooded scarlet at the accusation, leaving her mother to assume she had guessed correctly.

Mr. Henson started to speak, but Aurelia turned to him and smiled dangerously. "I find you infinitely de trop, my good man. I believe we would be better sans your company. I'm sure you would be much more comfortable in the... um…hall?"

Embarrassed, Mr. Henson found himself helpless to

protest, and fumbled through the words to excuse himself. Only after the door shut behind him did he consider that this was not the first time outside influences had prevented him from pressing his suit with Selma. Such was his confidence in himself that he was sure he would have succeeded in acquiring her promise to be his wife — if he could only be left alone with her for a sufficient amount of time.

Without warning, the massive front door opened and two rough-looking men stepped silently through the opening. One carried a long sack fashioned from some dark brown material in one hand and a can and rag in the other. The second man carried a blunt club in his massive fists.

"Here, I say." Mr. Henson puffed up and moved to intercept the two strangers. "Do you have business at this orphanage?"

Only after he blocked their way to the library did a premonition of fear drain the color from his face. He glanced from one swarthy countenance to the other and read only cold-blooded contempt in their eyes.

"You're probably not aware," he blustered, "but visitors are strictly controlled, to ensure safety for the children. I'll have to ask you to leave; I'm sure you understand."

In one swift motion, the man in the Red Cap closed the double dividing doors, flipped the key in the lock, and wedged a chair beneath the handles.

"If you'll tell me your business, I'm sure I can help you." Henson's voice raised to a shrill screech. He felt the sweat break out on his forehead and trickle from his armpits. He opened his mouth to scream as the man in the Red Cap turned back toward him and the other man raised the club in both hands."

Silence filled the room to crackling point before Aurelia finally spoke. "Have you no welcome for your mother, my dear?"

"Go back to England." Selma watched the woman before her as a bird watches a predatory snake.

"That's not very gracious, considering all the effort it took for me to get here, my darling." She purred, then waited, but nothing else was forthcoming. "As it happens, I haven't a feather to fly with, as the saying goes." A harsh laugh punctuated her sentence.

"I spent everything I own to find my adored daughter, who disappeared — without a trace, I might add — right after her husband's funeral." The words came out accusingly, but she raised her eyebrows in a coy manner most men found irresistible and Selma thought singularly revolting.

Selma could remain still no longer. She moved around the room, methodically opening the shutters on the giant windows at the end of the room. She froze in place, blinking into the bright light, staring at the melting snow beyond the glass panes, tracing the silver droplets as they trickled from the eves in bright traces of water.

"Can't you allow me a mother's natural concern?"

Selma cringed at the syrupy, sweet tone. "What do you want?" Her voice came out brittle, lifeless.

"Why, can you doubt that I came to assure myself that my only child is well — and to see how my dear grand-daughters are getting along? I'll bet they've grown in the..."

Brutally, Selma interrupted. "Don't! You never cared for them before. Why should I think you've changed?"

"You're very severe." Aurelia spoke lightly as she pulled out a long pin and lifted the modish hat from her perfect curls.

"Only truthful." Unable to remain still, Selma glided across the worn carpet to stop before the fire. She stared into the hypnotic flames, holding her cold hands out to the fire's warmth.

Aurelia's lips clamped together and her eyes narrowed like those of a cat watching a mouse. But she turned away from Selma and glided across the room to stop and stare at her reflection in the mirror above a credenza overflowing with books. Apparently pleased with what she saw, the calculating smile returned to her lips.

Through the mirror, Aurelia flicked a measuring glance at her daughter's stiff back and set shoulders. This was going to be harder than she had expected. She tried a new approach.

"I've come to make amends, my darling. When you left England, I realized how... wrong... I had been... how much I missed you... and Ruby and Arlene."

"Ruth and Anna." Selma felt the knife twist in her heart

and raised her eyes to the picture of a horse that hung above
the wooden mantel to keep the tears from falling from her
eyes. Even now, after all this time, she was amazed at the
power this heartless woman still held over her. She couldn't
trust her voice, even if she'd known what to say. Instead, she
remained stiff and silent.

"Oh, yes. So sorry." Aurelia began to prowl around the
room, looking at the books on the shelves and tattered doilies
lying across the backs of the antiquated chairs, flicking a
gloved finger at a span of dust on a table top.

"You don't belong here, Selma," she said. "You were
made for better things."

"Really?" Infused in that one word was all the bitterness
and loathing Selma had stored up through seven long years —
her entire lifetime — of neglect, misery, and abuse.

"You blame me, darling. But what else was I to do?"
Aurelia turned toward Selma, lifting her hands and shoulders
in a graceful shrug.

"Stop gambling? Get a job? Leave me free to make my
own life?" Anger had kept her voice steady, but it cracked and
broke on her next words as she turned to face her mother.
"Love me?"

"I do love you, Selma. I've always loved you."

"You have strange ways of showing it." Selma stared into
the green eyes set in the lovely face so like her own and realized her mother did not understand the meaning of the word.
Never had understood it.

"You never used to speak to me in this hoydenish fashion! Living in this wild, uncivilized country has not improved you." Aurelia thought she detected a weakness and pressed her attack. The commanding tone was back in her voice as she moved up behind Selma.

"Listen to the words you say to me. Look at the clothes you are wearing. See your hands? They belong more to a common laborer than to a lady."

Selma lifted her hands and stared at her fingers where a beam of sunlight shone through the window and highlighted her short nails. She turned them over, noting the calluses, and felt a thrill of pride for the look of usefulness her hands now bore.

"You're right. I am no longer a pampered, cosseted drone, Mother. I am a laborer and I'm happier here than I can remember ever being the rest of my life."

"You can't mean that!"

The truth of her own words struck deep into Selma's soul, searing her mind with their truth, filling her heart with strength and courage. In that single, warm rush, Selma felt lighter, freer, stronger than ever in her life. She breathed deeply and felt the constriction in her chest ease, then disappear as though it had never been.

Aurelia whirled away, unconscious of the change overtaking her daughter. She began pacing the length of the room and when she came level with the second bookcase, she decided to change the subject.

"That gentleman you were... kissing... when I came through the door. He looks very, um, substantial?"

A smile, strange to Selma's face, curled her lips, then disappeared. "Mr. Henson is my employer. But," she paused and licked her lips, considering her words before she spoke, "he has become very particular in his attentions of late. In fact, you just interrupted a proposal of marriage."

"Don't tell me you would honestly consider marriage with someone so... so low."

"Mother," Selma commanded her performance, then turned to face her mother, "this is not a country of lords and ladies. In America, a man is what he makes of himself. Mr. Henson is very wealthy, a prominent man in Superior society, head of the Board of Directors for this orphanage and, I daresay, other organizations. I've heard he has a huge house; a mansion, if rumors are true." She watched with disgust, but no surprise, as a gleam of avarice blossomed in her mother's eyes.

"I see." Aurelia turned and looked away, but she could not hide her sudden interest from her daughter. "He's more my age than yours."

"That didn't seem to bother you when you arranged my marriage to Lord Wraxmore."

"That was different."

"Really?" Selma shuddered, then forced such paralyzing thoughts out of her mind. "But you did not come here talk of Mr. Henson — or any of these 'heathens'. So tell me, Mother, why are you here?"

Aurelia detected the hint of a newfound strength in her daughter. She realized it behooved her to tread warily. Gracefully lowering herself onto the best sofa in the room, she paused a moment to consider her next words.

"Well, if you must be so ill bred as to pry, Lord Dewhurst came to visit me at the Countess Lieven's villa six weeks after Lord Wraxmore's funeral, God rest his soul."

"Lord Dewhurst?" Selma shuddered at the distinct memory of the sharp features and frigid eyes of this peer, a man singularly lacking any warmth or chivalry. His lewd suggestions had ruined more than one fashionable party where they had both been invited. Those had been the only times she was grateful to have a wedding ring to hide behind.

"A most estimable man, my dear, I assure you."

"Fat purse, mother?"

"You're indelicate, Selma," she admonished. "He was very interested to discover where you had gone to... mourn. He particularly wanted me to give you his regards and tell you he hopes to be able to pay his respects when your year of grieving is up."

She shifted in the stiff, brocaded chair. "I can't tell you how shocked I was to see you in the arms of... another man... with your dear husband buried less than six months. And wearing colors." She produced a theatrical shudder. "I'm so glad no one in London can see you. They would be appalled."

"Since none of them will ever be called upon to witness

my debauchery, your reputation is safe."

"How you do go on," Aurelia carefully straightened the folds of her skirt over her knees. "The wagging tongues of London are not my concern. But Lord Dewhurst is. Why, you should see his estate in Northamptonshire. At the fall hunt meeting, he confided in me that he felt it was time to settle down, take a wife, set up his nursery."

She arched her eyebrows suggestively, but Selma refused to look at her. "He especially made it obvious to even my mean intelligence that he thought you would be an eligible parti to take that exalted position."

"Did you gamble with him? Run up a sizeable debt?"

"I don't see that that is any of your business," Aurelia's offended tones did not deter Selma.

"Couldn't you... barter... yourself in my stead, Mother?" The bitter edge to Selma's voice was all the more galling because of its accuracy.

"This is not like you. You've changed—and not for the better, I might add." A thread of irritation, bordering on anger, sliced through her words. "Sarcasm ill becomes you, my girl. I'm still your mother, and when we get back to England, I think you'll see the wisdom of..."

Bluntly, Selma cut her off. "I'm never returning to England, Mother." She whirled around until her eyes bored straight into her mother's. "I am no longer the meek, biddable girl I was when you... arranged... my marriage. Here, now, I am my own woman! I make my own decisions! Live my own life!"

Selma sensed a final release flutter through her soul as the words passed her lips and she realized that she believed them. Finally free of her gilded bars, she had become a fully-fledged bird—loosed—never again to be caged. A rush of power and excitement rippled through her chest.

"Whatever you came here for, you won't get it. I can't say it's been a pleasure, but I wish you a safe journey back home. Now, Mother," Selma glanced at the clock on the wall, "I can't stay any longer or I'll miss my train."

"But…but… you can't just abandon me here… I forbid you to leave!" Aurelia shrieked as she pushed herself to the edge of the seat and jumped up.

Calmly pulling her gloves on, Selma walked to the door, ignoring the angry words and stunned expression on her mother's face. "Good-bye, Aurelia."

Selma stepped through the door and started to shut it, then peeked back around to smile at the furious woman. "And you may thank Lord Dewhurst for his kind inquiry. But please tell him I am not interested in furthering my acquaintance with him." On that note, Selma closed the door quietly in her wake.

Stunned and furious, Aurelia stood frozen in the middle of the room, looking at the silent door until she recollected herself enough to snap her slack jaw shut. She had spoken the truth when she told Selma that she had spent all of her money in the search for her daughter. But it was not love that had inspired her pursuit and it rankled that Selma was so undutiful a daughter as to not even consider Lord Dewhurst's offer. Aurelia was indeed deeply in dept to that peer and desperately in need of funds to recoup her place in society.

A hard, calculating expression settled over her face, then she shrugged fatalistically and stepped to the door, muttering softly beneath her breath. "There's more than one way to skin a cat, my girl. And I know most of them."

When Selma shut the door, she turned and almost tripped over Mr. Henson. He was sprawled on the floor, blood flowing from an ugly gash in his forehead. She whirled around as fear sent a chill up her spine. But before she could make a sound, a dark hood jerked over her head and was yanked down, tight around her shoulders and arms. Selma kicked out with one foot and heard a groan when her toe connected with bone.

Desperately, she thrashed against the ties she felt binding her arms tight to her sides. With no warning, Selma felt herself quickly hoisted in the air and flung over a beefy shoulder. Her breath heaved out in a painful humph when her torso swung helplessly upside down onto the back of a man. She took a gulp of air to scream and a sickly-sweet smell penetrated her throat and lungs. Nausea overwhelmed her, then darkness swirled around her. She thought she heard her mother's voice just before she passed out.

The library door opened and Aurelia Klintenberg stood in the opening. In one glance she noted her daughter's limp body slung across the broad shoulders of a man dressed like a chimney sweep. Then she lowered her eyes. A cold smile chilled her features as she clinically assessed the damage done to her daughter's ardent suitor. He still breathed, but Aurelia appeared singularly unconcerned whether he lived or died. Daintily, she lifted her skirts above the carnage and stepped around his prostrate form. She motioned the men to follow her, then walked briskly toward the entrance.

"Good work, Frank, Dick. Bring her along now, but be careful. She's not worth much to me if you damage her."

Dick opened the heavy door and stood aside for Aurelia to pass, then Frank carrying his unconscious burden. He glanced one more time around the empty hall before he pulled the door shut.

"The knockout drops, m'lady," Dick spoke in a thick brogue. "We sh'd prob'ly git t' sponge out a t'sack a'fore she suf'cates. I done kilt cats wi' them same drops."

"As soon as Frank gets her in the coach, we'll attend to that." Aurelia nodded at her faithful henchman, then stepped aside to allow the men to bundle Selma's inert form into the forward seat of the waiting coach. Aurelia climbed in and sat across from her daughter.

Dick jumped inside. Frank put up the steps and shut the door, then swung himself up and into the driver's box. He smacked the horses with the lash and slapped the reins on their steaming rumps. The startled horses leapt forward in their traces and the carriage bowled down the lane, through the gates, and onto the main road.

Inside, Dick carefully pulled the hood from Selma's ashen face and leaned his ear close to her parted lips while he braced himself against the bump and sway of the carriage. He held his breath for a moment, listening.

Aurelia, pretending unconcern, turned her eyes to survey the snow-covered trees outside the window. But finally, she grew impatient and pulled her gaze back to the interior of the coach.

"Well?"

"She still breathes, m'lady. An' 'er color's gittin' better." His deepset eyes glanced up at Aurelia, then quickly dropped again. "I'm thinkin' we might ought t' tie 'er 'ands and feet, if'n you don' wan' her runnin' off first chance she gits."

Reaching into her bag, Aurelia produced several lengths of strong cord and threw them across to Dick. "My very thoughts. Make sure the knots are tied well."

After almost sliding into the ditch on the first corner, Frank drove more carefully, easing his horses along the muddy, snow covered ruts, driving south.

Carl stepped down from the train into a light snowfall, then turned to help Amanda. From the corner of his eye, he saw a flying blur of blue and lifted his arms just in time to catch Anna as she leaped from the top step. She laughed when Carl shook her and set her on her feet. Unrepentant, she asked if she could do it again.

Ruth, more reserved, held to the rail and walked down the high steps in a very ladylike fashion. Reaching the platform, she moved up beside Amanda, took the blind woman's hand, and placed it on her own shoulder. For the last three weeks, she had been Amanda's eyes, guiding her everywhere. Carl could almost see the indelible bond that had formed between the serious little girl and her mischievous, adopted grandmother.

"Carl, I'm so excited to surprise Mother. I can hardly wait." Anna's childish accents reverberated between the wall of the train station and the gently steaming passenger car.

Before Carl could respond, the pounding of hooves caught his attention. Instinctively, he moved in front of Amanda and the girls. A split second later, a lathered horse plunged to a halt at the end of the station platform. Its rider threw himself off the swayback horse, charged up the steps, and pushed aside another man waiting at the window of the telegraph office.

Carl turned back toward the girls. Then he heard something that jerked his head up and made his blood run cold. Quickly, he told the girls to stay with Amanda, then he raced toward the telegraph office.

"Talk slower, man. I can't understand a thing you're saying," growled the telegraph operator.

"Kidnappers." Charlie gulped for air and tried to speak slower. "Attacked Mr. Henson. Took Mrs. Wraxmore." He swallowed, then Carl had him by the shoulders and whirled him around.

"What did you say about Mrs. Wraxmore?"

Charlie cowered before the blazing light in Carl's eyes and lifted one arm as though to protect himself.

Carl shook him. "I'm not going to hurt you. My sister and I are taking care of her children. Now tell me what happened to Mrs. Wraxmore."

"Two men and a woman," Charlie gasped. "They kidnapped her. Beat Mr. Henson. Knocked him out. Blood all over the place." The distraught servant started rambling incoherently. "Thought he was dead. Children screaming. Mrs. Cutfield..."

Carl shook him until his teeth rattled. "Get ahold of yourself and tell me about the kidnappers!"

By now a curious crowd had gathered, but Charlie kept his eyes on Carl. He swallowed a couple of times, then spoke more slowly and distinctly.

"Drew—one of the children at the home—saw a big man, dressed real rough, red stocking cap, carrying Mrs. Wraxmore to a carriage outside the orphanage. She was all tied up in a sack. Said he threw her into a coach with a woman and another man. Then the carriage drove away."

"What did the woman and the other man look like?"

Charlie concentrated on the steely gaze and his mind steadied. "She was tall and slender, fancy clothes, moved real smooth, Drew said. The other man was same as the first, but no hat, just long, shaggy black hair."

"Did he see which way they turned when they left the gate?"

"Right. Drew said he watched 'em 'til they drove into the grove south of the Home." Charlie breathed again and his stocky frame started to shake from the passing adrenaline rush.

"One more question. When did this happen?" Carl held his breath, waiting for the answer.

"No more'n two hours ago. As soon as I heard, I came fast as I could to wire the sheriff."

"Do that." Carl's eyes bored into Charlie's, making sure he understood. "Then I need you to take my sister and Mrs. Wraxmore's daughters to the orphanage." He pointed to where Amanda still waited with Ruth and Anna. "Ask your Mrs. Cutfield to look after them until I return."

Charlie followed Carl's pointing finger with uncomprehending eyes.

"Do you understand?" Carl's commanding voice finally penetrated the fog shrouding Charlie's distraught mind. The handyman shook his head and his eyes were steadier when they looked back at Carl.

"Yes, sir. I understand. I'm sorry. I'm just that upset. We all loved Miss Selma. I would have gone after them, but the old nag ain't up to a race and I thought it best to..."

Carl interrupted. "You did the right thing. Just do as I say now." He turned to go, but Charlie grabbed his arm, pulling him up face to face.

"Who are you?"

"Carl Stanton."

"Are you going after them?"

"The devil could not stop me!" Carl threw over his shoulder as he pushed his way through the assembled crowd and raced away.

"Then God speed you, sir. And don't worry about your sister or the little ones!" Charlie shouted as he watched Carl leap down the steps and speed toward the livery stable across the muddy street.

When Carl disappeared through the wooden stable doors, Charlie took a deep breath and carefully dictated his message to the excited telegraph operator. That done, he hurried down the platform to where a blind woman waited with two little girls.

Carl had accompanied his Uncle Thomas to the orphanage twice before, both times on tours of inspection. He knew the road from Douglas led south to the orphanage. Past the gates, the road forked. One branch continued south, the other veered off to the east. Carl slowed his horse when he reached the orphanage and carefully studied the tracks coming out of the gate. He saw where a carriage had come from the east and turned into the gates. More snow had fallen in those tracks, less in the tracks left by Charlie's horse. The only other disturbance in the new-fallen snow were left by wheels over horse tracks, sinking deep into the snow covering the road, headed south. He saw where the carriage slid sideways upon turning the corner, then settled behind the racing horses.

Carl kicked his horse to a trot, his hat dipped down to protect his eyes from the falling snow. His gaze constantly shifted from the tracks on the ground to the next bend in the road. He found where one of the horses had almost gone down, skidding and slipping in the snow. The driver had obviously slowed the pace after that, for the weaving tracks settled into a straighter line. No other tracks marred the fresh layer of white and Carl followed them easily when they turned on the next road heading east.

His horse was almost spent when Carl rode past the first house on the outskirts of Bower, fifteen miles southeast of the orphanage. He lost the tracks of the carriage in the melee of traffic when he neared the center of town. He asked a man crossing the street where the nearest livery stable was, then rode there. He exchanged the brown horse from Douglas plus five dollars for a tall, sturdy dun that looked like he could run forever. He slapped his saddle on the new horse and asked the ostler if a coach had passed this way recently.

"Yup, stopped 'bout an hour ago. Changed all four horses. They was sweated up real bad. I hated to trade 'im horses when he don't care no better for 'em than that. But," he shrugged fatalistically, "that fancy woman in the carriage had enough money to change my mind."

"Which way did they go?" Carl tensed, waiting for the

answer.

"You're lucky there, ya see, 'cause I asked…on account o' the horses."

Carl's fingers itched to reach out and shake the man into talking faster.

"Said they was headed for the rail station in Billingsgate. I took the woman's money and figured they couldn't hurt them nags even if they ran 'em all the way. It's just 'nother four miles east o' here." The neat little man cocked his head sideways and peered closely at Carl as he cinched the saddle down and dropped the stirrup into place. "How come you want t' know so much, if ya don't mind me askin'?"

"The woman took something that belongs to me. I plan to get it back."

The man thought to speak again, but stopped when Carl leaped into the saddle and turned the dun east. Fear kept a chilling grip on Carl's heart as he spurred the horse to a breakneck speed, leaving the stunned ostler staring wide-eyed at the corral gate.

If they reached the rail station and boarded a train before he caught them, he would never find Selma. He had no idea who would kidnap a young mother; had no idea where they would take her, only that he had to find her before it was too late. Four miles. A quarter hour at top speed in this snow.

Carl's mind raced beyond his galloping horse, calculating how far the carriage was ahead of him. Muddy ruts and trampled snow forced him to slow his speed in many places. He was only marginally consoled knowing that the carriage would be traveling even slower.

Giant white flakes were falling heavily when Carl passed a sign announcing his arrival in Billingsgate, population 11,422. He slowed his horse to pass down the main street. When the Knightsbridge Stableyard came into sight, he slowed even further to peer at a black carriage parked in the yard. The tracks leading to its resting place were fresh in the snow. In the distance, a youth was leading a team of steaming horses through the massive doors into the barn.

Panic edged his frantic thoughts and he gigged the horse into a gallop for the last three blocks to the rail station. Ruthlessly, he yanked the dun to a sliding stop. He leaped from the saddle, dropping the reins as he raced up the steps.

The last car of a slowly moving train cleared the end of the platform, headed east, as Carl skidded to a halt at the ticket agent's window. He banged on the glass, but kept his eyes on the train. No one came to the window. He looked inside and all was dark. A quick glance at the schedule posted beside the window told him the train just leaving the station was the last one out that day. And its final destination was written in bold letters: New York City, New York.

CHAPTER THIRTY

Thomas Mason's driver pulled his horses to a stop and turned to watch. Frederick Bronson, Mr. Mason's bodyguard, jumped out of the carriage, then turned, lifted out the wheelchair, and carried it up onto the porch. When he returned to the vehicle, he scooped Mr. Mason into his massive arms and carried him up to the waiting chair, much as a mother would carry a large child. Once Mason was settled in the chair, Duncan, his valet, laid a heavy rug across the shriveled legs. After Frederick lifted down the bags that were tied to the roof, the driver told the horses to 'git up' and headed for the stable.

Duncan held the door open while Fred pulled the wheelchair over the threshold. By then, several children had appeared and Mrs. Cutfield sailed out of her office to see what the commotion was all about.

"Mr. Mason?" Shock held Mrs. Cutfield frozen where she stood.

"It's a pleasure to see you looking so well, my dear Mrs. Cutfield." Mason dismissed Duncan and Fred, who headed to the kitchen area and the room Mason habitually used when he visited the orphanage.

"Why... was I expecting you?" Mrs. Cutfield racked her memory for any reason Mr. Mason should be visiting the orphanage, but could find none.

"No. I came here to speak with one of your employees. A Mrs. Wraxmore." Mason smiled with relish at the shocked expression that overpowered Mrs. Cutfield's normally placid expression and drained it of all color. Then his own face underwent a similar transformation as Amanda shuffled out of the library.

"Amanda?"

"Is that you, Uncle Thomas?" She moved further into the hallway, her cane tapping rhythmically from side to side. "I thought I heard your voice."

"What on earth are you doing here?" The gruff edge was back in his voice.

"I came here with Carl and Anna and Ruth." Amanda's wide eyes looked blankly over Thomas's head as she spoke.

"Is Carl here, too, then?"

"No... not right now."

"I thought he might be... he wasn't in town when I left." Thomas felt stunned and it took a moment for his mind to come back on an even keel. "No matter. Now, if you don't mind, I'd like to meet Lady Wraxmore. Is she busy or...

"Lady Wraxmore?" Mrs. Cutfield moved to stand before Thomas and searched his eyes carefully.

"Yes. I understood she was employed by Mr. Henson to sew clothes for the children here."

"Mrs. Selma Wraxmore works here. But... I don't think..."

"Good. Good." Thomas' face reflected his eagerness. "Well, don't stand there staring as though I'm a complete stranger. Call the woman! I believe she may be in some danger..."

Thomas stopped dead and his face paled at the stricken look on Mrs. Cutfield's face.

Before anyone could speak, a battered and disheveled Mr. Henson stepped out of Mrs. Cutfield's office and walked gingerly across the floor toward him. Thomas stared in shock at the dried blood that stained the front of Henson's shirt and spots where several buttons had been ripped away. One hand held a bloody cloth to the side of his bruised head above one eye that was swollen completely shut.

"Uncle Thomas!" The autocratic shipping baron twisted his ashen face to look at Amanda. "Selma...Lady Wraxmore... was abducted this morning!"

The dun shied when Carl leaped from the platform and grabbed for the reins. His rider barely had a foot in the stirrup when the wide-eyed horse leapt forward, pounding full speed after the departing train. The horse caught fire beneath his rider's hands and threw his whole heart into the race. His flashing strides carried him across the treacherous ground at a dangerous speed, but he gained on the train; quickly at first, then less and less as the train increased its own momentum.

The dun's nose came even with the platform on the last car, then his saddle, and under the frantic urging of the rider, his rump. Suddenly, Carl jerked the horse sideways toward the train, forcing the horse dangerously close to the murderous railroad ties where the horse could trip and break a leg, where a false step would likely spell death for both horse and rider.

Suddenly, the tiring animal stumbled beneath him and went down at the same instant that Carl launched himself toward the railing encircling the last platform of the train. Pain lanced through his ribs when all his weight smashed on the thin, metal rail. Desperately, Carl clung to the frozen steel with both hands and struggled to gulp air back into his bruised lungs.

Finally, one booted foot swung up and over the rail. Slowly, straining every muscle, he pulled the rest of his body up and over, crashing in a heap on the hard, cold steel of the platform.

Paralyzed for long moments, Carl watched his breath wisping away on the frigid wind. At last he struggled to his knees and turned to look back. The dun lay motionless, half on, half off the railroad tracks. The train sped on into the night as a fretful snow squall quickly moved to obscure the tragic scene. Carl felt a stab of desperate grief for the faithful beast and stared harder through the gathering fog.

Suddenly, the dun's head moved. Seconds before the fog shrouded him completely, the horse surged to his feet. He shook his head and turned to stare after the train as though sad to be left behind. In a whoosh of trailing smoke and fog, he disappeared and Carl slowly rose to his feet.

One hand rubbed his bruised ribs while the other dusted chunks of packed snow from his coat and pants. When he finally stepped through the door into the warm compartment, a conductor in uniform and peaked cap turned from where he was checking tickets and hurried down the center aisle toward him.

Carl only barely managed to sooth the man's flustered sensibilities, and that by purchasing a ticket from him. He apologized for catching the train so late, then excused himself and left the conductor staring after him with a confused frown on his face.

Carl moved slowly down the aisle, giving each passenger a quick, thorough inspection. The first and second car proved clueless, as did the dining car. When he reached the sleeping cars, a dawning realization chilled him. Even if Selma and her abductors were on this train, it might be very difficult to find her without opening every compartment door. And to do that would incite the wrath of every passenger and conductor aboard the train. He could think of no quicker way of getting thrown bodily from the train. Frustrated, he tried to curb his impatience and took up residence in the dining car.

Criminals or not, the people who kidnapped Selma had to eat. And it was four days to New York. They had to come out of hiding some time. He planned to not sleep, all the way to New York, if need be.

He was making good on his intentions, and the second crew of waiters had begun whispering and staring at him as though he meant to steal the silver, when a rough looking man opened the door from the sleeping cars, and stepped into the dining car.

Instinctively, Carl knew this was one of the men he sought. Surreptitiously, he took note of the red stocking cap that failed to hide strands of long, dark, greasy hair above a rough, brown, tweed coat stretched over massive shoulders.

Carl had done more than his share of boxing in the lakeside gym near his office. And the boxing master told Carl he displayed to good advantage. But he was under no misconception. If he were to fight this man, Carl would need a strong advantage, or he and Selma would both be lost. And the man from the orphanage had said there were two men.

Carl fretted impatiently while Red Cap slouched in a booth and drank coffee as though he had nowhere to go. Finally, a waiter brought two bags and set them on the table in front of Red Cap. Red Cap paid the waiter, lifted the bags, and headed back toward the sleeping car. Carl counted to three, then slipped out of his booth and followed.

By the time he stepped into the sleeping car, Red Cap

had disappeared. Carl sprinted forward, then jerked to a stop when he heard the latch on the door of the last compartment click shut. Squinting down the shadowy hallway, Carl held his breath until he was sure no one was coming out of the last compartment. Then he headed back to the dining car, in search of a conductor.

Ten minutes later, Carl opened the door to a room two doors from where he suspected Selma was imprisoned. Alone in the private room, he paced back and forth like a caged tiger, trying to formulate his next step. His biggest fear was that they might slip off the train without his knowing. If that happened, Selma would be lost to her daughters—and to him—forever.

Carl dimmed the lamp until the room was bathed in shadow. He propped the door ajar just enough to enable him to see and hear any commotion in the hallway, then flung himself down on the bunk to watch and listen.

Half an hour later, Carl was back on his feet and pacing again. Moments later, a lancing pain in the palm of his right hand revealed where his tightly clenched fingers had dug holes in the skin. He sucked in a ragged breath and forced his clenched fists to relax. Still, he felt like a watch spring, wound tight enough to explode.

Fifteen tense minutes later, Carl was considering and discarding increasingly more foolhardy ways of crashing into their room. Finally unable to wait longer, he opened the door and stepped into the hall. But the sudden opening of another door sent him scurrying back into his compartment.

Carl pressed his back rigid against the wall and peered through the slim crack in the doorway. His breathing froze when a woman stepped out of the very door that consumed his thoughts. Treading right on her heels came a man who could have been Red Cap's taller, swarthier cousin. Carl watched the man move forward, then shifted his eyes back to the woman. He felt vaguely disturbed by something familiar in the way the woman moved. Then she was past his door.

The woman was tall and slender, wearing fancy clothes, and she moved real smooth—wasn't that the way the caretaker from the orphanage had described her?

Carl shoved his hat onto his head, counted ten, then stepped into the hallway. For an instant, he peered longingly at the closed door of the last compartment. Taking a deep breath, he turned away and followed the odd couple toward the dining car.

The aroma of cooking food assaulted his senses the moment Carl stepped into the dining car, reminding him that he had eaten nothing since early morning. Quietly, he slipped into the booth nearest the door. Satisfied that the man and woman he was following would have to pass him to get to the sleeping car, he relaxed enough to signal a waiter and order a meal.

The woman and her companion settled into a booth in the mid-section of the railcar where they sipped at cups of tea. Several other diners finished their meals and exited the dining car until the only other occupant was a slender, western gent. The cowboy's face was effectively hidden by a newspaper held before his eyes and a battered, dun-colored cowboy hat pulled low on his forehead.

Carl glanced at the stranger several times, but could never get a clear look at the man's face. He sensed something furtive, almost devious, about the way the man kept his face hidden. He figured the cowboy was the sleeper; the ace any good gambler likes to have up his sleeve. Him against three men and one woman. The odds were getting worse.

When the waiter arrived with his food, Carl ignored the stranger and attacked the steak and fried potatoes set before him. After the first bite, Carl wolfed down the food. But though he rarely looked up from the plate, his attention never wavered from the woman and her companion.

When they pushed their cups aside and prepared to leave, Carl touched his napkin to his lips, stood, and dropped a tip on the table. He flashed a glance sideways and saw the paper in front of the western gent twitch back into place. No doubt about it; the cowboy was a sleeper.

Slowly, Carl moved along the aisle toward the kidnappers. The woman was walking toward him, her henchman following faithfully two steps behind. When Carl was six feet away, she raised her luminous eyes to his. Shock drained the blood from his face and his slack jaw threatened to drop open. Gliding confidently toward him, wearing a supremely confident look on her face, was an older version of the woman he was determined to rescue.

Her long, silken skirt rustled gently as she drew nearer. Jewels sparkled from her ears, neck, and fingers. A subtle hint of perfume greeted him before she did. A feline grin tilted the painted lips as her eyes met and held his for a breathless moment. In one, smooth movement her gaze traveled suggestively down the length of his body, then slowly back up. A provocative smile lit her eyes, signaling she was pleased with what she saw. Her pace had slowed as she came abreast of him, and she almost stopped while her glittering, emerald eyes bored straight into his. Carl felt himself helplessly drawn into the magnetism of her gaze for one incredible moment.

Then, just as suddenly as the spell had been cast, it shattered. Carl blinked his eyes as he realized that much of the woman's ravaged beauty was now the product of elaborate makeup. He could read the years of debauchery in deep lines etching her face and heavy bags beneath her eyes. Though skillfully disguised, they still displayed eloquent testimony to a life spent in dissipation.

"Excuse me." She purred as she moved to step past Carl in the narrow aisle. He turned to watch and she flashed him a calculating smile while her eyes measured the effect she might have had on him. Apparently pleased with what she saw, her eyes flashed once more, then she turned away.

Carl let out the breath he had been holding only to look up and find himself staring into the flinty glare of the hulking man following her. Unless he was mistaken, he had just read a death threat in the man's cold, menacing stare.

A door banged open and a corpulent, middle-aged woman sailed through the entrance at the opposite end of the dining car. The flower-covered hat she wore was every bit as wide as her hips. Bright lipstick outlined her full lips and served to emphasize the set of soft, double chins supported by a stiff lace collar. As Carl stared at her, he was reminded of nothing so much as a Spanish galleon sailing on the high seas with full canvas aloft. Her wide eyes and mobile mouth hinted at a good sense of humor coupled with a loquacious disposition.

Carl would have paid no more attention but for the interesting fact that her eyes coursed around the room until she spotted the man hiding behind the newspaper. Instantly, a gaze of longing flickered in her eyes and curved her bright lips. She carefully wedged herself into a booth at the other end of the car and tried to appear nonchalant, despite the longing glances she cast at the cowboy over her menu card.

Ideas had been whirling through Carl's mind as he contrived and discarded increasingly desperate ways to cut down on the odds. But now, as he moved out of the dining car, he smiled at a brash idea rapidly taking shape in his mind.

Back in his room again, Carl spent some effort composing a note. When he was finished, he reread his handiwork and nodded approval. Shoving it into his shirt pocket, Carl began to pace again, unprepared to wait much longer. Over and over, he discarded ways of getting into the room to assure himself that Selma was actually being held there. If she was not there... He would not, could not allow himself to believe he had lost her trail. Selma had to be in that room.

His curiosity about the older woman's possible relation to Selma merely added more questions for which Carl had no answers. The next stop came and went but no one from room eight exited the train.

Unable to stay cooped up in the small space any longer, Carl started pacing the hallway, hoping for an opportunity to see into their room. He had just begun his third lap when the door to number eight suddenly opened and both of the men stepped into the hallway, headed away from Carl toward the dining car. Carl was too far away from the door to catch a glimpse inside before the door closed again.

Carl followed the two men at a distance and watched them enter the dining car where they sat down at the same booth the woman had used earlier. Almost immediately, the waiter served coffee. When he turned away, the man with the long, black hair produced a flask from a coat pocket and poured some of its contents into his cup. Then he sloshed some into Red Cap's cup.

Carl looked beyond the hulking pair. The cowboy was still hunkered in his corner behind the newspaper and the plump woman was nibbling on a sweet roll. Carl stepped into the dining car just as the waiter turned toward him. Beckoning him forward, Carl whispered something in the man's ear. At the same time, he pressed the note he had prepared, along with a coin, into the waiter's palm. Not a muscle twitched on the waiter's face, but an infinitesimal nod told Carl all he needed to know.

Once out of the dining car, Carl rushed back along the corridor until he stood before the door to number eight. He sucked in a deep breath then knocked gently on the door. Nothing. He knocked again, louder.

Suddenly, the door flew open and Aurelia Klintenberg stood before him. Her look of surprise melted into something more devious and Carl was reminded of a snake he'd once seen in a cage. Slowly, methodically, it hypnotized a quivering mouse into frightened paralysis before launching its deadly strike. Though Carl did not move his eyes from Aurelia's once-beautiful face, his whole concentration was on the room behind her.

Aurelia arched a finely penciled brow and her voice purred from lips the color of a crimson rose. "Hmm, tall, handsome, and silent. What a delightful combination."

Suddenly, Carl saw what he was looking for. He paused only an instant while he glanced toward the dining car. The hall was empty. In one lightning move, he grabbed the seductive woman and hustled her bodily into the compartment, kicking the door shut behind him.

She made a hissing sound and lashed out savagely with her foot, delivering a nasty kick to Carl's left shin. In retaliation, he threw her unceremoniously onto the bench seat, then bent to rub his aching leg. Cautiously, he studied the seething woman as she struggled to sit up, watching her narrowed eyes shoot daggers of hate.

"Get out of here," she fairly spit at him. "You have no right to be in this room."

Carl's eyes stayed locked on the furious woman as he moved to the upper bunk on the other side of the narrow room. His finger touched a strip of blue material that protruded from the crack in the closed bunk. Then he yanked on the handle and the bed popped open. His pent-up breath came out with a whoosh as Selma tumbled down, all trussed up, to lay unmoving on the exposed bunk. Her eyes were closed. She made no sound, even when he pulled the gag from her mouth. An eternity crept by before he saw her chest rise and knew that she was alive.

Cold hatred blossomed in his heart as he glared at Aurelia. A thrill of premonition raced down his spine at the look in her eyes and he realized she would stick a knife in him or shoot him if she found any weapon at hand.

"Why?" The question ground between his teeth.

"I'm her mother!" The words hissed between her teeth. "I'm taking her back to England. She belongs to me. You have no right to interfere."

Her voice rose to a screech as she launched off the seat, hands thrust out like attacking claws aimed for his eyes.

Carl caught her arms and held her away. "If you were only a man... " He growled the words as he threw Aurelia back on the bench seat. "Don't move again or I swear I'll forget you're a woman!"

His naked threat made Aurelia's eyes gape open, blazing fire and anger shooting barbs across the room.

"If looks could kill…" Carl uttered a mirthless laugh then turned to the unconscious woman.

Quickly, he untied the cords that bound Selma's swollen hands. Impotent fury wrenched a knot in his guts at the sight of the bleeding bands carved into her pale wrists. When he glanced again toward the older woman, she involuntarily flinched and staggered back at the naked wrath burning in Carl's cold, silver eyes.

"You wouldn't dare!" Any beauty Aurelia still retained deserted her, replaced by an ugly sneer that matched the dark, frightened hatred in her eyes.

Carl whirled and reached for her hands. Suddenly, she unleashed her pent-up fury, clawing and kicking in her struggle to escape through the door. Carl wrestled brutally for a hold on the squirming body. At last, he threw her forcibly onto the floor and pinned her beneath him. His knees pressed into the small of her back as he ruthlessly trussed her up like a calf at a branding party. When he stood up again he was breathing heavily, but a savage grin curled one corner of his mouth as he surveyed his captive.

Suddenly, Aurelia opened her mouth to scream. But Carl had foreseen the intent and rammed a wadded handkerchief into her mouth. In a moment it was tied in place with the scarf from around her own neck. Satisfied, Carl lifted her easily and dropped her on the bench seat. Then he returned to Selma.

She was still unconscious. Quickly, he untied Selma's feet and lifted her down, laying her gently on the lower bench. Then he roughly hefted Aurelia, shoving her unceremoniously onto the hanging bunk.

Quietly, he inched open the door until he could peek down the hallway. Still empty. Carl shut the door and rifled through the only lady's bag in the compartment until he found what he was looking for. He held up the can of ether and a folded handkerchief and knew why Selma was still out like a light.

A devilish smirk twisted his features as he poured a few drops of the drug onto the handkerchief. When he turned to Aurelia, his eyes were blazing.

His frigid voice hissed between clenched teeth. "I never want to see you again. And I better never hear of you coming near Selma or her children — ever again!"

His voice chilled the air of the room and an answering shaft of fear shone in Aurelia's eyes. "Crawl back under whatever rock you came out of, lady, and don't you ever come back. Or I promise — you won't wake up next time."

Aurelia's narrowed eyes shot open wide and she thrashed futilely against the powerful hand that smashed the damp cloth over her nose. Bare seconds passed before her eyes fluttered back in her head and she relaxed completely.

Carl dropped the cloth and swiftly closed the berth, hiding Aurelia where Selma had been. Kneeling beside Selma, he whispered her name as he gently shook her. But her head only lolled on her shoulders. Carl checked the hallway once more, then lifted Selma's limp body over his shoulder and stepped into the hall. He paused only long enough to lock the door before shutting it.

His heart rose into his throat until he had crossed the few feet to the door of his own room and carried Selma inside. Gently, he laid his burden on the seat and watched her in silence for several moments. Finally, Carl moved to the window and gazed out at the unblemished snow. He was not fooling himself by thinking they were out of danger yet. He considered it almost impossible to find a way to get them both off the train and safely away before they were caught by the two brutish bodyguards.

Ten minutes later, Carl felt the train begin to slow. A shrieking whistle pierced the air, announcing their arrival at another stop. Selma moaned and one hand flapped an indeterminate gesture as her head thrashed from side to side. Carl held his breath when her eyes fluttered open. Once. Twice. Then they shut and she was out again.

Rapidly, he cocooned her in the blankets from the bunk, making sure neither her head nor feet were showing. One final time he peeked out the door. The corridor was still empty. Carl raced toward the dining car, sliding to a halt just short of the door. He peered through the small window to where Red Cap and his companion were just rising from the booth. Once on their feet, they swayed a bit more than the movement of the train justified, and Carl hoped they had liberally imbibed from their flask. Red Cap flopped back into the seat for a moment and shook his head slowly back and forth.

The cowboy had lowered his paper and was carefully watching Red Cap. The waiter was standing by the corpulent woman's table, offering her something from a small silver tray.

Carl waited no longer. He whirled and sped back to his room. Lifting Selma over his shoulder, he bolted back into the corridor. Just then, an elderly couple stepped out of their compartment at the end nearest the dining car. Their luggage was already sitting on the floor of the hall. Carl turned left and strode quickly down the length of the rail car, through the door and into the next car, through it and onto the platform of the last sleeping car.

The train was slowing rapidly and Carl could see the station platform ahead when he peeked around the edge of the baggage car.

Selma started making small movements and nonsense sounds as the train came even with the first pole of the station. Carl gauged the speed of the train and stepped down onto the dimly lit platform. He stumbled, but caught himself and hustled around the corner of the rail offices and out of sight of the sleeper car. It was only a matter of minutes, he knew, before Red Cap and his hulking cohort would be pounding after him. And Carl didn't fool himself into thinking he could survive an open battle with both men.

Black clouds hung low above the neatly aligned buildings. Scattered banks of thick, gray fog swirled in layers that hid a window here, a door there, and cast dark, threatening shadows haphazardly along the street. One shaft of light pierced the gloomy night and threw its pale light on the sign over the livery stable.

Carl hurried across the mucky street, slipping and sliding in the slowly freezing mud. His boots skidded sideways. He nearly went down, but caught himself just in time to slam against the open door of the stable.

His lungs were heaving from exertion and he leaned against the door long enough to catch his breath. Then he stumbled inside and turned back to peer around the door through the deepening fog. No one was following them. Yet.

Two horses and a mule sleepily shifted feet in the first three stalls, but the fourth was empty except for a deep layer of fresh straw. Carl hustled into it. Selma's body slipped from his shoulder as he lowered her to the straw. Pulling back the blankets from her face, he assured himself that she was still breathing. Tendrils of golden hair lay across her face and Carl gently swept them aside as he called her name. She stirred and her eyes fluttered open. They gazed at him without seeing, then slowly closed again. Even wrapped in the blankets, she started to shiver. He tucked the blankets close to her chin and turned to go in search of the ostler.

He had barely stepped around the edge of the stall when

a pile driver slammed into the side of his head. He hadn't seen the blow coming. It rocked him clear to the heels of his boots and sent him flying through the air to land heavily in a pile of straw.

Drunkenly, he shook his head, trying to focus his eyes as Red Cap charged down on him. A giant boot swung at him through the air just as he threw himself sideways. The wicked blow skimmed across his ribs, then he was rolling over and over. Like a cat, he scrambled to a stop and leapt to his feet.

Red Cap charged in like a mad bull, swinging his meaty fists. Carl waited until the last second, then sprang sideways, crashing his left elbow into Red Cap's back just below the ribs as he hurtled past. The thick coat absorbed much of Carl's blow, but the man still cried out in pain as he stumbled forward. In one lightning move, Carl whirled around and whipped his left foot into the broad butt, shooting Red Cap forward to crash headlong into a closed stall door.

Carl bounced back and forth on the balls of his feet as he warily eyed the bigger man who lay groaning in the straw. From out of nowhere, a stunning blow crashed into Carl's back, clubbing him to the floor and driving all the air from his lungs.

Warning bells clanged through his brain, screeching that Red Cap's friend had arrived, intent on pulverizing Carl's body. Gasping for air, Carl staggered to his feet and whirled to face his second antagonist.

The man was a giant and coming in for a second punch.

Carl backed away until the half door of a stall stopped him. From the corner of his eye, Carl saw Red Cap stagger to his feet, his face twisting into a mask of fury and hate. Deliberately, Red Cap reached into his coat and drew out an ugly gun that glinted black in the dim light. The giant stopped to watch. Carl instantly froze when the barrel leveled at his chest.

Time stopped for one heartbeat. Then another. Carl saw his final breath in that black bore of steel.

A sudden flicker of movement jerked all their heads sideways. Selma had struggled to the entrance of the stall where Carl had left her. She stood there now, horrified at the tableau before her. In that split second, Carl thought how deathly pale was her face, how helpless she looked with the single blanket drooping from her shoulders.

In that same instant, the cowboy from the train came pounding through the stable door and slid to a stop. His battered cowboy hat was missing, but a massive pistol extended from one slender hand. Then pandemonium erupted in a flash.

Red Cap and the giant whirled back just as Carl threw himself sideways. The report of two shots rang in time with a searing flame that bored a blazing trail through the flesh just above Carl's left hip.

Carl hit the floor rolling. The impossibility of surviving such unequal odds turned his blood to ice. Ignoring the fire in his side, he sprang to his feet and turned to face his three attackers. Shock stopped him cold. He swayed drunkenly for a moment and watched as Red Cap thrashed around in the straw, trading punches with the cowboy. The cowboy's gun had disappeared, but a streak of blood staining the ground beneath the struggling men told Carl the second shot had not been fired at him. Momentarily frozen in place, Carl found himself fascinated by the dark patchwork designs staining their coats as they rolled over and over.

Sluggishly, Carl shook his head, trying to clear away the haze blurring his eyes. A flicker of movement startled him and he shifted his gaze just in time. He launched himself backward into the stall with the mule just as a pitchfork slashed the air where his head would have been. The black-haired, black-bearded giant charged straight for him, the pitchfork thrust out in front. The terrified mule screeched and jerked its hindquarters back and forth. Red Cap's companion jabbed at the terrified animal and it slammed up against the far wall of the stall. But the diversion gave Carl just enough time to scurry over the side of the stall.

Carl raced out of that stall and right into the other pair of fighters. Carl smashed his right toe into Red Cap's ribs on his way past. With a blood-curdling scream, Red Cap loosened his chokehold on the smaller man and the cowboy rolled free. Carl didn't have time to help anymore. The giant was only inches away with his pitchfork when Carl whirled around the center post and faced his opponent.

The two men circled each other and the solid centerpost.

From the corner of his eye, Carl could see Red Cap and the cowboy doing the same dance two stalls away. His own assailant stood half a foot taller than Carl and looked to weigh at least another sixty pounds. The man reminded Carl of nothing so much as a hulking bear with beady black eyes sunk deep beneath overhanging brow ridges. The balled fists gripping the pitchfork handle exhibited layered scars and calluses from innumerable fights. Carl suspected this bear had probably won most of them. His throat was suddenly dry and he swallowed hard.

Slowly, they circled on the dirt floor, each weighing his opponent. Suddenly, the bear charged and Carl leaped sideways, delivering a powerful jab to the man's ribs as he passed. The bear whirled much faster than a normal man his size. But Carl was ready. He grabbed the shaft of the pitchfork and dropped to the floor, bearing down on it with all his weight. At the same instant, he swung his right leg against both his opponent's legs, sweeping the man's feet out from under him. The bear dropped the pitchfork and fell with a thud. Immediately, he writhed backwards to grab Carl's foot as Carl tried to scramble to his feet.

One giant heave flung Carl up and backward. He landed with a jarring impact on the hard packed floor. Forgetting about the pitchfork, the bear charged across the floor and flung his entire body on top of Carl. But he crashed onto bare floor. Carl had rolled to the side and now heaved himself to his feet. He whirled around, but the bear was already up and swinging. Carl felt dizzy at the speed the huge man moved. One beefy paw connected on the side of Carl's head and sent him sprawling through mounds of used straw. Dizzy and nausious, Carl struggled up onto his hands and knees, shaking his head to clear away the incessant ringing.

Then a shadow fell across Carl's hands. Through the haze, he saw a foot swinging toward his head and threw himself sideways. The blow missed his skull by a hairsbreadth. It collided with his shoulder and sent him sprawling across the floor again. Carl rolled over and over until he slammed up against a closed stall door. Staggering painfully, he pushed himself unsteadily to his feet.

The bear was charging toward him again. Head down, murder glaring from his beady eyes, arms extended way out to the side. Carl knew that if those huge arms ever closed on him, it was only a matter of seconds before he would lay in the dirt, broken and dying.

In one final, desperate surge Carl leaped into the air and grabbed onto a leather harness yoke hanging from the center rafters. One sweeping motion pulled his legs up then he crashed them down into the Bear's upturned face with all the power in his legs. The man let out a blood-curdling scream and toppled like a tree, writhing on the ground, blood oozing between the fingers covering his face.

Carl dropped heavily to the ground and staggered sideways to catch his balance. For several seconds he stared numbly at his antagonist, his lungs heaving and gasping for air.

An errant whisper of sound made him duck just as a wickedly curved knife slashed through the air and laid open a wide gash through the muscles across Carl's chest. Carl jerked his head around. In a split second, he saw the cowboy collapsed in a heap against the far wall and Red Cap, hatred gleaming from his eyes, preparing to strike again. Red Cap bellowed as he charged, the knife slashing through the air. Suddenly, a violent rage exploded in Carl's mind.

Launching himself high into the air, Carl whipped his right leg out to full extension as he whirled through the air. His boot heel caught Red Cap at the base of the throat with a sickening thwack. The knife clattered to the floor as Red Cap collapsed into a mound amidst the straw. He twitched for a few seconds, then lay still.

Carl stood rigid, head down, panting in the middle of the stable. Slowly, his legs buckled and he sank to his knees. His eyes moved down to his belt. For the first time, he noticed the blood soaking through his shirt and down his pant leg, almost to his ankle. His hand moved sluggishly to the gory hole torn by the bullet while a far corner of his mind reminded him that he'd been shot.

A groan caught his flagging attention. It took a great deal of effort to turn his head. The cowboy was up on his hands and knees, rocking back and forth, moaning. Carl struggled to stand again, then collapsed completely.

Suddenly, Selma was there. Her arms wrapped around

his neck as her lips pressed kisses to his face, crying words that he could not understand. He knew a moment of intense fulfillment as he wrapped an arm around her and pulled her close. Then his sight grew dim. The floodgates opened and a sea of pain washed over him in mounting waves. It was a struggle just to look past Selma as a crowd of men rushed through the stable door.

The cowboy had finally managed to pull himself to his feet, using a halter hanging from a hook on the wall. He tottered to the center of the floor where he stood between Selma and the crowd, swaying drunkenly, his head wobbling back and forth. He lifted one hand to run shaky fingers through his tousled hair just as a constable skidded to a stop beside him. The shocked man's eyes widened at the sight of four battered and bleeding men.

The men and the room spun faster and faster until Carl couldn't keep his eyes open any longer. He felt as though he was falling into a deep, dark well. He could hear the cowboy talking somewhere far away. Then closer, Selma's voice pierced the fog closing around his mind.

"Please, Carl. Don't leave me..."

Selma's voice, begging him to stay, while all he wanted to do was go to sleep. But he couldn't go without telling her. Desperately, he struggled to open his eyes one last time as he mouthed the words, "I love y..."

Then he slumped against the woman holding him and the hovering blackness descended and shut out the world.

Still queasy from the effects of the ether, Selma struggled to support the weight of Carl's unconscious body. But even though she held him tight, she could merely slow, not stop his descent to the straw-covered dirt floor. Through the fog clouding her brain, she recognized the danger he was in and was afraid Carl would bleed to death.

She cried out for a doctor. In the next second, the cowboy was beside her. He ripped Carl's shirt open, laying bare the bloody wounds. Selma was horrified as more blood slowly pulsed onto the ground beneath his body. The stranger ruthlessly shoved his wadded up handkerchief against the bullet wound and pushed. Carl groaned though his eyes did not open. Bile rose in Selma's throat and she scuttled sideways and barely reached a corner of the stall before she threw up.

Suddenly, the sheriff was shouting orders. He pulled Selma further aside as several men hustled in and lifted Carl from the floor. Hurriedly, they carried him out through the barn doors. Selma's head whirled sickeningly. She was shivering violently and started to collapse, but the sheriff lifted her to her feet. Selma was grateful for the arm he locked around her waist. He was a big man and supported most of her weight as he guided her in their wake.

Once outside the door, they moved into a bank of fog and Selma lost all sense of time and direction. She felt as though the sheriff had been half dragging, half carrying her for hours when they finally came to a door with 'Doctor

Preston' neatly printed on the shingle hanging over the doorway.

Feeling thoroughly befuddled, Selma looked up to see
the doctor himself throw open the door. He took one swift
glance at Carl's unconscious body and turned to lead the way
into his examining room.

"Well, don't just stand there, bring him on in," he bellowed.

The doctor went to work quickly while the sheriff
propped Selma beside the door and moved closer to watch.
Without his warmth and support, she started shivering
uncontrollably again, then slowly sank to the floor.

The doctor threw one glance over his shoulder at her
ashen face and spoke to the sheriff. "Look's like she's about all
done in." His head nodded in Selma's direction. "You go wrap
her in a blanket, lay her down, and prop her feet up—on that
old couch by the wall." His head indicated a faded, green sofa.
Then he returned his attention to the mangled flesh of Carl's
side.

The sheriff did as he was told, then left Selma to warm
up beneath a heavy layer of blankets.

"Well, doc. If you'll excuse me, there's a couple other
gentlemen I need to check on."

The doctor mumbled something, but never took his eyes
off of his work. The sheriff was gone almost an hour and
Selma was feeling toasty warm and much more awake by the
time he returned.

"Well, doc? What's the verdict? This guy gonna live?"

"I should think so." The doctor spoke as he rinsed his hands in a basin of water. "He's lost a lot of blood, but he was lucky. The knife wound is clean. Should heal fine. And the bullet passed right on through. Flesh wound, really, but nasty. No bones broken, though I should think these ribs are pretty well cracked." He indicated the livid bruising on the right side of Carl's chest above the bandage he had tied in place.

"He won't chew straight for a week." His shock of bright red hair nodded toward Carl's rapidly swelling jaw, cheek, and forehead," But his jaw is still in one piece."

"Looks like he's been through a meat grinder."

"He'll have a record quality shiner, but he looks worse than he is. I'm going to keep him here for a few days, make sure he gets to healing all right. Infection's his worst enemy, but with careful nursing, he ought to be up and around fairly soon." The doctor pulled a sheet and blanket up to Carl's chin and tucked his patient in securely.

"Good enough. Well, if you're done here, I'd appreciate it if you'd come on over to the jail. Both of them blokes that did this to 'im are locked up in a cell and bleedin' all over my floor. They were in pretty bad shape when I left. I'm thinking they're both gonna need more than a few stitches."

"Let me grab my coat and I'll come along right now."

Dr. Preston paused for a moment beside Selma and looked down at her. "Keep an eye on that young man for me while I'm gone." The smiling wink that accompanied his words warmed Selma's heart. "I won't be gone long."

Silently, Selma nodded then watched the sheriff and doctor pass out of the room. The door clicked shut. Gingerly, she stood up, holding one blanket wrapped around her shoulders and waist. The room spun. She was forced to hold tight to the arm of the sofa and wait while the room rotated twice. At last it settled into its proper balance and she took a cautious step forward. She looked across at Carl and wondered if she could walk that far without falling down.

Before she could move, the door opened again. This time it was the slender cowboy who stepped inside. Shoulder length blonde hair was slicked back from his weathered face. Fine lines from a lifetime spent in the sun radiated outward beside a pair of bright, darting brown eyes.

"My name's Ross, ma'am. Kirby Ross." He nodded at Selma as he stepped across to look down at Carl. Satisfied, he turned to face Selma.

"Thank you, Mr. Ross." The words seemed far too inadequate to express what she felt.

"My pleasure, ma'am." The cowboy blushed uncomfortably. His weathered face shaded to a dark red, emphasizing his own set of bruises. A jagged cut still bled a little at the corner of his mouth and his left eye was swollen almost shut.

"They would have killed him if you hadn't happened along when you did."

"Actually, ma'am, I didn't happen. I was late. I gotta apologize for that." He shuffled his boots, stared down at the floor, then looked back at Selma.

"I don't understand." Her head cocked sideways in bewilderment.

"I was sent to watch out for you."

"Sent? To watch out? For me?" Selma searched the dark, fathomless eyes for an answer.

"Yeah. Mr. Mason kinda figured somethin' like this might happen. My boss, Gunther Strauss, sent me to the orphanage to keep an eye on you. But I was late. I got there just after they grabbed you — but a mite afore this young-ster." He indicated Carl with a nod of his head.

"You know, he 'bout killed himself gittin' on the train. I don't know if the horse survived. Bravest thing I ever saw. Or the stupidest." Ross shook his head and smiled in awe at the memory.

Selma's head was reeling. She felt out of sync with the rest of the world and couldn't seem to find the rhythm to get back in step. "Wait. Start from the beginning. Mr. Mason? From the orphanage? Why... did Mr. Mason... how... ?"

"I dunno know all the details. But seems Mr. Mason knew this woman Klintenberg was gunnin' for you. I was supposed to stay close and scare 'er off if'n she showed up at the orphanage." His shoulders shrugged. "After they kid-napped you, I followed 'em to the train station. But every-thing was movin' too fast for me to make a play and the odds were in their favor. So, I was sittin' there, plannin' my moves when this youngster comes barrelin' along and jumps in with both feet. He's the one popped the cork."

"Cork?"

"You'll have to ask him how he got you away. I didn't see that. But when I saw them two blokes from the livery stable suddenly get all excited and jump off the train, I knew somethin' was up. I headed off to follow 'em." His brow wrinkled at the memory. "The whole party probably wouldn't have turned off so bad, but I got waylaid myself when I went to get off the train."

"Waylaid?" Selma felt sure she was in some sort of dream.

"Yes, ma'am. I got up to follow those two fellas when they got off the train. All of a sudden, the biggest... I mean, a woman — a very large woman — grabs me and starts chatterin' away like I'm her long lost love."

Ross blushed at the memory and his eyes dropped to study the floor. "Seems somebody slipped her a note," one of his eyebrows quirked up as he rolled his eyes at Carl for a moment, "that gave her some... ideas... made her think I was... I mean..."

"I don't think you have to explain." Selma's eyes began to sparkle and she couldn't suppress a small chuckle at the cowboy's expense.

An answering smile lightened Ross' weathered face. "I felt that bad, having to break the poor woman's heart. But she wouldn't take 'no' for an answer. I finally had to climb out a window. And the bloomin' woman grabbed my hat when I made a break for it!" Ross ran the fingers of his left hand through his hair.

"Ah might have to talk to that young man of yours when he's feelin' better. I liked that hat. I surely did. Took me near five years to break it in to fit my head. Howsomever, chances are he thought I was one of them and figured to cut down on the odds."

"It was an infamous thing to do." Selma glanced at Carl's immobile face, then back to the cowboy. "But you did arrive — and just in time. He's lucky to be alive."

"He is that, ma'am. Those two brutes had murder in their hearts."

Selma's voice chilled. "Why didn't you shoot the second man, too? You could have prevented... all of this." She waved her hand at Carl, at the bloody rags and clothes thrown in a pile and the ceramic basin full of bloody water beside the bed.

The cowboy dropped his head for a moment while he scratched the back of his neck. Finally, he peered up at Selma from beneath his eyebrows.

"I thought about it. I surely did. But I was thinkin' this young fella wouldn't have appreciated that none, ma'am. I figured he wanted to fight for his woman and he'd have been a sight disturbed if I didn't give him the pleasure."

Selma blushed furiously, completely stumped for words.

"However, I do apologize for not killin' that first fella right off. I thought the one bullet was plenty. Usually is. I was wrong. I miscalculated and it just about got us all killed.

Them two was tough as whip leather and mean all the way through."

He stared hard at Selma, then finally nodded as though at an inward thought. "But I've always said — and I'll stick by it to the day I die — when a woman goes bad, ain't no man can hold a candle to the evil thing her heart becomes. And that Klintenberg woman... well, you'll forgive me for sayin', but she's about the worst I've ever seen."

Selma blushed, at a loss for words. But Kirby just nodded, then stepped toward the door. "Take good care of that young'un. He's a keeper. Well, ma'am, I got one more chore to finish, so I'll be gittin' along."

Kirby Ross lifted his fingers in a brief salute and passed silently out of the room. Selma was left alone staring dumbfounded at the closed door. Several minutes passed before she finally shook herself out of the trance. Slowly, she crossed the room to stand beside Carl where he lay prone on the high table.

Trapped beneath the blanket, both of his arms lay straight down beside him. His face was very pale between the bruises and he reminded her too much of a dead person laid out for burial. His chest rose and fell in slow, rhythmic movements, but that was all the sign of life he gave.

She stared at him a long time, considering who this man was; what he was... From the depths of her memory, a picture flashed through her mind of the first time she had looked into his eyes from across a busy street. A tender smile lifted one corner of her mouth when she thought of the Christmas presents he had brought to her daughters before they had even met. The beautiful music carousel, though destroyed by fire, would forever live in her memory as a symbol of his kind and thoughtful nature.

She reached a tentative hand out and gently traced the line of his rough jaw from ear to chin. The skin was swollen and discolored. Tears welled up in her eyes when she recalled the dreadful fear that washed over her in the stable in those terrifying moments when she thought he might be killed. Second after second of stark terror forced her to realize just how much Carl had come to mean in her life. Hot tears trickled down her cheek, but this time she made no effort to stop them. Her fingers caressed the dark, curly hair that fell back from his brow, enjoying the rough texture of it between her fingers. Cautiously, she traced the bruise rapidly coloring and swelling from the right side of his head clear across his right eye.

A flicker of reflected light drew her attention to the bracelet on her wrist. Light from the lamp on the table had caught the ruby flame of the candle charm and turned it to glowing red. The heat from the tiny stone sparked a memory of Bertha, and Selma smiled as a chill rippled down her spine.

Slowly, deliberately, she bent and pressed her lips against a cut at the corner of Carl's mouth. His lips twitched. When she lifted her head, his left eye, the one he could still open, was wide and staring at her. She recognized a gentle fire blazing past his pain and into her soul. Slowly, his arms struggled to escape the confining blanket. Then his hands moved up until they gently held her shoulders, irresistibly drawing her closer. Tentatively, his lips touched hers and he tasted the salt from her tears.

"Selma Wraxmore," his deep, husky voice sent a shiver of electricity rippling up her spine.

"Yes, Carl Stanton?" She pressed a gentle kiss to his bruised cheek, then another to his chin.

"I think there is only one solution to this problem of yours." Carl felt he was drifting in a dream world and did not want to wake up.

"What problem is that?" Selma pressed a line of kisses to the livid bruise forming around his right eye.

"Where everyone you meet either robs you, tries to kiss you, or abducts you." Carl's voice was barely a whisper.

"Oh. That problem." She continued working her way across the bruises on his forehead and thrilled to the feel of his skin beneath her lips. "And what solution did you have in mind?"

"I think you need a full-time... guardian."

"Hmmm." Selma reveled in the sound of his voice. "Were you thinking of a guardian angel?"

"No. More the two-legged, no-winged, earth-bound type; the simple, ordinary kind who will be there every day to watch over you, keep you safe. A simple man who will love you with all of his heart and keep you safe for the rest of his life."

Selma froze at his words.

"And one more thing. You really don't want to live in Montana." Carl tightened his arms when Selma shivered.

"I don't?"

"No."

"Then where do I want to live?" Selma held her breath, as though she stood on the edge of a giant fissure in the center of the universe, knowing that if she once allowed herself to step through, her life — her soul — would never be the same.

"I have it on good authority that you want to live right here in Wisconsin."

"I do?"

"I'm sure of it!"

"Who said?"

"My future daughters — Ruth and Anna."

Selma gasped. Her eyes flew wide. Then she jumped when the door suddenly swung open behind her. She whirled around just as the sheriff stepped through the doorway.

CHAPTER THIRTY-ONE

Anna and Ruth were not told that their mother had been abducted. Mrs. Cutfield and Amanda agreed it would be better if the girls did not have to worry until they heard more news. Drew concurred, though it was hard to maintain his silence. It was even harder when Anna and Ruth decided to be his best friends and practically moved into his room.

Selma had shared stories of Drew with her daughters, but it amazed everyone at how quickly the three became fast friends. Anna and Ruth spent most of every day in Drew's room, which quickly became the social gathering spot of the orphanage. Other children gathered there out of curiosity to meet and play with Mrs. Wraxmore's daughters.

When they were alone with Amanda at night, Anna and Ruth wove dreams of their mother married to Carl, then adopting Drew to be their brother. Amanda could only listen in tearful silence and pray for Selma's deliverance.

But good things happened while Selma was away. The children of the orphanage soon discovered a fabulous story-teller in Amanda. It started the second day, completely by chance, with a short story she spun for the few children gathered in Drew's room. Her reputation spread quickly until she was spending hour after hour in the library, happily spinning captivating stories to an enthralled audience of wide-eyed children.

Late at night, when Anna and Ruth were sleeping peacefully, Amanda pondered her life and wondered why she'd never come here with Uncle Thomas. Gradually, she allowed herself to dream of returning here after her surgery. Unexpectedly, she now found herself surrounded by many, many children who needed the love she so desperately wanted to share. In Mrs. Cutfield she had discovered a soul mate and suddenly, a whole new world of possibilities laid open to brighten Amanda's future.

The eighth day after Selma's disappearance, Mrs. Cutfield stood by the door, watching Amanda captivate her wiggly audience. Along with the children, she listened to an adventure about a color-changing dragon trying to help a pair of unfortunate children. A fleeting shadow caught her attention and she glanced out of the window in time to see a buggy drive past. Softly, she tiptoed out of the room and closed the door. She was almost to the entryway when footsteps came pounding down the stairway.

Drew had seen the buggy drive up in front of the

orphanage from his perch beside the window of his room. He called Anna and Ruth to watch with him to see who would get out of the vehicle. He didn't recognize the man who gingerly stepped to the ground. Then the stranger turned to help a woman from the buggy and Drew's heart stopped as she turned her face up. Her eyes looked straight at the window of his room and she waved. His face split into a gigantic smile and his hand waggled frantically.

"It's Mrs. Wraxmore!" he shouted. "She's back!"

Suddenly Ruth and Anna shot off the bed. Trailing excited shrieks, they bolted out the door and across the hall, racing down the stairs. Both girls shot past a stunned Mrs. Cutfield and burst through the door just as Selma and Carl reached the top step of the porch. Without stopping, Anna and Ruth flung themselves into their mother's open arms, laughing, crying, and talking at the same time.

Mrs. Cutfield watched the reunion through an avalanche of tears. When her eyes moved to Carl's bruised face, her heart turned over at the gentle expression glowing from his silver-blue eyes; a mixture of love and pride, and something else she could not define. Feeling her gaze, he glanced over Selma's head at her and smiled.

Dashing away the tears, she moved forward, extending her hand. "Welcome to the Douglas County Orphanage, Mr. Stanton. I don't know if you remember me..."

"Of course I do, Mrs. Cutfield. Thank you for taking care of Ruth and Anna... " He paused as he looked past her toward the closed door.

"Yes, your sister is here. But I don't know if I'm ever going to let her leave. Amanda has become the main attraction in the library each afternoon. She has an amazing affinity for the children. Every day she tells story after story and the children love her. I love her!"

She chuckled at the shocked expression on Carl's face, then moved forward to hug Selma. At the same time, Ruth and Anna deserted Selma and charged into Carl's waiting arms.

"Are you all right, my dear?" she whispered, her voice tense in Selma's ear.

"Yes. Thank you." Selma moved her shining glance to hold Carl's eyes for several seconds as he stared past the little girls held in his arms. "Though, if it hadn't been for Carl..."

"I shudder to think." Mrs. Cutfield's face grew solemn as she held out her arms to usher them all out of the cold breeze and into the house, talking all the while.

"I confess that when Charlie got back from the telegraph office and told me Mr. Stanton had charged off in hot pursuit, my soul rested much easier than if we had been forced to rely only on the sheriff."

She shuddered in remembrance and turned her serious gaze to Carl. "None of us relaxed until we received your wire telling us Selma was safe. Thank you for that. It was very considerate."

Unexpectedly, her eyes fluttered and dropped. Her face

flushed in contrite discomfort as she shut the door and turned to face Selma. "I can't tell you how sorry I am that such a thing should have happened to you... here... " Tears burned her throat and she stopped speaking.

"Oh, my dear Mrs. Cutfield. This was no fault of yours. It was all my mother's plotting; none of yours."

"Mr. Henson told us he met her. I was that surprised when he finally told us all that happened. But still..."

"Let's not think of it any longer. I'm just happy to be back." Selma hugged her again, then stepped back, her eyes shining into those of her friend.

"Mommy." Anna was tired of listening to the adults talk and confused because none of it made any sense.

"Selma... ?" Suddenly, Mrs. Cutfield sucked in a breath and her head swiveled around to stare into Carl's shining eyes.

"Yes?" Selma could hardly keep from laughing, she was so happy.

"Mommy!" Anna and Ruth called at the same time. "Come see Drew. He's waiting for you upstairs."

"Are you... ?" Mrs. Cutfield began.

"Mommy... Carl... can we 'dopt Drew?" Anna begged and Ruth nodded in agreement.

"Yes." Carl and Selma answered at the same time.

The windy city was not living up to its name today. A gentle breeze urged the harbor smells a few blocks inland, then died completely, leaving the day brisk and sunny.

Amanda, her head swathed in snowy bandages, rode in her own wheelchair beside Thomas as two nurses pushed them along the paving stones through budding hospital gardens.

"I forgot how blue the sky is on a spring day." The awestruck smile on Amanda's face had been fixed there for the better part of two weeks — since the third day following her surgery when the doctors removed the coverings they had placed over her eyes. In a darkened room, everyone held their breath as Amanda slowly opened her eyes. Her eyes blinked, then moved back and forth for a moment. Slowly, they filled and overflowed with tears before she finally announced that she was able to distinguish light. Over the next several days, objects took blurry shape in her vision. For two miraculous days now, she had been seeing the world very much as she remembered it before the insidious tumor began to grow.

"Are the doctors treating you well?" Thomas asked.

"Oh my, yes. I think they view me as a particularly successful example of their skill. And they treat me as such." She reached across to lovingly squeeze his arm. "Thank you for being here. I know it was a long, hard trip. It means so much to know that you care."

"The two of you are the only family I have, Amanda... as I've told Carl often enough." Thomas signaled the nurses to stop, then shoed them away and jockeyed his chair around to face Amanda.

"Uncle Thomas, explain something to me." Amanda adjusted the dark glasses until they were more comfortable on her nose.

"If I can."

"What inspired you to concern yourself about Selma Wraxmore, a woman you'd never met?" She leaned toward him and reached out to hold one of his hands as she stared into his eyes.

"Don't misunderstand me. I will be eternally grateful that you entangled yourself in her affairs. Carl told me about the Texan who saved his life. I understand he was sent by you to watch over Selma." She took a quivering breath then continued. "If you hadn't sent that man, neither Carl nor Selma might be alive today."

The silver head turned away and Thomas stared off toward the sparkling bay beyond the greening trees. Amanda watched him for a moment before she spoke again. "I just wondered how... why... how you knew she would be in danger. Why... ?"

Thomas heaved a muttered sigh and shifted in his seat as a twisted grimace distorted his face. Amanda watched him and suddenly realized she had been holding her own breath. She forced herself to breathe just as Thomas began speaking.

"It all started when some vagrants camped out in the old shed in the alley at the back of our wharf building. I knew there was a woman down there. But I wouldn't have worried about her if Carl hadn't suddenly shown an inordinate amount of interest in her.

"You know I've hoped Carl would find a suitable woman

to settle down with. But not one of the young women he's ever met so much as turned his head. Then suddenly, the first woman he shows any interest in turns out to be a destitute vagrant with no home, living hand to mouth in a shack on the docks. I had no idea when I first sent Gunther to investigate... what he would find.

"Then, quite by chance, I ran into Selma at Henson's offices when she applied to sew for the orphanage. That's when I first recognized her and realized who she must be."

"But how could you recognize her, Thomas? She'd never been to America before. Surely you'd never met?"

Amanda waited long minutes while Thomas glared at a budding tulip from beneath his wrinkled brows. "Selma Wraxmore is my daughter."

The world stopped turning. When it started again, Amanda felt the jolt clear to her bones. "Your daughter?" The words stumbled out in a whisper.

"Aurelia Klintenberg — her mother — and I enjoyed a... romantic interlude... when I first went to England, twenty-four years ago. I had no idea what a heartless, scheming woman she was until the affair ended. My heart was broken. My ego a shambles. I'm ashamed to say that when I left for America, my tail was tucked securely between my legs."

"But how can you be sure Selma is your daughter?"

"Some seven years ago, I received a clipping from a news-paper story printed in England. The anonymous sender had scribbled a... note... in the margin."

He stopped talking and pulled his wallet out of the inside breast pocket of his coat. His fingers trembled as he extracted a frail, yellowed, newspaper clipping and carefully unfolded its sharp creases.

Amanda received it carefully from his hands. She held it close to her eyes until the words and picture came into focus, then she cried out. "This is Selma!"

"Yes. Taken with Lord Wraxmore on their wedding day, almost eight years ago. In the background you can just catch a glimpse of Aurelia."

"The likeness is incredible."

"In all things but one. Selma has a soul. Her mother has none!" Bitter loathing punctuated his words.

Amanda peered closely to read the hand written note in the margin. "Dear Mr. Mason," the words were faded and barely readable, but Amanda could still make them out, "Aurelia won't tell you, but I thought you should know that you have a daughter."

Amanda turned the paper over and back, then lifted her eyes to stare at Thomas.

"There's no name. Who sent this to you?"

"I'll never know for sure. But Aurelia had a maid who had been with her since she was a child. The old woman liked me for some reason. She actually warned me away from her mistress. But I was too love-struck to pay heed to her warning. I believe she's the one who sent it to me."

Amanda was stunned. Her mind refused to think further, but Thomas had begun to unburden his soul and could not stop now.

"Gunther discovered the woman I'd seen at Henson's law office and the woman in the alley were one and the same. Lady Selma Wraxmore. But by the time he figured that out, the fire had burnt down the shack and she was living in your house. Gunther was hot on the trail I'd asked him to investigate. And he didn't realize what a hotbed of snakes he was stirring to life when he sent inquiries to England requesting information about Selma.

"That was my fault. I didn't tell him all I knew. He unintentionally provided Aurelia with the very information she was desperate to know — where to find her daughter."

"Didn't she... doesn't she love Selma?"

"Love? That green-eyed witch practically sold Selma to Lord Wraxmore when she was little more than a child! To pay off gambling debts and assure herself of future financial stability."

"But that's criminal." Amanda was horrified. "How could a mother do that?"

She cringed at the picture Thomas Mason painted.

Harsh bitterness and self-loathing darkened Mason's voice as he continued to lash himself with guilt. "When Selma's husband died, Aurelia was left without her steady source of income. But it didn't take her long to attempt the same tactic that had been so successful before. She promised Selma as payment of a gambling debt — again — to some other licentious nobleman in England."

His voice dripped with irony. "Selma is, after all, very beautiful. Such a rare commodity brings a high price... in certain markets."

Amanda shuddered at his words.

"The only problem was where to find Selma. And Gunther unknowingly provided Aurelia with the final key to put her plot into action."

Thomas looked down at his hands and saw that he had gripped them together so hard that no blood was left in his fingers. He relaxed his fingers and wiggled them around, reveling in the pinpoints of pain as blood returned to the oxygen-starved cells.

"As soon as he told me he'd been in communication with Aurelia, I grew afraid. At my request, Gunther sent one of his men — the Texan — to keep watch over Selma." Thomas took a couple of deep breaths and threw his head back to stare at the sky. "We were almost too late. I still have nightmares of what would have happened if Carl hadn't shown up and Gunther's man hadn't arrived when he did. Argh!"

His large hands rubbed up and down the sides of his face then he shook his head to clear his thoughts. "It can drive a man insane!"

"What about Aurelia Klintenberg? What happens to her now?" Amanda felt breathless and strangely drained of energy, as though she had run an uphill race.

"Gunther's Texan escorted her to New York and made

sure she was safely aboard a ship back to England. I cabled $10,000 to him and he delivered it to her as an incentive — to get lost and stay lost. He also delivered my... instructions... that she is never to step foot in America again or try to see or contact Selma or any of her children — ever!"

The frigid tone of Thomas' voice told Amanda he was deathly serious and a chill shivered beneath the bandages around her head. "Does Selma know you are her father?"

"Not yet."

"Why haven't you told her?"

"For a number of reasons..."

"Give me one." Amanda had never seen her pseudo uncle/step-father so uncomfortable, so unsure of himself.

"Well, we've been busy..."

"That's not good enough, Uncle Thomas."

He seemed to shrink in on himself as he watched a honeybee investigate several likely flowers. When he finally spoke, a chill echoed his words. "I'm afraid."

Thomas lifted his eyes and she recognized the agony torturing his soul. Then, as she continued to gaze at him, a stunning thought occurred to her.

"Uncle Thomas, didn't you say Aurelia had green eyes?"

"Green as emeralds, like a cat's eyes. Probably glow in the dark."

Amanda nodded excitedly and reached out to squeeze his hand tight. "Well, my darling Uncle Thomas Mason," she slowly emphasized each word, "Selma has your eyes! And so does Anna. If I'd been able to see, I'd have known it long before now." She stared into his sapphire blue eyes and started to laugh. "You don't have to be afraid, Uncle Thomas."

She emphasized her next words and they pierced his heart with a dagger as powerful as a bolt from a wild, electrical storm. "I believe that all of your dreams for a family — of being a father and a grandfather — meet in Selma. She will love having you for a father. Ruth and Anna will adore you as a grandfather." She squeezed his hand in her own. " I know it!"

Amanda recognized the hope that blossomed in his eyes and watched him ponder her words. She knew it would still be a long time before the old man forgave himself for his part in Selma's dark history, but at the same time, she was sure they'd work at it together and be better for it in the end. She started to tell him as much, but a wild shout from the other side of the gardens caught their attention.

Thomas whirled his chair around easily, then tried unsuccessfully to keep from laughing as Amanda futilely struggled to get her own wheelchair to turn. In the end, she grew so frustrated that she jumped to her feet and jerked the chair around.

"Don't know why they make me sit in this dadratted contraption anyway!"

At last she plopped back into the chair and looked around to see who had called their attention. Coming toward them across the wide expanse of budding green lawn, arm in arm, walked Carl and Selma Klintenberg Wraxmore Stanton. Selma waved excitedly while Carl led a shiny, black pony with Ruth and Anna happily riding on its back. Squeezed tightly and securely between them, with a huge grin that showed every tooth in his mouth, rode Drew.

"Uncle Thomas?" Amanda spoke softly as she waved at the happy group.

"Yes, Amanda?" Thomas raised his right hand high in greeting as well.

"Look at her eyes and tell me what you think."

THE END